# A GRAVES UNDERTAKING

# A GRAVES UNDERTAKING

## By J.A. Lesser

Published by Sandia Press

Cover illustration by Nancy Twinem
Design by Cindy Monroe

ISBN: 978-0-9859749-0-9


Printed in the U.S.A.

For Donna

# Chapter 1

O n a crisp spring Sunday, dawn slipped between the leaves of an ancient oak, tipped its cap to a wormless and tardy robin, opened the window clasp, and strode into my bedroom with a hale "Good morning." Observing a distinct lack of response, it pried open a bloodshot eye and bent down to my uncovered ear; "Wake up, you bloody sod." I groaned, cursing the birds sitting in the same oak chirping mercilessly, and slowly raised myself into a more prone semiconciousness.

"Benjamin, we need to talk."

When the female of the species pronounces a need to talk, grim tidings follow.

The other eye opened, reluctantly, and beheld my wife, Cynthia. She stared at me as if I were a moribund goldfish floating in its bowl, wearing that "Right ho, time for your disemboweling" face all chaps know instinctively.

Being of stiff upper lip, a chap first listens and nods cheerfully as the fairer sex neatly sets one's entrails on the floor and dances upon them. Next, one is provided with a Chinese-like menu of guilt-assuaging platitudes, such as "I did not mean this to happen," delivered with a forlorn, whimpering puppy look, as if disembowelling you hurt her more than you.

Cynthia, as it happened, was quite a looker, if I may say so myself. A competitive swimmer, she glided effortlessly through the water like a seal. Well, at least I thought so, being one whose aquatic efforts consisted of weighing anchor.

The trappings of our marital union were typical for the youngish, up-and-coming London professional set: a large, well-furnished flat near Kensington, the paternal's Yorkshire country home visited over the longer weekends, and the requisite social life of those in our class. With the marauding hordes of nieces and nephews to fight off at holidays, neither of us had great zeal for offspring of our own.

The morning's grim tidings came in the form of a Spaniard, Rodrigo Lopreso de Vargas. Mister de Vargas was a salesman, foremost of himself, but also of various types of insurance through the London agency of Moore and Cromwell, Ltd., where Cynthia was employed. With his muscular build, mane of flowing jet-black hair, and silken accent, he oozed Iberian charm. He had left Spain, and a large set of unpaid debts, in search of female prey. Coming from one of the more emotional cultures, Mister de Vargas easily cracked the veneer of the fairer sex.

Well, one cannot whinge about what-ifs. Cynthia was like a baby gazelle one sees in those nature shows, separated from the herd and confused as to where to flee. She hadn't a chance. Rodrigo's efforts began stealthily—invitations to lunch with the lads, the casual chin-wag about life at home, and the odd cup of tea. In little time, she was ringing me up about this or that presentation the head of the firm required and not to wait dinner, and then not to wait up.

To be fair, I had engaged in the occasional bout of laddish behaviour prior to our marriage. I never subscribed to the *de rigueur* marriage-plus-mistress standard of the French. The care and feeding of one's wife is stressful enough, what with the various social necessities one must undertake: "surprise" gifts to be purchased on a regular schedule lest one be dismembered by the evil eye, flowers, chocolates, vague promises one provides in rather more delicate moments, &c. One imagines the French predilection for quick surrender arose because they were too knackered by the comings and goings of the wives and mistresses. A chap can only muster so much energy, after all.

Unluckily for me, like any voracious hunter, Rodrigo constantly required fresh prey. In one of those unfortunate turns of event, this took the form of Cynthia.

"Who's the chap?" Not that I really wished to know.

Cynthia's face softened. "His name is Rodrigo. He's head of accounts."

I stared at her, but said nothing. After all, what can one say standing in front of the marital firing squad?

"Oh, Benjamin, I didn't mean this to happen. I am so ashamed."

"Ashamed enough to stop seeing him?" I knew the answer, of course. But a Graves always maintains at least the appearance of dignity.

"I know it's wrong, but Rodrigo is so passionate, so alive, so romantic, so . . . When he speaks to me, I feel like I am in a garden of flowers. He's taking me back to Spain. It's difficult to explain."

I raised an eyebrow. I didn't doubt it. I mean, I have walked through my share of gardens. One hears the various fauna buzzing about and perhaps the odd curse from a gardener about deer hoovering up the edibles. But I confess to never having heard the whispers of Spain from a daisy or a geranium. Then again, the fairer sex tends towards more descriptive nonsense, what with entering poetry contests and endless goo-gooing over the romantic chaps that inhabit the Bronte sisters' novels. I lost count of how many times Cynthia had read *Pride and Prejudice*, crying over everything that fop Mister Darcy uttered. Thus, when the better half muttered nonsense about a Spaniard whose voice sounds like a geranium, I knew reason has been keel-hauled. Once she had introduced his thick accent and mane of Spanish hair to me, I knew the chap had deep-sixed our marriage.

Short of resurrecting Lord Nelson and declaring war on Spain, there was nothing to be done

Perhaps one has heard the expression "bad news comes in threes." Why this should be the case, I know not. However, having been cuckolded and now abandoned by the better half, the acrid scent of calamity was in the air. No sweet-smelling roses these, whatever the Bard may have called them. Cynthia had removed her belongings from our flat and taken up residence with Rodrigo awaiting their departure to Spain. The flat took on a rather shabby, forlorn look: blank walls where pictures had once hung, large gaps in the *objets d'art* that had once lined the bookcases, empty flatware drawers, and the like.

I would spend my days at the bank, evaluating whatever happened to be on the acquisition or sale menu that day, then return to the flat with a takeaway, and switch on the telly. Jack had become a dull boy, indeed.

A month after Cynthia left, I was summoned one afternoon by the firm's Senior Vice President of Accounts, Charles Winfield Peale, who had extended my original offer of employment. He was a portly, ruddy-faced and somewhat dishevelled sort, with one of those dual-tone, ha-ha sorts of laugh. I placed trepidation into the desk drawer and strolled down the quiet hallway to his office.

"You asked to see me, sir?"

"Ah, yes, Benjamin. Do come in, do come in. Would you mind getting the door? Ah, there's a good chap."

I sat down in one of the leather chairs facing his desk, an oak battleship type favoured by the traditional banking set. "Well, Benjamin, I have good news and bad news, you see."

"Yes, sir. Er, how about the good news first?"

"The good news is that your work has been exemplary, if I may say so myself. You've done a fine job for us."

I allowed myself a smile. "Thank you, sir. I have endeavoured to be of service and I greatly appreciate the confidence you have expressed in my work."

One could be forgiven for expecting to hear a "Starting today, we have increased your salary by £100 per week" or "We have decided to promote you to Deputy Bourser, with a commensurate increase in your salary, of course." What one most certainly does not expect to hear is, "It therefore pains me to inform you that your services at the firm are no longer required."

Fate, like all cruel mistresses, had struck for the second time. I had been lulled into an amnesiac state, having forgotten more grim tidings were due. Of course, Fate would not be what she was without such statements. I mean, who would not tempt Fate if her response was "Jolly good."

All I could do was goggle back at him, opening and closing my mouth, whilst unsuccessfully attempting to speak. Finally, I managed to splutter a single word: "Sir?"

"Yes, yes, a bit of a shock I know, and to me as well. But the Chairman announced that profit expectations have been increased, what with the market and all that, and we needed to trim up, attain our fighting weight, and the like. I'm sure you know what I mean."

Until that time, I had never considered pugilistic metaphors as applicable to a bank, especially as our Chairman weighed almost twenty stone. Other than squashing opponents like bugs, I was at a loss to imagine what "fighting weight" for the bank meant.

Still staring dully at him, I managed to engage the vocal chords. "I, I mean, why me, if my performance has been exemplary?"

"My point exactly, Benjamin, as I discussed the matter with the Chairman. I gather his nephew Arthur will be assuming your responsibilities."

"What? The chap found with the—"

"I remind you that no charges were ever brought in that incident. It was simply . . . youthful exuberance."

"—mannequin? And wasn't he expelled from Oxford for setting fire to a rector's chair, whilst the rector was napping in it?"

"Regardless of what Arthur may or may not have done, the Chairman has decided to appoint him Manager of Accounts. I can tell you that the Chairman is not without sympathy for your plight, and has authorised me to provide you with one month's severance. I am sorry, Benjamin, truly I am. One must understand these things, what."

"No, I mean—"

"Of course the firm will provide you with excellent references, should you request them. It's the least we can do. Now, if you'll excuse me, I have an engagement at my club. Miss Wilson will escort you out of the building." He handed me an envelope containing a cheque, which I grasped absently. I mean, it's one thing to be made redundant. But I was being replaced by a twit.

Miss Wilson glided in, gently gripped my elbow, silently escorted me to the main entrance, and wished me an officious good luck. So there I was, standing outside the bank with the envelope deposited in my pocket. Cold rain would complete the misery and, as if precisely stage managed, began falling steadily. I was unmarried and unemployed. The stiff upper lip, one is ashamed to admit, quivered ever so slightly. Desperate times were at hand and desperate measures called for.

# Chapter 2

I returned to the flat. Tossing my drenched suit into the rubbish bin, I put on dry clothes, poured a large whisky, drank deeply, and wandered back into the bedroom. There was a chair and small writing desk under one window. I sat down heavily and stared outside, watching the rain pour off the oak tree.

I inhaled another large dose and dropped the glass carelessly onto the desk. It rolled onto its side and the remaining whisky formed a small rivulet which flowed into the centre drawer. Cursing, I blotted the whisky with a sheet of paper and opened the drawer.

Inside was a set of postcards, banded together, that had been sent to me during my formative years by my Uncle Bill, whom I had never met. The postcards always had odd pictures, such as a giant hare with antlers, or ears of maize the size of a lorry. On the back would be his scribblings, such as "Happy birthday little pard'ner" or "Yee-hah, get a load of that jackalope!"

Uncle Bill was the black sheep of the family. He had moved to the States, New Mexico to be precise, and was never mentioned. To do so was considered an affront to polite society, not that polite society would have known who Uncle Bill was or cared a fig about *why he had been cast out by my grandfather* decades earlier. Even I was never told, other than the odd paternal muttering about what had happened to "poor Henry," the late Lord Admiral Sir Henry Throckmorton, an over-aged, over-whiskied, and self-important boor of the highest order, but one whose connections to the Admiralty had demanded fawning respect from all persons Graves.

Whenever my father saw one of the postcards, his eyes would bulge and he would emit a loud snort. I suspect Father was torn between a desire to tear them into bits and his respect for the sanctity of the Royal Mail, with the latter ultimately triumphing.

I had been captivated by the postcards, which, as far as I was concerned, came from a far end of the earth. True, one could find New Mexico on a map of the United States; however, I was left to wonder where in that foreign land Uncle Bill resided, not that I ever thought I would venture there myself.

Retrieving the whisky bottle, I poured another large glass and reread them all. Uncle Bill always fancied himself an American cowboy. He had once sent a book by Zane Grey, in which Wild West cowboys galloped away the hours on trusty horses named Paint and Buster; where Indians whooped and were "wupped"; and where the most romantic words spoken by a chap were "Howdy, ma'am."

As I stared at the yellowing picture of the Jackalope, Fate struck yet again.

"You're going where?" my father roared. "Have you gone barking mad?"

"I always favoured Uncle Bill. I even kept all of the post-cards he sent me from New Mexico."

A disgusted look descended onto his face. "You've never even met him. Your uncle is a derelict. What he did to Sir Henry, God rest his soul, was unforgivable. We were nearly shunned by all of polite society."

"And his fixation with American cowboys. Cowboys!" My father's glare lifted from me towards the ceiling. "He might as well have been switched at birth for a street urchin. We were told he married far beneath himself, a native woman named Lopez or Gomez, or some such thing. Pah!"

"And haven't you shamed the family enough, cuckolded by some idiot Spaniard and sacked from the bank? From a position I secured for you, or have you forgotten?"

At this point, the words "sod off" began to line up in the vocal chords. Fortunately, what few sensible neurons I possessed managed to wrestle them away before being uttered. In defence of my cowardice, Father's fondness for smashing breakables with the nearest fireplace poker, one of which was within grabbing distance.

"Well, do you have anything to say for yourself?"

"I, er—"

"Nincompoop."

"What?"

"Are you deaf, too? You were sent to the finest schools. And if it hadn't been for that gammy knee of yours—how did that happen again? Oh yes, fell out of a tree waiting to drop water balloons on little Thomas Parkingham—you would have been an officer in the Royal Grenadiers. You could have inherited my seat in Parliament. Instead, before me sits a thirty-year-old nincompoop."

"See here, I hardly think that is fair. I was twelve years old. As for drenching "little" Thomas, he resembled a larded goose and had a disgusting habit of sitting on me and breaking wind."

"Twelve or thirty, the pattern was established. When I was your age, your grandfather had me practicing speeches for Parliament."

"Stop shouting, Gerald," my mother said as she walked into the drawing room. "You should be proud of your son."

"Don't coddle him, Dorothy."

"Tosh, Gerald. Our son has had a run of bad luck, that's all. There's no need for your long-winded badgering. He wishes to travel to Mexico to see your brother. There is nothing wrong with that." She then turned to me. "But wouldn't you prefer Cannes, dear?"

My father's mouth opened and closed slowly like a grouper.

Though I appreciated mother's coming to my aid, another incendiary row between them was brewing, in which my part would drop from sight like an anchor.

"Er, New Mexico, Mother. Uncle Bill lives in New Mexico. America. In a town called Vaca Seca."

I shall not bore you with the mundane details of the departure preparations. I sent a telegram to Uncle Bill, who replied:
YEE-HAH PARDNER. STOP. BUNK AND SADDLE READY. STOP. DAISY AT FRONT DOOR. STOP.

"Yee-hah" was an expression I was most familiar with, thanks to the aforementioned postcards. And I knew what a saddle was. As for "Daisy at front door," I assumed he meant there were daisies around the front door of his home, rather like describing an individual English castle by saying "ivy on walls," "foul-tempered hedgehog under garden, or "drunken Irishman groundskeeper." I made a mental note of the floral identifier and proceeded with my plans.

I sold the flat to a fresh-scrubbed young couple, Orrin and Daedre, who reminded me of Cynthia's and my early days, eager to start their lives of wedded bliss. Avoiding any discussions of the marital debacle, I muttered diffidently about a transfer to the States and quickly moved on to listing the highlights of the neighbourhood, especially several of the better pubs. When Orrin smiled and Daedre scowled, I knew they would be at sixes and sevens in short order.

Several weeks later, with loose ends variously tied, I returned to say my good-byes.

"Well, father, I guess this is good-bye. I shall write, of course."

My father, whisky in hand, grunted. "I could speak with Sir Hugo Follansbee and arrange a position for you in New York."

"Thank you, no. I've had quite enough of banking."

"He's hopeless, you know."

"Sir Hugo?"

"What? No, my brother. Ruined by all of that cowboy nonsense."

"Now, Gerald," Mother said, "we shall have no more of that talk. You could be civil enough to wish Benjamin well on his adventure."

She turned to me. "Do be careful. There may be wild animals."

"I shall take pains to avoid them, Mother."

"Are you sure you wouldn't prefer Cannes, Benjamin?"

"Quite sure, Mother. A Graves always wants for a bit of adventure."

"Yes, dear, and adventure sent several of them to early graves, pardon the pun. If you must go, do return home soon. And do please send my regards to William."

"Dorothy!"

I shook my father's hand stiffly. Mother offered a somewhat tearful embrace, then rushed upstairs. I walked through the front door, future before me, adventure waiting.

I had booked Pan Am to New York City, then TWA to Albuquerque. From there, a dilapidated bus had taken me through Santa Fe and Española, and continued to head north towards Vaca Seca. The irony of the speeding greyhound displayed on the bus's side, when said bus's velocity could have been matched by a three-legged, inebriated tortoise, was not lost on me. I had presumed the New Mexico landscape would be an amalgam of the Gobi and Sahara deserts, only to discover foreboding mountain passes, eager to swallow buses like the chaps at Cambridge gobbled goldfish.

As we began to climb higher into the mountains, the macadam gave way to a gravel-strewn path that would have been perfectly at home in the Himalayas. All that was missing were Mongolian yak herders, or whatever shaggy beasts Mongolians herded in the Himalayas. In fact, careening through one especially vicious turn I was quite sure I espied a yak glued onto a particularly steep expanse. Well, perhaps it was an antelope. I mean, when one visits the London Zoo, the various hoofed fauna begin to look the same, save the odd horns or stripes. They certainly smell the same. In fact, the olfactory had detected vaguely similar odours onboard, which fooled me momentarily into thinking I was travelling on the Continent.

What with the vehicular to-ing and fro-ing, the stomach had raised the white flag, distracting my attention away from the passing landscape and rather more inwards. Finally, after what seemed like hours of tossing about in this vehicular miasma, I espied a rusty and bullet-riddled sign: "Vaca Seca, pop. 385."

The bus groaned to stop in front of a ramshackle building bordering what one might consider a town square. A rather skeletal and weathered chap exited slowly before me. I stepped off the bus, carrying two valises, and was greeted by a dusty silence. The driver got off and followed the first chap, who had shuffled his way across the macadam and through a door below a sign that read "Rudy's Bar and Package Liquors." A few minutes later, the driver emerged, right hand wrapped lovingly around a large bottle of beer. He climbed back into the bus, shut the door and drove off, leaving me encased in a choking cloud of diesel exhaust and dust I glanced about, a sense of dread settling heavily on the shoulders. The town itself seemed encased in dust. Everything—the pink-and-white buildings, a dog lying by the side of the road, the two white-haired chaps sitting in front of Rudy's—seemed to be covered with the same dusty veil. The jaw lowered like a drawbridge. A vision arose from within of sipping champagne whilst watching the sun descend below the Mediterranean; perhaps I should have heeded Mother's suggestion to visit Cannes.

Reality interrupted only too soon. A short, roly-poly chap, possessing a pair of rodentary eyes and a strong odour of beer, stood before me. His clothes, hat, and boots were the same dusty colour as the rest of the town. I glanced down at him. He offered a vapid smile which displayed an absence of several front teeth.

"Señor," he whispered, pulling on my sport jacket. "Señor."

"Eh? Yes?"

"I saw you get off Manny's bus. You sure you're in the right place?" He eyed me up and down, staring especially at the tweed jacket and tie. "Where do you come from, señor?"

"London."

"I was in London once." He grinned at me proudly.

"You were?" I could no more imagine him in London than on the moon.

"*Sí*, señor. London, Texas. But it was a long time ago."

"Indeed? Er, well, I'm from a different London. The one in England."

"England? That why you talk so funny?"

"I beg your pardon. I matriculated at Cambridge."

"Huh?"

"Look, perhaps you can help me find a chap in this town."

"A what?"

"A gentleman who lives here. This is Vaca Seca, is it not?"

"*Sí*, señor." He smiled and slowly turned, his arm arcing about so I might take in the splendour. "I lived here all my life."

He offered me a dust and grease-covered hand to shake. "Coronado de Vaca. My ancestor was the *conquistador*, Álvar Núñez Cabeza de Vaca. He discovered this valley."

"Indeed?" I glanced about, wondering what exactly the *conquistador* had discovered. "You must be quite proud."

I gingerly took his hand in mine, which he proceeded to crank up and down vigorously like a water pump. On its return, the hand was covered with the grimy mixture. "Yes, well, pleased to make your acquaintance, Mister, er, de Vaca. My name is Benjamin Graves. Now, perhaps you could help me find the gentleman. His name is William Graves."

"Is he your brother or something? I don't know nobody here named Graves."

"What? I know he lives here. He sent me a telegram."

He wiped his dusty-greasy hand on his shirt, which was already covered with the same mixture. "You sure you got the right town?"

"Look, William Graves is my uncle, not my brother, and he has lived here for many years." As the words spilled out, a sense of dread was shunted aside by despondency. Coronado shrugged his shoulders.

I pulled the crumpled telegram Uncle Bill had sent out of my pocket, smearing grease and dirt on the front of my trousers. "Damn and blast."

"What's wrong, señor?"

"I've ruined my trousers, that's what." I thrust the telegram into his face. "Look. The telegram is from William Graves, Vaca Seca, New Mexico."

Coronado seized the telegram and examined it intently, tongue lolling out of his mouth. Finally, after staring at it as if decoding some secret message, he returned it to me. The letters were barely legible and covered in grime.

"Well? Why would William Graves send a telegram from Vaca Seca if he didn't live here, eh?"

"I dunno, señor. I can't read."

"What? Bloody hell. Look, it says, "YEE-HAH PARDNER. STOP. BUNK AND SADDLE READY. STOP. DAISY AT FRONT DOOR. STOP.""

"Oh, *sí* señor. Why didn't you say so? You want El Vaquero!"

"I did say so, didn't I? Who, or what, is El Vaquero?"

"'El Vaquero is . . .' Once again he ran a greasy hand over his chin. '. . . a *vaquero*. He lives down that road, just a few miles." Coronado pointed towards a narrow dirt road between two old buildings across the square, which wasn't even a square but an exhausted parallelogram. "If you want, I can take you there. My pick-up is behind Rudy's."

"Your what?"

He looked at me as if I was some sort of alien. "My pick-up truck."

"You mean a lorry?"

"You don't need to say sorry, señor. I guess you don't got pick-ups where you come from. You should, 'cause they come in real handy, especially around here. Lemme get it and then

I can drive you to El Vaquero's ranch." He turned around and walked through the front door of Rudy's bar.

I waited outside, the minutes ticking by. Where he could have vanished? Then, as my gaze fell on the bent sign, I recalled the odour of beer enveloping Coronado. I abandoned the two valises and walked inside.

Though one might have naïvely hoped that Rudy's Bar and Drive-Thru Liquors would offer the same ambience as the Jolly Rooster, one's hopes were not so much dashed as stomped upon like an unwelcome bug. On the far wall was a large cooler. To the left, three men sat on rickety metal bar stools, hands wrapped around beer bottles in various states of emptiness, including, slumped over like a post-prandial flower, Coronado. He was mumbling a song about a lost *querida*, an ex-girlfriend who, apparently in a fit of sanity, had abandoned both Coronado and Vaca Seca to pursue a career as a hairdresser in Santa Fe. I walked over to Coronado and shook his shoulder. His head lolled about. "*Hola*, Señor Graves. You want a beer? You can grab one from the cooler."

"Thank you just the same." I wondered how many beers Coronado had managed to imbibe whilst I waited outside.

"Okay. Lemme finish this one, and then I'm gonna take you to see your brother."

"He's not my—yes, well, perhaps I should drive. You appear to be rather besotted."

"Huh? Oh, I can drive." He laughed and staggered to his feet, then fell onto the floor. The two other patrons sitting at the bar, neither of whom appeared to be capable of sentient thought, shifted in their stools.

I helped Coronado to his feet. Although I had seen him drinking beer, there was a pronounced odour of gin. "*Gracias*, señor. Maybe you should drive."

Even in the dim light of the bar, Coronado's face had taken on a greenish hue. This, I knew from contests with the chaps at the Jolly Rooster, presaged an emetic event. In such situations, one's best hope was to maintain a safe distance. "Where is your lorry, er, pick-up, Coronado?"

"I think it's behind the bar."

"Yes, yes, I realize that. How do we get there?" Rudy's was sandwiched between two other dilapidated buildings and I had seen no obvious route to the rear of the building.

"Out the back door, behind the cooler." He pointed shakily to a door on which was taped a small placard: "Do Not Enter."

Despite my trepidation—one always hesitates to open doors marked "Do Not Enter," after all—I grasped Coronado's arm and herded him through the door.

"Hey, shut the goddamn door. Don't you know how to knock?"

I pulled Coronado back and quickly slammed the door shut. "That's a bloody loo, Coronado."

Coronado stared at me. "It's just José."

"*Hola*, José, it's me, Coronado. I gotta get my truck. Can I come through?"

"Hang on, Coronado," José shouted. "Why can't you park your goddamn truck in front like everybody else?"

"There's never a place to park it. Besides, last time I tried parking in front, I ran over Sandoval's dog, Diablo."

"That's the only good thing you ever did. That dog ate my chickens, scared the goat, and pissed all over my house." Presently, I heard a loud flushing sound. "Okay, you can come through."

Coronado opened the door and we walked through. Well, Coronado staggered. José was a stringy-looking chap, dressed in what I had concluded was the unofficial town uniform of dirty jeans, soiled white shirt, and boots.

He was buckling his enormous belt and looked at me in a way I could only describe as unfriendly, although given the circumstances of our meeting, one could not blame him.

"This is Señor Graves. He's El Vaquero's brother."

"Brother?" El Vaquero never said nothing about a brother."

"Actually, I am his nephew."

"Where you from?"

"London, England. Perhaps you've heard of it?"

"Sure. I was there before our regiment got sent to Germany. Met some real nice girls. But they didn't talk like you." He paused and glared at me. "You think I'm stupid or something?"

"What? No, of course not. It's just, well, anyway, pleased to make your acquaintance Mister, er, José, is it?"

He stuck out his hand and grabbed mine. "José Gonzalez, but everybody just calls me Old Joe. El Vaquero's from London? He sure talks like a Texan."

"Not actually London proper. The ancestral home is nearby. I do hate to rush, er, Old Joe, however, it's been rather a long trip and I would like to get to Uncle Bill's ranch. I'm sure you understand."

Old Joe shrugged. "Tell him he stills owes me a six-pack."

"A what? Of course, just as soon as I see him."

I exited the rear of the loo, followed by the still staggering Coronado. The hallway was dark, lit only by a single bulb dangling from the ceiling. As we neared the door, where fresh air beckoned, Coronado stopped and, without warning, unleashed a torrent of vomit which the left trouser leg was unable to dodge. Rather than exploding with rage, as any reasonable chap might have under the circumstances, I merely sighed. It was an apt metaphor for the day.

"Sorry." We stepped outside into the bright sun. "I guess I had a little too much to drink. I feel better now."

"Quite. No doubt Uncle Bill will be delighted to welcome me into his home looking—and smelling—the way I do."

"You want to stop by my place and clean up, Señor Graves?"

"Eh? No thank you. I am quite sure I can have a wash and brushup at the ranch." The mind composed an image of Coronado's flat and shuddered.

We approached an ancient, rusted, and dented lorry which appeared to have once been blue.

"You know, señor, I think I feel okay to drive now."

"What? Are you quite sure?"

"Yeah. Besides, there are never cars on the road to El Vaquero's ranch."

As we would be travelling the aforementioned road in Coronado's lorry, I was unimpressed by his logic. However, he had already heaved himself behind the wheel. "Er, Coronado, I left my valises by the front door. Can you drive around so I may retrieve them?"

"Your what, señor?"

"Valises. Luggage. The large cases I was carrying in each arm after I stepped off the bus."

"You sure call things funny names."

He started the ancient vehicle. The engine groaned, sputtered, and finally came to life. Coronado reversed the lorry into a wooden fence, which looked as if had suffered this indignity daily, and inched forwards. He huddled over the steering wheel and stared resolutely through the windscreen whilst his head lolled.

He turned down a narrow alley and inched forward, knocking down several rubbish bins and scraping another fence. Presently, we found ourselves at the far end of the town square. Coronado slowly turned left, steering the lorry as if it were an ocean liner, and stopped in front of Rudy's. The white-haired chaps I had seen earlier were gone. I hopped out, picked up my luggage, and noticed a strange odour; a dog had relieved itself on both valises. Another apt metaphor, or omen, which I appeared to be collecting like one does stamps.

I shook my head and threw the valises into the back of the lorry. Then I climbed into the passenger seat, and slammed the door. "Do you know what happened whilst I was extricating you from this bar? A dog relieved itself on my luggage."

"You mean pissed on it?" He was unable to restrain a grin. "Paco, Señor Graves."

"Paco?"

"You see a scrawny yellow dog lying down out front when the bus came in?"

"As a matter of fact, I did."

"That's Paco. He kinda does that a lot." Coronado's grin grew more pronounced.

"I fail to see the humour in this. My trousers are ruined, I have been vomited upon, and now a dog has urinated on my luggage."

"Sorry, señor. Maybe that's why we don't get many visitors here."

We inched forward once again. He turned the lorry about and we drove to the end of the square, slipping between the two buildings he had pointed out earlier and down a road that was little more than an undulating, rock-strewn garden path. The truck bumped and banged down the road, leaving a huge trail of dust behind it. After several miles, we weaved our way into a narrow canyon, upon whose sides sat large boulders precariously balanced between small pine trees, as if waiting to roll down and crush the lorry like an egg. The canyon soon gave way to rolling hills. Finally, in the distance I espied a small, white house. "Is that Uncle Bill's ranch?"

"*Sí*, Señor Graves."

"Does he grow daisies?"

"Daisies? I dunno. He runs about fifty head, and grows alfalfa. But you never know with El Vaquero. He does some strange things."

# Chapter 3

As we neared the ranch house the road jostled the lorry violently. We passed a small sign nailed to a wooden post with the words "Cowboy Ranch" painted in black, along with an arrow pointing rightwards. Presently, Coronado slowly turned onto a narrower and more rutted path, promptly steering the lorry into a large boulder.

"You seem to have rather a problem with sharp turns, Coronado."

"*Sí*, Señor Graves. My truck don't steer real good. I think I gotta bad tie rod."

I had no idea what a tie rod was, nor had any particular interest in knowing. "Yes, well, perhaps we should back up and try again."

Coronado put the lorry into reverse gear and pressed on the accelerator. We did not move. "I think we're stuck."

"Quite. Well, let us have a look, shall we?" I opened the door and slid out. The lorry had nosed itself downward onto the boulder and the right rear wheel was fully airborne. Coronado had come around for a look. He rubbed his hand over his chin and grimaced.

"*Híjole*. Maybe if one of us gets in the bed it will push the back down, Señor Graves."

He returned to the driver's seat, which meant me.

"Right, shall I climb in?"

I hauled myself up and sat on the side over the right rear wheel, which slowly lowered itself back onto the dirt. Coronado pressed the accelerator. The lorry lurched backwards, knocking me off the side and into the two malodorous valises. Then, roaring forwards, he continued to the other side of the road, until another boulder helpfully stopped the lorry again.

It is on occasions like this one wonders whether God is bored and in need of amusement. I righted myself again, noticing that my right trouser leg was now ripped, in addition to being grease stained. I climbed down, drew in a largish breath, retrieved the two valises, and began walking down the narrow path.

"Don't you want me to drive you to El Vaquero's house?" Coronado shouted.

"No." The molars were firmly clenched. "The walk shall do me good. Thank you again for the lift."

"Sure. Maybe I'll see you in town again soon."

"No doubt you will. Good day."

I heard the lorry's wheels spin violently as Coronado pulled back onto the road. The sound of the engine soon faded into the distance and another odd silence, much like the one I had experienced in town, descended, broken only by the buzzing of locusts in the nearby trees. Fatigue had overtaken me and I was desperate for a pint to wash away the ever-present dust.

My spirits lifted as I drew closer to the house. The yard appeared to be fenced all 'round. A small wooden gate lay ahead. I walked up to it, lowered the valises to the ground, and stared at the house. It was rather low slung, with green-shuttered windows and a covered veranda. Had the roof been sod, it would not have looked out of place in rural England.

Exhausted and filthy, I approached the gate, then stopped suddenly and gaped. Lying on the veranda was a massive sow, which appeared to be asleep. A large, brightly coloured hat, which looked like a garish straw-boater was tied about its whitish-pink head with a pink ribbon. Although the olfactory detected a thick odour, the sow seemed harmless enough. I opened the gate, hoisted the two valises, and walked through, closing the gate behind me. When I turned around, the previously somnolent sow was now standing at full attention. It grunted loudly. Not your friendly, welcome-to-the-ranch grunt, but a more menacing, cheesed-off sort.

I was agog that something of such bulk could right itself so quickly. Concluding that discretion, if not outright panic, was called for, I gently lowered the two valises and retreated slowly towards the gate. The sow grunted again. Heeding Admiral Nelson's advice to forgo manoeuvres, it trotted down the steps that led off the veranda and came straight at me.

"Gah!" I turned around and dove over the gate like one of those Olympic pole-vaulting chaps. As I cleared the top, I felt the left trouser leg ripping apart on a wooden slat. I landed on the ground, extremities splayed. Too frightened to move, I heard the sow squealing behind me. She crashed into the gate with a loud thud. Begging the legs to engage, I scrambled to my feet and ran behind the nearest tree, ready to engage any long-lost tree-climbing abilities I might still possess.

Peering from behind the tree, I stared in horror. The sow had grabbed the larger valise in her mouth and was shaking it like a ragdoll. Then, with a toss of her hatted head, she sent the valise sailing over the gate and crashing down where I had been standing just seconds before.

The practice round completed, she grunted contentedly and retrieved the smaller valise. No doubt expecting to break the world record for valise-tossing, over the gate it sailed, landing heavily perhaps ten feet behind me. It exploded upon impact, sending a shower of shirts, trousers, socks, and a coddled bottle of eighteen-year-old Scottish malt into the air. The raiment fell onto nearby bushes, trees, and what appeared to be fairly fresh deposits of a bovine nature. The bottle crashed on a large rock, surrendering its contents onto a nearby anthill.

"Oh, please, not the whisky." I whimpered, watching the golden nectar vanish into the soon-to-be-inebriated ants' lair.

I gazed back towards the enclosure. Declaring herself the valise-tossing gold-medalist, the sow returned triumphantly to the veranda and flopped down with a contented grunt.

By now, the jaw was in full-drop mode. If this behemoth was the porcine equivalent of a tail-wagging dog, I shuddered to think what stood inside. Not that it mattered, of course, as I had no idea how I would ever get past the guard.

Whilst pondering my options, which appeared to be either a several-hours walk back to town or a jumping off of the nearest cliff, the front door of the house burst open. A late fiftyish chap with piercing blue eyes and a leprechaun-like grin stepped out.

His voice boomed. "Daisy, what in tarnation is going on out here?" He wore a large white cowboy hat, a white long-sleeve shirt with ivory buttons, and blue jeans attached to a massive silver belt buckle.

Hearing the word, "Daisy," I knew it was Uncle Bill.

Bill looked at the sow. She raised herself up, threw her head back proudly, and sauntered over to him, curly tail wagging. "What's up, little girl?" he cooed, scratching a pink ear that had flopped out from beneath the hat. "You see a coyote or some-thing?" He looked around the fence, and espied the remains of my large valise.

"What the hell is that?" He walked towards the gate and opened it. "I say, is that you Uncle Bill?" I peered from behind the tree, fearful that Daisy would charge.

"What?" He looked around searching for the voice, until his eyes fixed upon my countenance, which was in a sorry state.

"Cheer-o Uncle Bill. Afraid, I am rather poorly now."

"Well, I'll be goddamned! Bennie, is that you?" Uncle Bill grinned and sauntered towards me, swaying to and fro in his cowboy boots, and extended his arm. He shook my hand vio-lently and delivered a friendly blow to my shoulder with his left arm. "Howdy, pard'ner! I was wondering when you would show up. Sorry I don't have a phone out here. Never saw the need."

"Er, hullo, Uncle Bill. I don't suppose you could restrain your sow, er, Daisy, could you? Rather afraid the introductions did not go well."

He burst out laughing. "Don't worry, she's as gentle as a lamb."

Having never encountered a man-eating, valise-tossing merino, I remained skeptical. "Er, are you quite sure? I seem to have set her on edge, if you know what I mean."

"Nah, she's just a bit protective, that's all. We just gotta show her that you're part of the family. C'mon out from behind that tree and give her a scratch behind the ears. She likes that."

I stepped out from behind the tree, ready to spring behind it again, should the gentle lamb desire a round of luggage-owner-tossing to amuse herself.

"Jesus, what happened? You look like someone beat the crap out of you."

"What? Oh, no, nothing like that. She directed her fury at the valises. Seems to have a fondness for tossing objects about."

I paused, wondering if I was actually saying anything cogent or had fallen into delirium.

"It's rather a longish story. Chap from town gave me a lift here."

Coronado's name had escaped me momentarily, the result of the accumulated trauma. "Odd fellow, looks like a plumpish sort of rat. Said the town's founder is his direct ancestor."

Uncle Bill raised a brow. "Coronado de Vaca drove you out here? How drunk was he?"

"Yes, that's the chap's name. Coronado. Rather inebriated—sick on my trousers—dog urinated—lorry—large rock—sow attacked, what?" The words spewed forth in a river of babbling.

Bill walked over and placed a work-roughened hand on my back.

"Come on, boy, let's get you inside. Looks like you could use a whisky."

"Whisky? Oh, God yes, please." The thought of a smooth single-malt to wash away the day's trauma provided a much-needed mental boost. Uncle Bill took my arm, but the legs remained frozen, terrified that Daisy would hoover me up like an appetizer if I dared move. But the sow just grunted softly and ran her snout down my trousers. I stiffened, presuming she was gauging my fitness as an appetizer.

Instead, she put her massive head under my hand.

"What did I tell you, Bennie? She just needed to get to know you. Go ahead, scratch her behind her ears."

I dutifully moved the fingers under her hat and scratched. Apparently, all was forgotten, at least whilst Uncle Bill was present.

"Er, Uncle Bill, what exactly is this?" I pointed a shaky finger at Daisy's hat.

"That? Called a *sombrero*. Keeps her cool in summer. You gotta remember, Bennie, this ain't England."

"Quite. What did you call it?"

"*Sombrero*. That's Spanish for hat. Now, let's pick up your things. She sure did a number on those bags or yours. Daisy's always enjoyed tossing things around. Keeps her amused."

"Er, yes."

I picked up my clothes and stuffed them back into the exploded valise, whilst Uncle Bill retrieved the other. Daisy led the way, climbing the stairs of the veranda and returning to her slumber.

I followed him into the house into what looked to be the sitting room. There was a fireplace along the wall, in which stood a large wood stove. A large wooden wagon wheel was mounted above the fireplace mantle.

Uncle Bill motioned me to sit down and continued into the kitchen. I eased myself into a large chair, sighing noticeably. In front of me was a davenport covered with what looked like a Hudson's Bay blanket. Not what one would have expected in New Mexico. Then again, nothing I had found here, including Uncle Bill, was what I was expecting. Presently, he returned, carrying two glasses and a bottle. He sat down on the davenport, placed the glasses on the small table between us, and poured two bracing doses.

"Cheers," he said, knocking his glass against mine.

"Cheers," I replied hoarsely, promptly downing half the glass.

"Whoa, Bennie," Uncle Bill said. "That stuff's got a kick."

The taste buds and oesophagus suddenly realized what I had imbibed was not a well-aged single malt.

"Gah!" I coughed violently and gasped for air. "What is this?"

"Whisky."

"It tastes like petrol." Fighting off the urge to do what Coronado had done to me earlier, I picked up the bottle and read the label. "Dusty Trail Blended Whisky. Real cowboys ask for it by name."

I sighed and sat back in the chair. "Not a Speyside tipple, I gather."

"That stuff's for toffs. This is what a real man drinks." He finished his glass and poured himself another.

I considered adding "and dies soon afterwards," but suppressed the vocal chords. After all, I was his guest. Plus, he had saved me from a deranged sow.

"I brought you a bottle of eighteen-year-old single malt, but it did not survive the blast."

"Eighteen years old, huh? Guess I coulda drunk that, too."

"Er, Uncle Bill, I am rather curious. Your accent. Rather American, it isn't it?"

He looked up at me, narrowing his brow. "Do you think I should speak like an English gentleman?" he asked, with an Oxbridge accent.

"No. I mean, well, I hadn't expected it, that's all. We are British, after all."

"You may be, but I ain't. Not anymore. I left England for good. Must be thirty-five years or so. Never spoke to my father again, the bastard. When mother told me he had died, I got drunk. She died five years later. Didn't even make it back for her funeral." He paused, emptied his glass again, and stared ahead at nothing in particular.

"But you knew about the family. You sent me those postcards."

"Sure I did. Your mother still writes now and then, which enrages your father—my pompous brother. She tells me about the goings-on. Sorry about that wife of yours, by the way. I remember when I read that the two of you had married. Dorothy said she was a nice girl. Maybe a bit quiet."

He poured himself a second glass. "Always watch out for the quiet ones, boy. They'll sneak up behind you and bite you in the ass."

"What? Oh, yes, I suppose so." I was suddenly reminded of Cynthia and wondered where she and the flower-chatting Sergio were. Much as I had been gobsmacked by her running off, I still thought of her fondly.

Uncle Bill continued. "My brother—your father—was as much a horse's ass as your grandfather. I wanted you to know there was something else out there besides clubs and polo, and God knows what else these days, even if it was just those silly postcards. Always hoped you would visit."

"Well, it's awfully good of you to let me stay here. I needed to get as far away as I could from London, at least for now." I drained the remaining Dusty Trail from my glass and gasped. "Not what I expected, this New Mexico."

He laughed. "Yep, it's a pretty unique place, especially around here. I can never figure how this town survives, but somehow it does, even if Coronado drives everybody crazy."

"Might I trouble you for a bit more?" I asked, pointing to the bottle. The need for inebriation had overtaken any qualms about the quality of the tipple.

"Here you go, pard'ner. Cheers."

"Er, Uncle Bill, how exactly did you end up . . . here? I mean, this place? Seems rather like the end of the earth, if you ask me."

"That's one way of putting it. I'll tell you sometime, Bennie. It's a long, long story. Well, how about we rustle up some grub? You must be starved."

"Rustle grub?"

"Didn't you ever read any of those Zane Grey books I told you about? I sent you some, didn't I? Well, you'll learn, soon enough." With a haughty sniff, he laughed and reverted to the Oxbridge accent. "Shall we dress for dinner? You are most unpresentable."

"Rather a mess, I'm afraid."

"I got a pair of jeans and a clean shirt that ought to fit you." Then, espying what had been black leather shoes, he added, "And a pair of boots. This ain't country for fancy shoes. Too many goddamn snakes."

"Snakes?"

"Yep. Rattlesnakes. Most times they'll try to get away from you. But now and then you'll accidentally step on one hidden in the brush or sunning itself on a rock. They like ankles."

"Ankles?" Mine began to tingle.

Uncle Bill raised himself up. "C'mon back with me Bennie. I'll show you your room."

After a much needed wash-and-brush-up, I was properly attired with fresh shirt, jeans, and a pair of cowboy boots. From the kitchen wafted a rather delicious odour. I followed it eagerly, albeit rather ploddingly, given the unfamiliarity of the boots, and found Uncle Bill standing over a large pot, which he stirred slowly.

He looked up at me and grinned. "Fits you pretty good, I'd say. Got beans and *tortillas* for dinner. You've probably never tasted anything like it."

"Well, I was always rather fond of beans on toast. What is a *tortilla*."

"Think of it as Mexican toast. C'mon, let's eat."

I pondered the idea of Mexican toast and sat down at a small wooden table in the corner of the kitchen. Uncle Bill placed a steaming bowl before me, then removed a small towel from the oven, wrapped in which were round flatbreads.

He grunted and tucked into his bowl of beans. I swallowed a large spoonful and soon detected a burning sensation in the mouth. It became increasingly acute until the flames seemed to leap out the forehead.

I gasped, desperate for the nearest fire extinguisher. "Gah! What's in these?"

"Green chile. Most folks 'round here use it in everything. You'll get used to it. Go pour yourself a glass of milk. Water doesn't help." I retrieved a bottle of milk from the fridge, poured a large glass, and gulped it down, followed by a second.

After dinner, the mouth continued to smoulder, but I was too fagged to notice. I simply collapsed on the davenport.

The next morning, I awoke with a start. Uncle Bill was in the kitchen and the aroma of coffee had wandered over. Stretching rather languidly, I glided into the kitchen.

"Mornin'. I didn't have the heart to wake you up last night. That Dusty Trail can sneak up on you, if you're not used to it."

"Good morning." I yawned. "Actually, I seemed to have slept rather well. I say, is that coffee?"

"Would you rather have tea?" There was a hint of sarcasm in his voice.

"Er, well, yes, but Americans aren't overly keen on serving it. I asked for a cuppa at a shop near the bus station in Albuquerque. The chap looked at me like I had two heads. Finally, he brought over a cup of tepid water and a small tea bag that, when combined, created the most horrid cuppa I have ever tasted. Completely undrinkable."

"Well, I don't have any goddamn tea, anyway. Coffee's what real men drink, and I make it cowboy style."

"Cowboy style?" I was not sure I wished to know what he meant, given the previous evening's experience with cowboy whisky.

"Yep. You throw in some ground coffee into a pot and boil it for a while. Hot and strong. Here, try a cup."

He handed me a ceramic cup, which had a picture of a rooster on it. I took a tentative sip. Although I had survived the green chile of the night before, neither the throat nor the stomach were prepared for another assault. "A bit, er, bitter, it seems."

"You'll get used to it."

"Why do cowboys like bitter coffee?"

"What? How the hell should I know? 'Cause it's hot and strong, that's why. Gets a man going in the morning. Anyway, that's how I make it. Always have. If you don't like it, maybe you can get some tea at Garcia's General Store in town. I need you to go there anyway to get a few things. I could use some help around here."

"Of course. Happy to do my part."

"Good. Finish your coffee. We've got a bunch of chores to do. Then we'll grab some breakfast." He smiled somewhat deviously. "Think I'll have you feed Daisy her breakfast. That'll put you in her good graces."

"Feed her? She was ready to devour me yesterday."

"Don't worry. Once she sees you've got her breakfast, she'll be your best friend."

The thought of a *sombrero* wearing, valise-tossing monster as one's best friend did not warm the cockles. Perhaps, if I showed her a picture of a slab of bacon or a large ham, she would understand a Graves was not to be trifled with.

I followed Uncle Bill, who carried a large bucket of leavings, to the small barn behind the house. Daisy was loitering nearby and trotted over to greet us, grunting contentedly. The *sombrero* had slipped and now lay askew on her enormous head.

"How are you, girl?" He straightened the hat. "Ready for breakfast?" The sow, which looked permanently ready for breakfast, luncheon, high tea, and dinner, grunted loudly. She appeared to be dividing her attention between anticipatory glances towards the empty trough and suspicious ones directed towards me. The feeling was quite mutual, at least regarding suspicion, and I searched for the nearest scalable tree in the event evasive manoeuvres were required.

We walked into the barn. Inside was an amalgam of baled hay, wire fencing, buckets strewn about, an ancient, rust-coloured tractor, and a rather forlorn-looking grey mare.

"Morning Marjorie," Bill warbled, walking over to the horse and patting its side. "This is my nephew, Bennie. Say hello to Marjorie, Bennie. She's always been one for proper introductions."

Never having been schooled in equine etiquette, I was not sure of the proper behaviour when one was introduced to a mare. A kiss of the hand, er, hoof, seemed rather out of the question. Perhaps a neighed "Charmed, I'm sure."

I looked at the horse and cleared my throat. "Er, yes, Marjorie. Benjamin Graves at your service." I offered the horse a quick small bow.

"Pat her on her neck. She likes that. It's not like you're meeting the goddamn Queen."

I approached the horse, right hand extended warily towards her neck. "There's a good horse." The horse stared at me, eyes bulging, and moved away whilst shaking her head violently. Presumably, she was ascertaining which of my strategic parts she would target.

"Give it time, Bennie." Uncle Bill patted Marjorie's side. "Like I said, once you feed 'em, they're your friend for life."

"Now, grab some of that hay and put it in her stall." He pointed to a large metal bucket next to the stall. "Then go fill that bucket with water. The pump's to your left as you go out the door."

I did as I was told. The horse stared at me and remained motionless. "There you are, Marjorie." I feigned cheerfulness. "Hay, water, everything a horse needs, what?" She continued to stare, although the previous eye-bulging, surprised look had been replaced with one of utter equine contempt.

"C'mon over here, Bennie. I'll show you how to mix Daisy's mash." I walked over to a large work table, which was covered in dirt, mice droppings, small tools, several rodent-gnawed paper bags, and a large old coffee can.

Uncle Bill pointed to various bags and buckets as he spoke. "See that coffee can? Fill it twice with feed from that bag and dump it into this bucket. Then dump this bucket of slops into the other bucket and mix it all with that old paddle. When it's mixed real good, pour it into her trough."

I mixed the porcine witches' brew together, wondering how anything could relish eating it. After returning the mixture to Daisy's trough and pouring it in, the beast pushed me aside. She ate ravenously, whilst emitting loud grunts. Soon, the contents were gone and the trough licked clean. I stared at Daisy. She grunted again, nodding her head in the affirmative. Perhaps Uncle Bill had been correct and I was now her friend. But the Graves naval background suspected a false flag operation.

"Right, then," I said as I walked back into the barn. "The natives have been fed and watered. Anything else?"

"As a matter of fact, yes. You can muck out Marjorie's stall as soon as I let her out to pasture. I haven't had a chance to do that for a few days."

"Er, muck out, you say?"

"That's right." He pointed at a small, rusty shovel. "Go grab that big shovel hanging on the wall. You get the stall mucked out while I take some hay to the cattle."

"Cattle?"

"Yep. Got about 50 head now. Good stock, too. Taken me years to build up that herd."

I recalled Coronado's saying Uncle Bill "ran fifty head" and a dim light flickered inside the brain. "What are they for?"

"What the hell do you think they're for? I sell 'em. Have you ever eaten a steak?"

"Yes, of course. I rather enjoy a good fillet steak."

"Well, somebody's got to raise cattle so you can enjoy your god-damn fillet steak, don't he?" He shook his head.

"Er, yes, sorry. I mean, living in London all these years, one rather forgets such things." I imagined Marjorie rolling her large eyes at me, equine contempt rising. "Well, I had best start mucking out the stall, as you say. Er, what exactly does one do when one mucks out a stall?"

"Shovel out the dirty hay and crap into that wheelbarrow. About fifty feet behind the barn there's a pile where you can dump all of it. Then grab a fresh bale and spread it in the stall."

"You mean the dung?"

"That's exactly what I mean. Once you're done, go on back to the house. We'll have our breakfast and then head into town." With that, Uncle Bill walked out of the barn, leaving me to the rather malodorous task.

I spent half an hour in the stall, mucking it out whilst unsuccessfully attempting to keep the olfactory closed. I mean, one encountered the occasional canine, er, droppings in the streets of London; this horse was in a prodigious class by itself.

Presently, chest heaving and having finished the appointed task, I stepped into the fresher air outside the barn, and breathed deeply. Returning to the house, I poured myself another cup of coffee, which in the interim had further evaporated into a brownish sludge, and sat down. Despite having been relinquished of the spouse and made redundant, the civility of London, and the absence of threatening and contemptuous barnyard creatures, began its soft siren's song.

# Chapter 4

As we breakfasted—fried eggs, bacon, beans, and toast, almost British in its civility—Uncle Bill set out the day's schedule. We would first visit Garcia's General Store for various fence-mending components, without which the bovine population might escape their confines. Next would be a visit to the ranch of Ernesto Morales, from whom a large trailer's worth of hay would be purchased to feed said bovines, as well as Marjorie. Then, a brief detour to Rudy's Bar and Drive-Thru Liquors to resupply the larder with Dusty Trail. Uncle Bill had misinterpreted my ingestion of several glasses as an endorsement of its restorative qualities, and was determined I should be able to share it with him each and every evening.

He scraped the last few beans from his plate with an edge of toast. "We ought to be moseying into town."

"Eh? I thought we would be motoring to town in your lorry?"

"That's what I meant. You'll learn the language soon enough, Bennie. No more of the Queen's English for you."

"Well, the *lingua franca* spoken seems rather odd. I prefer the Queen's English, thank you very much."

Uncle Bill looked at me with surprise. "You won't fit in speaking like that. Hell, folks 'round here barely speak English, much less the Queen's English. Took me a few years to adapt. It's good, though, and a hell of a lot less pretentious. Like the West."

There was certainly an air of familiarity amongst the populace, almost frighteningly so. Not that I was of the "familiarity breeds contempt" school, mind you. I had already dealt with enough toffs in my life, including the familial ones, to understand the difference between class and, well, *class*.

Having finished breakfast and stacked the dishes, we opened the front door and stepped onto the veranda. Daisy rose up instantly. She walked over to Uncle Bill, offering several cheery grunts, whilst giving me the porcine equivalent of the Gypsy's curse, despite my having recently breakfasted her. Granted, one prefers a Gypsy's curse to being tossed about like a ragdoll. Still, one presumed a modicum of gratitude would be in order.

"Bennie and I will be back soon, girl," he said, straightening the gaudy *sombrero* and scratching her behind the ears. "You keep an eye on things." Suitably placated, Daisy returned to her usual position and flopped down heavily.

"Woe betide the feckless chap who sets foot in her porcine lair," I thought.

We walked to the far side of the house and up the drive to the garage. It was a forlorn-looking structure with a noticeable lean. On the roof, a small, rusted, and bent weathervane in the shape of a trotting horse meandered aimlessly in the breeze. To the left of the garage, a large metal trailer sat parked.

Compared with the decrepit lorry that Coronado had coaxed about Vaca Seca, Uncle Bill's was Rolls Royce-like in appearance. He climbed in, started the motor, and reversed it out of the garage. He soon had the trailer connected and we trundled slowly down the dirt road towards town, avoiding, unlike Coronado, the nearby boulders. We stopped first in front of the general store, which shared the same run-down Vaca Seca architectural style. Next to the front door sat a gaunt and barkative dog. Uncle Bill stepped out of the truck and put his cowboy hat on. The dog began wagging its tail wildly.

Uncle Bill bent down to pet it. "*Hola*, Pedro. There's a good dog." He pulled out a smallish dog biscuit from his shirt pocket and gave it to the dog, which despatched it instantly.

Sensing this beast was harmless, I extended my hand and petted its head. "This dog looks famished. Doesn't his owner feed him?"

"Well, nobody really owns Pedro. I suppose you could call him the town dog. He's pretty good at scrounging for food. Between the trash at Rudy's and the leftovers he steals from the cafe, he survives." Pedro, presumably contented, strolled over to the lorry, lifted his leg and urinated on the front tyre, then returned to his post in front of the door.

"I say, Uncle Bill. That dog just relieved itself on your front tyre."

"As long as Pedro doesn't piss all over me like that damn Paco, I don't care." He laughed softly. "Funny thing about Vaca Seca, it attracts strays who somehow survive."

"Might that include you, Uncle Bill?"

He looked at me silently for a moment, then offered a wry grin. "I suppose you could call me a straggler of sorts, Bennie. Never really thought of it that way."

"My apologies. I, er, meant no offense, of course."

"Forget it, Bennie. I always thought of myself as a refugee from snobbery. But I guess I was a straggler here, too, at least when I first arrived." He snorted. "C'mon, let's go get our supplies."

We walked past Pedro and into the store. Inside, the shop looked as though a typhoon had roared through. Boxes were strewn hither and yon. It looked like a combination of ironmonger's, grocer's and chemist's shops. Boxes of wire were perched next to a display of ladies' bonnets. Tins of beans were stacked next to an assortment of pills and plasters. A selection of cowboy hats, white and black, hung over largish bags of feed for chickens, horses, and pigs.

"What a bloody mess," I muttered, as we navigated our way precipitously along an aisle stacked with all manner of fence posts, wire, and odd-shaped tools that looked as if they were taken from the Marquis de Sade's mediaeval sitting room. "How does one find anything in here?"

"You get used to it." Uncle Bill's eyes wandered along the aisle searching for well, whatever bits were required for repairing fences. "Now, where's that damn crimper I need?"

He continued to scour the aisle for a crimper, whatever that was. Finally, he finally shouted, "Hey, Joe, I need a new crimper. Where you hiding them?"

For a moment, there was only silence. Then, to my dismay, I found myself staring at Coronado de Vaca, wearing a too small white apron and inching his large form through the detritus to greet us.

"*Buenos días*, El Vaquero. Long time. ¿*Que no*? And you're here with your brother. Hola, Señor Graves. You look a whole lot different today." He extended a relatively clean hand to mine and shook it.

"Brother?" Uncle Bill turned to me with a confused expression. "He thinks we're brothers?"

I shrugged. "I attempted to explain the familial relationship, but without success."

"Where's Joe, Coronado? I can't find the wire crimpers I need."

"Joe went over to Rudy's to get a cup of coffee. Can I help?"

"Look Coronado, do you know where Joe keeps the wire crimpers?"

"I dunno. What are they for?"

"For fixing my goddamn fence. I can't have fifty head wandering all over the county."

"Okay, El Vaquero." Coronado hesitated. "You need some chicken wire, too?"

"No. I need a pair of wire crimpers. They look like pliers but with twisted jaws." I could see the frustration building on Uncle Bill's countenance, like a kettle about to boil.

"Pliers? Oh, sure, they're on the next aisle." Coronado turned around and crabbed away. A few minutes later, he came back, holding a large pair of pliers in his chubby hand. "Here you go, El Vaquero. Pliers, like you want."

"These aren't wire crimpers. They're just pliers. I need ones with the twisted jaws."

"But these are nice and straight."

"Oh, to hell with it. I'll go find Joe myself. You said he's over at Rudy's?"

"*Sí*, El Vaquero. He should be back later."

I felt as if I were in the middle of a nightmare, with Coronado a dim-witted Lucifer whose utter vapidity caused his charges to scream and writhe in agony. Uncle Bill, perhaps because he was used to Coronado's barmy behaviour, simply shook his head in defeat and glanced at his watch. "C'mon, Bennie, let's walk over to Rudy's."

We walked out the door. Pedro had not moved. Espying Uncle Bill, his tail began to thump the ground wildly. He raised himself up stiffly, walked over to the lorry, and urinated on the other front tyre.

"Bad dog," I shouted.

Pedro looked at me indifferently, then sauntered over towards me, tail still wagging. He casually urinated on my boot.

"You bloody canine bastard!" I shook off my boot and rubbed it on the dirt tarmac in front of the shop. "Do you have some sort of reserve bladder?"

The dog feigned ignorance and lay back down.

"Don't mind him, Bennie. After you've lived here a while, a little dog piss on your boots will be like a splash of perfume."

"I suppose we must deal with that other disgusting cur I encountered in front of the bar?"

"Paco? Well, there's always a chance Nestor Martinez is too drunk to have let him out this morning."

As we approached Rudy's, we discovered Nestor must have remained mildly sober. There stood Paco outside the front door. He growled and was surely manufacturing copious quantities of urine to be despatched forthwith.

I let Uncle Bill go, well, over the top one might say, whilst I guarded the rear. He walked up to the growling Paco, shouted "shut up," and delivered a stern kick to Paco's behind, which convinced the dog to slink away. Normally, I abhorred animal cruelty, RSPCA member, and all that. Paco, however, had tested my canine sympathies.

We walked inside. It took a minute for the eyes to adjust to the dimness. Uncle Bill walked into the bar an approached a rather scrawny, unshaven, and semiconscious chap.

"Hey, Joe! I need a pair of wire crimpers. Where you hiding them?" Joe Garcia looked at Uncle Bill with a vague hint of recognition. "Wire crimpers? Aisle three with the rest of the fencing crap. Ask that *pendejo* Coronado. He can get 'em for you."

"I asked Coronado. He brought me a pair of pliers. Hell, he wouldn't know crimpers from crackers. Now, can you come back to the store and find them for me? Otherwise, my whole herd's gonna escape."

Joe offered Uncle Bill a rather fatigued look. "Let me finish my beer." He raised the bottle to his lips and emptied it. "Hey, Rudy," he shouted to no one in particular, "I gotta get back to the store and find some wire crimpers. I'll pay you later."

Joe staggered out the front door, followed by Uncle Bill and me. Paco had relocated himself a discreet distance away, and was casting a wary eye towards us. Walking into his store, Joe yelled for Coronado, who was gnawing on something as he stepped from behind a counter.

"*Hola*, Joe. You're back early."

"Coronado, do you know where the wire crimpers are?"

"Sure, Joe," Coronado replied, smiling. "Aisle three."

"Can you get a pair for El Vaquero."

"Okay." Coronado walked back to the third aisle, where Uncle Bill had initiated his search. Within two minutes, he returned, holding what appeared to be pliers with twisted jaws

Uncle Bill's eyes bulged as he glared at Coronado. "I looked all down aisle three. I asked you where they were. You didn't even know what they looked like. Where the hell did you find these?"

"Sorry, El Vaquero. Guess I forgot. They were behind the flour."

"What? But how did you know what they were?"

Coronado shrugged. "I know where everything is, El Vaquero." I thought you wanted a pair of nice pliers. You should have said you needed fence crimpers."

Uncle Bill's face turned a mottled shade of purple. "But I told you that. I said I needed a pair of crimpers to fix my goddamn fence and that they LOOKED like pliers." He shook his head and stopped. For me, the conversation was already framed in unreality, like one of those Salvador Dali paintings, what with the limp clocks lying about everywhere.

Joe eyed the crimpers. "You're wasting your time. That's four dollars."

"I need a hundred-foot roll of fence, too, Joe. And instead of me looking around the whole goddamn store to see if Coronado put it behind the laundry soap or next to the toilet floats, can he load it into my truck?"

Joe sighed. "Coronado, go load a hundred-foot roll of the welded fence into El Vaquero's truck."

"*Okay*, Joe."

"How much for the fence?"

"Ten dollars."

Uncle Bill took out his wallet and handed Joe fourteen dollars. He grabbed the fence crimpers tightly and walked out the door. Following closely, I heard a forceful stream of invective, generously laced with Coronado's name.

We walked back to Rudy's. "I gotta get some whisky, Bennie. You mind waiting here? Make sure that idiot brings the fence with four-inch squares. If he brings out real thin stuff that looks like little diamonds, that's chicken wire. I don't want that."

"I say, Uncle Bill, a bit early in the day for a tot, is it not?"

"After dealing with Coronado, no time is too early. But I'm just gonna buy a couple more bottles of Dusty Trail, especially since you took a liking to it."

The memory of the battery acid-like fluid I had imbibed the previous evening sent waves of fear through the neurons. "Er, most kind of you. No need to bother. I thought I might swear off the stuff. Tee-total and all that."

"Well, I need more whisky. You want any beer?"

"Beer? A few pints of bitter this evening would be grand, thank you."

"I can get you a six-pack if you want."

"A what?"

"Haven't you ever had a can of beer?"

"Beer in a can? Are you joking?"

"You're not in England anymore. The only pub is Rudy's. Folks round here drink beer mostly from cans and bottles."

"Barbaric."

"I'll get you a six-pack. Maybe some Milwaukee's Best. That stuff's not too bad."

As Uncle Bill disappeared into Rudy's, Coronado came out dragging a large roll of metal fence.

"*Híjole.* This fence is real heavy."

I could see beads of perspiration falling from his ears. "Here, Coronado," I said, taking an end of the roll. "Allow me." Together we tossed it into the back of the lorry.

"*Muchas gracias,* Señor Graves. I guess El Vaquero is mad at me, huh?"

I hesitated, debating the efficacy of an honest response against a convenient falsehood. The mind recalled an incident when I had accompanied Cynthia to a dress shop, as she wished to purchase an evening dress. After trying on a half-dozen or so, she came out beaming, wearing a reddish dress that one could only describe as hideous. A more careless chap would have made an inopportune remark, perhaps even several. When she asked how she looked, I said, "No one else could wear that dress, my love." This endeared me to her, albeit temporarily.

"Not angry, Coronado, merely a bit fatigued."

"I wouldn't want El Vaquero mad at me. I seen him mad before." Coronado paused and shook his head. "*Híjole.*" He walked back into Garcia's store.

Presently, I espied Uncle Bill walking back from Rudy's, carrying a large paper bag. He stepped up into the lorry and placed the bag carefully between us on the seat. "Let's go get that hay."

We motored off once again, this time heading north. Some five miles down the road, Uncle Bill manoeuvred the lorry and trailer sharply onto a small dirt road, which seemed in worse condition than the trail that led to his own ranch. The ride felt endless. When we arrived, the kidneys were in full retreat.

Uncle Bill backed the lorry up to an enormous barn, whose doors were wide open. Inside, yellow bales of hay were stacked neatly throughout and the air was redolent with the smell of newly cut grass.

He sounded the lorry's horn and slid out. From the back of the barn emerged a gigantic chap, who lumbered over towards us like a dinosaur.

"How's it going, Ernesto?" Uncle Bill said. "Looks like you've got plenty of hay."

Ernesto broke into a wide grin. "El Vaquero, how's that herd of yours?"

"If I don't get my fence repaired soon, my herd's gonna wander all over the county. Otherwise, it's real good." .

Uncle Bill pointed towards me. "Ernesto, I want you to meet my nephew, Bennie. He just arrived from England. Finally came to his senses and got the hell out of there. He's gonna be helping me out for a while."

Ernesto extended a gaping maw of a hand, which engulfed mine. "*Bienvenidos*, Bennie. I'm Ernesto Morales. So, you're gonna help El Vaquero, huh? That's good. You ever been to New Mexico before?"

"Er, afraid not." I tried to ignore my throbbing hand. "Rather different than what I had expected."

"Yeah, there's nothing like it. My family's been here for almost two hundred years. I wouldn't want to live nowhere else."

Although the mind boggled at the concept of two hundred years in Vaca Seca, surrounded by two hundred years' worth of Coronado's ancestors, I simply smiled. "Yes, well, I believe Uncle Bill is of the same opinion, Mister Morales. A most interesting locale. Quite different from London."

"Glad you like it. You need anything, just ask. Now, let's go load up that trailer."

He picked up four bales of hay and carried them into the trailer. Uncle Bill followed, carrying two bales, whilst I struggled merely to grab one, which was quite abrasive. After struggling, I managed to carry two bales, although the arm and shoulder muscles complained loudly. By the time all of the hay was loaded, I was all in.

Ernesto piled the last bales near the top on the trailer. "You thought anymore about the cafe, El Vaquero?"

"Yeah, I've thought about it. Still don't know. I got my hands full with the ranch."

"I understand. Wish I could, but everything's tied up in the ranch. I just bought a new breeding bull. He's supposed to be a champion." Ernesto stepped off the trailer, took off his hat, and wiped his forehead with a large blue and white spotted handkerchief. He performed a bit of mental arithmetic with his giant fingers. "Let's see, two hundred bales. That's forty dollars."

Uncle Bill took out his wallet and retrieved the funds. He shook Ernesto's hand, thanked him, and we returned to the lorry and rumbled off.

"I say, Uncle Bill, what's this about a cafe?"

"What? Oh, nothing really. Just something I've been thinking about, that's all." He looked at his watch. "Don't know about you, Bennie, but I need some grub. Let's grab a bite to eat on our way back home."

After another jarring ride and screaming complaints from the kidneys, we arrived in town. We parked in front of a small building. It, too, sagged noticeably, looking even more decrepit then Rudy's. Above a small curtained window and painted on the wall in faded white paint were the words "Dos Abuelas Cafe."

"What does "Dos Ab—, Ab-u—how exactly does one pronounce that word?"

"Dohs Ah-bwah-las. It means two grandmothers. The place is named for the owners. They're sisters."

"Jolly good. I'm feeling rather peckish. A grandmotherly luncheon would be excellent."

Uncle Bill slid out of the lorry and brushed off the bits of hay clinging to his shirt and trousers. "Yep, it sure would be." He sighed and we walked inside.

# Chapter 5

An acrid odour permeated the small confines of the cafe, reminding me of the fish-and-chip takeaways I had frequented in the college days. The outside sag of the building carried through inside. There was a distinct incline to the floor towards the back, almost as if the building itself were encouraging patrons, of which there were no others, out the door. One doubted the establishment would find itself listed in the *Michelin Guide*.

We sat down at one of the tables. It was covered with a red and white checkerboard plastic tablecloth. Uncle Bill removed his hat and placed it on the table. I set my forearms down, only to discover that a glue-like substance had attached the shirtsleeve to the tablecloth.

"Gah! What is that?"

"Probably honey. Sometimes happens. Just ask Maria for a cloth to wipe it down."

"Maria?"

"She's one of the *abuelas*. Maria Amador. You'll meet her, and her sister Esperanza, soon enough."

"Rather quiet in here. Shouldn't someone be greeting the customers, offering them menus, and all that?"

Uncle Bill said, pointing to a bruised, blue-grey door on the back wall. "Why don't you go knock on the door to the kitchen? They may not have heard us come in."

"Odd way to run a business." I stood up. "Right, I'll see if anyone is about."

Uncle Bill looked at me with a wry smile. "You do that, Bennie." I walked up to the door and knocked gently. "Hullo," I said, speaking into the door. "I say, anyone about?"

The door was the type that swung in either direction, so I gently pushed it open and peered into what looked like a casualty of the London Blitz. "Hullo?" I retreated into the dining room. Suddenly, the door swung open wildly. I turned around. Before me stood a rather shapeless woman of medium height, with greyish-black hair and an aquiline nose. She wore a filthy apron and was holding a large metal spoon, which was dripping a reddish-yellow liquid onto the dirty floor. The ashy remains of a cigarette dangled from her lips.

"¡*Pendejo*! What the fuck are you doing in my kitchen?"

"I, er, I beg your pardon, madam. I only wished to enquire if someone was about and, er, to ask for a cloth with which to clean the table at which my uncle and I are sitting."

Her brow, which was rather thick, furrowed noticeably. "What the fuck are you talking about? And how come you talk so funny?" She turned around and went back into the kitchen, hurling the door at me. I stood there motionless, feeling rather flummoxed. Just as suddenly, she pushed the door open again and threw a dripping wet rag at me, which soaked my shirt and then fell to the floor. I picked up the rag and walked slowly back to our table.

"I see you got a rag to wipe the table down."

I ran the cloth over the offending spot and then the entire table. "What do you think I should do with the cloth?"

Uncle Bill laughed, "Well, one thing's for sure, I wouldn't go back into the kitchen."

"Who is that bloody viper? Surely the grandmothers wouldn't approve of such a cross employee."

"Nope, they wouldn't. But she ain't an employee. You just met Esperanza Fuentes, one of the *abuelas*."

"Good God! I mean, aren't grandmotherly types supposed to be gentle, roly-poly sorts? That woman looked as if she was ready to do me violence."

"If you had stepped any further into the kitchen, she might have. 'Course, she seems to be in a pretty good mood today, from what I saw."

"Eh? She threw a wet cloth at me like a star player on a cricket pitch."

"You're lucky she didn't throw a pan at you. Her sister Maria once threw a large butcher knife at a customer who complained about his meal." Uncle Bill pointed towards the side wall. "Flew by his head and stuck in the wall, right over there."

"Then why we are sitting here? I mean, one may be peckish, but not so much that one is willing to be eviscerated by flying cutlery."

"Calm down, Bennie. Esperanza just takes some getting used to. Now, Maria, she's a bit tougher, like a wild horse. Best not to cross her. A long time ago, before I got here, she almost shot a guy at Rudy's. She was tending bar and, well, he got a bit grabby. So, Maria pulled out the shotgun from under the bar and pointed it at his family jewels, if you know what I mean. Told him to get out and never come back. He ran out of the bar and never set foot in town again."

I grimaced. "Well, I am all for yobs receiving their comeuppance. However, this Maria sounded positively deranged."

A few minutes later, the kitchen door flew open, followed by Esperanza. She marched over to our table, looked at Uncle Bill, and then glowered at me. "This *pendejo* belong to you?"

"Be nice, Esperanza. This is my nephew Bennie. He just arrived from England yesterday. Staying with me and helping out at the ranch."

"He don't look like he can do much work." She surveyed me up and down, like a cut of beef. "You know anything about ranching? You even know what a steer looks like?"

"I know perfectly well what cattle look like. As for ranching, I am quite sure Uncle Bill will teach me everything I need to know."

"Oh, a big city *pendejito*," she replied, laughing derisively. "What do you want for lunch El Vaquero?"

"Green chile *enchiladas*."

"*Bueno.*" She turned to me again. "What about you, *Pendejito*? Do you want some baby food like my granddaughter used to eat?"

"I beg your pardon, Madam. I have no intention of being insulted." Esperanza rolled her large eyes. "*¡Ay, cabron!* What do you want?"

"May I see a menu, if that's not too much trouble?"

"We got *enchiladas*, *tacos*, or a bowl of *frijoles*. What do you want?" Not knowing what a *taco* was, and having barely survived the inferno that was Uncle Bill's beans last night, I settled on *enchiladas*, whatever those were. "I will have the, en-chy-ladas, thank you."

"En-she-lahdas, *Pendejito*. You better learn to pronounce Spanish if you stay around here."

Tempted as I was to interject that she needed a course in English grammar, personal safety suggested discretion. "Er, yes. Well, thank you for correcting my pronunciation, madam."

"What do you want to drink?"

"Tea would be grand."

"I'll have tea, too, Esperanza."

When Esperanza had disappeared behind the kitchen door, I turned to Uncle Bill. "A most sour disposition. And why does she keep calling me *Pendejito*? What does it mean?"

Uncle Bill stared up towards the ceiling of the cafe, which looked as if it might come crashing down at any moment. He rubbed his hand over his chin. "It's just a term of, ah, endearment, Bennie." He looked at me, then stared back at the ceiling. "Kinda tough to translate into English. I guess 'little one' is the closest definition I can think of."

"Joe Garcia referred to Coronado as a *pendejo* when we saw him in Rudy's. Not endearingly either, as I recall."

Uncle Bill grimaced and smacked his lips. "Nah, it's not exactly the same. You see, '*ito*' is a diminutive. You add it to the end of a word to mean something small. Now, Coronado is heavyset, so Joe couldn't call him little one."

I was about to respond, when the kitchen door flung open again and Esperanza set down two large glasses with ice before us.

I looked at the glass. "I asked for tea."

"What the fuck do you think this is?"

"Madam, I may not know what *enchiladas* are. However, I assure you I know my tea. Tea is hot. It is served in a cup, generally with milk."

As I stared at her, I felt a sharp kick from under the table, which had connected with the tibia. "Gah!" I looked over to Uncle Bill, who was gently shaking his head back and forth.

"You want *hot* tea?" We don't serve no *hot* tea." She glared at Uncle Bill. "Maybe you don't want hot *enchiladas* neither."

"Of course we do, Esperanza. Bennie's just used to hot tea in England. I'm sure he'll like iced tea fine once he tries it. Right, Bennie?"

Uncle Bill stared at me intently. I was sufficiently cognizant to understand I should agree wholeheartedly.

I stammered. "Er, yes, iced tea will be quite nice, thank you. Just not used to it."

"*Pendejito*," she muttered, and stormed back into the kitchen.

"Term of endearment, eh?"

Uncle Bill shrugged, poured sugar into his glass, and stirred.

We sat at table silently, drinking our iced tea, which certainly did not taste like proper English tea. Presently, the kitchen door exploded open again. From behind it emerged not Esperanza, but a woman who bore an uncanny resemblance to one of those *Grimm's Fairy Tales* witches. She was bearing down upon us like a dreadnought. Had she had a broom, I have no doubt she would have flown to our table.

She was carrying two large, steaming oval plates. Setting the plates down sullenly, she walked away, saying not one word. As quickly as she had appeared, she vanished back into the kitchen.

"Thanks, Maria," Uncle Bill shouted.

"That's the infamous, Maria, of shotgun fame?"

"Yep. Not the most talkative person, but that's probably for the best. Well, we better eat, while it's still hot."

The steaming mass before me was like nothing I had seen before. There was no discernible beginning or end to it, although I did recognize a small mound of beans on the plate, which looked suspiciously like the ones I had eaten the previous evening. The odour was quite pleasant, although I noticed a slight burning sensation in the tonsular region as I inhaled. Not quite sure how to tackle the meal, I observed Uncle Bill, who had dove into the mass with his fork. The top was covered with a sauce of sorts with dark green bits and flowing ribbons of what appeared to be cheese.

With temerity, I took the fork and knife and cut into the mass, returning a largish bite to the waiting jaws. It was rather hot in temperature, so I instinctively reached for the glass of iced tea. The taste was pleasing, although difficult to describe.

And then I felt an explosion. The flames that had leapt out of the cranium the previous evening whilst consuming Uncle Bill's beans paled miserably in comparison. The mouth felt as if it had been overrun by lava, which was now spreading upwards through the cranium and destroying everything in its path. I reached for the glass of iced tea and drained it, to no avail. My eyes bulged and teared. I glanced across the table. Uncle Bill was cheerily tucking into his *enchiladas*. I was unable to speak and perspiration gushed down my forehead.

I pounded the table. Uncle Bill looked at me and chuckled. "A little too spicy, Bennie? You'll get used to it. Like I told you last night, try some milk. Go on back into the kitchen and ask Esperanza for a glass." I shook my head violently in opposition. Not even the prospect of being crisped to a cinder was worth the wrath that awaited behind the kitchen door.

"I'll go get you a glass." He stood up and bow-legged his way to the kitchen.

"Esperanza," I heard him shout. "Can I get a glass of milk for my nephew? He's not quite used to Maria's *enchiladas* yet."

Uncle Bill came back bearing a glass of milk, which I made short work of. The effect was minimal, at best, although it did manage to stop the advancing march of the lava.

"What is in these? I have never tasted anything remotely as incendiary."

"That's just good ol' New Mexico green chile. Esperanza and Maria do like the hotter varieties. But, then, that's what folks around here are used to."

"How does anyone get used to this inferno? I mean, look at you, tucking into your plate as if it's a pudding."

"I've been eating it for years. You should have seen me the first time I ate here. I was what they called a greenhorn, and was I ever."

"Back then, Esperanza's and Maria's father Ernesto was still running the place. His green chile was even hotter than this. But I kept coming back. The taste just grows on you, I guess."

Oddly enough, as Uncle Bill said that, I felt a suicidal desire for another forkful, knowing full well what lay in store. I gingerly manoeuvred the fork into position and extracted a much smaller quantity. Although the lava-like heat reappeared, it dissipated surprisingly quickly.

"See what I mean. There's something about that green chile that makes you want more, no matter how damn hot it is."

"I must admit, the taste is rather intoxicating. But how does this place stay in business? Those sisterly vipers cannot possibly encourage customer patronage."

"Not exactly. Maria does most of the cooking. She uses Ernesto's recipes. The food's good, so folks put up with the gals."

"Have they always been this vituperative?"

"Well, they were never what you would call soft and cuddly. Maria's a widow. Lost her husband, oh, about ten years ago, I guess."

"Sorry to hear that. What about Esperanza?"

"She's divorced. Her ex-husband is a truck driver. He never spent much time at home anyway."

"One can understand why the chap would not have wanted to. Rather hard to imagine Esperanza as the doting wife and motherly type."

"Anyway, the place could be doing better. Trouble is, those two get nastier and folks come in less and less."

I was pondering the business circumstances silently, when a tall, grey-haired chap walked in the door. He espied Uncle Bill and sauntered to our table.

"El Vaquero," he said extending his hand. "Where you been hiding?"

"*Hola*, Rudy. I've been around. Stopped in your place this morning, as a matter of fact. Had to find Joe so he could get me a pair of wire crimpers. You weren't around."

"Yeah, I had to get a part for my truck up in Crístobal. Starter's shot." Rudy looked at me and smiled. "Who's the new *gringo*?"

"Rudy, this is my nephew Bennie. He came all the way from England. Gonna help me out on the ranch."

He shook my hand. "*Hola*, Bennie. I'm Rudy Sandoval. Your Uncle, he's one crazy *gringo*. But we sure like him."

I smiled. "A pleasure to meet you, Mister Sandoval."

"Just call me Rudy. I own the bar down the street."

"Yes, I actually stopped in yesterday after I arrived."

Rudy laughed. "Yeah, I'm the first stop for a lot of folks who come to Vaca Seca. I guess they're all real thirsty when they arrive. Goes with the name."

"Yes, well, I had to retrieve Coronado de Vaca, who had offered me a lift to Uncle Bill's ranch in his lorry."

"Coronado spends a lot of time in the bar, that's for sure. Still hasn't paid off his tab." Rudy shrugged his shoulders.

"How are the *enchiladas* today, Bennie?"

"How did you know I ordered the *enchiladas*?"

"A bartender always knows his customers, even the *gringo* ones. Besides, nobody ever orders Maria's *tacos*."

"Is something wrong with them?" I began to ready myself for a bout of ptomaine.

"The only thing wrong with Maria's *tacos* is that they're not her *enchiladas*. Nobody makes *enchiladas* like Maria."

"Nobody serves them like her, either, I should imagine."

"Huh? Oh, Maria's okay, Bennie. Just don't ever touch her. A long time ago, she was bartending. This young *cabrón* kept pawing at her, like a bear. So, she pulled out the—"

"—shotgun that was kept under the bar?"

"I already told him the story, Rudy. Figured it's best to know some things right away."

"Yeah, I guess that makes sense." Well, don't be a stranger, El Vaquero. Guess I better go see about some *enchiladas*."

Rudy walked over towards the kitchen door. "*Querida*? Are you in there?"

The door opened violently and Maria glowered at him.

"*Sí*, Rudy. *Enchiladas* today?"

"*Por favor, mi querida*."

"*Vete a la chingada*, Rudy. I'd rather sit on a cactus." She slammed the door into him and disappeared.

"What did she say, Uncle Bill?"

"Just a bit of friendly banter, Bennie."

"It's just a little game they play. He's been saying that for years, and her answer is always the same. Well, almost always. I've heard Maria say she would rather drink bear piss, drink goat piss, drink dog piss, eat a tarantula, kiss a rattlesnake, sit on a firecracker, shoot herself with a shotgun—after shooting him in his *cojones*, you get the idea."

"Sounds like true love."

"I think she actually likes him, Bennie. He always gets extra *enchiladas*."

Rudy sat down at one of the other tables, grabbing hold so as not to slide down the incline, and waited for his luncheon. Uncle Bill walked over to the cash register that sat on a small table in the corner of the restaurant, counted out five dollars, and slid the money into the table drawer.

"Thank you Uncle Bill. A most interesting luncheon."

"You're welcome. You get to work it off this afternoon. We're gonna mend that fence."

Uncle Bill started to walk towards the front door, when it opened before him, admitting Coronado. There was a near collision, as both stopped suddenly.

"El Vaquero. I guess we almost wrecked into each other."

"Yep."

"Sorry about your pliers this morning. Joe got pretty mad at me after you and Señor Graves left."

"No matter. I got my fence crimpers and I got my fence. Bennie and I, we've got plenty of work to do."

"*Sí*, El Vaquero. I'm just here to get some lunch for Joe. He's too busy to come over." Coronado directed his rodentary gaze towards me and smiled.

"*Hola*, Señor Graves. Did you eat lunch? Maria's *enchiladas* are real good, huh?"

"Er, yes, Coronado. They were. Rather on the spicy side."

"That's what Joe told me to get. He always gets the same thing."

Coronado walked over to the table Rudy was sitting at and dropped down heavily onto an old wooden chair.

"Odd duck, Coronado. Bit of the Churchillian riddle-wrapped-in-a-mystery-inside-an-enigma type."

Uncle Bill put on his hat as we walked out into the bright sunshine. "He's odd all right. Not sure about the riddle in the enigma crap. Dumb as a post, if you ask me. Well, let's get back to the ranch and get to work."

# Chapter 6

O ur work that afternoon, and over the next three days, consisted of repairing seemingly endless lengths of rickety wire fence strung between poles made out of tree limbs. The copious quantities of blood that dripped off my hands and arms introduced me to barbed wire. Nor were our repairs performed anonymously. Whilst we worked, small groups of rather befuddled-looking cattle would meander over to wherever we were making repairs. They would observe us, masticating the contents of whatever particular stomach they favoured at the time, whilst swishing their tails about to ward off ever-present flies. The flies, suitably rebuffed, would then alight on my neck in search of a meal.

The work was entirely foreign to me. I mean, rare is the banker type who deals with barbed wire—although some of the clients may have disagreed. Yet, I found myself rather enjoying it, despite the bleeding arms and biting flies. The air was fresh, other that the malodorous droppings of our bovine audience, redolent of sagebrush and pine.

At the end of each day we returned to the ranch house, whereupon Daisy would trot up to Uncle Bill, grunt her loud welcome, and be rewarded with ear scratching and realignment of the ever-present *sombrero*. She still glared me in her less-than-welcoming porcine way. However, I no longer felt as if I were being regarded as a two-legged valise. Progress, I reminded myself, comes in small cloven-hoofed steps.

Uncle Bill and I would discuss the day's progress and the next day's goals over large glasses of Dusty Trail. Despite its appalling taste, by the end of the day I did not care. One can only imagine what the chaps at the Jolly Rooster, to say nothing of the club, would have said had they observed my fall from single malt grace to—what was the word in the States?—glorified moonshine.

After a third night, having finished the repairs, we sat in the drawing room.

"Uncle Bill, my father mentioned you were married. Someone named Gomez or Lopez or such? I say, did you suffer my fate?"

He lowered his glass slowly, steadying it on his right knee. "It's a long story, Bennie. Her name was Celestina Lopez and she was a damn fine gal. We met in Arizona. I was working on a ranch near Flagstaff as a hired hand. Celestina, well, she had been hired on as a maid. Helped out with the cooking, too."

Uncle Bill paused and took a large swallow of whisky.

"We got to know each other working there, and pretty soon, I made sure my day off was the same as hers. We'd head into town, not that there was much in Flagstaff, and grab a bite to eat, maybe a movie. All the typical things when you're dating a gal.

"I had taken a real liking to her and she seemed sweet on me, so about a year later, I proposed. We were married by a Justice of the Peace in Flagstaff the next week. We both wanted to get the hell out of there and get our own place. So, I worked real hard and so did she. Celestina's grandfather owned a cattle ranch in northern New Mexico. He wanted her to come back. Said there was a small house on the property he'd fix up if she returned.

"After we were married, she sent a telegram to her grandfather, saying she had decided to come home. We left the following week."

"Did she inform her grandfather she was already married?"

"She may have conveniently forgotten to tell him that, as a matter of fact." He paused again and shook his head. "Been a while since I thought about this, Bennie."

I raised my hand. "No need to continue, Uncle Bill. I don't wish to stir up unpleasant memories and all that."

"Nah, the memories are real good. Just been a long time since I thought about 'em."

"So, you were on your way to the grandfather's ranch?"

"That's right. Now, you have to remember that Celestina was Spanish and I was, as Rudy said in the cafe, a *gringo*. And there weren't many *gringos* living in northern New Mexico at the time. Still aren't."

"Er, yes, I rather gathered that, at least in the local environs."

"So we arrived on the bus in Santa Fe, all hot and dusty. Celestina's grandfather was there to meet her. She spotted him, took me by the arm, and we walked over to where he stood."

I cringed. "I gather the grandfather chap was rather taken aback?"

"Yep. 'Grandfather,' she said, 'this is my husband, Bill.' Well, she said it in Spanish—I don't think he spoke any English. His eyes narrowed and I think if had been carrying a pistol I would have gone to my heavenly reward right then. I extended my hand, smiled, and said, 'Howdy, Mister Lopez,' trying to be as friendly as I could be. "He wasn't going to have any of it. He started shouting at Celestina.

I didn't know what he was saying, but he sure as hell wasn't offering his marital blessing. She was jabbering right back at him. Then she slapped his face—hard. That stopped him cold. His eyes got real wide and he just stared at her. Then he looked at me. Then he looked back at her. Finally, he looked back at me and spit on the ground."

"I say, that sounds rather menacing."

"That's what I thought, Bennie. But the old guy had a real soft spot for Celestina. Whatever she said to him must've worked. Finally, he walked over to me and extended his hand, staring at me like he would have shot me dead if it wasn't for Celestina standing next to him. In a low voice he said, 'Sabino Lopez.' So, I replied, 'Bill Graves,' and shook his hand. He didn't say another word to me for the next three months."

"What did you do?"

"We moved into the little house and started fixing it right up. I figured if I worked my tail off, maybe he would change his mind about me, or at least think about something besides shooting me.

"Anyway, I don't think I ever worked as hard as I did those next couple of months. I'd come back to the house each night dog-tired. Sometimes, I was too tired to eat. And that was saying something, because Celestina was one hell of a cook.

"One morning, I was with her grandfather repairing a couple hundred feet of fence that had been knocked over. He still wouldn't talk to me, but there was always work to be done and I was pretty good at it. I had dug new post holes and was starting to put the fence posts in them when I felt a hand on my shoulder. '*Momentito*, Guillermo,' he said. I stopped, wiped the sweat off my forehead, and looked at him, wondering what I was doing wrong. But the old guy just looked at me and nodded his head. Then he took my hand—Jesus, but he had a grip like iron—and shook it hard. '*Bienvenidos a la familia*,' he said, 'Welcome to the family.'

"'*Muchas gracias*, Señor Lopez, *muchas gracias*,' I replied. That was enough for him. He said, '*Vamos a volver al trabajo*,' 'Let's get back to work.' So, I started putting the fence posts in the holes I had just dug." From then on, I was okay in his book."

"The Graves charm won him over, eh?"

"Maybe. For all I know, Celestina had threatened to slice off his *cojones* if he didn't start acting civil towards me. But I like your explanation better."

"Well, one wonders if the vaunted Graves charm is overrated. At least in my instance, it could not compete with the charms of a certain Iberian type."

"Don't be so hard on yourself, Bennie. You remember Tennyson, 'Tis better to have loved and lost—"

"Yes, yes, burned into the neurons, that. Though I rather doubt Tennyson's wife ran off with a Spaniard." I paused for a large swallow of Dusty Trail. "So, after you were officially welcomed by the paterfamilias, what occurred next?"

"For the next year, not too much. Celestina and I kept sprucing up the little house and little by little, her grandfather started relying on me more to run the ranch. Some days he was a bit forgetful, asking me about whether I checked on the water or the fences, even though he had asked me the same thing a few days earlier. I never did know how old he was."

"Any offspring in the works by that time?"

"Nope. We figured we would let Nature take its course. And we were both happy. I don't think I was ever happier in my life.

"Well, one morning, this was a few months later, Sabino rides out on his horse. Said he was heading to the upper part of the ranch to check on the cattle. We had moved them there a few weeks before because the grass had come in real sweet with all of the summer rains.

"Around dinner time, his horse showed up, but no Sabino. Celestina and her grandmother Lupe were beside themselves, of course, so I jumped on his horse and rode back. There was still another hour of daylight and I figured that would be plenty of time to find him and get him back home. I just assumed he had gotten off his horse to take a *siesta*. There was one spot along a small creek with big cottonwoods and nice grass. Sometimes, he and I both would stretch out there for a while. I headed straight there.

"Sure enough, as I rode up, I saw him lying under that cottonwood. I got down and walked over to him. I could tell right away he was dead. But, if he had to go, that's probably the spot he would have wanted."

"Poor bugger. What did you do?"

"Well, for a while I just stood there frozen. Couldn't think what to do at first, but it was getting dark. I knew I had to get back and I couldn't leave him there for the coyotes. So, I managed to lay him over the horse and we rode back. It was pitch black when I arrived. Celestina had been in the main house with her grandmother. They both came out when I rode up. As soon as they saw Sabino on the horse, the wailing started.

"You can probably imagine the aftermath. Sabino's oldest son—I think it was Miguel, he was Celestina's uncle—lived in Santa Fe. Another son, Alejandro, was in the Navy, and nobody ever knew where he was. Anyway, Miguel worked for the state and had never been interested in the ranch. He came back and first thing he starts talking about is selling the ranch and having Lupe move to Santa Fe and live with his family.

"Now, if I had had the money, I would have bought the ranch from Miguel straightaway. But I didn't. Your grandfather was still alive at the time. He forgot to write me out of his will, but that's another story. "Well, it turned out that Sabino had written me into *his* will, giving me an equal share of the ranch as his own two boys. Miguel didn't like that, but there wasn't much he could do. Plus, I think Celestina would have sliced off his *cojones*, too. Damn, she was a spitfire, my Celestina."

"She certainly sounds like one. I take it Miguel succeeded in selling the ranch?"

"Yep. I told Miguel I would buy both his and Alejandro's shares out. Pay 'em back over time. Miguel wouldn't even consider it. Well, to make a long story short, the ranch got sold and I used my share to buy this place in Vaca Seca. Not nearly as big, of course, and I sure missed that creek and the big cottonwoods, but it was ours."

Uncle Bill yawned, then drained the last bits of Dusty Trail from his glass. "Time for me to turn in. You know, Bennie, I think you're gettin' the hang of things."

"It is rather odd. City chap like me, distinguished lineage, ex-wife who ran off with an Iberian charlatan, banking career lost to a twit with an unnatural fondness for store mannequins. And here I am, west of nowhere, working on a cattle ranch overseen by a *sombrero*-wearing pig. Where shall it end, one wonders?"

He laughed. "Six feet underground, like everybody else. After I first arrived in the States, I travelled around a lot. Earned my keep working different jobs. Doing this and that. I'd even hop freight trains like some of those hobo types. One day, I found myself in West Virginia in some little no-name town. I had a few dollars saved up, so I wandered around and found this little cafe.

"I walked in and saw a gal standing behind the counter, smoking a cigarette. Nobody else was in the place. I sat down and she handed me a menu. It all looked real good, of course, 'cause I was so damn hungry.

"She was about to ask me what I wanted when a little girl, who couldn't have been more than four years old, burst through the door to the kitchen yelling, 'Mommy, Mommy.' She looked at me and blushed a bit, then scooped up her daughter. 'Mommy, I'm scared,' the little girl said. 'What you scared of, Ellie?' she asked. 'I heard a noise in the kitchen, Mommy. I think it was a mouse.' 'A mouse? Is that all? You don't have to be scared of a little ole mouse. Now, Ellie, Didn't we put those big girl panties on you this mornin'? We did, and 'cause you're wearing them, you don't need to be scared of any mouse.'"

"Big girl panties?"

"It means, Bennie, that the only place I know where it all ends is in a pine box. Until then, you've got to wear those big girl panties."

"Er, yes." By now, my head was suffering from the effects of the Dusty Trail. "The mind boggles, really. Well, I shall simply bid you goodnight."

The next morning, Uncle Bill was sitting in the kitchen drinking coffee, when I walked in. "Morning," he said, rather too loudly for the brain, which was still becalmed in a whiskied sea.

"Eh? I suppose it is. Any more coffee?"

"Yep. I made extra this morning. Figured you'd need it. You were guzzling whisky last night like it was water."

"I was? I mean, I don't recall. Well, perhaps a glass or two. Did you say something about women's knickers?"

"What?"

"I'm quite sure you relayed a story concerning a large woman's knickers."

"Maybe you had better stick to coffee from now on."

"Are you quite sure?"

"About the coffee?"

"No, about the woman's knickers. I say, was it your wife we were discussing?"

"What did you say?"

"Right. Best change the subject. I presume we have a full day's work ahead of us?"

"Well, since you're here, I've been thinking we could repaint the barn. I need to call the vet, too. Daisy's acting a bit funny. She didn't even finish her slops last night."

"Off her feed, eh? Perhaps it's just a touch of porcine indigestion, if such a thing is possible." As best I could tell, the beast was a four-legged locust, devouring anything and everything in its path. "Is there a vet in Vaca Seca?"

"Nope. Nearest one lives near Sierra Bonita. He's been out here before to check on the herd and Marjorie, but never Daisy."

"Best warn him to keep his bag out of sight. Wouldn't want Daisy to use it for sport."

"Yep. She wasn't all too neighbourly the last time he was here." He paused. "Bennie, you mind driving into town this morning? Joe Garcia sells some stuff. Does a pretty good job of calming animals. Maybe I'll try that first. It comes in a big brown bottle. Can you get me a few? Oh, and I need a half-dozen bags of oats for Marjorie, the fifty pound ones. Tell Joe to put it on my tab."

"Of course. Anything else?"

"What's today? Saturday?"

"Yes. Why?"

"My *tamales*."

"What?"

"It's *tamale* day. Maria only makes them on Saturdays. Half the town lines up for 'em."

Knowing this involved the sisters of Hades, I grew apprehensive. "Er, I take it these are a type of comestible?"

"Made by the hand of God. They're that good."

"Indeed? I rather thought the hand of God did not go tossing large kitchen knives into walls. However, as the saying goes, He, or perhaps She in this particular circumstance, works in mysterious ways."

"I always get a dozen." He reached into his pocket and extracted a large leather wallet. "Here, let me give you some money for them."

"Put it away, Uncle Bill. I am fully boursed. In fact, I set up an account with a bank in Santa Fe before I departed. One advantage of having been in the business."

"Thanks, Bennie. That's mighty nice of you. And don't worry about Maria. Besides, lots of folks will be around."

"Would they be willing witnesses in court?"

"By the way, can you drive a pick-up?"

"Though I have never driven a lorry, er, pick-up, I do know how to drive. Besides, if Coronado can keep his decrepit lorry on the road, in a manner of speaking, I am quite sure I can too."

"Good. Key's hanging up in the kitchen. Should have plenty of gas. You do know we drive on the other side of the road here, don't you?"

I sighed. "I have observed that, yes. Americans must always have their own way of doing things. Nevertheless, one presumes the motoring principles are the same."

After breakfast and a quick wash and brush-up, I retrieved the key to the lorry and exited the house. I walked over to where it was parked and slid into the driver's seat. Inserting the key in the ignition, I cranked the engine, which started with a low rumble.

I released the brake and eased off on the clutch. The engine promptly stalled. Again, I tried, this time pressing more diligently on the accelerator. Rather than stalling, the lorry lurched forward, hurtling towards a large pine tree, which I missed only by slamming my foot down on the brake pedal and wrenching the steering wheel to port.

By this time, Daisy had raised herself from her usual sleeping position and was following my progress from under her *sombrero*. Again I attempted the manoeuvre: clutch out, accelerator in. This time, perhaps in resignation, the lorry complied, and we bounced slowly forward. I absently waved my arm at Daisy—realizing subsequently I had just waved good-bye to a pig—and turned onto the rutted dirt road that led into town.

# Chapter 7

Easing the lorry to a stop in front of Garcia's store, I stepped out, turned around. Immediately, I collided with Coronado's bulk and crashed to the ground.

"¡*Híjole*! Sorry, Señor Graves." Coronado extended a pudgy hand to help me up. "Are you okay?"

I brushed myself off. "Fine, Coronado. A bruise or two to the dignity is all."

"I got a bruise on my arm last week, Señor Graves, but it's getting better."

"What? Oh, yes, quite. Er, why the rush, Coronado?"

"I got to get over to the cafe 'cause there won't be no *tamales* left. Where's your brother, El Vaquero, Señor Graves? He never misses *tamale* day."

"My brother, I mean, my uncle sent me in to purchase a few supplies at Garcia's store and asked me to purchase the *tamales* for him whilst in town."

"Well, if you want some, you better come now."

"Why? I glanced at my watch. "It's only, what, ten o'clock in the morning?"

"*Sí*, it's real late. Come on, you don't want El Vaquero not to get his *tamales*."

I began to protest, but Coronado had already started to run, or at least waddle quickly, towards the cafe like a famished penguin. I followed him, espying a mass of perhaps forty locals who were gathered in front of the cafe. The two local dogs, Paco and Pedro were milling about. Pedro wagged his tail hungrily, whilst Paco sought out unsuspecting loiterers to urinate upon.

In line, if one could call it a line, the citizenry of Vaca Seca waited in anticipation, as if *tamales* were Vaca Seca's answer to ambrosia.

I neither knew what *tamales* were nor why they elicited such odd behaviour amongst the townspeople.

I walked up to the group, maintaining a weather eye on Paco, and found Coronado, who was clutching his hands together, as if in prayer. Nearby stood the massive form of Ernesto Morales, who smiled and tipped his cowboy hat. "Hey, Bennie," he shouted. "El Vaquero must be getting lazy, sending you into town for his *tamales*. ¿*Que no*?"

"No, I mean yes, Mister Morales. I mean he asked me to obtain a few items from Garcia's store and mentioned the, er, *tamales*. Asked if I might procure a dozen on his behalf."

"A dozen? El Vaquero is getting greedy, Bennie. Or maybe he has gotten sweet on Maria and hasn't told anyone, especially Rudy. I'd be careful about asking Esperanza for that many *tamales*."

"What?" I replied, lost in the *tamale*-laden fog into which Ernesto Morales had vanished. "Coronado, may I ask you something?"

"Sure, Señor Graves."

"What exactly is a *tamale*? Why the frenzy?"

"A what, Señor Graves?"

"Frenzy. I mean, why is everyone desperate to obtain them."

"You don't know what *tamales* are, Señor Graves?"

"No. That is why I am asking you."

"Well, *tamales* are—" Coronado paused, deep in thought, or what passed as such within his brain. He made a slow rolling motion with his hands and moved his fingers. "They're *tamales*, Señor Graves."

"Yes, thank you. What they are made of?"

"*Tamales* are made from *masa*."

"And what might that be?"

"*Masa*?"

"Yes."

"*Masa* is made from corn."

"Do you mean maize? I see."

"I'm glad, Señor Graves. What do you see?"

"Eh? What tamales are made from. Maize. Corn."

"*Sí*, Señor Graves. Corn."

I looked at the rumbling crowd. "So, all of this is for something made from maize?"

"Maria puts other stuff in them, too, Señor Graves." Coronado's eyes widened. "Pork."

The word conjured images of Daisy and brought a smile to the face. I wondered how many of Maria's *tamales* the sow's ample girth would supply. Could they be carried home in a valise as vindictive irony? Well, one is allowed to dream.

"So, *tamales* are made from maize, *masa*, and pork. Is that it? Sounds rather pedestrian."

"Huh? Señor Graves, maybe you should just try one."

"I believe I shall."

The crowd continued to mull about whilst awaiting for the cafe to open its doors. I rather expected to see puffs of white smoke coming out of the chimney signifying the newly crowned Pope Tamale XII. At about eleven o'clock, Esperanza opened the front door of the cafe. The crowd surged forward until Esperanza raised her hand like a Roman emperor about to pronounce sentence on a hapless Christian. Silence descended, as everyone waited for her to speak.

"Everybody," she shouted. "We ran out of corn husks. All we got is ten dozen *tamales* today. So, nobody get greedy."

The murmurs began anew. "But, Esperanza," an older woman wearing a shawl said, "My Tito can eat a dozen by himself. What should I tell him?"

"Carmen, your Tito is a *comilón*. And it shows, too. Tell him to eat more beans."

Rudy called out. "Esperanza, tell my Maria I hope she saved extra tamales for her *querida*."

"You tell her, Rudy. You'll be lucky to get any *tamales*. Okay, who's first?"

A young girl, who looked no more than ten years old, emerged from the crowd and walked up to the door.

"*Bueno días*, Anna," Esperanza said, bending down slightly and with a surprising hint of softness in her voice. "How's your Uncle today?"

"*Bueno días*, Mrs. Fuentes. He's okay, I guess. I wish he didn't cough so much."

"I know. But he's real lucky you and your mother are helping take care of him."

"Can we have three *tamales* today?"

"How about six, instead? But don't let your Uncle eat all of them. You and Aunt Rosa have some, too."

"Thanks, Mrs. Fuentes." The little girl went inside and soon emerged with a large paper bag.

"Next!" Esperanza commanded. Now it was Joe Garcia's turn to walk up to the door. "How many you want, Joe?"

"Half a dozen, same as always. By the way, the cafe owes me a lot of money. When you gonna pay?"

"You don't want no *tamales* today, Joe? So, why you here?"

"Dammit, Esperanza, don't give me that. You and Maria got to pay your bills, just like everybody else, including me. You want more *masa* for Maria's *tamales*, you start paying me what you owe."

Esperanza growled under her breath. "*Vete a la chingada.*"

"*Y tu, también.*" Joe disappeared through the door.

The processional continued. Rudy stood outside, serenading Maria, whom I presumed was inside. "Save some *tamales* for your true *amor*, Maria."

"*Vete a la chingada, Rudy,*" came the muffled reply from inside the cafe.

"It's true love," he shouted to the crowd.

Finally, the line reached Coronado and me. Coronado muttered politely and walked through. Esperanza looked at me. "*Pendejito*, did El Vaquero send you to get his *tamales*?"

"Yes, he did. And must you continue to call me that? I mean, not especially neighbourly, is it?"

"You ain't my neighbour, *Pendejito*. Do you even know what a *tamale* is?

"As a matter of fact, I do. A mixture of, er, *masa* and pork."

Her eyebrows rose. "*Bueno, Pendejito.* Come in, so you can tell Maria you know her secrets."

"What? Please Esperanza, I have several other items I need to obtain for Uncle Bill. I really haven't the time this morning." With that, I turned around and began to walk away.

"Wait, *Pendejito.* El Vaquero will be real mad if he don't get his *tamales.*"

Somewhat taken aback, I walked into the cafe, followed by Esperanza. Maria sat at a small table, glowering at no one in particular. In front of her lay a platter of yellowish-brown, sausage-like objects, their ends tied off like Christmas crackers.

"*Hermana,*" Esperanza said, "*Pendejito* is here for El Vaquero's tamales. You got his dozen?"

I looked at the platter. "Given your earlier protestations about a shortage of—did you say corn husks?—would that not deprive your remaining customers of their due? I mean, it appears you have barely a dozen left."

"*Sí,* but El Vaquero, he always gets his *tamales.*" Maria nodded silently.

The moral compass spun—should I obtain the usual quantity for Uncle Bill, which made me wonder if the *tamales* were not a payoff for some debt incurred, or should I be magnanimous, and accept a lesser quantity? After a brief internal interlude, and to the great displeasure of my vindictive half, magnanimity prevailed. "Look, Esperanza, I am quite sure Uncle Bill can survive one week on short *tamale* rations. Perhaps just four."

"You don't understand, *Pendejito.* El Vaquero, he always gets a dozen *tamales* on Saturday."

"Stuff and nonsense. El Vaquero, I mean, Uncle Bill, will quite understand the situation. Besides, I will tell him I refused to accept the usual amount you had offered."

Maria looked at Esperanza, offering a slight nod in the affirmative to her sister. "Okay, *Pendejito.* But El Vaquero, he ain't gonna like it."

"I don't suppose you will tell me why you and Maria owe him this weekly tribute?"

Both sisters shrugged their shoulders. "You better ask El Vaquero," Esperanza replied in a defeated tone. "He swore us to secrecy."

Now, one is all in favour of secrecy—spies, payoffs, coded messages, current accounts hidden from the spouse for expenditures on the mistress—but this was Vaca Seca, and the payoffs were in *tamales*. As for random thoughts of either Esperanza or Maria as someone's— anyone's—mistress, well those were quickly Greco-Romaned to the ground and despatched.

"Say no more. How much for the four *tamales*?"

They stared at me silently. "Ah, let me guess. You don't charge Uncle Bill for them, do you?"

Both heads shook simultaneously. "We don't charge him nothing," Esperanza said.

"Right. Mum's the word, as they say."

"*Gracias.*" Esperanza suddenly looked pensive. "You want to try some *tamales* now, in case El Vaquero don't let you have none? You sit down with Maria. I gotta see who else is waiting in line."

"Eh, I should probably be on my way." I was not sure whether I wanted to be left in Maria's shotgun-wielding and knife-throwing care. Maria stood up to retrieve a plate and cutlery. Convinced a refusal on my part would be met with some form of unpleasant mayhem, I sat down. "Er, well, why not. Most kind of you."

Maria motioned for me to sit down at one of the nearby tables and disappeared into the kitchen. I waited, wondering whether her *tamales* would be as incendiary as her *enchiladas*.

A few minutes later, Maria returned with a plate upon which two steaming *tamales* sat. She set the plate down before me, folded her arms sternly, and waited. I picked up the knife and fork, not at all sure how I was supposed to tuck into them. I gently touched one of the ties trying to loosen it, treating the *tamales* as ordinance to be defused.

I slipped the left tie off the first *tamale* and delicately placed it on the edge of the plate. Next, I turned my attention to the other tie, probing it oh-so-gingerly with the knife. I was about to begin the removal process when, without warning, Maria grabbed my knife and fork, gestured with her knife hand for me to get out of the way, and despatched both the remaining tie and corn husk wrapping instantly. Sitting before me was a small, reddish-yellow mass. My first thought was, "*This* is what the frenzy is about?" Maria returned the fork to me, folded her arms sternly again, and waited. Given the appearance, at least, I was rather taken aback at the reverence the townspeople held these in.

I cut into it, revealing a dark brown centre which I assumed was Daisy, er, pork. I cradled the just cut piece with my fork, placed it carefully on the tongue, chewed diligently, and swallowed, wondering how much time would elapse before my entire upper digestive system was enflamed.

The taste was quite extraordinary, simultaneously sweet and spicy. I nodded an affirmation to Maria, whose stern demeanour relaxed, if only slightly.

"I say, Maria, this is most savory." I speared another bite. "M'mm, yes, one can understand why the town queues up every Saturday morning."

"You like it. *Bueno.* You and El Vaquero get *tamales* every week." Maria stood up sharply, turned around, and disappeared through the kitchen door.

Other than cursing at Rudy, this was the first time I had heard her speak. I quickly consumed the second *tamale.* As I was finishing, Maria came out again, bearing a small paper bag.

"A dozen *tamales. No hay más.*" She dropped the bag on the table next to me and again vanished through the kitchen door.

I sighed, having asked just for the four, then retrieved the bag and walked out the door. A few latecomers, turned away by Esperanza, still hung about, muttering amongst themselves. Walking back towards Garcia's store, one could feel the untoward glances in my direction. No doubt the natives were upset at the unknown *gringo* who had somehow absconded with Vaca Seca treasure.

I placed the bag of *tamales* on the seat of the truck and went inside the store. Joe was nowhere to be seen, which meant he was sitting at Rudy's bar. I awaited Coronado's appearance with trepidation.

He emerged from aisle two. "*Hola*, Señor Graves. Did you get El Vaquero's *tamales*?"

"Indeed I did. I even consumed two whilst in the cafe. You were correct, they are most delectable."

"You didn't like them?"

"No, I mean, yes, Coronado. They *are* good."

"I told you, Señor Graves. You need something today, besides *tamales*?"

"Er, yes, I need half a dozen of bags of oats and something Joe sells to calm Daisy's stomach. Apparently, she is suffering from indigestion."

"Again? Maybe El Vaquero needs to get a new pig."

"I couldn't agree more. However, Uncle Bill seems rather attached to the beast."

"When Daisy was little, she would ride in the truck to town with El Vaquero. She would jump out and chase Paco." Coronado laughed. The mind imagined a compact Daisy sitting in Bill's lorry like a small dog, as her current girth would fill the entire bed. As for chasing Paco, perhaps that would explain the cur's fondness for urinating on the lorry's tyres.

Coronado disappeared down one of the aisles. He returned soon thereafter with two largish brown bottles and handed them to me.

I read the label and directions. "Miller's Concentrated Farm Calm. For the distressed farm animal. Mix one part Farm Calm with one part water. Do not use near open flame."

I raised an eyebrow and opened the bottle, curious as to what Miller's Farm Calm contained to warrant its inflammability. A shallow inhale quickly revealed the answer: a large proportion of grain alcohol. I inserted a finger into the bottle to confirm my suspicions. Not only was the alcohol overpowering, it was quite sweet, like a concentrated Christmas punch. A bracing dose of this would calm Daisy, and no doubt many of the local farmers.

"Er, thank you, Coronado. I imagine Farm Calm is quite the popular item."

"*Sí*. All the farmers say it works real good. We never had no animals when I was a kid. Just a few chickens. I guess we were lucky."

"How do you mean?"

"Everybody who had horses and goats and pigs always talked about how sick their animals would get. They sure bought a lot of this stuff. Said it was the only thing that worked. Our chickens never got sick. Except the coyotes got them."

"A miracle cure, no doubt. Would you mind bringing the bags of oats around to the lorry?"

"Sure, Señor Graves. Coronado pecked at the old cash register. "That's gonna be fifteen dollars, Señor Grave." He put the bottles into a large paper bag.

I retrieved the money from my trouser pocket and handed it to Coronado. He stuffed it into the cash drawer, closed the register, and disappeared down another aisle.

I took the bag and walked outside to the lorry. When I opened the door to place the bag on the seat, I recoiled in horror. The bag of *tamales* had disappeared.

# Chapter 8

I looked under the passenger seat, wondering if the tamales had somehow hopped down from the seat. I then knelt down and looked under the lorry. Perhaps someone opened the bag mistakenly and, realizing they were *tamales*, had set it down on the macadam.

Growing more desperate, I circled the lorry, peering into the bed, between the tyres, everywhere, really, searching in vain. My head was next to the front tyre when I heard Coronado arrive, wheeling around the bags of oats.

"You looking for something, Señor Graves?"

"Someone nicked my bag of *tamales*," I shouted. "A bloody thief. Who would do such a thing?"

Coronado rubbed his hand over his double chin. "*Híjole.* How come a thief would cut your *tamales* with a razor?"

"What? No, someone stole the bag of *tamales*, whilst I was inside the store purchasing oats and Farm Calm."

"El Vaquero, he's not gonna like this. You think maybe it was because Maria couldn't make enough?"

"I did see some townsfolk glowering at me when I came out with the bag. Did you see anyone outside recently? Perhaps when you wheeled around the bags of oats on the hand trolley?"

"No, I didn't see nobody outside. Except Anna Flores."

"Anna Flores? I knew it. So, she's the local thief, eh?"

"I dunno, Señor Graves. She's just a little kid."

"Wait. I recall a little girl named Anna standing in line. For her sick Uncle or some such thing, wasn't it? Esperanza gave her a bag of six *tamales*."

"*Sí*, that's Anna Flores. Her Uncle Ramón lives with Anna and her mother Carmen."

The mind whirled. Could the angelic behaviour I had observed earlier have been entirely for show? Perhaps she had been trained by her mother and Uncle. After all, no one would suspect an innocent, well-behaved child of breaking into cars and lorries to nick their contents? But why not take the bottles of Farm Calm, too? Too noisy? Too heavy? What was it Sherlock Holmes had told Watson—eliminate the impossible and only the possible remains? Or did one eliminate the possible and whatever remained, even if impossible, must be the cause?

"You okay, Señor Graves? Your face looks all twisted up. We could go to Rudy's for a beer, if you want."

"Eh?" I came out of the Holmesian trance. "Yes, er, fine Coronado. I was just thinking about the *tamale* thief. Eliminate the suspects, that's it. Whomsoever remains, well, that's the thief you pinch."

Coronado scratched his head. "If you say so, Señor Graves. Maybe you should go back to the cafe. Maria and Esperanza usually keep some *tamales*, even if they tell everybody they got no more. That way El Vaquero can still get his *tamales*."

"A reserve, eh? Thanks, Coronado. I shall go there presently."

I hoisted myself into the lorry and sped over to the cafe, parking the lorry in front of the urine-stained front steps. Steeling myself to face Esperanza again, I walked inside. A family sat at one of the leaning benches.

"I say, have you seen Esperanza or Maria?" They stared at me silently.

"Esperanza or Maria? No? Right." I walked towards the kitchen door, paused, knocked firmly, and walked in.

I found both standing next to the gas cooker, cigarettes dangling from their mouths. Bits of ash had fallen onto the top of the cooker and to the floor. Esperanza was pawing an onion whilst Maria held a large chef's knife.

They turned simultaneously. "*Pendejito*," Esperanza growled, removing the cigarette from her mouth. "You know how to knock on a door?"

"I did knock."

"Unless you're gonna help cook, get the fuck out."

"Well, I shan't be but a minute. You see, it's the *tamales*."

Maria furrowed her brow menacingly, but said nothing. "What's wrong with our *tamales*?" Esperanza snarled.

"Nothing, I mean, they're gone. Nicked. Stolen. I left the bag on the seat of the lorry when I went in to Garcia's store to buy Farm Calm for Daisy. I came back outside and they were gone."

"Somebody stole the *tamales* out of your truck? So?"

"So? You told me Uncle Bill would be most disappointed if he did not receive his weekly ration."

"We gave you El Vaquero's *tamales, Pendejito*. You lose them, too bad."

"Look, Coronado told me you may still have a few lying about. Of course, I shall pay for them."

"I told you, we don't got no more." Esperanza pointed to a large pan on the cooker. "We ran out of corn husks. You want more *tamales*, go to Garcia's store and get us some more corn husks. Then come back here and make your own fucking *tamales*."

"Me? I haven't the faintest idea how to make *tamales*."

"Anybody can make *tamales, Pendejito*, even you. We got plenty of *masa* and pork, so all we need is corn husks. So, you want them or not?" Esperanza crossed her arms over her chest and looked even more menacing.

"Well, I . . . yes, I suppose, why not? How many corn husks do you require?"

"Get as many as Joe has. He won't sell none to us."

"Why not?"

"Didn't you hear him this morning? We owe him too much money. I don't know what we're gonna do. No supplies, no cafe."

"In arrears, eh? Can't help you there. However, I shall purchase the required corn husks and return directly."

I turned around, walked out the door, and launched myself back to Garcia's store.

"Coronado?" I shouted as I entered. "Coronado, are you here?"

"*Momentito*, Señor Graves," came a muffled response from the back of the store, followed by a distinct loo-flushing sound.

Soon thereafter, Coronado wandered up. "*Hola*, Señor Graves. Did you forget to buy something?"

"No, I mean, yes. I need corn husks. How many do you have?"

"For *tamales?*" Coronado displayed an even more puzzled countenance that usual.

"Quite so. Do you have any?"

"*Sí*, Señor Graves. Aisle two. I can show you."

He waddled down the aisle, stopping about half-way. Sitting on a shelf, next to several large tins of lard, were two packages of cornhusks. I retrieved one of the packages and read the label: Dry Corn Husks, Dist. by *Sabrosa Foods*, Santa Fe, NM Contents: 100.

"Are these what Maria uses?"

"*Sí*. Only, Joe won't sell her no more 'cause she and Esperanza owe Joe too much money."

"How much do they owe?"

"I dunno Señor Graves, but Joe says it's a lot. He told me I can't sell nothing more to them ever until they pay their bill."

"Sounds rather serious. How long have they been in arrears?"

"Huh?"

"How long have they owed Joe money?"

"I dunno. Forever, I guess. As long as they been running the cafe." Slowly, the puzzle pieces and Uncle Bill's role as *capo di tamale*, began to fit together.

"Er, Coronado, has Joe ever threatened to stop selling them supplies for the restaurant before?"

"*Sí*. I guess it was about a couple years after Ernesto— he was their father and owned the cafe—died."

"When was that?"

Coronado began counting his fingers, stopping abruptly after one hand. "Long time ago."

"What happened after Joe's threat?"

Coronado shrugged. "Nothing, really. A few weeks later, Esperanza came in with the money she owed. So, Joe started selling stuff to her again."

"Thank you, Coronado. Most interesting."

I paid for both packages and returned to the cafe. The family who had been eating their lunch previously had left and the cafe sat empty.

"Esperanza? Maria? I have the corn husks. Are you in the kitchen?"

Esperanza opened the kitchen door violently and motioned me inside. "*Bueno, Pendejito*. You got the corn husks from Joe? Okay, now you can make El Vaquero's *tamales*."

I walked into the kitchen. Esperanza tore the packages from my hand. A cloud of cigarette smoke rolled along the ceiling, enhanced continuously by Maria's chimney-like emanations. She was standing at a counter near the sink, mixing something in a large metal bowl. I heard her muttering something unintelligible, although the ears discerned the words "Garcia," "*pendejo*," and "*cojones*" amongst the utterances.

The combination of smoke and spice was crisping the eyes, which were watering profusely. "How can you work in here with all of that cigarette smoke?"

Maria looked up, stared violently at me, shook her head in disgust, and returned to the mixture in the bowl.

Esperanza sent a large blue-grey cloud in my direction. "You don't like smoke, *Pendejito*, too fucking bad. You want El Vaquero's *tamales* or not?"

"Yes, yes," I replied, in a defeated tone, futilely attempting to wave away the smoke from my face. "Do you have a gas mask left over from the war, by any chance?"

"Huh?"

"Nothing. Now, will you kindly instruct me as to how I am to make these *tamales*?"

Maria motioned me over towards the counter where she was working. "*Masa* and pork." She waved her chef's knife towards the fridge. I opened the large refrigerator. Inside sat two large metal bowls, which I retrieved as ordered, and placed on the counter.

"*Bueno.* Now you get the corn husks. Put them in warm water." Maria picked up a large rock, which had been casually minding its own business by the sink.

"Gah!"

Maria looked at me disdainfully and shook her head. "*¿Por que tienes tanto miedo?*"

"What?"

"Maria asked you what you are afraid of. The rock is to weigh down the corn husks, *Pendejito*, not to beat you over the head."

"Well, one cannot be too careful."

"*Pendejito.*" With the diminishing embers of her cigarette, Esperanza pointed towards another metal bowl. "You see that bowl on the counter? Fill it with warm water, put the corn husks in the water, and then put the fucking rock on top of the corn husks. Otherwise they float."

"Right," I said, resisting the urge to salute.

"Soak the corn husks for five minutes. Then we make *tamales.*"

I waited in silence, staring at nothing in particular. Maria resumed her chopping and muttering, and Esperanza pawed at a number of largish cans of lard, pinto beans, and another type of corn, called hominy. When five minutes had passed, Esperanza recalled me to reality.

"Bueno, *Pendejito.* Time for you to learn." Esperanza removed several corn husks from underneath the rock and spread them out on the counter. She retrieved two tablespoons from a drawer and shook them at me.

"First, you take a spoon of *masa* and spread it on the corn husk. Don't go to the edge of the corn husk, otherwise the *masa* falls out." She spooned out what appeared to be a large walnut's worth of the *masa* mixture from the bowl, spreading it over the husk.

"Now, take a spoon of the pork filling. Spread it in the centre of the *masa.*

"Now we fold it into a *tamale*." Then, rather like the magician performing an origami trick, she rapidly folded a long side over the other long side, and folded the larger short side over the shorter short side. Next, she tore a second husk intro long strips and tied the two ends of the tamale. Esperanza picked it up and shoved it under my nose.

"You try."

I removed a corn husk from the bowl of water and set it down. Retrieving a walnut-sized spoon of *masa*, I turned my attention back to the corn husk, the edges of which had curled inwards to form a cylinder. With my left hand, I spread the curled edges apart and applied the *masa* mixture, lamely attempting to smooth it to a uniform thickness. From the corner of the eye, I espied Esperanza looking at Maria. Both were shaking their heads mirthfully.

No matter. No *tamale* was going to defeat Benjamin Graves. I retrieved a spoon of the pork mixture and ladled it onto the wavy surface of *masa*. Now I faced the task of wrapping the bloody thing. Slowly, I folded the long edge over to the other side.

I had before me what appeared to be a flattened cylinder. I then attempted the cross-folding. As I did, the mixture inside oozed out the ends and onto my fingers like mud, which it somewhat resembled. I picked up a thin strand and tied off one end, causing further oozing, then tied the other end. "Ooze, ho!" it seemed to shout. The final result resembled less a Christmas cracker and more something mucked out of Marjorie's stall.

Esperanza and Maria stared at my effort. "*Pendejito*," Esperanza gasped, between hyena-like gales of laughter, "is this what a tamale looks like where you come from? It looks like horseshit."

"Yes, well, practice makes perfect as they say."

"For you, practice makes horseshit." Esperanza and Maria erupted in another gale of laughter.

As the laughter calmed down to muted cackles, Esperanza looked at me with a mixture of pity and contempt. "*¡Díos mio!*

Maybe you better stick to roping cows with El Vaquero. Okay, let's try again. This time, you watch me."

I clenched the jaw. "Perhaps if you would proceed a bit more slowly, I might actually see how you fold the bloody thing."

She demonstrated her technique once again and, to my amazement, stopped after each fold to let me see her progress. "You want to try again, *Pendejito*?"

"Thank you, yes." For this second effort, the mixture remained within the corn husk. The final product, though not offering the pleasant congruency one might expect of a *tamale*, at least did not look like it had been mucked out of a stall.

Esperanza and Maria examined the results of this repeat effort. "Not bad, *Pendejito*," Esperanza said. "Try again."

I did. And again after that. And yet again. The results of my final effort were, not to brag, most satisfactory. The Graves perseverance had conquered the *tamale*, albeit at a rather glacial pace.

"*Bueno*," Esperanza said with a short whistle. "I gotta admit, *Pendejito*, I didn't think you could do it. So, now you can make a dozen for El Vaquero."

Apparently, I had earned a grudging—if only temporary—respect from Maria and Esperanza. After an hour of tamale folding and spindling, I walked out of the cafe with the new bag, guarding them as if they were the Crown Jewels themselves. The bags of oats and the bottles of Farm Calm were still in the lorry. I placed the bag on the seat, started the lorry, and returned to the ranch.

As I drove behind the house, observed closely by Daisy from the porch, a glance at the watch informed me I had spent the entire afternoon at the cafe. Under Marjorie's baleful eye, I stacked the bags of oats in the barn. Finally, gathering the bottles of Farm Calm and the bag of *tamales*, I walked in the back door, placed the *tamales* in the fridge and the Farm Calm on the countertop, and limped into the drawing room.

Uncle Bill sat reading a Zane Grey novel. "Where in hell have you been all day, Bennie? I was ready to hoof it over to Felipe Aragón's and borrow his truck to find you."

"Yes, well, apologies for the delay. However, when I relay the events of the day, you shall understand, and perhaps sympathize, with my endurances."

"Jesus, all you had to do was buy a few things at Garcia's store and pick up a dozen *tamales*."

"Ah, yes, the *tamales*. Interesting story, that."

"You got them, didn't you?"

"Oh, quite. In fact, made by my own hands." I raised my hands into the air and manipulated the metacarpals for emphasis.

"What do you mean, you made them? Dammit, it's *tamale* day."

I held a hand up again in a gesture of calm. "Yes, however *tamale* day was abbreviated, owing to a shortage of corn husks. It seems Esperanza and Maria are suffering from a large arrearage of funds owed to Joe Garcia. Joe has therefore decided he will no longer advance additional supplies, including corn husks, until he is repaid in full."

"How much do they owe?"

"I enquired of Coronado who, whilst unaware of the precise value, suggested the sum was substantial."

"So how did you—"

"—make the dozen *tamales* now residing in your fridge? Quite simple. I purchased several packages of corn husks from Garcia's store, returned to the cafe, and received rather acidic instructions as to their manufacture."

"Maria and Esperanza showed you how to make *tamales*?"

"Quite. In fact, they were rather insistent upon my doing so."

"Let me get this straight, Bennie. You went to the cafe this morning, right? "Yes."

"And you waited in line for *tamales*, along with everyone else, right?"

"Most assuredly, yes. Whilst queued, the ears were entreated to several, what I gather were, colourful epithets uttered by the grandmothers Grimm. One rather doubts Joe Garcia will be receiving a Christmas card this year."

"So, they ran out of *tamales* while you stood in line."

"Er, well, not exactly. In fact, I was still able to secure your dozen, despite the limited supplies. Esperanza also insisted I try them. They were delicious, I must admit."

"Goddamn, Bennie, you're talking in riddles. You told me you had to make a dozen tamales, but you also got a dozen this morning. What happened?"

"Ah, yes. Well, those tamales were nicked from the lorry."

"Somebody stole my *tamales*?"

"Apparently. I hadn't been in the store but five or ten minutes to secure oats and Farm Calm—a most interesting product that, by the way. On returning to the lorry, the bag of *tamales* was gone. Nicked.

"I was at wits end, really. I mean, one doubts the locals authorities, if there are such in Vaca Seca, would be exercised by reports of a *tamale* thief in their midst. Coronado suggested I return to the cafe and ask for replacements, owing to his belief the grandmothers maintain a *tamale* reserve, as it were."

"Did they?"

"No. Hence Plan B, which involved me purchasing several packages of corn husks from Garcia's store, returning to the cafe, and receiving a rather churlish lesson in *tamale* manufacture. Said lesson also provided boundless quantities of hyena-like laughter from Maria and Esperanza, I might add. Thus instructed, I proceeded to fold and spindle the dozen *tamales* now resting comfortably in your fridge. I say, would you object to my pouring a large whisky?"

Uncle Bill's jaw had dropped several notches. "Pour me one, too."

I retrieved the open bottle of Dusty Trail and poured each of us a large glass. Even battery acid could provide a calming effect for a brain that has endured extreme mental trauma, and I considered an afternoon spent in the embrace—a regrettable choice of words, I admit—of Esperanza and Maria to be just so.

I swallowed a bracing does. "Uncle Bill, I believe I have stumbled upon a mystery. And although I am no Sherlock Holmes, there are rather some odd goings-on associated with *l'affaire tamale*."

Uncle Bill looked at me quizzically. "What mystery?"

"The cafe. And your weekly tribute of a dozen *tamales*. When you offered me funds to purchase said *tamales*, you knew I would not be asked to pay for them. Moreover, the cafe's present cash flow crisis is not the first. In fact, I gather a similar situation arose some years ago, which was mysteriously resolved."

Uncle Bill remained silent, except for a slight gurgling sound as he drained his glass.

"You loaned Esperanza and Maria the funds to settle the cafe's debts with Joe Garcia, didn't you? And, their weekly loan repayment is in the form of one dozen *tamales*?"

"Yep. But I swore those two to secrecy and that applies to you, too."

"I presume there was a reason for the loan, and the ensuing veil of secrecy?"

"There was. Suppose I gotta tell you what it was all about. Pour us some more whisky and pull up a chair."

# Chapter 9

Fortified with a second whisky, Uncle Bill began his tale. "It was after Celestina and I had moved here. I had used most of Sabino's inheritance to purchase the ranch, so she started to look for a job. Well, being that she was a damn good cook, she spoke with Ernesto, who had opened the cafe a few years earlier. Of course, it was called Ernesto's back then. In fact, if you look real close on the outside wall, you can see where 'Ernesto's' was painted over and replaced with 'Dos Abuelas.'

"Celestina told him about her work on the ranch in Arizona. She said she would cook, do dishes, waitress, whatever it took. When he first opened the cafe, Esperanza and Maria were helping out. But they were both recently married and starting families of their own."

"Rather difficult to imagine the maternal instinct emanating from either of those two," I said, shuddering.

"Yeah, well, that might explain why Esperanza's ex-husband was a truck driver. Never really knew much about Maria's husband. She took his death pretty hard, though. Never talks much. But you know that."

"As they are the eponymous 'Abuelas,' I take it there are children?"

"Esperanza's daughter married a guy in the Air Force. I know he was stationed in Roswell for a while. Then he got sent to Texas. From there, he was stationed in Germany. Last I heard, they were back in Texas somewhere. She's got a son who lives in Albuquerque. He works construction."

"What about Maria?"

"One son. Always had a drinking problem and a nasty temper. Story is he was in a bar in Gallup one night and got into a fight with a Navajo. Smashed the fellow's head with a whisky bottle. Just kept hitting him with it. Wasn't like those old western movies where the bottle breaks on the bad guy's head. So, the police charged him with manslaughter. He spent, oh, maybe ten years in prison. Would have gotten out sooner, except he was always fighting.

"After he was released, he moved to Texas. Settled down for a few years. Even got married. Then he started drinking again. Beat up his wife, so she took their daughter and high-tailed it home—Arkansas I think. One night, he got real drunk and drove home. Never made it. The police found his pick-up upside down in a creek the next day."

"No wonder the poor woman is a bit addled."

"Maria's had a rough time of it. Probably why she spends most of her time at the cafe cooking. Comfortable, I guess, like slipping on an old pair of boots."

"I shall endeavour to remember that the next time she is menacing me with her chef's knife. I take it Ernesto hired Celestina?"

"Yep. Like I say, she was a spitfire who wouldn't take no for an answer. I think Ernesto saw that in her. Plus, he needed help. The cafe was doing real well. Ernesto had a gift for cooking. He's the one who started *tamale* day.

"True to her word, Celestina helped cook, waitress, and washed a hell of a lot of dishes. I think Ernesto thought of her as his third daughter." Uncle Bill paused, looking lost in thought.

"I had bought a bull one year. Not one of those champions, of course, but he was pretty good. Well, one morning I got between him and one of the gals on the other side of the fence. Smashed me into that fence and stuck one of his horns into my lower leg."

Uncle Bill rolled up his trouser leg and displayed a large oval scar. "Gah! You were lucky not to be killed by that beast. What happened after you were gored?"

"Well, I just crumpled into a heap. Once I was out of the way, the bull just knocked the fence down and had himself a good time with his gals."

"But what does this have to do with Ernesto?"

"Yeah, that's what I'm gonna tell you. Celestina hadn't gone into town quite yet. I was hollering for her, but she couldn't hear me inside the house. But when she came outside to leave, she sure did.

"I was laid up for about three weeks or so. Ernesto wouldn't let Celestina work. Told her to stay home and take care of me. He would come by every afternoon, between lunch and dinner, with plates of food—*enchiladas, burritos,* green chile stew, *tamales.* After the first week, I told him I could look after myself. I knew he needed Celestina's help. But he said no, even though I could tell he was exhausted.

"I convinced him by driving into town, limping into the cafe with my cane, and insisting Celestina come back to work. Told him he needed her help more than me and that I wasn't gonna allow him to work himself to death while I ate all of the food he kept bringing us. Said I would always be in his debt."

"Did he agree?"

"Yep. He looked at me and broke out in the biggest goddamn grin I ever saw. He motioned for Celestina to go into the kitchen. When the door closed, he told me how lucky I was to have a wife like her.

"Well, I agreed with him, of course. I *was* damn lucky and I knew it. But then he just stood there for a minute. Finally, he said she was lucky to have a husband like me, too. Then he shook my hand, commanded me to sit down at a table—that was before the floor started leaning by the way—and said I was going to eat a plate of his *enchiladas* or else he would shoot me."

"Interesting chap, this Ernesto. I take it Celestina returned to work and all went well?"

"For a while. About a year later, Ernesto had a heart attack. It didn't kill him, but he was laid up for weeks. Celestina took over running the cafe. Esperanza and Maria helped, of course. Maria took care of the cooking, Esperanza took care of the supplies, and Celestina did a little of everything. Together, they kept the cafe running.

"After about three months, Ernesto desperately wanted to work at the cafe. But he was still weak. Every day, he would come in and try to help for an hour or two, but it was too hard. Eventually, he stopped. He would show up now and then to see how things were going. Every Monday, Celestina would show him the books and tell him everything was fine.

"That's how things stayed for a few years. The three gals ran the cafe. Ernesto would stop in, reassure himself the place was still standing, have some *enchiladas* or a few *tamales*, and then head back home."

When one hears a story like Uncle Bill's, one awaits for the other proverbial shoe to drop. "What happened then?"

"One afternoon, I was in the pasture repairing some fence that had been knocked down. I heard a truck pull up. A voice started shouting, 'Bill! ¡*Venga aca*!'—come here!

"I heard him—it was Rudy actually—and ran back towards the house.

"'What's going on, Rudy?' I shouted."

"'It's your wife. She collapsed in the cafe. Come on, I'll take you there.'

"We sped off in his truck back to town. Rudy screeched to a stop in front of the cafe and I jumped out and ran inside."

He stopped, wiped his eye, and stared at Celestina's picture, which sat atop the mantelpiece. Then he drained the remaining whisky in his glass.

"She was gone, Bennie. Esperanza said Celestina had complained of a bad headache and then collapsed. The doc told me it was a blood vessel or something in her brain. Just burst. Said there was nothing on God's green earth could have prevented it, or even known it was there. My beautiful spitfire. Taken from me like that."

"Uncle Bill, I am so very sorry. I do wish I could have met her."

"You would have liked her, Bennie."

"And after she was gone, the cafe began to falter?"

"For a while things went okay. Folks would still come in. Maria and Esperanza tried real hard and Ernesto did what he could, but he took Celestina's death as hard as I did. Told me he felt like he had lost a daughter.

"Well, about a year later, Ernesto had a second heart attack. That one did him in. Esperanza and Maria still had kids to raise, so they closed the cafe. There it sat, collecting dust, for years."

"What made them decide to open it again?"

"Me. Every time I drove by the place, seeing it all boarded up. Just wasn't right. Celestina wouldn't have wanted that."

"What did you do to convince them?"

"I was in town one day. Needed to get supplies at the general store, so I stopped in at Rudy's for a drink. We got to talking about things, including the cafe. Rudy told me how much he missed it, and Maria's *enchiladas*."

"Sounds rather callous. I mean, you had lost quite a bit more than the cafe."

"Nah. Rudy knew how much I missed Celestina. He even arranged a blind date for me with his sister Anna. Well, it wasn't so much a date as dinner over at his house. She was nice enough, but the spark wasn't there—not like it had been with Celestina. Anna ended up marrying a rancher in Colorado.

"Anyway, one day Rudy asked me if I thought we should ask Esperanza and Maria to open the cafe again. He said the town just wasn't the same without it. Told me we should try to convince 'em."

"I take it you did just that."

"Convince 'em? Wasn't easy. The next Saturday, Rudy and I went to see Maria. We figured, 'cause she would have to cook, if we couldn't convince her, there wasn't much sense talking to Esperanza.

"Maria answered the door. Rudy removed his cowboy hat, bowed low and said, '*Buenas tardes*, Maria. Could Señor Bill and me speak to you for a few minutes?'

"She looked at Rudy with distrust, but motioned us inside. '*¿Que?*' she asked.

"'Maria, *mi querida*,' Rudy replied, in as smooth a voice as possible. 'Would you consider opening the cafe again?'

"'I'm not your *querida*.' She looked at me, and I could see she was sympathetic. 'That cafe is cursed, anyway.'

"'Maria,' I said, 'It's not cursed. But it's a damn shame it sits there all closed up. Ernesto wouldn't want that. Neither would Celestina.' "'I just cook. I don't know how to run things. Esperanza's got to do that. You ask her?'

"'No, not yet,' Rudy replied. 'If you won't cook, there's no sense asking Esperanza.'

"Maria shook her head. 'I dunno. It's been so long.'

"'Maria, you still know how to cook,' I said. 'Every Christmas, the whole town talks about the *tamales* you make.'

"'*Ay cabrón*,' she muttered with a sigh. 'You talk to Esperanza. See what she says. Besides, we got no money to open the cafe again.'

"'Maria, Rudy and I can help with the money. Will you come with us now? We can all talk to Esperanza.'

"Maria shook her head no, but stepped outside anyway. 'Okay, but Esperanza's never gonna agree.'

"'She will if you cook, Maria,' Rudy said.

"She looked me in the eye, but pointed angrily towards Rudy. 'Okay, but only because of Celestina. Not this *pendejo*.'

"Esperanza lived in a small, nondescript adobe house around the corner from Maria. The three of us walked over, probably looking like a New Mexican version of the Wizard of Oz. We knocked on the door. Esperanza opened it, then stepped back.

"'*Hermana*,' she said, 'What are you doing with these two?'

"'They want us to open the cafe again. I said ask you, 'cause I don't know how to run it. I just cook.'

"'It's been closed for years now,' Esperanza said to us. How come now?'

"'Why not, Esperanza?' I replied. 'The town needs the cafe,' Rudy added.

"'Where we gonna get the money to open? The place needs to be cleaned up. We need supplies. We got no money.'

"'You can borrow what you need from Rudy and me.'

"Esperanza turned away from us and looked silently into the tall cottonwood that grew along the side of her house. 'I dunno. How can Ernesto's be the same without my father or Celestina?'

"'It can't, Esperanza,' I replied. 'But it can be yours and Maria's cafe.'

"'I got to think about it,' she said, looking at all of us. 'Maria and me, we'll talk about it.' Then she motioned Maria into the house.

"'Thanks, Esperanza,' I said. 'You, too, Maria.'

Uncle Bill eyed the empty whisky glass in his hand, contemplating a refill.

"How long did it take them to agree to open the cafe?" I asked.

"Not long. A few days later, Rudy drove out here. Esperanza had come into the bar earlier and let him know. That's when the real fun began. Most every day, Rudy and I both wanted to shoot 'em both, especially Esperanza. She was the one running the show, not Maria. Maria just screamed at us from the kitchen."

"Easy? I gather you became rather adept at avoiding collisions with airborne knives?"

"I don't remember her throwing any knives at me. Saucepans. A couple of rolling pins. She liked throwing them. We had to replace the front window twice."

I cocked an eyebrow. "Indeed? At the bank, one would estimate a cash reserve needed for unanticipated expenditures."

"Well, they sure went through a lot of cash. Nobody had set foot in the cafe—other than mice, birds, and roaches—since it had been closed. Took weeks to clean up the place. The roof had leaked. We had to install a new roof. The whole building had sagged, too, I dunno, maybe cause of the leaks.

That's why the floor leans. But, hell, the building's been around for a long time, so we didn't bother jacking up the foundation. We repaired the holes on the *portal*. Figured that folks falling through before they even came inside would be bad for business."

"Well, one's gustatory inclinations might be off-put by a pre-entry injury, as it were."

"Yep. Once the building was fixed, we had to work on the inside. We bought tables and benches, a new stove and two new refrigerators, sink, put in new storage shelves, new pots and pans, knives—"

"—two sets, one for throwing and one for meal preparation?"

Uncle Bill laughed. "Nope, we saved money by having Maria use the same ones for both. Anyway, once we had everything fixed and in place, we had to buy her supplies for cooking. Made Joe Garcia real happy."

"It all sounds frighteningly expensive. How did you and Rudy obtain the necessary funds?"

"Remember I told you your grandfather forgot to remove me from his will? As for Rudy, hell, with the way folks drink around here, he makes plenty of money from that bar."

I sighed. "Well, I assume my father has already expunged me from his will. No doubt, I top his list of disappointments in *extremis*."

"Forget it, Bennie. It doesn't matter. Look at me for Christ's sake. If there was ever a black sheep in the family, it was me. And I wouldn't change a goddamn thing."

"Kind of you to say, Uncle Bill. Perhaps your assessment is even accurate. However, one's instincts lead one to seek the paternal blessing regardless." I emptied my glass. "In any event, at this point the cafe was ready to commence operations."

"Yep. We thought everything was all set. We were wrong."

"What happened?"

"If Rudy and I had had half a brain between us, we would have foreseen it."

"I don't understand."

"Maria."

"What?"

"Maria was the complication. Everything was ready, but she refused."

"You said she had agreed."

"We thought so. Rudy tried to talk to her. She told him, well, you can guess what she told him."

"What about Esperanza? Given what you have told me, it seems Maria had entrusted Esperanza to make the final decision."

"That's what we thought. But Maria wouldn't come out of her house. She just yelled at Rudy. Esperanza talked to her, then came back and told us Maria had changed her mind. I couldn't believe it. Rudy even threatened Maria with his shotgun."

"How did you change her mind? One presumes Rudy did not shoot her."

"Nope. Damn close, though. Maria was cursing at him and Rudy was cursing back. 'Course I didn't understand everything they were shouting, but I could tell Rudy was giving as good as he got. Never saw him so mad. Thinking about it now, it was damn funny. Rudy and I were standing outside Maria's front door. Maria was in the doorway and Esperanza behind her. Maria was shaking a big knife at him and Rudy was pointing his shotgun at her. I thought we were gonna have another gunfight at the O.K. Corral."

"Eh?"

"O.K. Corral. It's a famous story. Happened in a place called Tombstone, Arizona, around 1880. Feud between the Earps and the Clantons. I'll tell you the story sometime."

"Precisely how did you and Rudy change Maria's mind?"

"Vanity."

"What? Vanity and Maria seem rather incongruous."

"Yeah, but it worked."

"How?"

"Her cooking. She was afraid it wouldn't be good enough, that everyone would compare it to Ernesto's or Celestina's."

"But hadn't you complimented her already, regarding her *tamales* at Christmas?"

"Sure we did. Luckily, Rudy knew Maria pretty well. He told her maybe she was right. Said he would go to Santa Fe and find somebody who could cook real good, especially *tamales*. 'How hard can it be for somebody to make *tamales* better than yours, *querida*?' Rudy told her."

"Did he suffer any physical injury?"

"Not right away. Rudy turned to me and said real loud, 'Let's go to Santa Fe. I got a friend who owns a bar there. He'll know somebody.' We turned around and started walking away.

"We got about ten, maybe twenty, feet from the door when a cast iron frying pan came flying through the air and hit Rudy's right shoulder, followed by more cursing. Rudy grimaced—that fry pan hurt like hell—but then he smiled at me. We had Maria dead to rights.

"Rudy turned around and looked at Maria as she walked towards him, cursing and jabbing her finger at him. Maria yelled she could make *tamales* better than any *pendejo* from Santa Fe. I saw Esperanza standing on the *portal*, shaking her head and smiling. She knew right away what Rudy had done.

"The next week, the Dos Abuelas cafe opened for business. Half the town must have shown up. Folks were cheering and clapping when Esperanza opened the front door. Maria's cooking was great, of course. I was stoppin' in every day. Maria would turn out *enchiladas*, *tacos*, *burritos*, *carne adovada*, and *posole*. Damn it was good. Poor Rudy, though, he was afraid to show up in case Maria came after him. So I was always bringing food to him over at the bar."

"Sounds like a smashing success. What happened?"

"I don't rightly know. I think the success got to be too much for both of them."

"Not sure I follow you. Wasn't Maria especially concerned that the townspeople would find her cooking wanting compared with her father's?"

"Yep, that was true. Thing is, when Ernesto and Celestina were running the cafe, they kept pretty calm. Maria and Esperanza, they were like a couple of stallions that hadn't been broken. Real high strung."

"High strung stallions?"

"What I mean, Bennie, is they just couldn't take it in stride. Running a restaurant is a hell of a lot of work. Ernesto and Celestina knew that, but it didn't matter to them. It mattered a lot to Maria and Esperanza."

"Surely they could have hired someone to help. Why didn't they?"

"Would you work for those two?"

"Ah. But surely they had not yet descended into their present, er, dyspeptic states?"

"No. Well, I guess Maria was already there. Didn't take much to get her into that corral. She just stayed in the kitchen and cooked, except to let Esperanza know when she running out of lard or beans, or chile, or God knows what. And, you gotta remember, Esperanza is the younger sister. She grew up with Maria bossing her around, so didn't take kindly to it. I know what that's like."

"A bit of sibling rivalry?"

"Maybe. Esperanza was having to take care of everything— supplies, tallying up the receipts, sweeping the floor, washing dishes, all of it—while Maria cooked. Of course, folks came for the food, not the swept floors. So, Esperanza just started to 'forget' things Maria had told her to buy. Then Maria would scream at her and Esperanza would scream back. Those two would go at it like a pair of alley cats, sometimes right in front of customers."

"Not an aid to the digestion, I should think."

"Nope. Not good for business, either. Got to be folks in town were plain scared to go in. The place started losing money, so Esperanza stopped paying Joe Garcia for all the supplies. After a few months, Joe told Esperanza she had to pay up or he wasn't gonna let her buy anything else.

"Problem was, Esperanza didn't tell Maria what was going on. She just said that Joe wouldn't sell them anything more. Because Maria didn't know why Joe wouldn't sell them anything more, she erupted. Even threatened to burn down his store."

"Murder and arson, eh? Always a good crime novel combination. At the bank neither would have been conducive to an extension of credit. Hence, your first loan to Scylla and Charybdis?"

"Yep. I couldn't let the cafe go. So I paid Rudy what he was owed, then went to have a talk with Maria and Esperanza. I don't think I've ever been as mad in my life. Told both of them they ought to be ashamed of themselves, how Ernesto and Celestina would be ashamed of what they did to the place, how the town was rootin' for them, and all they did was drive everybody away 'cause they were so god-damn selfish."

"Were they contrite?"

"Sort of. Maria started to yell back at me, about how she never wanted to reopen the cafe anyway. I just let her yell. Finally, when she was done, I said something to her that I never said to a woman, either before or since: '*Vete a la chingada*, Maria.'"

"Gah!" The Graves code simply did not allow for such things to be said to the fairer sex. "Well, Maria obviously failed to shoot you. What did she do?"

"She just stared at me, open mouthed. Esperanza looked like she was in shock. Sat real still and stared at the floor. Finally, Maria looked me in the eye. I don't think I ever saw her look that angry, and I thought, "Jesus, what's she gonna do?' But all she said was 'Okay.' Then she stood up and walked away."

"That was the entirety of her response?"

"For Maria, that was as good as an admission of guilt. I told them they had one more chance to make things right. I would pay Joe Garcia what he was owed. But that was it. The two of them had better act like goddamn adults. And they were not to tell anyone about the loan, ever."

"I am loathe to say it, Uncle Bill, but it seems you were simply rubbishing perfectly good brass. But why the secrecy over the loan?"

"Celestina. I didn't want to let her down. I know that sounds crazy, but as long as the cafe was open, she was still with me. I suppose that doesn't make much sense."

"On the contrary, it makes perfect sense. Rather romantic, really. And thus the *tamale*-payment-in-kind was begot. Yet, it would seem that I am correct. Your loan provided a temporary respite. However, history appears to have repeated itself, one might say."

"I just can't let the place go."

"But Uncle Bill, you've tried. Herculean effort, above and beyond the call, and all that. Esperanza and Maria are simply incapable of running the cafe."

"I know. That's why I want you to run it."

# Chapter 10

W hat? Are you mad? You want me to work with those cobras?"

"Look, you studied at Cambridge. You worked at a bank. You know all about business."

"In case you've forgotten, the bank made me redundant in favour of a dim-witted pyromaniac who takes liberties with store mannequins. The only experience I have with the food and drinks business was the odd dinner with Cynthia. Well, there was the Jolly Rooster, but inebriation rarely qualifies as business acumen."

"You made those *tamales*. Good ones, too."

"I made one dozen *tamales* whilst receiving instruction from a mad-woman. Of what possible relevance can that have?"

Uncle Bill's eyes sparkled. "Bennie, I know it will work."

"It's barmy."

"Dammit, Bennie, listen to me."

I groaned. "Uncle Bill, I know nothing of running a business. Moreover, you appear to have forgotten two immovable objects, called Maria and Esperanza, and one Sisyphean task, namely convincing them. Do you actually believe you can sit them down for tea, offer them a biscuit, and then without so much as a 'by your leave' announce, 'Oh, yes, Bennie here will be running the cafe from now on?' The London Blitz would be a walk in the park by comparison."

"I can convince them."

"Before or after Maria has used my head as a chopping table?"

"Hell, you're carrying on like a frightened rabbit. Where are your *cojones?*"

"Present and accounted for, if you must know. Bravery is one thing; going over the top to be machine-gunned because of some loony general's idea of derring-do is quite another."

Uncle Bill put his hands together silently, as if in prayer and blew into them softly. After sitting quietly for several minutes, he looked at me with a Cheshire cat-like grin. "What if Maria and Esperanza asked you—begged you—to run the cafe?"

"Allow me to repeat myself: you are mad—barking, howling, loony-bin mad. Setting aside Maria's propensity for homicidal violence, Esperanza despises me. Why else would she constantly refer to me as *Pendejito.*"

"I thought I told you it was a term of endearment."

"And a broken clock tells the correct time twice a day. I have heard that particular word with sufficient frequency that, though I may not know its precise definition, it is certainly not a term of endearment."

"Fine. It means you're a little asshole."

"Bloody hag."

"Don't get your knickers in a twist, Bennie—my God, I haven't said that in years. She calls half the folks in town the same damn thing."

I sighed. Dante himself could have created a tenth circle of Hell where one was forced to work with Esperanza and Maria. How Uncle Bill could possibly convince them to request my help was simply beyond comprehension.

"Well, will you run the cafe if they beg you?"

"One might as well ask if I will manage the cafe if the Queen herself requests it. And I remind you again I know nothing about running a business, least of all a cafe."

"You think those two know anything? That they can do a better job running the cafe than you? Last time I checked, you hadn't lost thousands of dollars."

Pride is a terrible thing to have, because it is always prone to injury. "Very well. Pray tell me how you will accomplish this miracle?"

"You let me worry about that. I got an idea. Now, I need to get some sleep."

I retired for the night, managing only fitful bouts of slumber interrupted by nightmarish visions of knife-wielding *tamales* and choruses of *pendejito*-shouting *enchiladas*.

The next morning, in fact the following week, was uneventful. There were the usual chores involving the care and feeding of Daisy and Marjorie. Daisy, with her ever-present *sombrero*, began to regard me as a mere annoyance, like the obsequious waiters one encounters in overpriced restaurants. I did, however, notice a distinct spring in her hoofed steps, if a twenty-five stone pig can step springily, whenever I approached with her daily dose of Farm Calm. Uncle Bill remained silent regarding his plan to "convince" Maria and Esperanza into requesting my managerial services.

Mid-week, we voyaged into town for additional supplies.

---

**CLOSED
YOU WANT SOMETHING
TO EAT GO ASK
PENDEJO JOE GARCIA**

---

As we motored past the cafe, I espied a small sign hanging in the window, on which, written in bold letters said:

Uncle Bill parked his lorry in front of the cafe and stared at the sign. "Damn those two."

"I should think Esperanza is more to blame for the sign. Maria seems inclined to express her displeasure in a physical manner. By the way, have you formed your plan yet?"

"What? Yeah, I'm working on it. I need to talk with Rudy. Let's head over to the bar and see if he's around."

We walked in. The bar, dimly lit as always, appeared to be populated by its usual patrons, including Joe Garcia.

"Hey, Joe," Uncle Bill said, tapping him on the shoulder. "You seen the sign?"

"Yeah, I seen it." He exhaled a cloud of smoke. "Goddamn Esperanza. You know how many people I had come into the store asking me, 'Hey, Joe, what's for lunch?' or 'How about some *enchiladas*, Joe.' Worst thing is that some of the *estupidos*," he jerked his thumb towards the two figures who were slouched over bottles of beer poised in front of them, "are serious. They think I opened a goddamn restaurant. I asked Rudy if maybe he can talk some sense into them."

"You know where Rudy is? I gotta talk to him."

"I saw him go into his office a little while ago."

"Thanks, Joe." Uncle Bill wandered down a dim hallway to Rudy's office, whilst I remained at the bar.

Joe turned to me. "So how's it going, Bennie. El Vaquero driving you crazy, yet?"

"Eh? No, on the contrary, it's been quite the adventure, really."

"Coronado told me you bought out all my corn husks, so Maria could make more *tamales*. You a *penitente* or something?"

"A what?"

"*Penitente*. They're a real serious group of Catholics. Carry crosses around at Easter, that kind of shit."

"Ah. Actually, I'm a Church of England man, myself."

"What kind of religion is that?"

"Protestant, I suppose."

"So how come you bought all of the corn husks?"

"Well, the *tamales* I had obtained for Uncle Bill were stolen from the lorry whilst it was parked in front of your store. I went to the cafe to purchase additional *tamales*, but an apparent shortage of corn husks had limited that morning's supply. So, I, er, purchased the corn husks. That way, Uncle Bill was able to enjoy his usual dozen."

Joe picked up the bottle of beer in front of him. "You know why they couldn't buy them?"

"Yes. I gather from Coronado they are in arrears."

"Huh? No, 'cause Maria and Esperanza owe me money. A lot of goddamn money." He drained the remaining beer from the bottle, then threw it into the rubbish bin behind the bar.

As I contemplated how to respond, a childlike voice spoke to me.

"You gonna order a drink or just sit there on your ass?"

I turned towards the voice, which belonged to a small lad who could not have been more than ten years old. "I say, you're rather young to be a publican."

"What are you talking about, *pendejo*?"

"I beg your pardon. Where are your manners, young man?"

He folded his arms across his chest. "You either buy a drink or get the hell out of my grandfather's bar." Apparently, this yob-in-waiting was Rudy's grandson. "Well? Do I have to throw you out?"

Although I considered reaching across the bar and thrashing the diminutive sod, doing so would have likely been met with approbation by the other patrons, none of whom appeared to care one whit if their publican was a child.

"Fine. I'll have a pint of bitter."

"You want a pint of bitters?"

"Not bitters, bitter. It means beer. Didn't your grandfather teach you what beer is?"

Apparently unused to disgruntled customers, and likely sober ones, his lip quivered slightly. Immediately I felt rather yobbish myself for raising my voice.

"We got Schlitz, Bud, and Best Milwaukee. What do you want?"

"Look, sorry lad, I didn't mean to raise my voice. What is your name by the way?"

"Antonio."

"Well, Antonio, which do you recommend?"

"I dunno. My grandfather only lets me drink Coke. A bottle of Best Milwaukee costs an extra quarter, so my grandfather always tells me to try to sell those."

"Keen businessman, your grandfather. Right. I'll have a bottle of Best Milwaukee."

The lad placed a dark brown bottle in front of me. "Do you have a glass?"

"Nobody ever drinks beer from a glass."

"Yes, well they do where I come from."

"Where's that? Albuquerque?"

"No, London. Do you know where that is?"

"Sure. Coronado told me about the time he went to London. You're from Texas. I guess that's why you talk so funny. Did you meet Coronado there?"

"Er, no. Big city and all that. How much for the beer?"

"A dollar."

I retrieved two dollars out of the wallet. "There's a good chap."

He smiled at the tip and stuffed the extra dollar into his trouser pocket. "Thanks, señor."

I turned my attention back to Joe Garcia, who appeared to be in a semi-coherent state. "Er, Joe, how much do Esperanza and Maria actually owe you?"

"Huh? Three thousand, four hundred, sixty-two dollars and eighteen cents, plus interest. And they call me a *pendejo*."

I was shocked by the amount, and wondered how much Rudy and Uncle Bill had paid to erase their debt on the previous occasion. "Didn't this happen some years ago, as well, Joe? They owed you money, but then repaid you."

"Yeah. Esperanza came in one afternoon. Paid me almost fifteen hundred that time. I should have never let them run up another tab, but I felt sorry for 'em."

"Where did Esperanza get that kind of money?"

"I dunno. She said something about some uncle dying. I didn't care. All I knew was she paid."

"Quite." I poured the beer into the small glass Antonio had left for me and drained the glass in one pull. "Gah! Is this what passes for beer?"

"Hey, that's Best Milwaukee, the Cadillac of beers."

"Alcoholic swill," I muttered.

"What?"

"Nothing. I say, I really should see what's become of Uncle Bill."

I tried to ignore the foul aftertaste lingering on the taste buds like a boring relation, lifted myself off the stool and walked down the hallway where Uncle Bill had disappeared earlier.

"Hullo? Uncle Bill? Mister Sandoval?"

Uncle Bill's voice from behind the door at the end of the hall. "C'mon in, Bennie."

I walked in. The air was thick with cigar smoke.

"How about a cigar, Bennie?" Uncle Bill said, pointing to a box on Rudy's desk. "Montecristos."

"Montecristos, you say? Not something Cynthia ever allowed me to have, actually. Although at Cambridge, I always enjoyed a good smoke."

I sat down in a vacant chair by the desk, performed the ritual cigar review, put flame to the tip, and delighted in the taste.

Rudy smiled at and blew a large cloud towards the ceiling. "El Vaquero has been telling me about his plan. For a *gringo*, you got *cojones*, Bennie. Working with those two ain't gonna be easy."

"I haven't actually agreed. Besides, Uncle Bill insists they will ask, if not beg, me to run the cafe. Hell will be overrun with glaciers before that occurs."

"I dunno, Bennie. El Vaquero has a pretty good plan."

"Really? Well, Uncle Bill, what's this plan of yours?"

"I'm dying, Bennie," he groaned.

"What?" Good heavens, Uncle Bill, why didn't you tell me? Have you seen a specialist?"

Uncle Bill and Rudy burst out laughing.

"This seems rather macabre, if you ask me. Hardly a laughing matter."

"Sorry, Bennie," Uncle Bill said. "You should have seen your face. It's perfect."

A thick fog had settled upon the cranium.

"I'm not really dying, Bennie. But I'm gonna tell Esperanza and Maria I am."

"Eh? I don't understand. You tell them you are dying and then they beg me to run the cafe? That's your plan? Do you actually expect their response will be 'Oh dear, we had better beg Bennie to run the cafe for us?' It's daft."

"Calm down. There's more to it than that. You see, first, I'm gonna put the cafe up for sale."

"How? Maria and Esperanza own it."

"Not if they owe me money, they don't."

The cranial fog began to lift. "Oh, I see. You intend to put a lien on the property. They must pay what they owe you but lack the funds to do so. Most clever."

"Yep. So, they have to sell the place to pay off their debt."

"But I still don't understand why you must pretend to be dying."

"If those two think they have to sell the cafe 'cause they owe me money, what do you think they're gonna do?"

"It will surely be most unpleasant."

"Yep. So, I tell them I'm dying and I'm leaving the ranch to you. I'll tell 'em how sorry I am to make them sell the cafe, but you're gonna need the extra money to run the ranch."

"Bit of a sympathy play, eh?"

"Yep. But I ain't done yet. I'll tell them I know Ernesto and Celestina would have wanted the cafe to keep going. Then I'll tell them that I wanted you to buy the cafe and keep the memories alive, but that you don't have that kind of money. Starting to make sense to you now?"

"It's despicable and dishonest. You could have had a most successful career as a banker. So, faced with the prospect of a sale, you then suggest an alternative solution to remove the lien."

"Yep. 'Course, I'll tell them you refused and you intend to sell the ranch and return to England."

"As I said, most despicable and dishonest. Perhaps it will work."

"El Vaquero," Rudy said, tapping his skull with his cigar finger,"*es muy astuto*."

"You mean astute? I am inclined to agree, Rudy." I turned to Uncle Bill. "Although I am impressed with the degree of cunning, you've over-looked two important considerations."

"Such as?"

"First, having failed miserably and either infuriated or terrified all of their customers, what makes you think Maria and Esperanza will not do so again?"

"What's the second?"

"I still have sufficient remaining sanity to refuse. How would I possibly control their behaviour? A cudgel? Heavy irons, perhaps?"

"Look, Bennie, if they know the cafe will be sold, they'll behave. Okay, maybe they'll behave if we're lucky. But there's nothing to lose."

"Nothing to lose, you say? Do you recall the fable about the scorpion and the frog?"

"C'mon, Bennie, they're not that bad."

"I observed Esperanza being kind to a small child. But as you may observe, I am not a small child. Furthermore, confronting a knife-wielding Maria and an enraged Esperanza regarding, well, the mind boggles at the possibilities, is not something any sane person would do."

"Bennie, *mi querida* Maria, she's got a good heart," Rudy said. "You'll be fine."

"Rudy, you have so much business acumen, what with owning the bar and liquor store. Wouldn't it make more sense for you to run the cafe?"

"And deal with those two? Are you crazy? I mean, I got my hands full, running the bar."

"Your ten-year-old grandson serves drinks. How full can your hands be?"

"He turns eleven next month. Already knows how to water down drinks. Look, Bennie, this is one of those family things. But if you need advice, you just ask."

I sighed and shook my head.

"Just try, Bennie," Uncle Bill said. "The town needs the cafe. I need the cafe. Please."

I was hopelessly outmanned and outgunned; surrender was the only option.

"Very well," I said. "But if my *cojones* are paraded about town on a stick by those serpents, I shall be most displeased."

"Don't worry, Bennie," Rudy said, "We'll make sure your *cojones* are safe."

# Chapter 11

Over the ensuing week, I remained ensconced at the ranch, tending to the needs of the domestic fauna. On Tuesday afternoon, I found myself again repairing fences that the cattle had decided to rubbish. Uncle Bill had travelled to Santa Fe to deal with some matter involving registration of his herd. I heard a vehicle approach the house. Assuming he had returned, I continued my repairs.

Presently, I heard a woman's voice calling me. "Señor Bennie, where are you? We got to talk to you."

I walked back to the house and froze. The voice belonged to Esperanza which, because of its almost pleasant tone, I had failed to recognize. I could see a lorry parked next to the house, in which sat Maria, who was smoking aggressively.

I feigned good cheer. "Esperanza, if you're looking for Uncle Bill, he's gone to Santa Fe for the day. I don't expect him until evening."

"Oh." Esperanza stuttered. "Uh, Maria and me, actually wanted to talk to you *Pendej*—I mean, Señor Bennie."

Uncle Bill had put his plan into operation. As Esperanza and Maria were here, to say nothing of Esperanza's shunting aside her venomous by addressing me by my Christian name, his plan must have taken hold.

"You wish to speak to me? Why?"

"Uh, Maria and me, we're real sorry about El Vaquero."

I adopted the appropriate mournful expression. "Yes, it was quite the shock when he informed me. He still seems so, er, vigorous. Rather difficult to fathom."

"Has he told you anything else?"

"No. I assume he told you about his condition?"

"*Sí.* He said he has the cancer."

"Is that it? I mean, yes, such a tragedy." I sighed as convincingly as possible. "But his spirit remains indomitable, having received the diagnosis. Would you not agree?"

"Huh? Oh, sure, I guess so."

"Well, it was most kind of you and—" I glanced towards the lorry where Maria sat chimneying away "—Maria to come out here and pay your respects."

"Uh, Okay. He didn't tell you nothing else?"

"Not that I recall. Of course, after he informed me of the prognosis, I was in a state of shock."

"He didn't tell you nothing about the ranch?"

"No. A shame he has no heirs. I assume he has a will. Naturally, I will not enquire until the proper time. Of course, I shall return from England to take care of the final arrangements with the family."

"You're gonna leave? You can't."

"Oh, I shan't abandon him, if that is what you mean. I will make sure he has proper care and will set up a trust with the bank to administer the expenses."

"*Estamos jodidos,*" Esperanza muttered under her breath.

"Sorry?"

"Huh? Oh, nothing. Don't El Vaquero want you to stay here at the ranch? With him?"

"As I said, I shall ensure his affairs are in order." I paused, hoping to increase her discomfort. "I say, Esperanza, did Uncle Bill say something to you about the ranch? Something I should know about? Perhaps he forgot to tell me."

"Oh, yeah. He, uh, said you were a big help. Wants you to stay here."

"Really? Well, that is most kind of him to say. I do hope someone purchases the ranch when the time comes."

"Maybe he's gonna leave the ranch to you."

"Me?" I forced a laugh. "I cannot imagine why Uncle Bill would do such a thing, especially since I know nothing about ranching. Besides, I rather doubt owning a ranch here will be of much value when I'm in England."

"Maybe you could stay here."

I looked at Esperanza, suppressing an intense urge to tell her to bugger herself. Yet, it was now time to bring the cannons to bear, as it were.

"If I didn't know better, Esperanza, I should think you would prefer I stayed. Of course, despite my being a—what did you call me, *Pendejito*?—I know better."

"*Sí*, Señor Bennie. Maria and me, we're sorry. It's just, it's been tough with the cafe. Especially now it's closed again because that *pendejo* Joe Garcia won't give us no more credit."

"How long have you been in arrears?"

"Huh?"

"How long have you owed him money?"

"Ever since El Vaque—a long time, I guess."

"Esperanza, before I came here, I worked for a bank. One cannot borrow funds without an expectation of timely repayment. Wouldn't you agree?"

"I dunno. I told Joe business was no good, so we couldn't pay him, but if we had to close the cafe, then he wouldn't ever get nothing."

"Well, there is a basic principle in banking of knowing when to cut one's losses, as it were. I mean, Joe Garcia has to pay for the items he sells you. If you cannot, or will not, repay him, surely you understand he then faces the same problem."

"Joe? He's rich. Maria and me, when we go to Santa Fe, we look at what they charge for pintos and *posole*. Even corn husks for Maria's *tamales*. Joe charges lots more."

"Then why didn't you buy your supplies in Santa Fe?"

"'Cause those stores in Santa Fe won't give us no credit."

"Ah. Rather a quandary, that." The water was becoming less murky. "You gotta know a lot about business, Señor Bennie, working in a bank. ¿*Qué no*?"

"Well, banks are rather different from other businesses."

"You think you can teach Maria and me?"

"Teach you what?"

"About business. Maybe then we can open the cafe again."

"I know nothing about the cafe business, so I doubt there is anything I could offer. Besides, your fundamental problem is constrained access to capital."

"Huh?"

"You have no money. You have to pay Joe Garcia what you owe him before you can establish a small line of credit with the store. You'll need enough money to purchase lower-cost supplies from Santa Fe. That will improve free cash flow and introduce the spectre of competition to Joe, which will cause him to moderate his prices, further benefiting you. Does that make sense?"

"We just need money to pay *pendejo* Joe Garcia and buy supplies from Santa Fe. You know where we can get some of that free cash?"

"No, no, you don't understand. The cash isn't free. Think of it this way. You sell Maria's *tamales* for, what, fifty cents each?"

"*Sí.*"

"So, if it costs forty cents to make each *tamale*, your profit is ten cents."

"Yeah, I guess."

"Quite. Suppose you can make each *tamale* using corn husks from Santa Fe. They cost less. So, perhaps each *tamale* costs only thirty-five cents to make. Now your profit per tamale has increased by fifty percent to fifteen cents. Lower cost, higher cash flow, and Bob's your uncle."

"I don't got no Uncle Bob. *¿Quien es?*"

"No, I mean, what I am trying to say is, with a good business strategy, the cafe will be right as rain."

"Business strategy? What's that? It's just the cafe."

"The cafe is a business. Every business needs a strategy."

"So you got a strategy with the money we need?"

"Er, no. Terribly sorry. Afraid I'm not in a position to extend credit to you and Maria. What money I have I need for my return trip to England."

I espied Maria was walking towards us, ever-present cigarette listing to starboard.

"*Hermana*," Esperanza said, "Señor Bennie says we got to have a business strategy."

"*¿Que? No entiendo.*" Maria shook her head and exhaled a tremendous cloud of smoke.

"He says we need this strategy to pay *pendejo* Joe Garcia." Maria shook her head. "*No más. Estamos jodidos.*"

"What did she say?"

Esperanza turned to me. "She said, uh, maybe it's not worth trying no more. Look, Señor Bennie, if we got the money, could you help us with this strategy shit and everything? Maria and me, we want to open the cafe again. Our father would be real proud. So would your Uncle, El Vaquero, 'cause of his wife Celestina. *¿Por favor?*"

"I suppose I might be of temporary assistance—"

"*Bueno!*" Esperanza and Maria both smiled, at least their somewhat abortive versions of a smile. "*Muchas gracias*, Señor Bennie. We can get the money tomorrow from El Vaq—our family. Then you can run the cafe and make sure we got a strategy thing. Maybe we can even open for *tamale* day."

Maria nodded her head in agreement. I was rather amazed at the speed at which Esperanza had jumped from asking for my help with cafe strategy to managing its operations, rather like a flea jumping from one dog to another.

"I say, did you just ask me to run the cafe for you?"

"*Sí.*"

"I'm flattered, of course, but I know nothing about running a cafe."

"We can show you."

"Then why do you need my help?"

Esperanza opened her mouth, then reclosed it silently. To my surprise, Maria spoke instead. "Señor Bennie, I cook. Esperanza, she makes sure we got supplies. But, we need something else. You figure that out so we don't got to close no more. Okay?"

I stared pensively at both of them. "Do you really think I can help?"

They both shrugged their shoulders. "*¿Por qué no?* Esperanza said. "Nobody else in this shithole town can."

I raised an eyebrow. "Very well, I shall endeavour to help you. However, we shall need to agree on various operating principles. Is that understood?"

"Okay," they responded simultaneously, not having the vaguest notion of what I was saying.

"You come to the cafe tomorrow," Esperanza said. "Maria will make you some *enchiladas*."

The mention of Maria's *enchiladas* induced an almost Pavlovian response in the stomach. "I should enjoy that very much."

"*Bueno*. Maria and me, we'll see you tomorrow."

As I watched them disappear down the road, I felt a quandary. If Maria's cooking could prevail over her violent disposition, and Esperanza's predilection for, well, making life miserable for everyone within shouting distance could be tamed, perhaps the cafe could succeed. Then again, optimism was the proverbial fool's errand.

I resumed the fence-mending chores, anxious for Uncle Bill to return. To my astonishment, his plan had succeeded, and I now found myself facing, well, that was the trouble. I had agreed to run the cafe, which meant containing the worst instincts of Maria and Esperanza, if such a thing were possible. It seemed rather like trapping enraged lions in a paper bag.

As dusk descended, I returned the tools to the barn, much to the chagrin of Marjorie, who eyed me warily. I heard Uncle Bill's lorry arrive.

I walked back to the house and stepped into the sitting room. Uncle Bill was pouring himself a large bracer of Dusty Trail.

"Pour yourself a whisky, Bennie. Cheers." He drained the glass. "Damn, I needed that. Any visitors today?" He winked.

"I should think you already know the answer. We will be discussing the details of my role at the cafe tomorrow. I am promised a luncheon of *enchiladas*."

"What did I tell you? Did they beg you to help?"

"Funny thing, that. It was the taciturn Maria who elucidated, with almost surgical precision, why they needed my help, not Esperanza. I was surprised, to say the least. Not begging, mind you. Rather a matter-of-fact declaration of need, really."

"You gonna help them?"

I grimaced. "Against my better judgment, yes. No doubt, the few bits of sanity I have are already packing for an extended holiday."

Uncle Bill stood silent and nodded his head. "Thank you, Bennie, from Celestina and me." He poured a second glass of whisky and sat down on the davenport.

# Chapter 12

I arrived at the cafe at high noon, noon being *de rigueur* for shoot-outs between the yobs populating Zane Grey novels and the Gary Cooperish types defending truth, honour, and the fairer sex.

The cafe appeared lifeless until the front door opened, revealing Esperanza, ever-present cigarette dangling listlessly from her mouth. She motioned me inside. As I stepped through the door, the folly of the task before me glowed, bearing an uncanny resemblance to the ends of both sisters' cigarettes.

"You really gonna help us, Señor Bennie?"

"I shall do my best. Where's Maria?"

"She's in the kitchen, making your *enchiladas*. You want something to drink, a Coke maybe?"

The memory of the lava-like heat of Maria's green chile erupted, and I quickly agreed. "Yes, please. Might I have a glass of milk?"

"Milk? Sorry, we don't got no milk. Don't worry, Maria made her chile less hot, the way you *gringos* like it."

"Er, well, most kind of her." As we spoke, the kitchen door burst open, followed by Maria, who was carrying a large, *enchilada*-laden plate. She placed it before me. As the steam rose, I was smitten by the sweet fragrance of the green chile.

Maria exhaled a large cloud of cigarette smoke, which enveloped the entire table and abruptly ended the olfactory rapture. A large clump of cigarette ash fell dead centre onto the plate.

"So," Esperanza said, oblivious to the ash, "you got some ideas for your strategy?"

I stared at the ruined lunch. "Perhaps the first item of business should be your cigarettes."

"Cigarettes?"

I pointed an accusatory finger at the ash deposit. "May I suggest not smoking whilst serving customers? Granted, I'm English, but I prefer my meals to be served sans cigarette ash."

Both Maria's and Esperanza's smiles faded into oblivion. Maria took the cigarette from her mouth, dropped it to the floor, and attacked it with her shoe. Then she swooped up my plate and returned to the kitchen. Esperanza placed her cigarette in the ashtray that sat on the table next to mine.

"No cigarettes? I been smoking since I was twelve. I don't even remember when Maria started smoking."

"Look, you asked for my advice, didn't you? I'm not suggesting you rubbish the habit entirely, but good God, who wants to be served a side dish of cigarette ash with his *enchiladas, tamales,* &c. Surely you've had complaints in the past?"

Esperanza shrugged. "Maybe a couple times. We just took their food back to the kitchen and spooned off the ash. Then I brought the plate back. One time, Maria put a cigarette butt in *pendejo* Joe Garcia's *enchiladas* 'cause I asked her to. He didn't come back no more."

I felt the onset of a tremendous headache and massaged the wrinkling brow. I had expected the task to be impossible; it had now progressed to suicidal, rather like Scott walking about the Antarctic in swim trunks.

"Er, yes." I raised my voice in frustration. "Nor, one suspects, would any customers of his to whom he discussed that particularly juvenile incident."

"Huh?"

"Why do you think no one dines here anymore? Or perhaps you think that customers says, 'Right, let's motor to the cafe and see whose dinner will have the cigarette butt.' Or, perhaps—just perhaps—Joe told his customers about his *enchiladas?* Perhaps—just perhaps—someone might be put off their feed, knowing they might find a small 'surprise' with their meal? I suppose you never considered that possibility, eh?"

"You think Joe Garcia would tell people? ¡*Que Pendejo*!"

"Of course he would bloody well tell people!"

Esperanza raised her voice. "Don't shout at me, *Pendejito*."

Maria came through the kitchen door, plate in one hand and chef's knife in the other. I stared at Esperanza, curling the lip. "I see Señor Bennie has devolved to *Pendejito*. That didn't take long. Do you want my help or not?"

Esperanza took a large pull on her still smouldering cigarette. "*Hijo de puta*." She glanced at Maria, who dropped the plate of what I hoped were ash-free *enchiladas* in front of me, and glowered. Oddly, I did not feel intimidated in the least.

"Sorry?" I replied calmly, returning Maria's glare.

"Okay. Esperanza and me, we want your help. *Por favor*."

"Apology accepted. Look, I realize it will be difficult for you and Maria to, well, experiment with a new approach." I paused. "But that is why you asked for my help, is it not?"

"*Sí*," Maria replied, lowering the knife and returning to the kitchen. I enjoyed a forkful of the *enchiladas* and turned my attention to Esperanza. "Well?"

"What?"

"These are quite delicious. If we can match the service with the taste, the cafe might even prosper."

"I don't understand."

I retrieved another forkful. "I mean Maria's cooking is not enough to ensure success. The atmosphere must be agreeable so people will want to eat here."

"People come for *tamale* day."

"True. They line up outside the cafe as if it were gaol, secure their *tamales*, and then leave hurriedly."

"Huh? You think the cafe is a jail? That don't make no sense."

I was about to respond, when Coronado's rodentary visage shimmered before the front door.

"*Hola*, Esperanza. Are you open again?" He turned and looked at me with surprise. "Señor Graves, are you here? Hey, you got some *enchiladas*." He sniffed with anticipation, reminding me of Daisy. "They sure smell real good."

"Hullo, Coronado. I'm sorry, but the cafe is not actually open today. However, perhaps Maria would be willing to prepare a plate for you anyway. Please sit down."

Coronado lowered himself carefully into a rickety chair. Esperanza glared at him and then me. "You think you're gonna get a free meal, *gordo*? Get the fuck out."

Coronado glanced alternately between Esperanza and me. "But Señor Graves, he told me to sit down. I got money."

"Esperanza, please ask Maria to prepare a plate of her *enchiladas* for our guest."

"For him? Are you crazy?"

"Perhaps. However, do you remember what we discussed earlier?"

"*Sí*, but is this your strategy, a free *lonche* for El Gordo?"

"As a matter of fact, it is."

"*Hijo de puta.*" She shook her head and walked into the kitchen. "Señor Graves, I don't understand. How come you're here?" He paused and stared at me wide-eyed. "Esperanza, she doesn't take orders from nobody. How come she—"

I raised my hand to end the questions. "Allow me to explain. Esperanza and Maria would like to reopen the cafe. They have asked for my help."

"*Híjole.* You give them the money they owe Joe, Señor Graves?"

"Are you mad? I mean, I was told they obtained the funds from, er, a family member. No, they asked me to run the cafe." Coronado continued to stare. "You see, although Maria's cooking is excellent, as you well know, they need help running the cafe on a day-to-day basis. As I have some experience, I accepted, at least for now."

"You owned a cafe, Señor Graves? Did I eat there when I was in London?"

"What? No, I never owned a cafe in London, and certainly not London, Texas. I did evaluate several restaurants to determine their profitability."

The kitchen door opened and Coronado glanced over with anticipation. Esperanza came out with a steaming plate of *enchiladas* and gracelessly set it down before him.

"*Muchas gracias*, Esperanza. They smell great. You got anything to drink? Maybe a Coke?"

"Now you want a free Coke, too, you f—"

"Esperanza," I interrupted sharply. "Please bring our guest a Coke. Thank you very much."

She bent down and hissed in my ear. "You crazy? Giving him *lonche* for free? How are we gonna make any money giving away food?"

"Trust me."

Esperanza cursed under her breath and disappeared into the kitchen. Presently, she returned with a bottle of Coke, which she slammed down in front of Coronado.

"Here."

"*Gracias*, Esperanza." Coronado tucked into his *enchiladas* voraciously. "I'm glad the cafe is gonna open again, Señor Graves."

"You are quite welcome. Would you let Joe know you ate lunch here."

"I dunno, Señor Graves, Joe used to get mad at me when I ate lunch here."

"Indeed? Well, I shall speak with him myself. Now, Coronado, may I ask you something?"

"Sure."

"Did you enjoy your lunch?"

"*Sí*. Maria's *enchiladas* are real good." He patted his ample waistline and smiled.

"I didn't mean lunch today. You said you used to eat lunch here, when the cafe was open. Did you enjoy doing so?"

"Yeah, I guess. Sometimes, I would bring a *burrito* from home and eat in the store. Or, maybe have a couple of beers at Rudy's."

"Did many people eat lunch at the cafe, when Ernesto and Celestina ran it?"

"*Sí*. Some days, it seemed like the whole town was here."

"How about when it was just Esperanza and Maria?"

"It was pretty crowded for a while. Then not so much."

"Why not? Wasn't Maria's cooking just as good?"

"*Sí*, Maria's cooking was always real good." He paused and stared at a wall.

"What is it, Coronado?"

"I dunno. I guess everybody missed Ernesto and Celestina, your brother El Vaquero's wife. She was a real nice lady."

"Thanks. Are you returning to the store?"

"*Sí*. I got some money for the *enchiladas* and Coke." He rooted about in a greasy trouser pocket.

"No need, Coronado. You were our guest. I appreciate your help."

"I dunno what I did."

"I know what you did. Do tell Joe you had lunch here today."

"Okay, Señor Graves. I hope he don't get mad at me."

"If he does, tell him I invited you. Understood?"

"*Sí*. Thanks again for the *lonche*." He raised his bulk and walked out slowly, smacking his lips. Our first customer, rodentary as he was, had returned.

As soon as the front door had closed behind, Maria and Esperanza burst through the kitchen door and marched towards me like dreadnoughts at full steam.

Esperanza began the tirade. "What were you thinking? Why you give him free food? He's gonna come back every day."

"Precisely. We, well, you and Maria, have gained a loyal customer, which the cafe desperately needs."

"We don't need no customers who don't pay," Esperanza yelled. "We need money. That lunch cost us."

I removed my wallet and retrieved a ten-dollar bill. "Will this be sufficient?"

Esperanza snapped the bill from my hand like an iguana shooting out its tongue to capture an unsuspecting beetle.

"Don't let that *pendejo* around here anymore."

"Why not? We need to attract customers, rather like that disgusting bit of flypaper hanging in Maria's kitchen attracts flies."

"We don't want no customers like him."

"Why not?"

"Because he don't pay."

"I just paid you for both of us."

"You wait. When we open again, he's gonna try to run a tab, just like at Rudy's."

"First, we shall not allow any customers to run a tab. Second, Coronado is an important customer. I specifically asked him to mention his lunch to Joe Garcia."

"That *pendejo*? How come?"

"Allow me to explain. Coronado will tell Joe about his delicious repast. He will also tell Joe I am running the cafe. Though Joe will be suspicious, he will conclude the cafe will soon reopen, offering him the opportunity to sell us needed supplies."

Esperanza looked at me quizzically. "But you said we were gonna get supplies from Santa Fe."

"We shall. Next week, we will bring a lorry's worth of supplies from Santa Fe to restore the larder. In fact, I may ask Coronado to help stock the shelves, offering him lunch in exchange, on the condition that he say nothing to Joe about where the supplies were purchased."

"You think Coronado isn't gonna tell Joe? He's gonna tell everybody in town."

"One certainly hopes so. Coronado, who I gather spreads gossip like jam on bread, will inform Joe of our purchases. Joe will realize the seriousness of his position. Then, Joe will inform everyone who comes to his store, providing additional publicity for us. In fact, I should not be surprised if Joe himself graces us with his presence soon thereafter."

Maria shook her head with a rather defeated looking motion. "I got to go cook," she mumbled, walking back into the kitchen.

Esperanza scratched her head. "You talk real fancy. Maybe I don't understand, but people here, they don't do what you expect."

"What do you mean?"

"You ever think if you do something to somebody, they're gonna do something else.

"Er, well, yes, I suppose I have. Why?"

"'Cause in Vaca Seca, they're gonna do something real different. And then you're gonna wish they hadn't. *¿Comprende?*"

"You mean there will be unintended consequences."

"I dunno. People here got their own way of doing things. You better remember that, *Pendejito.*"

She turned around and disappeared back into the kitchen. I sat at the table, draining the last drops of Coke from my glass, wondering what form the unexpected that Esperanza had warned me about would take.

After five minutes or so of unsuccessful attempts to divine the future, I took my leave. I walked to the kitchen door, knocked politely, and pushed through.

"Ladies, thank you again for the delicious lunch." I expected to find them both puffing away in high dudgeon. Instead, I encountered only emptiness. "Maria? Esperanza? Hullo?"

Nothing. Not even the remains of fresh cigarettes. The door at the back of the kitchen opened into an alleyway of sorts. I stepped through; perhaps they had wandered outside, the better to raise their voices whilst avoiding my prying ears. Never one of those chaps who believed in alien abductions, although at the time I would have cheerfully escorted both Rodrigo and Arthur of mannequin fame to the nearest alien spaceship and waved them off, I was nevertheless taken aback by Maria and Esperanza's disappearance.

I returned to the kitchen and locked the back door. I even peered into the fridge, which was appallingly filthy and thus one more problem to address. Here was another Vaca Seca mystery, "The Case of the Missing Vipers," perhaps worthy of Holmes himself. Unfortunately, the Baker Street detective was unavailable and I knew nothing of the local constabulary.

I wandered over to Rudy's Bar. As the eyes adjusted to the dim light, I saw the usual suspects floating over their beer bottles in a semi-conscious state. A ceiling fan spun slowly overhead, groaning with each revolution. The bar itself was untended.

I walked down the hallway to Rudy's office and knocked on the door. No answer. Next, I went to Garcia's store, wondering if I would find it, too, empty and silent. But as I entered and peered about, I heard Coronado's voice.

"*Hola*, Señor Graves. Thanks again for lunch. It sure was good."

"Er, did Maria or Esperanza come in several minutes ago?"

"No."

"How about Rudy?"

"I saw him at the bar this morning. Maybe he went home for his *siesta*."

"What about Joe??"

"I think he went to Santa Fe."

I grimaced, unsure how to proceed. "I say, Coronado, Maria and Esperanza seemed to have vanished. I finished my lunch and, when I went back to the kitchen to bid them fare-well, they had disappeared."

"*Híjole*. They were kinda mad at me, huh?"

"More with me, I should think."

"How come, Señor Graves?"

"Er, nothing to concern yourself with. If you see them, would you be so kind as to let them know I'm looking for them."

"Was Esperanza's truck parked behind the cafe?"

"What? I mean, no, I do not recall seeing it."

"I guess they drove off."

I sighed. "Er, yes. Any ideas where they might motor off to at this time of day?"

"No. Maybe they went somewhere."

"Of course they—" I closed the jaws in futility.

"Well, I suppose I shall return to the ranch."

"Maybe El Vaquero knows where they are, Señor Graves."

"How could he possibly—" I stopped myself before edging over another verbal precipice. "I mean, yes, I shall enquire of him. Good day, Coronado."

"*Adios*, Señor Graves."

# Chapter 13

With the grey matter overwhelmed by the stress of Maria and Esperanza's mysterious disappearance, as well as from the conversation, if one could call it that, with Coronado, I returned to the ranch. Daisy, *sombrero* well-attached, eyed me from her usual post on the patio. As I motored around the side of the house, I espied Esperanza's lorry.

The sounds of Esperanza's cursing drifted outside and into the lorry's open window, where it attacked the eardrums. Well, a Graves girds the loins when called upon, and what awaited me would no doubt challenge the most resolute of girders. Inhaling a large snifter of untainted air into the lungs, I opened the back door and walked inside.

My presence, hidden in a fog of smoke and sound, went unnoticed. Uncle Bill was sitting quietly on the davenport, armed with a large whisky. Maria and Esperanza stood athwart the front door. Esperanza was simultaneously gesticulating, yelling, and puffing.

"Giving away Maria's *enchiladas* for free to Coronado? You got to talk to *Pendejito*, El Vaquero."

Before Uncle Bill could reply, I waltzed in cheerily. "I say, ladies, I wondered where you had vanished. Kind of you to venture here to speak with Uncle Bill. How charming. I didn't mean to interrupt."

Uncle Bill looked at me, rolling his eyes.

"Uh, Señor Bennie," Esperanza said, "sorry, uh, Maria needed something from her house. We, uh, had to talk to El Vaquero."

"Quite understandable. Do you mind if I sit down?"

"Uh, okay. I guess we finished talking."

"Might your discussion have something to do with the cafe? Of course, you wouldn't want to burden Uncle Bill, especially in his condition, would you?"

"Huh? I dunno."

I turned to Uncle Bill "How are you feeling today, Uncle Bill? I asked with artificial sympathy. May I get you anything?"

"Maybe a whisky, Bennie." He winked. "Ladies? Would you care for a whisky?"

Esperanza looked at Maria, who shrugged in the affirmative. "Okay, sure I guess."

I poured each of them a large glass. "Here you are. Cheers."

"*Salud, gracias*," they replied in unison, draining their glasses in one quick motion.

"Right ho. Another round?"

"*Sí, Pendejito*," Esperanza replied. While Maria took a sip, Esperanza drained her glass instantly.

"Well, what did you think of our earlier discussion of business strategy?"

Esperanza waived her glass through the air. Maria looked at the floor.

"How to encourage new customers? Providing Coronado with a free lunch. That sort of thing."

"*Pendejo* Coronado," Esperanza blurted, bilious lava erupting, "you don't know what you done."

"Ah, so you've come to Uncle Bill. Have him rein me in, eh? Well, I do need to return to England. Quite understandable you wish to address things yourselves. I am curious, though."

"Curious?"

"Yes. Maria, yesterday you told me the cafe needed something else, although you and Esperanza didn't know what that was. I gather you have decided that something else is not advertising. What then?"

Maria stared at me, glassy-eyed, and remained silent.

"Esperanza?"

"Huh?"

"What do you suggest?"

"We ain't gonna give away no more free food."

"But the cafe needs *something* to succeed. You and Maria said that yourselves."

"I dunno. You got some more whisky? Maybe that will help me think of something."

I turned to Uncle Bill, who shrugged his approval, then poured Esperanza another large glass, which she summarily drained. I raised an eyebrow. The woman clearly possessed an iron-clad liver.

Esperanza slurred, waving the empty glass at me. "Look, *Pendejito* . . . just 'cause El Vaquero is dying, we don't got to . . . " She collapsed heavily into a chair, nearly rolling backwards onto the floor.

"She never could pace herself," Uncle Bill remarked dryly. "How long will she sleep it off, Maria? A few hours this time?"

"*Sí.* She always does."

"Good. Then maybe we can get somewhere."

"What do you mean?" I asked.

"Once Esperanza gets liquored up, there's no reasoning with her."

Uncle Bill turned to Maria. "Can you talk some sense into your sister, once she wakes up?"

"I dunno. I can try."

"I don't think I fully understand. Maria, weren't you the one who was furious at me for offering Coronado lunch?"

"No. Esperanza, she was real mad. She don't like Coronado. Señor Bennie, you sure he's gonna help?"

"Well, that's the idea. We must try something."

"Okay. I just want to cook. Esperanza, she likes to be the boss."

"But she asked for my help."

"*Sí.* But Esperanza, she don't like help from nobody."

This was all rather topsy-turvy. I had assumed that Maria, what with her history, would have been the enraged one, whilst Esperanza would have been the voice of reason. Apparently, I was mistaken.

"Do you still want my help?"

"*Sí.*"

"Are you sure?"

"We don't got no choice. *¿Que no?* No help, no money, no cafe."

"Yes, well, an accurate assessment, I suppose. Right. We shall let Coronado work in his, er, mysterious way, whilst we discuss other changes."

"What changes?"

"Well, the menu for one thing."

Maria's brow furrowed deeply. "You don't like what I cook?"

"No, no, that's not what I mean. However, as I recall from my first visit to the cafe, the menu was— how shall I put this?—rather limited. When I asked for a menu, Esperanza snarled. She informed me my choices were *enchiladas*, *tacos*, or a bowl of *frijoles*. Surely when your father ran the restaurant, the menu was, well, more expansive?"

"Damn right, it was," Uncle Bill said. "*Burritos*, *carne adovada*, *rellenos*, *posole*, stuffed *sopapillas*. My favourite of all was Ernesto's half-breed."

"His what?"

"Half-breed. Steak and *tacos* together. You remember, Maria?"

"*Sí*, I remember. I could never cook the steak right."

Uncle Bill sighed. "And Bennie, for breakfast, Celestina made the best damn *huevos rancheros* you ever tasted."

"I'm sure she did. What are they?"

"*Huevo* is the Spanish word for egg. 'Course, it can mean something else, if you know what I mean."

"Er, yes." I grimaced involuntarily.

"Anyway, to make *huevos rancheros*, you put fried eggs on a fresh flour *tortilla*, and smother the whole thing in red and green chile. There was a woman working at the cafe. All she did was make fresh *tortillas*. Maria, what was her name?"

Maria crossed herself. "Lupe Mondragón. We called her *Tia* Lupe, but she wasn't really our Aunt. She was my mother's friend."

"The cafe served breakfast as well?" I asked, agog at the prospect of a three-meal-a-day commitment.

"Only on Fridays and Saturdays," Uncle Bill replied. "Celestina would leave the house at five o'clock those mornings."

"Was breakfast popular?"

"Hell, yes. Celestina told me that folks sometimes drove all the way from Santa Fe."

"Blimey! I say, Maria, why did you abandon all of these menu items?"

"Too much work. Esperanza, she wasn't much help."

"Did she cook?"

"Maybe some, when our father told her. But when it was just Esperanza and me running the cafe, she worked out front."

"But surely you could have hired—" I paused. "Ah, nub of the problem."

"*¿Que?*"

"Er, nothing."

I was about to suggest a new strategy, when Esperanza began to snore, emitting a sound reminiscent of the large pneumatic drills one sees chaps using to repair roadways. "Does she always snore so loudly?"

"*Sí*, even when we was kids."

Listening to the clamour, I could well imagine where Maria derived her fondness for kitchen knives. "Perhaps we should continue our discussion in the kitchen . . . or the barn."

Uncle Bill raised himself off the davenport, groaning slightly. "Let's go in the kitchen. I need some coffee anyway."

"You okay, El Vaquero?" Maria asked, evincing concern.

"Hell, yes, Maria. Just a little stiff, that's all."

I had temporarily forgotten about Uncle Bill's fiction of dying, which had precipitated the current situation, and I wondered if he had forgotten it as well.

"Er, Uncle Bill, in your condition, one mustn't hesitate to ask for assistance, should one need it."

"Huh? Oh, yeah. Thanks, Bennie. Mighty nice of you. But I ain't dead yet, despite what that goddamn doctor says."

"Stiff upper lip, eh, Uncle Bill? That's the spirit."

"Uh, yep. Maria, you want some coffee?"

"*Sí, gracias.*"

"Bennie?"

"Yes, please. Now, whilst you are attending to the, er, 'cowboy' coffee of yours Uncle Bill, perhaps Maria and I can continue our discussion of the menu."

"Fine with me," he said. "Maria, how about *carne adovada*? Celestina would make it at the house sometimes. Can't be that tough."

"*Carne adovada*? No, it's real easy. You just got to make the red chile sauce the right way."

"*Carne avocado?*" I asked.

"*Adovada*," Maria said sharply. "Pork in red chile sauce."

"Did you say pork?" My thoughts drifted lazily towards the porcine nemesis slumbering on the patio.

"*Sí.*" Maria extended her thumb towards the slumbering Daisy on the patio and grinned. "Señor Bill, You got lots of *carne adovada* on your *portal*. *Tamales*, too."

"Nobody's cooking up my little girl. She's part of the family."

I glanced at Maria and offered a surreptitious finger-across-the-throat motion. Apparently, we had discovered an item of mutual agreement. "Of course, not, Uncle Bill. Did the cafe offer any equine-based delicacies?"

"*¿Que?*"

"Jesus, Bennie, you're goddamn heartless. Marjorie, too?"

"Just having a bit of fun. Although we will need to find a good source for beef and pork. Any locals you would recommend? Maria, do you remember where your father bought meat for the cafe?"

"*Sí.* We got beef from Archuleta's ranch. Maybe twenty miles north."

"What about pork?"

"Zafarano Wholesale in Santa Fe. Later on, Esperanza and me just got it from Joe. It wasn't real good."

"H'mm. Perhaps the Archuletas know someone who raises pigs. We could motor there tomorrow and discuss it with them."

"I think Arturo Archuleta died a few years ago. He took over the ranch from his father, Jaime. Arturo's son, Jesus, I think he's running it now."

"Very well. We might obtain more favourable prices if we offer him the opportunity to be our exclusive supplier. Which reminds me, Maria, where did your father store all of this meat? There doesn't seem to be a freezer of any sort in the kitchen and the refrigerator is quite small."

"Rudy's. He got a big freezer in back. We owned the building next to the cafe. Had a refrigerator, shelves, lots of space."

"Owned, as in you no longer own it?"

"No, we still got it."

I turned to Uncle Bill. "Did you know about the building next door?"

"Nope. Ernesto never said anything about it. Neither did Celestina."

"A stroke of luck, I should think."

A tremendous groan emanated from the sitting room, followed by a snort that sounded like Daisy before her morning trough. I peered into the sitting room. Esperanza was cradling her head like an egg and moaning.

"Rather in our cups, eh, Esperanza," I said loudly.

"*Dios mio.*" She glanced up towards me, still cradling her head. "*Pendejito*, you got some aspirins maybe? What kind of whisky was that?"

"Dusty Trail, of course. Only the best for El Vaquero. Would you care for another glass?"

"Are you crazy?"

"Always. Then again, I didn't pass out in the chair."

"Where's Maria? Smells like coffee. You got some more?"

"In the kitchen, and yes. We were chatting a bit about business strategy whilst you were asleep."

Esperanza groaned again as she raised herself up, looking like Frankenstein dressed for Hallowe'en night, and offered me a dishevelled, squinty-eyed look. "No more strategy. Maria and me, we're gonna figure something out."

"Really? You've made rather a hash of it so far. Besides, have you discussed this with Maria? She seems rather keen."

"What do you mean?"

"Well, whilst you were unconscious, we discussed options for the new menu, for one. Seems your father offered a wide array of dishes, including ones so popular the cafe attracted diners from as far as Santa Fe. Rather different than what you offered on my first visit."

"Maria couldn't cook everything. It was too much work."

"Indeed. And your not helping her in the kitchen? Perhaps that contributed to Maria's overwork."

"*Vete a la chingada, Pendejito*. I thought you were gonna get me some aspirins." She began to move slowly towards the kitchen.

"Charming as that expression may be, it does not endear me to provide assistance."

"Huh?"

"Do you have any concept of basic manners?"

Esperanza ignored me and shuffled into the kitchen. "*Hermana*," she whispered, still holding her head, "let's go. I told *Pendejito* we don't want no help. I'll go talk to Joe to get some supplies."

"No," Maria replied bluntly. "I want Señor Bennie's help. Tomorrow, we're gonna go to Archuleta's ranch. You can stay here."

"*Pendejito*, he don't know nothing. He said so himself."

"No. I want to cook *carne adovada* again."

"So cook it. You don't need anybody's help for that."

"And *tortillas*, like *Tia* Lupe's." Maria appeared rather entranced, as if stepping back in time, imagining herself in the cafe with her father and Celestina.

"Okay, we'll make *tortillas*, too. You think *Pendejito* is going to make them?"

"Goddamn it, Esperanza," Uncle Bill interjected. "You're more stubborn than that old nag I got in the barn. Bennie's offered to help you, despite his reservations. If he leaves, there's no more cafe. I don't want that. Do you?"

"We don't need no help, El Vaquero, just some more money. Then we can open again. Maybe I can hire somebody to help Maria cook."

"Hire someone? You remember the last time you hired someone? That poor girl quit after the first day. If it wasn't for Rudy, her father would have shot you."

"This time, we'll get somebody good, not like that lazy Carolina."

"Jesus! Who the hell in this town is gonna work for you? And how are you going to pay 'em?"

"Maybe we can sell the building next door. Then we won't owe you no more money and we won't need no fucking strategy, or whatever *Pendejito* calls it."

By this time, I felt like a chap who had been wrongly declared dead by the authorities, then admonished by said authorities for bringing the error to their attention. "Excuse me. Whilst you are all nattering about my role, or lack thereof, in the cafe's future, you may wish to hear my thoughts on the matter."

Esperanza, for whom the staff of life was something to be kneaded into a dagger, jumped. "Maria and me, we always done things without nobody's help."

"What about the previous loans?"

"We paid that money back."

"Bollocks. Had you repaid it, I would be enjoying a peaceful afternoon, rather than listening to your ravings. However, if do not want my help, I am only too delighted to oblige."

I glanced at Maria and detected the rumblings of a violent eruption forthwith. She turned to Esperanza and growled. "¡*Callate*! You ain't gonna decide no more, *hermana*. I want Señor Bennie's help. He got good ideas for the cafe, and I want to cook again."

Esperanza's jaw dropped.

Listening to the two sisters, I was possessed of a strong urge to grab Uncle Bill's arm and run to safety, much as one might climb the nearest tree to avoid an enraged pig. Surprisingly, however, Maria remained steady. "No cooking, no cafe. You want to run the cafe, you go find somebody else to cook. I can start my own cafe with Señor Bennie's help."

"What?" I said, reeling.

Esperanza stared vacantly at Maria. "*Hermana*, you always let me run things."

"*No más*. We got one more chance." She pointed at me like one of the witches from *Macbeth*. "Señor Bennie."

I felt as if I Maria had elevated me to "lead us out of Egypt and part the Red Sea, there's a good chap," status.

Now it was Esperanza's turn to glower, not at Maria, but at me. I shrugged.

"Ladies, I don't wish to be the cause of internecine civil war. You both have your respective skills cafe-wise and, no doubt, will be successful combining forces. Think of England and Spain uniting to battle the French."

"When was that?" Esperanza asked.

"Well, it was one of those wars—thirty years, one hundred years— really not sure. They did rather run together. The point is that the cafe will be more successful if you work together."

"We worked together and the cafe was no good," Maria said. "You're gonna fix it."

"Yes, well, wasn't that the point of our discussion at lunch today?"

Esperanza spat violently. "*Bueno*. We'll let *Pendejito* run the cafe. Then we'll see what happens."

"Will you cooperate, Esperanza?"

"What do you mean?"

"I mean, will you help, lend a hand? All for one and one for all, that sort of thing?"

"Which hand you want, *Pendejito*?" She raised the middle fingers of both.

"Quite. My point, Esperanza, is that if we work together, we might make a go of the cafe. Or should I simply pack my luggage and depart your charming little town?"

Esperanza shrugged. "This ain't gonna work, *Pendejito*, so you're gonna be packing soon anyway."

"I don't suppose you would be willing to address me using some other term besides *Pendejito*? My Christian name, perhaps?"

Esperanza grinned slyly. "How about *cabroncito*?" Maria laughed, lowering her head to avoid my gaze.

"One supposes you might have a few rather choice nicknames, Esperanza. However, in the interest of fulfilling Uncle Bill's wishes, I shan't speculate."

I turned to Uncle Bill, who himself had succumbed to the jocularity of this alternative epithet. The battle had been engaged.

# Chapter 14

E speranza and Maria drove off, the grey-blue cigarette smoke mixing with the greyer smoke of burning oil from Esperanza's lorry. Uncle Bill breathed a large sigh of relief, and I felt as if I had successfully defused an unstable, grandmotherly bomb. We enjoyed a celebratory whisky and settled in for the evening.

The next morning, preparations, backed with Uncle Bill's brass, began in earnest. Having passed the concept phase, as we banking types like to say, the time had come for execution, an admittedly awkward term given Esperanza and Maria's proclivities. The heavy lifting of spiffing up the cafe into something presentable, with an actual menu and paying customers, seemed a daunting, if not suicidal, undertaking.

The first task was to be the floor and its distinct list to starboard. A bit of experimentation showed that a plate of Maria's *enchiladas*, set upon a dampish table-top, would begin a slow but inexorable slide towards the table's edge if the floorboards were vibrated by footfalls. My naïveté rejected the temporary solution, which was to level the tables and chairs with bits of wood glued to their respective leg-bottoms.

Instead, because the list extended into the kitchen and under Maria's cooker, I suggested we repair the cafe's foundation, thus levelling the floor properly. However, my knowledge of tasks of a carpentry-like nature consisted of futile attempts at inserting small picture hooks into the sitting room walls of the old flat, using a large hammer. The result had been several craters and an obscenely large bill from the local carpenter, whom Cynthia rang up after witnessing the destruction I had wrought.

On an otherwise cheery morning, Esperanza and I argued how best to proceed. "Everybody knows the floor ain't level. Nobody in Vaca Seca's got a level floor. So what?"

"Because I do not want anyone shouting 'man overboard' when customers fall off their chairs whilst sitting at their tables. Besides, Maria should have a level surface on which to cook, especially as she will be called on to prepare a variety of menu items."

"You want to fix the floor, go the fuck ahead." She shrugged disdainfully.

"Yes, well, is there a carpenter in town?"

"*Sí*, Pedro Martinez. He built a shed for his Uncle Nestor."

"Nestor? As in Nestor Martinez, who owns that foul cur Paco?"

"*Sí*. It's a nice shed. Nestor keeps some chickens in it. He's got a rooster, too. Francisco."

"Is he sober?"

"Francisco? I dunno. Sometimes he rolls around in the pen. Maybe Nestor gives him beer."

"No—oh, never mind. Can you ring him?"

"Who?"

"Pedro."

"He don't got no phone."

"Naturally. Could you find Pedro and ask him to come to the cafe?"

"*Sí*. When?"

"Nothing like the present, I always say. How about this afternoon?

Does he live in town?"

"*Sí*. He lives with Nestor."

I again considered Pedro's sobriety. However, one tries not to condemn the innocent, at least not immediately. "How about if you find Pedro, wherever he may be hammering and sawing today, whilst I take inventory of our supplies? Ask Pedro to come over here, say at two o'clock."

"Okay, *Pendejito*—I mean Señor Bennie." Esperanza walked over to the empty cash register, retrieved her keys, and strolled out the front door of the cafe.

I concluded the inventory quickly, as we had so few supplies. Then, feeling rather peckish, I motored back to the ranch for a spot of lunch, from whence I would return in time for the appointment with Pedro.

Back at the cafe, two o'clock arrived, drummed its fingers upon a table top, glanced at its watch, yawned, and bid me adieu. Three o'clock sighed, and then left whilst mumbling an excuse about time waiting for no man. Four o'clock grumbled and, when I suggested waiting a few minutes more, told me to sod off. Finally, at two minutes before five, I heard a half-hearted knock on the front door. I opened the door.

Before me stood a thirtyish chap holding a bottle of beer and a cigarette in his right hand. Next to him sat Paco, who had gleefully relieved himself in front of the still-dripping door.

"Ah. You must be Pedro. Kind of you to bring Paco over here."

"Huh? Oh, yeah, he's got a thing about doors. I thought he only peed on Rudy's. You the *gringo* who needs a carpenter?"

"Yes. You were supposed to be here three hours ago."

"Uh, yeah, sorry. I stopped at Rudy's for a beer."

"No doubt. Did Esperanza tell you what we need done?"

"Yeah. You want the floor levelled. No problem. All I gotta do is jack up the building, repair the foundation and the floor joists, and set it down again, all nice and level."

He exuded confidence, along with a stale odour of alcohol and cigarette smoke.

"Right. When can you start?"

"Maybe tomorrow. But I need some money first. I gotta get some jacks."

"How much do you need?"

"I dunno. How about two hundred bucks?"

I grimaced. "Very well. I can write you a cheque."

"Can I have cash? I don't like banks much."

"I haven't that much cash. I suppose I can go to the bank tomorrow and get it. Why don't you like banks?"

"I dunno. My uncle never trusted them. Guess I don't either."

"Yes, well, what time shall I expect you tomorrow?"

"When can I get my money?"

"I believe the bank opens at ten o'clock. How about half ten?"

"When?"

"Half ten. Thirty minutes past the hour."

"Okay." He turned around rather woozily and began to walk back towards Rudy's.

As he walked away, I shouted. "Pedro, could you leave Paco at home, or wherever he tends to be left?"

"Okay, but he kinda goes where he wants."

Indeed he does, I thought.

The following morning, Uncle Bill retrieved the cash Pedro had requested and delivered it to me at the cafe. I had asked Maria to motor up to the Archuleta ranch herself and discuss our beef and pork supply, whilst I tended to the construction project. I sat and waited, fooled again by Pedro's unique sense of time. Around one o'clock, I walked over to Rudy's for a spot of lunch. Uncle Bill rolled through the bar's front door soon afterwards, ordered a beer from young Antonio, and enquired of the absent Pedro.

"You know, Bennie, you gotta get used to *mañana* around here."

"To what?"

"*Mañana.* It means 'tomorrow.' What it really means is, well, nobody around here does anything until they damn well feel like it."

"How are we to repair the floor, if Pedro chooses not to show up?"

"He'll show up, just not when you want him to."

"Eh? That's madness."

"Yep, I suppose it is. Not like the British Navy."

I grunted. "I'm feeling rather flummoxed. I mean, one cannot simply drum my fingers on the table for days waiting. Surely there must be an alternative?"

Uncle Bill considered the question over several pulls of beer. "Well, if we start the work ourselves, make it seem like we don't need him, then Pedro will be all over us like a dog on a bitch in heat."

"Rather a repulsive metaphor."

"Call it what you want. It's the truth."

"Er, my carpentry skills are, well, rather limited."

"You repaired all that fence, didn't you?"

"One would hardly consider repairing a bit of fence carpentry."

"Why not? We just need to get some jacks, so let's see if Joe's got any."

We finished our lunch of desiccated sandwiches and beer, then went to Garcia's store. Joe, not surprisingly, was nowhere to be found, and we found ourselves greeted by Coronado.

"*Hola*, Señores Graves." He grabbed both of our hands and shook them vigorously. "You need something?"

"Yes. We need several jacks to raise the cafe off its foundation."

"I got a scissors jacks for a car. But I think you're gonna need a house jack."

"A what?"

"A house jack. It's kinda like a car jack, but lots bigger."

"Well, do you have any of those?"

"Sorry. Maybe you could use some floor jacks. Try the Texaco. Luis Chavez can probably loan you a couple."

"Yes, floor jacks are precisely what we need. But why would one find them at a petrol station?"

Uncle Bill shook his head and grabbed my arm. "They're a kind of car jack, Bennie. It just rolls on a floor. They use them at gas stations. But they'll work for what we're gonna do."

"They will?"

"Like I said, all we need to do is start working. Pedro will show up." We motored over to the Texaco station, which was located at the south edge of town. It was a smallish place and, unlike the rest of the buildings in Vaca Seca, appeared to be freshly painted and scrubbed.

Luis Chavez came out from the small garage and walked over to the lorry.

"El Vaquero," he boomed, extending a greasy palm to Uncle Bill, "what kinda trouble you in now?"

"Damned if I know Luis. By the way, this here's my nephew, Bennie. He's been helping me out on the ranch. He's gonna help re-open the cafe."

Luis's eyes popped. He whistled and moved his palm towards mine. "¡Ay, cabrón! You gonna work with the abuelas?"

"Er, act of mercy, really." I shook his hand lightly. "I have a bit of, er, business experience, and they begged me to help them."

"The abuelas begged you for help? Hijo de puta. I can't see them asking anybody for no help, much less begging. Things must be real bad."

"You have no idea, Luis," Uncle Bill said. "That's why we're here. You got a couple of floor jacks we can borrow? Won't need 'em real long."

"Sure. Your truck acting up again? I can take a look for you."

"Truck's fine. Bennie and I, well, we just need them over at the cafe."

Luis laughed. "What you gonna do, jack it up and change the oil?"

"The cafe is several quarts low," I added.

Having secured two floor jacks, we motored back to the cafe. "Er, Uncle Bill, what we do with these? I mean, I know how to jack up a vehicle and all that. Rather afraid I have little experience with buildings."

"Well, the foundation is made of rocks. So, so we're gonna knock out a few and slip one of the jacks into place. Grab that shovel that's in the truck."

Our goal was to be observed. I began to pound on several of the rocks that comprised the foundation, just to the right of the front porch and entrance. Whilst I pounded, several lorries drove by, each slowing down for a better glimpse of the goings-on. In short order, we had knocked several rocks from the foundation, creating a large enough space into which we could insert one of the jacks. I pumped the jack until it made contact with the building itself. With Herculean effort, at least for me, I pushed the handle down so as to raise the floor. Several boys, including young Antonio, had gathered around to observe.

Suddenly, I felt a warm liquid on my forehead as I strained on the handle. I raised myself up and espied a thin, reddish stream of fluid spewing from the jack onto my shirt front, whilst the jack sank.

By now, Rudy had wandered over. "What the hell are you doing?"

"Gonna level the floor, Rudy," Uncle Bill said. "We need to jack up the cafe off its foundation first."

Rudy looked at the flaccid floor jack. "You're not gonna use that floor jack, are you?"

"That was the idea, at least until we get some real house jacks."

"You get that jack from Luis, El Vaquero?"

"How'd you know?"

"I borrowed one of his jacks for my truck. Damn thing leaked hydraulic fluid all over. I don't think you could jack up a lawn mower with it."

I turned around towards Rudy, displaying my fluid-stained shirt. "Perhaps we were lent the same jack."

Rudy burst out laughing, as did the rest of the swelling crowd. "It's all a bit of a show, really. I've engaged Pedro Martinez for the work. He was supposed to begin this morning. I don't suppose he is sitting at the bar, is he?"

"Haven't seen him today. Never been a regular. But I've never known Pedro to be on time for anything. He takes his *mañana* seriously."

"Will ever show up? He seems to have no sense of time."

"Yeah, Bennie, he will. You just got to be patient. Things 'round here move a little slower than in big cities like London."

"Well, we seem rather becalmed at the moment. If you should see Pedro, would you please tell him—oh, bollocks. I need a whisky." I looked again at my shirt, which was dripping hydraulic fluid onto the ground.

The next morning, hope, and the strong odour of Uncle Bill's cattle, hung in the air. I returned to the cafe at mid-morning. Pedro was nowhere to be seen. Paco, however, was sniffing about and pawing at the foundation. He began to bark wildly.

I stepped out of the lorry, grabbed the electric torch Uncle Bill kept in the glove box, and strode cautiously towards Paco. I turned on the torch, bent down and shined the light into the hole, slowly arccing it about. The light reflected on two beady eyes in the far corner.

"Gah!"

The eyes began to come closer. I straightened up and retreated hastily across the road. Paco stuck his snout into the hole and continued to bark wildly.

"Paco, come here! Paco!"

The dog ignored me entirely and continued his barkative behaviour. Then, without warning, he yelped and ran up the road.

I turned back towards the hole as a large skunk nonchalantly emerged.

Fearing for my olfactory safety, which had already discerned why Paco had disappeared, I retreated further. The skunk looked at me, and shuddered its tail. Then it turned around and disappeared back under the foundation.

"Gah!"

As I stared at the hole, unsure what to do, Pedro rolled up in his lorry.

"*Buenos días, gringo*" I hear you tried to raise the building with one of Luis's leaky floor jacks. I could have told you that wouldn't work." He laughed, and stepped out, extending his hand.

"Hello, Pedro. Well, since you didn't show up as agreed, we decided to start without you."

"Did I say I would show up yesterday? I had to get some house jacks. Went down to Santa Fe for 'em. They're in the back of the truck."

"What? I thought you needed cash for that?"

"You got some cash? Great." He stuck his hand out in anticipation. I retrieved my wallet and extracted two hundred dollars.

"Er, there's a bit of a problem, I'm afraid. Your dog discovered a skunk. Apparently, it's made itself at home underneath."

Pedro sniffed the air. "Damn. I hope my Uncle don't let Paco into the house. He don't got a real good sense of smell."

"How do we rid ourselves of it?"

"As soon as I start jacking up the building, it'll leave. Skunks don't like a lot of noise."

He began removing his tools from the lorry along with the large house jacks and large blocks of wood.

"Aren't you concerned about getting sprayed whilst you are working?"

He shrugged. "It'll stay on the other side of the building while I'm working. Probably leave tonight. Skunks are pretty smart."

Not being familiar with skunk intelligence, nor how one would measure it, I accepted Pedro's authority on the subject. I mean, one doesn't go around quizzing skunks on naval history, or the Prime Minister's latest speech.

"Right. I shall leave you to it."

I walked back to the lorry and motored to Maria's small house. I needed to confer about the negotiations with Jesus Archuleta for our beef and pork supplies.

Maria informed me that he had agreed to supply the cafe with beef, and would arrange for pork, at what Maria considered to be most favourable prices. Apparently, the agreement involved Maria's supplying him with several dozen *tamales* each week, which I considered sound negotiating strategy on Maria's part. I returned to the cafe, observed Pedro setting up the house jacks, and returned to the ranch. When I returned the next morning, the front of the building was jacked up several feet. Wondering if the skunk had departed, I retrieved Uncle Bill's electric torch, walked over to the front and began to scan underneath the building. I had almost convinced myself the skunk had departed, when, in the farthest, darkest corner, the torch revealed the same two beady eyes. They were staring back at me rather less charitably. "Damn and blast!"

It was time to take matters into my own hands. I walked over to Garcia's store to purchase whatever one needed to rid oneself of a skunk.

As I walled inside, Coronado's rodentary visage greeted me. "*Hola*, Señor Graves. You still fixing the cafe? I saw Pedro working over there."

"As a matter of fact, yes. However, repairs have been delayed owing to a recalcitrant mephitine."

"*Híjole*. That sounds real bad."

"Quite bad. Although, I must admit there has been one ancillary benefit, as it summarily despatched Paco."

Coronado removed his cap and held it to his breast. "That's too bad, Señor Graves. I kinda liked that dog. Does Nestor know?"

"Eh? Rather difficult for him not to know, unless his olfactory no longer functions."

"He was here a couple days ago. Said his TV don't work no more."

"What? Do you have any idea what I am talking about?"

"No, Señor Graves, but it sure sounds bad. Paco's dead and Nestor don't know 'cause some old factory don't work no more."

"Dead? Factory? Paco's not dead, not that I would mourn the loss. He ran off because of a skunk. Smells bloody awful."

"Skunk? Oh, Paco got skunked, huh?" Coronado paused. "I don't like skunks."

"That's why I'm here. You see, the skunk is under the cafe. It crawled through the hole in the foundation and refuses to leave. Do you sell anything that will encourage it to leave?"

"Everybody here just shoots 'em. You want me to shoot it for you? I got a shotgun in my truck."

Although Coronado's offer set off the internal alarm bells, there seemed little choice. "Er, yes, I suppose. Pedro has lifted the building up enough so someone can crawl in and retrieve the, er, carcass." I shuddered. Though I had become accustomed to my daily porcine and equine interactions, skunks were a different matter. No doubt one reason I had preferred life in an upstairs flat.

"You want me to shoot it now?"

"Now? Don't you have to man the store?"

"Joe won't mind. Nobody's here."

"Yes, but what if—quite."

"Lemme get my shotgun, Señor Graves. I'll meet you at the cafe." Coronado's eyes shone brightly. There was a spring in his step as he walked to the back of the store.

I returned to the lorry and retrieved Uncle Bill's electric torch. The unwelcome visitor had not moved from its spot in the far corner. No doubt, it was feeling churlish, what with the torch's light reflecting off its eyes once again. I quickly switched off the torch and retreated to a safe distance across the street, waiting for Coronado's arrival.

Coronado arrived a half hour later, stopping his decrepit lorry in front of the cafe. He retrieved his shotgun and slid out of the driver's side seat.

"I stopped to get some bigger shells. See this? He extracted a large, bright green shell from a box, which resembled a nuclear tipped suppository. "They got more powder. More shot, too."

"Er, quite. Are you sure they will work?"

"*Sí*. These shells are real good. Lots of folks here use 'em."

I pointed to the foundation as we crossed the street and walked up to the cafe. "The skunk is in the far left corner."

Coronado proceeded silently towards the foundation, like a rotund lion stalking its prey He pointed the shotgun menacingly towards the foundation.

I switched on the torch and scanned underneath. "It is still in the corner. Can you reach it?"

Coronado bent down and grunted, peering into the darkness. "*Sí*, Señor Graves."

He pointed the gun towards the corner and fired. The gun lurched upwards with a deafening blast. A cloud of dust rose around the edges of the foundation. As it cleared, I scanned underneath with the torch and saw a flash of white moving along the back wall.

"Damn, you missed. The bloody thing is moving towards the other corner."

"I got it, Señor Graves." He grinned wildly and pointed the gun towards the foundation. Then he began shooting as if at a carnival gallery. The loud retorts echoed off the buildings. Bits of wood and stone were raining down upon us. Coronado reloaded the gun and resumed his fusillade. A blast smashed into one of the house jacks, destroying the wood blocks between it and the wall. Then another blast, and the right-most house jack vanished. Coronado continued firing wildly, reloading his shotgun until he had exhausted his ammunition, a shotgun cannonade that would have warmed Lord Nelson's heart.

As the dust cleared, I espied a large hole in the uplifted front wall. Both front windows were gone. And then I heard an ominous creaking. The remaining house jacks groaned and collapsed. The uplifted walls followed, smashing down upon the rock foundation, which proceeded to crack apart. More dust and debris billowed outwards. We retreated to the other side of the street, where a crowd of wide-eyed onlookers had gathered.

As the air finally cleared, I inched towards the cafe to inspect the damage. Gaping holes peppered the foundation. Large pieces of plaster that had coated the outside walls were strewn about. One piece, with the word "*Dos*" painted on it, lay near the front door, itself ripped from its frame and propped against what remained of the porch.

Jaw dropped and stowed, I surveyed the damage, amazed that the entire cafe was not a pile of rubble. One could only imagine the bits of skunk that were buried underneath.

And then, as I goggled in disbelief, a small head emerged, phoenix-like. The beast shook itself, sniffed, blinked its eyes at me with an air of casual indifference, and walked down the street, disappearing into the nearby bushes.

I watched its slow procession and shook my head in disbelief. Presently, Coronado stood next to me, shotgun spent and lowered.

"I guess I missed."

# Chapter 15

We were now faced with rather more involved repairs. Coronado's errant fusillade had struck everything but its intended, malodorous target. The crowd began to disperse, tongues clicking. Coronado disappeared with them, no doubt destined for the dim confines of Rudy's Bar.

I continued to stare at the debris, jaw agape. The prospect of a hasty return to London, despite Uncle Bill's wishes, tugged at the subconscious, which suggested immediate surrender and retreat to civilization. Of course, no Graves would allow himself to be accused of failing to engage the enemy; sterner stuff infused the Graves spine. That, and bracing doses of whisky, which I now sorely needed.

I returned to Uncle Bill's lorry, not knowing how I would inform him of this latest debacle. I heard the sound of squealing brakes behind me and turned. Esperanza and Maria were staring goggle-eyed at the cafe through the windscreen of Esperanza's lorry. They jumped from the cab and ran over to inspect the damage, accompanied by a staccato of shouted invective, hair pulling, and fist shaking, interspersed loudly with the hissing of Coronado's name and phrases such as "*estamos jodidos*" and "*hijo de puta.*"

Esperanza came about and directed her ample wrath towards me.

"You asked Coronado? To get rid of a skunk?"

"He said a shotgun was the standard method by which the locals rid themselves of such pests."

"*Sí*, but not Coronado. ¡*En boca cerrada no entran moscas!*"

"Pardon?"

"It means keep your mouth shut, especially around Coronado. Now, how are you going to repair our cafe?"

'Eh? Your cafe, is it?'

"*Sí*, our cafe, *Pendejito*. ¡*Ay, Cabron*!"

"Look Esperanza, I understand your, er, concern—"

"You don't understand nothing. Who's gonna fix this fucking mess, *Pendejito*?"

"Pedro? After all, he had begun work on the foundation."

"You know how long it's gonna take Pedro? Maria and me, we'll be dead by the time that *borracho* is finished."

"Surely there must be someone else in town possessing the skills to effect the necessary repairs in a timely manner."

"*Todos son borrachos, Pendejito*."

"Would you kindly stop referring to me that way? It is rather tiresome."

"If I had Coronado's shotgun, I would shoot you." She turned to Maria. "Let's get the fuck out of here." They slammed the doors of the lorry. Esperanza roared the engine and drove altogether too close to me.

"¡*Vete a la chingada*!" she screamed.

An emergency bracing of alcohol was required to lift the Graves spirits. I walked to Rudy's. Sitting down in the dim light, I espied Coronado, huddled over several bottles of beer in an even dimmer corner.

Rudy was behind the bar. "Guess you gotta a little skunk problem, huh, Bennie?" I slid onto a rather sticky bar stool, gesturing over towards Coronado's bulk.

"Er, yes. The skunk problem has evolved into a bloody nightmare. Esperanza wishes to shoot me, even more so than usual. God knows what Maria is thinking. If I had any sense, I would return to London immediately. However, I promised Uncle Bill."

From his corner, Coronado moaned. "Sorry, Señor Graves. Really. I was just trying to hit the skunk. I'll help you fix it."

He put his head down on the small table, knocking the empty bottles to the floor, and sobbed.

Without even asking, Rudy poured a large glass of whisky and set it in front of me; I inhaled it greedily.

He drummed his fingers on his desk. "Folks in this town, they got their own way of doing things. And they usually don't like strangers, especially *gringo* ones. But when things are really bad, they always come through. And, El Vaquero, he's one of us. Has been for a long time."

"Kind words, Rudy. However, whilst Uncle Bill may be one of you, as you say, I am rather a fish out of water, as it were. The *gringo* with the foreign accent. Besides, even if the entire building does not now require razing, it's well on its way. One doubts whether Uncle Bill has the brass for such an all-encompassing repair effort."

Rudy shrugged. "All you *gringos* have foreign accents. Besides, I can get everybody in town to help rebuild the cafe. Like a barn raising."

"A what?"

"In the old days, folks out west, they would all come together to build a barn. Make a day of it. You been in El Vaquero's barn?"

"Of course. Part of my daily equine duties, not that Marjorie appreciates it, mind you."

"Everybody in town helped build that barn."

"But this is the cafe, not a barn."

"So? Ray Ortiz and his brother Manuel, they're both masons. They can fix the foundation. Pedro is a pretty good carpenter, once he shows up. Enrique Esquivel, he does a lot of stucco work. Even Coronado. He can't shoot a gun for shit, but he's a pretty good painter. Painted the entire bar."

Coronado moaned again and raised his head. "*Sí*. Good paint. Benjamin Moore, not the shit we sell in the store. Two colours, enamel on all the doors." He returned his head to the comfort of the beer-sodden table.

"Well, it all sounds quite charitable. *Noblesse oblige* and all that. But we're talking about an act of charity for Esperanza and Maria? I mean, one can only turn the other cheek so far."

"I know, but folks really like Maria's cooking." Rudy winked at me. You want another whisky? Then we'll go see how bad the damage is."

"Right ho."

I downed the second whisky, albeit in a more dignified manner. Rudy retrieved an electric torch from beneath the bar. With Coronado lolling behind us and continuing to mew his apologies, we walked over to inspect the cafe.

The trench that Pedro had dug to expose the foundation was choked with debris—rock, wood, shards of glass, and plaster. The front door lolled off its frame. We pushed the door out of the way and stepped inside. The same stew of debris that filled the trench covered the floor. An acrid smell of gunpowder and skunk hung in the air. Pictures that had been hanging on the walls—including a picture of Ernesto, Celestina, and Uncle Bill that had been taken in front of the cafe—lay smashed on the floor.

"Jesus, Coronado." Rudy said, eying the destruction. "You use a shotgun or fucking artillery?"

"The naval term is softening the target," I said.

Coronado sniffed. "I said I was sorry, Señor Graves. I'll repaint everything. I promise."

I turned to Rudy. "What do you think?"

Rudy jumped up and down. "Floor seems Okay, except for that big hole in the corner." He pointed to the front corner, near the now vacant front window. The wood had shattered and split apart when the jacks gave way, leaving a largish hole.

He switched on the electric torch and put his head through the hole. "I see some joists that got to be replaced. And we're gonna need to fix the foundation walls. I bet Ray Ortiz could cement some cinder blocks where the rocks are gone. Probably be stronger, too."

Rudy stood up, brushing off his trousers. "You know, since we gotta fix the floor, we could cut a nice big hole in it and then work on the foundation from the inside. Pedro could reinforce the joists, put some cross-braces in. Then we can lay a new floor."

Although I did not understand the specific terms, Rudy's tone reflected, if not hope, at least not hopelessness. "I take it you believe we can affect the repairs successfully?"

"I've seen worse. Why don't you go back to the ranch? Let El Vaquero know what's going on, if somebody hasn't already been out there. I'll go find Ray Ortiz." He turned to Coronado. "Get this floor swept up and clean the *portal*, too."

"*Sí*, Rudy. I'm real sorry, Señor Graves."

"Yes, yes, I know Coronado. No need to apologise again. Stiff upper lip, as they say."

"Huh?"

"Just do what Rudy says."

"Okay, Señor Graves. You let me know what colour you want me to paint. Maybe light blue walls and red doors."

"Yes, thank you. But let's not concern ourselves with the paint scheme at present."

I returned to the ranch, expecting that Uncle Bill would have already been informed on the morning's events, and the disaster thereof. Apparently, however, the smoke signals, cactus drums, or whatever served as the preferred New Mexican mode of communication had not yet reached him.

Uncle Bill received the news far better than I had expected. After perhaps thirty minutes furiously cursing Coronado's existence and threatening to end said existence using Coronado's shotgun, plus two large glasses of Dusty Trail, he had regained his calm.

Nor did I escape Uncle Bill's wrath, as Coronado's manic behaviour whilst operating any sort of firearm was the stuff of local legend. He had singularly despatched dozens of windows, two dogs, a chicken coop and its inhabitants, the Model A Ford Luis Chavez had painstakingly restored, Josefina Ramirez's refrigerator, and Elizardo Romero's coffin. Had I been aware of Coronado's destructive prowess, I would have tipped the proverbial cap to the cafe's bullet-proof skunk and bid it good day.

As we sat in the drawing room, I explained Rudy's offer. "Mighty nice of Rudy to offer that, Bennie. I'll head into town tomorrow and talk to him. Give him some money. They'll need it for the materials. What about Esperanza and Maria?"

"Rudy said he would speak with the both of them. Esperanza was in fine form, positively incendiary. Maria was silent, but smouldering."

"Jesus. I just want to get the cafe going again."

"We shall, Uncle Bill, we shall."

On a bright Saturday morning a fortnight later, the cafe-raising began. Coronado had removed the debris. Pedro had enlarged the hole in the floor and braced the joists underneath. The Ortiz brothers began to repair the crumbling foundation, complaining all the while of the still-pungent odour.

Rudy appointed himself gaffer, which was seconded by all, if not for his knowledge of construction, then surely his promise of liquid refreshment at the end of the day. Coronado wandered over from across the street, where he had been observing the repairs stealthily in case Esperanza and Maria espied him. Although Maria was nowhere to be seen, Esperanza had motored by several times during the day to inspect the progress.

"Looks good, huh Señor Graves," Coronado said, maintaining his vigil. "I can start painting real soon. I sure like that light blue colour."

"Thank you, Coronado. Let's consider the paint colours after the other repairs are made."

Whilst the Ortiz brothers applied their masonic skills, Pedro nailed braces between numerous joists and installed support posts throughout. By Sunday afternoon, a newly strengthened subfloor was in place.

Rudy jumped up and down on the new floor, to the cheers of the crowd. "Good as new. Even better."

By the following week, the cafe was structurally sound and refenestrated. The interior walls were ready for painting and

Enrique Esquivel had stuccoed the outside walls of the cafe. The front door had been replaced. Pedro would install a new floor over the old one, once Coronado finished painting the interior as penance.

Coronado continued to insist on his light blue with red trim colour scheme. I acquiesced, although not without trepidation. Before allow ing him to put paint to brush, I insisted on inspecting every can, lest I discover that he was colour blind, as well as illiterate.

Uncle Bill and I focused our attention on the ranch. Several of the more boisterous steers had knocked down the fence again, and the herd was gorging itself on Felipe Aragón's well-irrigated alfalfa. Daisy, for her part, had excavated a large cavern under the *portal*, exposing the support post unfortunate enough to bear her twenty-five stone weight. And Marjorie, although not having actively destroyed or damaged anything, continued to provide copious quantities of muck wanting removal.

As we repaired the fence, Uncle Bill was rather pensive, much unlike the boisterous relation I had become accustomed to. "You think I'm crazy, Bennie? This whole thing with the cafe—maybe I'm just an old fool."

"Daft," I mumbled, catching my palm on a wire barb. "I mean, no, Uncle Bill. Just yesterday Rudy said Esperanza had calmed down. Apparently, she has been stopping at the cafe to curse Coronado only once each day. Rudy considers that real progress."

"It's not that, Bennie. I kinda roped you into this, didn't I? What I mean is, you don't have to stay here. You're young and you got your whole life ahead of you."

"Uncle Bill, you didn't, er, rope me into this, as you say. Well, you did. But I acquiesced, did I not? In for a penny, what?"

"You sure?"

"Have you ever known a Graves to abandon ship? Besides, I want to see things through. I mean, this place is bloody mad, yet—"

"You don't have to explain, Bennie," he interrupted. "I know exactly what you mean."

Several days later, Uncle Bill and I were in the barn, restacking hay. We heard Coronado's decrepit lorry crawl to a stop beside the house.

"El Vaquero? Señor Graves?"

"In the barn," we replied in unison.

Coronado manoeuvred his bulk into the barn. "*Hola*, Señor Graves, El Vaquero. I got the cafe all painted. I think you're gonna like it. Remember I told you light blue and red would look real good, Señor Graves?"

"Er, yes." Despite my having carefully inspected the paint, I remained fearful. "You didn't change the colours, did you?"

"No, Señor Graves. Like I said, light blue and red trim. Maybe you and your brother El Vaquero want to see it now? It looks real good."

I glanced at Uncle Bill, who nodded his agreement. "Let us finish here and then we'll meet you at the cafe. Shall we say two hours from now?"

"Coronado smiled. "I think you're gonna like it." He started walking back towards his lorry with an almost child-like excitement, then stopped suddenly.

"Señor Graves?"

"Yes?"

He raised his bare arm. "I dunno what time it is."

I peered at my watch. "Eh, two o'clock, Coronado. We'll be there at four o'clock."

"*Gracias*, Señor Graves." He waved his fleshy hand and motored off.

After only a trail of dust remained, I looked at Uncle Bill. "Dare we entertain hope?"

"I dunno, Bennie He's an idiot, but he means well."

"My greatest fear."

We finished stacking the hay, had a quick wash and brush up, and journeyed into town. I braced myself for a horrid colour scheme and Esperanza's wrath visited upon me like one of the Biblical plagues. As we drove by Joe Garcia's store, I espied a crowd across the street in front of the cafe.

The heart began to pound, expecting some new horror awaited us. Perhaps the skunk had returned and was lolling about the *portal*, daring anyone to cross the threshold. Or perhaps Esperanza and Maria were positioned on the patio, threatening to shoot anyone who came near.

I glanced at Uncle Bill. "Restless natives?"

"Guess we're gonna find out."

We pulled around the corner and parked. As we stepped out of the lorry, the crowd clapped. Rudy nodded and pointed to the cafe. Even Esperanza and Maria were smiling, well, at least not scowling overtly. Uncle Bill and I turned our heads. Painted on the freshly plastered wall was a new sign

"Señor Graves, El Vaquero. You like my sign?"

"You painted that?"

"*Sí.* I done it last night and this morning."

"It's grand, Coronado." I hesitated, thinking back to my initial encounter and Coronado's inability to read Uncle Bill's telegram from. "Coronado, you told me you couldn't read."

"No, I never learned."

"Well, if you can't read, how did you paint the sign?"

"Esperanza wrote it for me. She got some stencils from the school."

"What is that other writing?" I peered closely at the sign. The words *y un gringo* were painted in smallish cursive. I eyed Esperanza and Maria.

---

**DOS ABUELAS**

(*y un gringo*)

**CAFE**

"You"re real lucky," Esperanza said. "I was gonna have him paint, *y un Pendejito.*"

"Yes, well, I suppose it can be painted over when I depart."

Maria raised her ample eyebrows. "She didn't mean nothing bad, Señor Bennie. You're still gonna stay and help us? *¿Que no?*"

"Yes, Maria. As I told Uncle Bill, a Graves never abandons ship. Well, almost never."

# Chapter 16

We opened the new front door and walked inside. The walls glistened. Coronado's colour scheme was spot on. The combination of light blue walls, coupled with the red trim, including the new front door, gave the room a cheery ambience.

His rodentary eyes gleamed. "Do you like it, Señor Graves?"

"Coronado, you are a most accomplished painter. Where did you learn to paint so well?"

"I dunno, I always liked to paint."

"Innate ability, eh? Well, whatever it is, thank you."

"Sure, Señor Graves. I'm really sorry about everything."

I raised my hand up to end the verbal groveling. "Water under the bridge. Let's hear no more about it."

Behind us, the crowd had assembled, apparently waiting for Uncle Bill to say something. Someone shouted, "¡*Viva El Vaquero*!"

Uncle Bill turned around. He cleared his throat and croaked,

"*Muchas gracias para todos*. I wish Celestina was here to see the cafe now. She wouldn't believe her eyes." He turned to Rudy. "*Tu eres un caballero y un amigo especiál. Muchas gracias*."

Rudy smiled and the crowd clapped. Their eyes turned towards me in expectation. I had little practice with public speaking, for the simple reason that I dreaded it.

"Yes, ah, some of you know me as Uncle Bill's, I mean, El Vaquero's nephew." I began to perspire profusely. "I, er, that is, we hope to reopen the cafe quite soon. I, er, thank you for all of your help rebuilding the cafe. Most, er, unexpected."

"Jesus, *Pendejito*," Esperanza shouted. "For somebody who talks real fancy, you sure sound stupid."

The crowd erupted in laughter. I felt my stature shrinking rapidly to that of a small beetle drowning in perspiration.

I cleared the throat. "Speaking of sounds, Esperanza perhaps we should discuss your intoxicated state at the ranch several weeks ago. Your snoring was loud enough to wake the dead."

A small woman, who had greyish air and was wrapped in a bright red shawl, shook her cane. "You should've seen her at her daughter's wedding. She was drunker than Nestor Martinez."

Esperanza's eyes glowed red. Luis Chavez, who was standing near the back in his greasy coveralls, shouted, "Make sure you lock up the tequila. And don't let her eat no *frijoles*."

The crowd erupted in laughter and I feared an explosion.

"Well, we've all had a bit of fun," I shouted. "Thank you again, all of you, for your help. As soon as we finish the repairs, you're all invited to our grand opening. Dinner will be on the house, as they say. No charge."

The crowd began to applaud its approval, shouting, "¡*Viva El Gringo*!" They began to disperse, already anticipating the free meal I had spontaneously promised.

Esperanza refocused her anger towards me. "You know what you did, *Pendejito*? Free food? For all of those *lobos*. You know how much they're gonna eat?"

"A gesture of charity, Esperanza. Without their help, the cafe would still be in ruins."

"It's gonna be in ruins after the first night. You see Carmen Flores?"

"Who?"

"The little *vieja* with the red shawl. The one who joked about me at my daughter's wedding. I never saw nobody eat so much. She could eat that whole goddamn pig of El Vaquero's."

"And Luis Chavez? He's right, you better hide the tequila. 'Cause he'll drink it all. I saw him empty an entire bottle like it was a Coke." She jerked her thumb toward Rudy. "Ask Rudy. He saw it, too."

Rudy nodded. "Yeah, Luis does like his tequila."

Esperanza's face had turned a mottled crimson. "Stay calm, Esperanza. All will be well."

"I'm real calm, *Pendejito*. You're gonna see what happens. We're gonna give everybody a free meal and then close the next day, 'cause there won't be no more food."

"Well, let's not cross that bridge quite yet. I am sure we can exercise some control over our guests."

A veil of trepidation descended over me. Would a new plague be visited on the first born sons of those foolish enough to manage run-down cafes in misbegotten corners of the world?

Despite the progress, much work remained. Pedro was finishing the new pine floor, having promised to forgo his usual multiple-day absences. Maria and I discussed the opening night menu—I suggested her *tamales* would be a most welcome addition, to which she concurred—and the supplies we would need on an ongoing basis. Although she had already made arrangements with the Archuletas, we needed to replenish the larder with numerous staples—beans, rice, *masa*, cooking oil—the list spanned five handwritten pages.

The morning after the near fisticuffs between Luis and Esperanza,

Maria and I were in the supply room off the kitchen when we heard the front door open.

"*Hola*. Anybody here?" I recognized Joe Garcia's voice. I came out of the kitchen, followed by Maria. "Good morning, Joe. Come to observe the progress?"

"*Sí*. Looks good. Coronado did a real good job painting."

"Indeed he did. Surprising, really."

"Yeah. I don't think nobody's gonna ever figure out Coronado."

"No, I suppose not. Well, it's kind of you to stop by, but Maria and I are rather busy planning the menus and determining the supplies she shall need."

"Uh, yeah, that's how come I'm here. Now that I been paid, I figure you're gonna need me to get a bunch of supplies for you, just like before."

"Ah, that. I mean, we've already identified a preferred supplier, Sabrosa Foods in Santa Fe."

"Huh? You don't want to buy nothing from me?" He began to breathe heavily.

"Er, it's not that we don't *want* to buy from you. Rather, I mean, we need to keep our costs down. Your prices are rather high."

Joe's face darkened. "You gonna buy from those *cabrones* at Sabrosa Foods? Maria, what do I get for all those times I gave you and Esperanza credit? '*Por favor*, Jose, we're gonna pay you back. I promise. Just one more week, Jose.' All I did for you and your sister. Now, I'm no good no more?"

"*Vete a la chingada*. We don't owe you nothing. Señor Bennie, he told me we gotta control the cafe's margin. I dunno what that is, but he says it means we got to buy stuff from Sabrosa Foods, 'cause they don't charge as much as you."

Joe turned around and glowered at me. "What the fuck is margin?"

"A term we in the banking world use, the difference between revenues and costs. Now, one also needs to account for depreciation and taxes, gearing and the resulting interest payments on debt, that sort of thing. Of course, whilst I was employed at the bank, we never evaluated a cafe. However, I am quite sure—"

"What the fuck? You're gonna be real sorry, Maria. You too, *gringo*." He pointed a finger menacingly, then turned around and stormed out the front door, slamming it so hard I feared the new windows would shatter.

"Er, Maria, is Joe the vindictive type?"

"Huh?"

"Well, he just threatened us, didn't he? Doesn't that concern you?"

"Jose? He ain't gonna hurt nobody. Besides, I got my shotgun in the kitchen." She patted my shoulder forcefully. "You want to finish the list of stuff we need?"

I forced a smile. Despite Maria's twelve-gauge assurances, the brain imagined the cafe filled with contented diners, meals suddenly interrupted by a gunfight worthy of one of Uncle Bill's Zane Grey novels.

The following day, we motored to Santa Fe and Sabrosa Foods in Maria's lorry to secure supplies. We returned that evening, stopping the heavily-laden lorry in the alleyway behind the cafe. I searched for any sign of Joe Garcia, fearing he would emerge from behind a doorway waving an axe above his head, drooling like some rabid dog.

On Saturday, Pedro returned to install the new floor. Whilst he pounded various boards into place, Maria, Esperanza, and I argued in the kitchen over the date on which we should open.

"Monday, *Pendejito*." Esperanza dropped cigarette ash onto the new floor.

I glanced down at the pile of ash. "Monday? Impossible. Pedro may not be finished, especially if you continue with your attempts to burn down the cafe. Second, Maria needs time to prepare, as we intend to serve her *tamales*. Third, who dines out on a Monday? We'll want to schedule the grand opening for a Friday or Saturday night."

"Too many people on Friday or Saturday. Monday's good, 'cause we won't give away so much free food."

"What? As I've attempted to explain, the purpose of the complimentary meal is to express our appreciation for their help and encourage the townspeople to dine here again."

"Even if you give them free food, they're still not gonna come here again."

I sighed. "Perhaps you are correct. Why even bother? Call the whole thing off, shall we? Stuff and nonsense, reopening the cafe, eh?"

"Señor Bennie," Maria said, waving her ubiquitous chef's knife, "don't listen to her. We open when you say." She turned to Esperanza. "*¡Callate, hermana!* You screw this up and I'm gonna shoot you."

Esperanza stared at Maria. "Okay. But you didn't see what I did, *hermana*. You just worked in the kitchen. I ain't saying we shouldn't open again, *Pendejito*. I'm just saying it's not gonna work."

"*Hermana*, it better work. *¿Comprende?*" Maria moved her chef's knife in a slow arc.

"Ladies, let's calm ourselves, lest Pedro's new floor be covered in a pool of blood."

I turned again to Esperanza, suddenly overcome with fatigue. "Esperanza, we may fail. Spectacularly so. That said, we shall sail into battle, guns ablaze. If you wish to be relieved of duty, so be it. Er, *comprende?*"

"What the fuck are you talking about, *Pendejito?*"

"Will you at least try to make this work? If not, then, well, just go away." I motioned her towards the front door.

"You telling me to leave, *Pendejito?*"

"Unless you are willing to help, then yes. We shall attempt to find someone—anyone—else." A rather vicious thought then appeared in the grey matter. "Perhaps Luis Chavez would exchange his greasy overalls for a waiter's white jacket, if only for a night."

With the mention of Luis Chavez, Esperanza exploded. "You think you're gonna get that *hijo de puta* to replace me?"

"Why not? He seems a friendly sort of chap."

Maria began to laugh. Esperanza's face chameleoned into a vivid crimson. "I ain't stupid, *Pendejito*. I know what you're doing."

"Perish the thought. Stubborn? Certainly. Vituperative? Absolutely. Puerile? Definitely. Now, having reached this *modus vivendi* of sorts, shall we endeavour to continue our planning efforts?"

"I don't understand nothing you say." Esperanza inhaled deeply from the remaining stub of her cigarette, dropped it on the floor, and crushed it violently. "Okay, when do you want to open, *Pendejito?*"

With Esperanza's Eeyore-ish attitude temporarily in check, we embarked on the final preparations. We settled on Thursday for the opening night, which seemed a reasonable compromise. I despatched Esperanza to ask Coronado if he could create a suitably festive sign announcing our opening. We were also in desperate need of new tables and chairs, the existing ones having been grievously injured by Coronado's fusillade. I asked Esperanza to locate suitable replacements in Santa Fe.

Meanwhile, seeing I was possessed of idle hands, Maria engaged my help.

She pointed to a large burlap bag filled with green chiles. "We gotta roast and peel those."

I removed a redolent chile from the bag for an unenthusiastic inspection. "How does one roast such a thing?"

"Use the broiler. The skin blisters and starts to turn black. Soon as it does, you flip 'em over so we get both sides. *Comprende?*"

"You mean you burn them?"

She pointed with her knife to a large baking pan on the counter. "Put the chiles on that pan and stick it in under the broiler."

I spread the chiles on the pan and placed them in the oven as commanded.

"You gotta watch them real close. Too burned and they're no good. It's gonna take maybe four or five minutes."

Whilst the chiles roasted under the flames, I alternated between inspecting them and consulting the wristwatch. After four minutes, I pulled the baking sheet out.

"Er, how is this?" The exposed side of the chiles had taken on a greyish-black appearance.

"Not done. One minute more. *No más.*"

I returned the chiles to the oven for precisely one minute, then pulled the sheet out again for Maria's inspection.

"*Bueno*. Now you flip them over. Do the other side. It's not gonna take as long."

I flipped the chiles with a fork, and returned them to the oven. After four carefully timed minutes, I retrieved them for inspection. They steamed and sizzled.

Maria stared at the chiles and scowled in silence. "Something wrong? They smell quite good."

"I dunno. Maybe they're okay. Peel one."

"How?"

"Run it under some cold water. The skin is gonna come off if you roasted it good."

Once again, I did as commanded. I picked up one of the larger chiles, which quickly proceeded to sear my fingertips.

"Gah!" I dropped the chile on the floor. "It's bloody hot."

"¡*Cuidado*! Pick it up and wash it off."

"Sorry. Afraid my culinary experience is rather limited." I retrieved the still smouldering chile off the floor and held it up.

"You better learn to cook real fast, or we not gonna open."

"Yes, all right." I placed the chile under the tap. The skin slid off easily and I held it by a blackened stem. "Well?"

"Pull the stem off. Some of the seeds inside should come out, too. Then put it in that bowl." She pointed to a large ceramic bowl with the knife. "Now you know how to roast and peel chile. Get to work."

Feeling like an assistant scullery maid, I proceeded to roast additional batches of chiles. After an hour, and just three additional batches, the heat in the kitchen was stifling. The eyes burned, which caused me to rub them unceremoniously for relief.

"Gah!" My eyes suddenly felt as if someone had bathed them in acid. Instinctively, I shut them tightly as the pain exploded.

"Put some water on your eyes," Maria shouted. "Go over to the sink."

With my eyes still tightly shut, I groped my way towards the sink, waving my arms about like a blind drunk.

My left hand encountered something untoward on Maria's person. "You do that again, you ain't gonna have no hand."

"Sorry."

I hastily withdrew the offending metatarsals. "Can you at least guide me to the sink?"

She grunted, then grabbed my shoulder tightly and led me to the sink. I found the tap and deluged the eyes with cold water until the acidic sensation began to abate.

"Don't rub your eyes no more."

"Yes, well, easier said than done, as they say."

"We got some rubber gloves under the sink. Nobody uses them, but you can."

"Gloves sound quite sensible, thank you." I rooted about under the sink and located them, a pair of thick yellowish gloves that smelled strongly of mildew. "These?"

She glanced at me. "*Sí.*"

"Perhaps I should wash them first?"

"How come?"

"Er, well, they do have a rather unpleasant odour about them."

"¡*Madre de Dios*! We don't got all day. ¡*Andale*!"

"Eh?"

"¡*Andale*! Go. We got lots of work to do."

I pulled on the gloves, gave them a quick rinse, and then, machine-like, for the next four hours continued to roast and peel until the entire bag was emptied.

Exhausted and overheated, I asked Maria what she would do with the overflowing bowl of chiles.

"We gotta chop it all up. Half we're gonna freeze. The other half, we're gonna make green chile sauce. Go get some onions, garlic, and tomato. You make the sauce."

I cringed, praying for deliverance from this culinary purgatory. No doubt, God had switched off His heavenly hearing aid rather than listen to my fulsome blather. After chopping my first onion, the front door opened and a voice cried out.

"*Hola.* Señor Graves?" The unmistakable voice of Coronado called out.

I put down my knife, went through the kitchen door, and walked into the dining room. Coronado's eyes widened. "¡*Híjole*! What happened, Señor Graves?"

"What do you mean?"

"Your eyes, they're all red, like you got beat up or something." He lowered his voice to a whisper. "Did Maria hit you, Señor Graves?"

"What? No, nothing of the sort. I roasted a large quantity of green chile and mistakenly rubbed the eyes."

"Maybe you should wear gloves when you peel them. I seen *gringos* do that."

"Er, yes. Thank you for the suggestion. We are rather busy at present, Coronado. What exactly do you want?"

"I made the sign for the grand opening. You want to see it?"

"The sign? Oh, yes, I had forgotten."

Coronado unfurled a large piece of paper and held it aloft with a large grin. "I made it look like the sign on the wall, Señor Graves. You like it?"

I glanced at the sign. "Er, Coronado, several words are misspelt. Did Esperanza help you again?"

"*Sí*, Señor Graves. I used those stencils." His grin vanished, replaced by one of those forlorn, lip-quivering looks one sees on a child whose ice cream treat has just fallen onto the macadam. Coronado looked at the sign and lowered it slowly.

"The word opening is missing the second 'n' and Esperanza has completely misspelt the word 'night'. Can you repaint it?"

"I guess so. You want me to bring the stencils? Esperanza, she'll get real mad at me if I ask her for help again."

"Well, a misspelt sign simply won't do. I'll help you with the spellings. There's a good chap."

"Okay. I can bring the stencils tomorrow."

"Good."

"Señor Graves?"

"Yes?"

"Can you teach me to read and write?"

```
┌─────────────────────────────┐
│                             │
│       DOS ABUELAS           │
│         CAFE                │
│                             │
│        GRAND                │
│        OPENIG               │
│       THURSDAY              │
│         NITE                │
│                             │
└─────────────────────────────┘
```

"Eh? Teach *you* to read and write? I mean, of course, I'm flattered, Coronado. However, I doubt I am the, er, teaching type, if you know what I mean."

"But you talk so fancy, sometimes, I don't even know what you're saying."

"Er, well, the, uh, fancy talk is not overly appreciated in Vaca Seca. Besides, once the cafe is on a steady course, I shall be returning to England." I coughed artificially. "Right. Come back tomorrow and we shall mend the sign."

"Okay, Señor Graves." Coronado looked at me again. The previous child-whose-ice-cream-has-been-rubbished forlorn look had been replaced with an even more puppy-in-the-window one. He turned around and slowly walked out the door, leaving the misspelt sign on one of the tables.

I returned to the kitchen, encountering Maria leaning against the cooker, arms crossed and cigarette dangling from her lips. A large bowl of onions sat nearby, as did a bowl of tomatoes, both having succumbed to violent chopping.

"Sorry, Maria. Had I not abandoned my post, we would have had a misspelt notice for the grand opening."

"So what? Half the town don't know how to read."

"Well that means half do. Mustn't offend them."

"We gonna offend everybody if we don't got enough food."

"Right, well, we have plenty of time, what? It's Monday afternoon.

Pedro has finished the floor. We should have new tables and chairs tomorrow. Green chile is chopped and being sauced. Am I forgetting anything?"

Maria reacted to my cheerful blather with a combination of contempt and disbelief. "¡Ay, cabrón! We got to make *tamales*. We got to get everything for the *enchiladas*. We got to cook *frijoles* for the *refritos*. We got to have everything ready to make *tortillas* and *sopapillas*." She stopped and sighed. "Maybe I'm too old for this."

"Now, now, Maria, stiff upper lip, as we English like to say. Perhaps a good night's rest would help. Fresh start in the morning, eh?"

"Huh? I need a beer. You be here tomorrow morning at seven."

"Seven it is, then." Maria hung up her filthy apron and walked slowly out the kitchen door. Despite feeling all-in from the day's exertions, a crackle of excitement ran though me. It may have been the neurons offering a final gasp before collapsing, but the restaurant entrepreneur had begun to emerge. Besides, the nadir was surely past proclaimed the entrepreneurial self.

The internal cynic chortled. "Indeed? I suppose you believe the *Titanic* was unsinkable, too."

# Chapter 17

"How go the preparations for the grand opening?" Uncle Bill asked as we nursed glasses of Dusty Trail in the sitting room.

"Ah. I am of two minds. One, having seen the cafe rise, phoenix-like, thanks to the generosity of the townspeople, and you of course, sees the milk of human kindness, glass half full, and all that. The other, alas, bides its time waiting for the glass to fall to the floor and shatter."

"Yep, this town can have that effect on you. You need anything more from me?"

"The patience of Job, perhaps; a second whisky, most certainly." Uncle Bill reached for the bottle and refilled my glass.

"One thing I did not anticipate is spelling."

"Spelling?"

"Quite. Coronado, who cannot read, is painting the sign for the grand opening, helped by Esperanza, who cannot spell. Most disconcerting."

"Hell, Bennie. Half the folks in this town can't read. And the other half don't give a damn."

"You sound like Maria. A slave-driver, that one. I am to be at the cafe at seven o'clock sharp. We shall be boiling chickens and preparing pork. Speaking of which, if demand for *tamales* is especially great, we may need some additional pork."

"You go tell Daisy. See if she agrees."

"A bit of fear to dampen recalcitrant porcine behaviour, I always say." As if she had been listening, Daisy, who had been asleep on the patio, grunted loudly.

"Hear that, Bennie? I don't think she's the one who ought to be afraid."

"Perhaps not of me. I doubt even Daisy would care to trifle with a frenzied Maria."

"I don't suppose anybody in their right mind would. 'Course, lots of folks here aren't in their right mind, at least not all the way. Maybe some pigs, too."

"Wiser words were rarely spoken, Uncle Bill."

"Well, I got a pot of beans on the stove. You want a steak, too?"

"That sounds grand."

"You want green chile with your steak? You know what they say 'round here. '*Comida sin chile no es comida.*' Means a meal without chile isn't a meal."

I paused, contemplating the ocular spasms Maria's chiles had inflicted. "Just remind me not to rub my eyes. I discovered the perils of such this morning."

"Yep, most folks only make that mistake once," he replied, retrieving two steaks from the fridge.

I staggered into the kitchen at five the next morning, head throbbing from the previous evening's intake of Dusty Trail. Uncle Bill, who was either immune to its affects or masked them far better than I, extended a large mug of his coffee.

"God's cowboy nectar," I said, inhaling the brew. I glanced out the kitchen window. The sky was filled with stars and one could discern the silhouettes of several steers behind the fence. All was right with the world, I thought.

Later, with coffee coursing through the veins, Marjorie fed and watered, and Daisy sleeping off her breakfast, I motored into town to resume the day's culinary servitude. As I passed by Garcia's store, I noticed Coronado stepping outside, and stopped.

"I say, Coronado, rather early to be opening the store, is it not?"

"*Buenos días*, Señor Graves. Store's closed. I had to get some more paint for the new grand opening sign. I'm gonna ask Esperanza to help me this morning, so I don't make no more mistakes."

"Say no more, Coronado. I would assist you myself, but Maria has much for me to do."

"Thursday night's gonna be real good, huh, Señor Graves."

"One can only hope, Coronado, one can only hope."

"I hope Maria makes lots of *tamales*."

"As a matter of fact, we shall be preparing them today."

"*Híjole*."

"I agree completely." I handed him a small sheet of paper. "Coronado, please make sure Esperanza spells 'night' correctly. I wrote it down for you."

Coronado grasped the paper with his fleshy hand. "Okay. I'll give it to her. *Gracias*."

I parked the lorry in front of the cafe. Peering through the window, I could see light from under the kitchen door. It was quarter-past the seven, I hoped my slight tardiness would not further sour Maria's mood.

I unlocked the front door and turned on the lights.

"Good morning, Maria," I warbled, walking through the kitchen door, expecting to see her savaging an onion or dismembering a chicken.

Instead, she was standing by the back door, eyes bulging and face ashen. "Good heavens, Maria, you look as if you've seen a ghost."

She remained frozen and mute. "Maria, I say, are you—"

Then, without so much as a "beg pardon," the legs cemented themselves to the floor and refused to move. I heard a pebbly sort of rattle coming from the floor, which caused me to glance downwards.

"Gah!"

"¡*Callate*!" Maria hissed through clenched teeth.

Between us, head up, its vibrating tail the source of the rattling, was a coiled serpent. I mean, I had seen the odd garden snake in my day. And the London Zoo had a herpetology exhibit filled with the beasts, along with gruesome descriptions and pictures of how they devoured their prey.

I remained motionless and looked at Maria, whose face remained ashen. "What do we do?" I whispered.

Maria's voice trembled. "You got to kill it. I hate snakes."

"Kill it? How?"

"Chop its fucking head off."

"With what?"

"My knife. By your left hand."

I glanced over and willed the left hand slowly towards it, one of Maria's larger, more menacing ones, so as not to enrage the coiled assassin. My fingers reached the handle and enveloped it.

"What am I supposed to do? Pick up the snake and place it on the chopping block? I rather doubt it will cooperate."

"Throw the fucking knife at its head."

"I don't know how to throw a knife, much less throw one to decapitate a snake."

Perhaps sensing we were discussing how to slay it, the snake began to flick its forked tongue rapidly. The tail-rattling increased in volume and it turned towards Maria, who was attempting to merge into the door. Then the snake returned its serpentine attentions to me.

"Gah!"

I was about to recite the Twenty-Third Psalm, when I heard the front door open.

"*Hola*. Anybody here?" It was the unmistakable voice of Coronado.

"In the kitchen," I replied in a hoarse whisper.

"*Híjole*. Where is everybody?"

"*¡Ayudanos, pendejo!*" Maria shouted furiously. "*Estamos en la cocina.*"

Hearing Maria's command for help, Coronado accelerated through the kitchen door, his bulk nearly crashing into me.

"Señor Graves, what's wrong?"

Espying the snake, he stopped quickly. "Looks like a rattlesnake. How did it get in here?"

The snake turned its head towards Coronado.

"I neglected to ask. Can you kill it? Without using your shotgun?"

"Sure. There were always rattlesnakes around when I was a kid. Most of the time, they leave you alone. Just don't get 'em mad."

As he spoke, the snake raised its head higher, rattling its tail with greater determination. "This particular snake seems rather ill-tempered at the moment."

"Okay, Señor Graves." Coronado took the knife from my hand and with a surprisingly quick flip of his fleshy wrist, launched it downwards. The blade struck home several inches behind the head and continued until it was lodged in the floorboard, killing the beast instantly.

"My God, Coronado, I've never seen anything like that before."

"Thanks. Like I said, we always had snakes around. I never liked to kill 'em, except when they got in the house."

"I am afraid this serpent left you little choice. Most fortuitous of you to show up when you did." I shook his hand vigorously.

"I like to help."

Maria still had not moved, although colour was slowly returning to her face. "All clear, Maria. The prince has slain the evil dragon, as it were. And his reward shall be extra *tamales*."

Maria's eyes smouldered. "I hate fucking snakes." Reaching down, she pulled the knife free and held it in front of Coronado.

"You ruined a good knife." She tossed it into the sink, retrieved a cigarette, lit it, inhaled deeply, and blew a huge cloud of smoke towards the serpentine carcass.

"Sorry, Maria. If you want, I can get you a good price on another one from Joe."

"That *pendejo*? I got one at home."

"You seem to be rather well-versed in all things serpentine, Coronado. How did that snake get into the kitchen?"

"I dunno." He pointed towards the back door. "Did you leave the door open?"

Maria growled. "It's locked every night. No fucking snake's gonna get through there."

Coronado looked about blithely. He pointed to the small, high window above the door, which was cranked open several inches. "Maybe a hawk dropped it through that window."

I eyed the window. "Rather precise aerial bombardment, don't you think?"

"I dunno, Señor Graves. Rattlesnakes don't crawl up walls. Maybe we could ask Joe. He knows lots about snakes."

"Joe Garcia?"

"*Sí*. He used to catch 'em a lot. The government would pay for live rattlesnakes so they could get the venom for making anti-stuff."

"You mean anti-venom?"

"*Sí*, that's it."

As Coronado recounted Joe's serpentine expertise, a monstrous thought distilled in the grey matter. "When did this government, er, 'roundup' take place?"

"Maybe five years ago. Joe told me you can still get money for them. If I hadn't killed this one, I could have given it to him."

I glanced down at the reptilian mass. "Has Joe mentioned any recent snake-catching activities to you?"

"How did you know? He told me yesterday he was gonna try and catch some 'cause he needed some more money."

"Indeed."

I glanced at Maria, whose brow was now knitted tightly enough to hold an anchor.

"I'm gonna shoot his *cojones* off."

"Maria, surely not even Joe would lower himself to such a contemptible act. I mean, simply because we were not buying supplies from him?"

"*Híjole*. You think Joe put the snake in here, Señor Graves?"

"No, Coronado. Well, he was rather angry with us yesterday." Maria growled.

"I can ask him if you want, Señor Graves. He should be at the store pretty soon."

"No! I mean, thank you, anyway, Coronado. Er, Maria and I shall stop by to ask Joe ourselves later today."

"Okay. I guess I better get over to Esperanza about your new sign." Coronado waddled out the back door and into the alley, oblivious to the possible criminal acts which had been perpetrated by his superior. Maria's face was boiling with anger.

"Let me speak with Joe, Maria. We can't have you tossed into gaol before we open."

She grunted, lit another cigarette, retrieved a broom from the closet, opened the kitchen door, and catapulted the snake's remains into the alley. Next, she retrieved a pail, filled it with hot water and soap, and began scrubbing the floor viciously whilst cursing Joe's existence. I told Maria I was going to see Joe and would return thereafter to continue our preparations. She cursed him again, then turned around and walked into the storeroom. I walked out the front door and took a deep breath. The morning air was crisp and fresh. As I stepped off the *portal*, I almost collided with Rudy.

"Jesus, Bennie. I was coming over to check on you and Maria. Coronado just told me you had a rattlesnake in the kitchen."

"My first, and I fervently hope last, encounter with such a beast. According to Coronado, Joe Garcia may have been the instigator. Apparently, he has some facility at catching serpents. I intend to have a chat with him about this."

"Why would Joe want to put a rattlesnake in the kitchen?"

"Yesterday, I informed him we would be purchasing our supplies elsewhere because of his rather high prices. I am attempting to reinvigorate the cafe's accounts, after all. Still, one cannot believe a businessman like Joe would engage in such an act of sheer villainy."

Rudy whistled softly. "Yeah, but Joe's had it pretty good around here for a long time. And he's got a real hot temper. Hell, he threw a brick through my window once."

"And you let him still drink in the bar?"

"Sure. His money's good as anybody's."

"Er, yes. What are we supposed to do? I mean, it was a bloody snake. Maria and I could have been killed."

"Was it a big snake?"

"Pythonish, in a coiled up sort of way. Maria was absolutely terrified."

"Yeah, she's always been real afraid of snakes. About the only thing she's afraid of. I'll go calm her down. You sure it was Joe? Maybe Maria left a door open. Snakes sometimes like to find someplace nice and warm, like a kitchen."

"No, Maria is quite certain she closed the kitchen door. The window above the door was open. Apparently, the snake gained entrance through it."

"Window, huh? That sounds like Joe."

"What? Surely stuffing a venomous snake through an open window is a criminal act, even in Vaca Seca?"

"I dunno. We could ask Tiny Roybal. He's the county sheriff. But I don't think he's gonna want to get involved. He doesn't like to get involved in most things. He and his brother Jimmy used to eat at the cafe a whole lot. You'll probably see him Thursday night."

"What type of sheriff prefers not to investigate criminal activities?"

"You don't know Tiny. Maybe if you or Maria had been bitten and died, he might look into it."

"How very comforting. Well, if Maria has her way with Joe, Tiny may have a murder to investigate. And I may assist her."

"Look, Bennie. Take my advice. Calm down. God knows we don't need any more feuds in this town. Joe's gonna calm down. I bet he'll even offer to sell you stuff for the same price as Sabrosa Foods. That's what he did for me."

"Yes, but a rattlesnake?"

"I'll go talk to Joe. Why don't you go over to the bar and get yourself some coffee? Antonio's there. Just ask him."

I exhaled loudly. "Fine. You may wish to inform Joe that Maria intends to shoot his *cojones* off. Given what I know of Maria's past, I rather doubt she engages in idle threats."

"Yeah, I guess Joe wasn't thinking too straight. He was pretty drunk when he left the bar last night." Rudy paused and scratched his chin. "You go get that coffee. I'm gonna see if I can calm everybody down."

"Thanks, Rudy. Coffee would be most welcome."

I strode into the bar. Resisting the urge to drown the morning's events in whisky, I confined myself to several large cups of coffee and then returned to the cafe to face Maria.

Maria was wrestling with a large bowl of filling for her *tamales*. "You talk to that *pendejo*? I got too much work to do, otherwise I'd go shoot him now."

"Er, no, actually. I spoke with Rudy and apprised him of the situation. He counseled patience. Said he would speak with Joe and try to, er, restore a bit of sanity to the situation. Apparently, your sheriff, a Mister Roybal, is less than keen to investigate such matters."

"Tiny? Only thing that he knows how to do is eat. He ain't gonna do nothing."

"Maria, please remain calm. If you shoot Joe, we're finished. No one could ever cook as well as you. If the cafe is a success, and I know it shall be, Joe will no longer matter."

Maria sighed, lowering her head towards the bowl she was stirring. "If Joe ever comes in here, I'm gonna shoot him."

"Well, that seems, er, a reasonable compromise. Now, how may I assist you with preparing the *tamales*?"

By mid-afternoon, Maria and I had assembled several hundred *tamales*. My folding technique had improved to the point where Maria even complimented my work; grudgingly, but complimentary nevertheless. More importantly, she had cooked several for our luncheon, which I devoured greedily, along with several fresh tortillas.

As we continued our preparations, a sudden thought entered the mind. "Maria did you speak with Esperanza this morning? We still need the new tables and chairs."

"No, but I saw her truck this morning. It was piled real high."

"Ah. I had begun to wonder, actually. Simply wouldn't do not to have anywhere for the customers to sit."

"Yeah, I guess." She examined the platters of *tamales* we had made and the remaining ingredients. "We got enough for another dozen. You do it. I gotta get the *frijoles* ready."

Shortly thereafter, I heard the front door open. "*Hola*. Señor Graves, I got a new sign."

"Just finishing up in the kitchen, Coronado."

He walked into the kitchen and zeroed in on the platters of *tamales*. "Those sure look good."

Coronado eyed the platters like a dog staring at an unguarded beefsteak. "I get real hungry just looking at them. I didn't eat lunch today."

Maria, looked at Coronado and shook her head. "Get the fuck out of my kitchen. I'll cook some *tamales* for you."

"*Gracias*, Maria. I got the sign ready, Señor Graves. I made sure Esperanza told me how to spell the words right this time."

"Let's have a look."

I followed his waddling form into the dining room. The sign was propped up against the wall under the window.

"Do you like it, Señor Graves? I showed Esperanza your note. She set up all of the stencils for me."

I stared at the errant sign. The jaw lowered itself like a reefed sail.

"What's wrong, Señor Graves? I painted the sign exactly like what Esperanza told me. I was real careful."

"Ah. Well, 'night' is indeed spelt correctly. Regrettably, the sign now reads 'Grand Night Thursday Opeing.'"

"But I was real careful with the stencils." Coronado's lip began to quiver.

"I am sure you were. Not your fault. I'll speak with Esperanza." As I contemplated what to do next—and despite my earlier admonitions to Maria, shooting Esperanza came to mind—Maria walked through the kitchen door with Coronado's *tamales*. She stared at the sign and mouthed the words silently. She slammed the plate of *tamales* on the table. Coronado cringed.

```
DOS ABUELAS CAFE

GRAND NIGHT
THURSDAY OPEING
```

"What the fuck are you doing?"

"Don't blame him, Maria. Your sister set the stencils out for Coronado to paint."

"Esperanza knows how to spell. She did real good in school."

"Not a case of poor spelling, I should think."

Maria shook her head and returned to the kitchen.

"Forget the sign, Coronado and enjoy your *tamales*. I shall deal with it."

I weighed several options silently. "Coronado, why don't you just tell everyone we open Thursday night? Spread the word, as they say."

"Sure, Señor Graves."

"And tell Luis Chavez, too. He must encounter numerous people at his petrol station. I'll speak to Rudy, of course, although we probably do not want customers who are overly inebriated."

"Should I tell Joe, too? Lots of people come into the store."

"Er, no need. I'm quite sure Joe is already letting everyone know."

# Chapter 18

After Coronado had waddled away, I dashed back into the kitchen. "Maria, do you have any idea where your sister is presently? We must have those tables and chairs. And I intend to speak with her about Coronado's errant sign." I held up the garbled sign. "I mean, look at this bloody thing. Why must she continue to sabotage our efforts?"

Maria retrieved another cigarette from a pocket in her skirt, lit it, and inhaled deeply. "I dunno. Sometimes, our father, he couldn't figure her out. She always got real mad about money."

"Why? Uncle Bill told me the cafe was always quite popular."

"*Sí.* But Esperanza, she always think we're gonna run out or something." Maria shrugged. "I got to get back to work. You get the menu done yet?"

"Menu? Damn and blast. I forgot completely."

"You forgot? We're gonna need menus, no?"

"No. I mean, yes, of course we shall." I looked about the kitchen for no reason other than to avoid Maria's dagger-like stare. "Right. Er, what if we hung up a blackboard and simply wrote down the menu items? That way, if we run out of an item, we can simply erase it."

"You said we got to have real menus."

"Well, the menu shall be real enough. I mean, the first time I was here, when I asked Esperanza for a menu she just snarled and then recited my three options."

"*Sí.* But you said we're gonna do things right this time."

"Er, perhaps, we could use a blackboard to display the day's specials, as well as regular items?"

"Okay. What's gonna be special?"

"That's up to you. *Tamales,* perhaps?"

"I always make *tamales.*"

"Yes, but they were available only on Saturdays, were they not? So, on Saturday, we write *tamales* on the blackboard, unless of course you wish to serve them on other days. What about holidays, like Christmas? Any particular festive dishes you would make?"

"*Sí. Empanadas, posole, tamales,* and *biscochitos* for dessert."

"Right. Those could be written down on the blackboard at the appropriate time. Who knows, we could even serve steak-and-kidney pie or bangers and mash."

"Steak pie? Bangers? What the fuck is a banger?"

Memories of delicious aromas coursed wistfully through the neurons. "Merely some favourite English dishes."

"Maybe you cook them for me sometime. We still got to get a menu. And we don't got no blackboard."

"Yes, that is rather a problem. School."

"Huh?"

"There must be a primary school in Vaca Seca."

"We got an elementary school. So?"

"Well, schools have blackboards. And, most schools have banda machines.

"You want to steal a blackboard from the school? What's a bandage machine? You think people are gonna cut themselves?"

"What? No, a banda machine, a duplicator." I mimed rotating my right arm in a circle. "Rather messy at times. One types out one's lesson or examination on a purplish sheet, inserts the sheet onto the roll of the machine, then cranks it to produces copies."

"You mean a ditto machine?"

"Is that what you call it here in the States?"

"*Sí.* I seen one of those. The school's got one."

"Excellent. Now, what about the blackboard? Does the school have a portable one?"

"I dunno. We could ask Carmen Esposito."

"Who?"

"Carmen. She runs the school."

"Shall I speak with her?"

Maria shook her head. "She don't like strangers, especially *gringos*. We gotta get Esperanza. She used to babysit Carmen's kids."

I thought of the woebegone waifs whom Esperanza babysat and shuddered. "Right. I'll ask Esperanza about securing a blackboard from the school and then return here as soon as possible."

Maria waived me off, tracing large arcs of cigarette smoke about her, and returned to the kitchen.

I walked out the front door and stepped into a shimmering pool of urine. Paco was sauntering casually towards Rudy's Bar, no doubt intending to leave his mark there as well. Resisting the urge to flatten the cur with Uncle Bill's lorry, I set off for Esperanza's home. When I arrived, I espied her lorry parked in front yard, the bed piled high with a potpourri of tables and chairs in various shapes and colours. I rolled to a stop, stepped out of the lorry, walked up to her front door, and knocked loudly.

"Esperanza," I yelled. "Maria and I need your help." Silence. "Esperanza, please. I can smell the smoke from your cigarette."

After another long silence, I heard loud, plodding footsteps come towards the door, which then opened violently. Before me stood a shirtless, grey-moustachioed chap, whose imposing size and muscularity bore a strong simian quality, if not matching intelligence. His left hand dwarfed the beer bottle around which it was wrapped.

"Who the fuck are you?"

I stepped back instinctively. "Er, do I have the correct home?" I pointed to the laden lorry. "I mean, that's Esperanza's lorry, isn't it? I really must speak with her."

He curled his lip. "You gotta be that *gringo*. Esperanza told me about you."

"Er, yes, I suppose I am." I extended my right hand hesitantly. "Benjamin Graves, not that Esperanza ever calls me that."

He enveloped my puny hand, which distressed the metatarsals in the extreme. "Hector Castillo. I'm Esperanza's boyfriend."

"Gah! I mean, Esperanza hadn't, er, mentioned you before. Pleased to make your acquaintance, Mister, er, Castillo. Might I have a brief word with Esperanza? It's rather important."

"Sure. You can come in if you want. I think she's gettin' dressed."

"Ah, I mean, no. I don't wish to intrude. Happy to wait outside." The thought of seeing Esperanza in a partially clothed state, or worse, was not something the stomach would endure. That, and the thick haze that hung in the room, counselled maintaining a discrete distance.

"Okay." He shut the door heavily.

Whilst I waited, a mental picture of Esperanza *in flagrante delicto* briefly surfaced, before being pummelled into oblivion by the more sensible neurons. I turned around and stared off towards the pine trees, inhaling the far more pleasant fragrance they provided.

Suddenly, a voice boomed, causing me to jump. "What the fuck do you want, *Pendejito*?"

I turned around. Esperanza was leaning against the doorway, dressed in a short, pink satin robe tied loosely about her waist. The ever-present cigarette smouldered between her fingers.

The eyes reeled. "I, er, Esperanza, I mean, I apologise for the interruption, but Maria and I need your help."

"What kind of help?"

I looked towards the lorry. "Those tables and chairs, for one. They'll want cleaning and setting up. We open Thursday, you recall."

"I got a real good price for those, *Pendejito*. Saved a lot of money."

"Yes, thanks. Keeps margin low, and all that."

"Is that it?"

"Er, no, actually. We need a blackboard from the school. And the use of the banda, I mean, ditto machine."

"Blackboard? What the fuck do you want a blackboard for? And why do you need a ditto machine? You gonna give everybody a test, *Pendejito*?"

The molars ground themselves tightly. "We'll use the blackboard to write out tomorrow night's menu. As for the ditto machine, I want to use it to copy a temporary menu, until we can have something printed professionally."

Esperanza blew a large cloud of smoke into my face. "We always just told people what we got. Who needs a fucking menu?"

"Maria, that's bloody who. Look, whilst you've been otherwise, er, engaged, Maria and I have been working quite diligently to prepare for the opening tomorrow night. If you wish to be part of the cafe's putative resurrection, we need your help. Now."

"So, you growing some *cojones* now, *Pendejito*? You met my boyfriend Hector? He came up from Santa Fe last night. He requires my help, too. *¿Que no?*"

Though I was accustomed to an Esperanza hurling invective, an Esperanza prancing about like an aged prostitute was above and beyond the call, but I doused an emetic urge.

"I am sure he is most, er, appreciative."

"Look, perhaps I could take your lorry and unload the tables and chairs whilst you—well, just join us as soon as possible."

"Your face is all red, *Pendejito*. You embarrassed or something? Maybe you need a girl. Or you one of them who don't like girls?"

The emetic urge flared into a conflagration. "What? No, I mean— May I borrow your lorry?"

"Suit yourself, *Pendejito*. Keys are in the ignition. Tell Maria I'll come over later." She turned around, walked inside, and slammed the door shut.

Desperate to escape Esperanza's carnal Hell, I dashed over to her lorry, started the engine, and motored slowly back to the cafe.

The tables and chairs were intertwined like a jigsaw puzzle, and spilled onto the macadam as I pried them apart, discovering that several had been amputated. Maria came out from the kitchen to inspect the progress. She stared at the debris.

"What the fuck are these? How come some of these chairs don't got legs?"

I threw several of the absent-legged chairs into the lorry. "Excellent questions all."

"Where's Esperanza?"

Images of the pink-robed Esperanza flooded the brain like pike-wielding sailors overrunning an enemy's ship. "She was, otherwise engaged with her, er, boyfriend, a Mister Castillo. She informed me she would be here later today."

Maria shook her head. "Hector? That *borracho*? She gives him money, that's how come he sticks around."

"Well, she made a point of telling me she provides him more than just money."

"I'm gonna go over there and tell Hector to get lost."

"Are you sure that's wise? I mean, he's a rather large, ill-tempered chap."

"Hector? He's real scared of me."

"Yes, well, whilst you deal with your sister, I shall clean and set up our new furniture, at least the unbroken bits."

Maria walked back into the cafe and I heard the roar of her lorry shortly thereafter. I turned my attention to the disorderly pieces before me, deciding to group them by colours, rather than style. After a half hour of sorting, I moved the surviving tables and chairs into the dining room, and arrayed them in what I hoped were the least visually disconcerting combinations.

Whilst moving the tables about, I began to notice a commonality amongst them: even the ones with all of their legs wobbled noticeably, no doubt another reason for the discounted price. I turned the tables larboard and starboard, but Pedro's workmanship had produced a level floor. The tables wobbled no matter how they were rotated.

Feeling mentally fatigued, I pulled a nearby chair towards me. It had a tall, straight back and looked uncomfortable. I sat down heavily. The chair's uncomfortable look was well-deserved. I attempted to adjust the posture to compensate, but to no avail. Then, perhaps a minute after I sat down, I heard a sharp crack and found myself supine on the floor, dazed and surrounded by various woody debris. One could almost hear the rap-rapping of the invisible hammer pounding yet more nails into the cafe's coffin: unsteady tables and disintegrating chairs made an inestimable combination.

I remained on the floor, staring blankly at the ceiling. Whilst the grey matter pondered the relative merits of a return to the vertical against maintaining the present position, I heard the front door open. Assuming Maria had returned with Esperanza, I decided to remain at my new post to provide visual evidence of Esperanza's latest folly. Footsteps approached and I espied a pair of bronzed and rather shapely legs standing beside me.

"Are you Bennie?" a smooth, honey-dipped voice asked.

"Eh?" I rolled over onto my left side and pushed myself into a sitting position, brushing off the bits of wood that clung to the shirt. Before me stood a shapely young lass, with large brown eyes and reddish-black hair that curled about her shoulders.

"I mean, yes, I'm Benjamin Graves. Most everyone calls me Bennie." I stood up, brushed more bits of wood off the trousers, and extended my hand. "And you are?"

"Loretta Alvarez," she said softly, extending a silken hand. "My aunt said you need a waitress."

"Your aunt?"

"That's right. *Tia* Esperanza. She said you needed some help."

"Gah. Esperanza's your aunt?"

That a relation of Esperanza's could be so comely and pleasant-voiced gave pause to the grey matter. I struggled to avoid staring at Loretta like a slavering Neanderthal.

"You sound surprised? Is there something wrong?"

"Surprised? No. I mean, yes, we need a waitress. Are you experienced? I mean, as a waitress?"

"I worked at La Cena in Santa Fe for a few years, after I graduated from high school. Then I worked in a doctor's office as a receptionist. But Dr. Montoya had a heart attack a few months ago, so the office closed. I've been looking for work ever since, but there's not much around. *Tia* Esperanza said I could probably work here."

"She did?"

"I guess she didn't tell you. That's okay, thanks, anyway."

Loretta turned around and began walking towards the front door. "Please, Miss Alvarez. Wait. Your aunt's correct, we do need a waitress. And, no, we haven't hired anyone yet. So, er, the job's yours, if you like."

"Really? Thanks!" She threw her arms around me in a most pleasant embrace.

"I say—"

"I'm sorry. I didn't mean to do that."

"No need to apologise, Miss Alvarez. I, er . . ."

"Please call me Loretta."

"All right, Miss, er, Loretta. I was rather expecting your aunt, well, both of them really, to show up. Have you seen them?"

"No, sorry. *Tia* Esperanza called me—I'm staying at my mom's house—and told me to see you right away."

"Ah. Well, I have been attempting to devise a strategy to prevent the tables your bloody aunt—er, *Tia* Esperanza—purchased from wobbling."

"I know a trick. Do you have some napkins?"

"Napkins? You mean serviettes?"

"Um, I guess so. *Tia* Esperanza said you talked funny, but I like your accent."

"Well, your aunt does have a way with words. Anyway, yes, we refer to them as serviettes. Regardless, how do we fix the wobbling tables?"

"Easy. You fold enough napkin under the table leg to make it stop wobbling and then you tape it to the bottom. Works for chairs, too."

"Er, yes, I should have thought of that myself. Rather obvious. We've serviettes in the storage room. As for tape, I don't know. I may have to purchase a roll. Anyway, the storage room is off the kitchen."

I led the way into the kitchen, unable to reconcile the incongruity between Loretta and her aunts. Then again, families often breed an odd mix, as my own certainly proved.

"I never realized Esperanza had a niece."

"Actually, I'm just related because my oldest sister is married to her son, Miguel. They live in Albuquerque. They got married when I was ten. I always called her *Tia* Esperanza."

A wave of relief washed over me. "Were you raised here?"

"Yeah. It's a funny little town, but I like it."

"Yes, I've discovered it's rather unique. Much different from London."

"What's it like?"

"London? Rather difficult to describe. I mean, I suppose it is like your New York City in a way, a gateway to the country."

"I hope I can go there someday."

"It's quite popular with the tourists."

I cringed after saying that, distraught that I seemed capable of only dim-witted babble at present.

"*Tia* Esperanza said El Vaquero is your uncle. He doesn't sound anything like you."

"Uncle Bill? Rather a long story that. Coronado—I gather you know him—thinks Uncle Bill and I are brothers. I gave up correcting him."

Loretta laughed. "Everybody knows Coronado. Does he still work at my uncle's store? I remember at Hallo'ween, Coronado would carve really scary pumpkins. But he always had lots of candy for us."

"Pumpkins, eh? Artistic bent, I suppose. He painted the—gah! Did you say your uncle's store?"

"Yeah. Uncle Joe's store."

"Joe Garcia is your Uncle?

"Uh-huh. He's my mom's brother."

Fate had delivered another vicious blow. Cynthia's running off with Rodrigo had soured me on the fairer sex. And observing Esperanza—in heat as it were—was enough to put any chap "off his feed." Now, the attractive and charming lass who had walked through the cafe door and awakened the Graves heart from its long coma, was the niece of the fiend who had almost succeeded in despatching Maria and I with an ill-tempered rattlesnake.

"You've quite the collection of aunts and uncles."

She laughed again. "I guess so. Have you ever seen a rattlesnake?"

"What did you say?"

"Uncle Joe used to catch rattlesnakes. He sold them to people in Santa Fe who to make anti-venom. Anyway, sometimes Uncle Joe would put a couple of them in this pit he had dug so we could watch them. Sometimes, the snakes would attack each other."

The ventricles pounded "Fiend," I muttered. "I mean, imagine that. I suppose they are quite fearsome."

"Uncle Joe told us they were more afraid of you. He said just leave them alone and they wouldn't bother you. Are you okay? You look pale."

"Me? No, I'm fine. A bit warm, perhaps. I say, Joe must have an encylopaedic knowledge of rattlesnakes." I drew in a large breath to combat an upwelling of nausea. How could I tell Loretta her beloved uncle was a psychotic loon?

I opened the door to the storage room, switched on the light, and espied a large package of serviettes. "Here we are, servi—I mean, napkins. As for tape, perhaps you could walk over to your Uncle's store and purchase a roll."

She offered me one of those winsome smiles that chaps fall prey to. "Okay, Bennie. Do you need anything else?"

"Eh? I mean, no, the tape will be quite sufficient, thank you."

Alone once again, I wondered why I had ever agreed to attempt this culinary resurrection. Retrieving a broom to sweep up the remnants of the disintegrated chair, I sat down in another, taking care to test its strength first. There I remained, in a stupor, until the front door burst open, followed by Maria and Esperanza's heavy footsteps.

They scanned the dining room and espied the remnants of the broken chair.

Esperanza cackled. "You break one of my chairs. *Pendejito*? You eating too many *tortillas*? Your new waitress ain't gonna like that."

Her voice had the dulcimer tone of nails drawn down a blackboard. "Had you bothered to purchase something other than cast-off rubbish, I wouldn't have to deal with one broken chair and others which are waiting to disintegrate beneath unsuspecting customers. Nor would I have to deal with mis-matched, listing tables. Your niece has gone to her uncle's store to purchase some tape, so we may at least solve that inconvenience."

"Don't get mad at me, *Pendejito*. I was just trying to save you some money. Ain't that part of your business strategy, or whatever the fuck you call it?"

"We open Thursday night and we have no bloody chairs. What do you suggest to do?"

"Maybe everybody can eat standing up. They won't eat so much that way."

I stood up and held the broom tightly, as if I were stran-gling it. "I am beyond the limits of my patience. You and Maria asked for my help, yet you continue to sabotage my efforts. I'm not a student of psychology and psychopaths. I don't know why you're doing this. Nor do I care at the moment. You are a menace and a carbuncle."

"*Vete a la chingada, Pendejito*. This is my cafe, not yours."

"*Hermana*," Maria said, her voice steady and firm, "this is our cafe, not yours. Señor Bennie, he's been working real hard. Maybe you should spend less time with Hector and more here."

"Don't talk to me about Hector. You're just jealous."

"For the love of God, Esperanza, we open in two days. Either help, in a constructive manner, or . . ."

"Or what, *Pendejito*?"

I glared at her malevolently. "Or I shall borrow Maria's shotgun and shoot you. And stop calling me *Pendejito*. Do I make myself clear?"

Esperanza's face reddened. She was about to erupt, when Loretta walked in.

"*Tia* Esperanza. I was just at Uncle Joe's getting some tape. Bennie hired me as a waitress just like you said he would. And I'm going to help him fix the tables that wobble. Isn't that great?"

An excruciating silence ensued. Finally, Esperanza said, "Yeah, Loretta, I'm real glad he hired you. We need an experienced waitress, especially one who has worked in Santa Fe."

"I thought you were gonna waitress," Maria said.

"Yeah, but we're gonna be real busy, so having Loretta here is gonna be a big help. *¿Que no?* You don't want just me and *Pend*—Señor Bennie working, do you?"

Maria's face began to contort, until she shook her head. "I gotta get back to the kitchen. You gonna be a big help to us, Loretta. *Gracias*." She walked slowly back to the kitchen.

Esperanza turned to me. "I guess I'm gonna go. You don't need my help now."

"As a matter of fact, there are a number of things we need help with. I was about to discuss them with you and Maria before your charming niece returned to help me repair the tables. The chairs, alas, are beyond repair. Shall I continue?"

"Uh, okay."

"Please go to the school and borrow a portable blackboard. I also need you to obtain ditto masters so I can write a rudimentary written menu until we can have something more permanent printed. Assuming, that is, we stay in business. Whilst you attend to those tasks, Loretta and I will repair the tables. Then we shall have to find structurally sound chairs somewhere in this town. Is that clear?"

Esperanza cursed under her breath, "Okay. I'll be back soon." She turned around and walked out the front door, slamming it loudly.

"You don't like *Tia* Esperanza, do you Bennie?"

"What? No, I mean, well, your aunt does have a rather, er, forceful nature. She and Maria asked that I run the cafe in hopes we can make a go of it this time. I'm afraid your aunt and I disagree on the appropriate strategy for doing so."

"Yeah, I know, she can be a real bitch."

The eyebrows raised. "Well, I wouldn't say that, of course. Merely that your aunt can be somewhat, er, obstreperous." I cleared my throat and gazed out the front window.

"That's okay, Bennie. Before I walked in, I heard you threaten to shoot her." Loretta giggled, as my countenance assumed a crimson-like state. "Don't worry, you're not the first. She and Uncle Joe don't get along real well, either. And I've seen *Tia* Maria scream at her. And Luis Chavez—he owns the gas station just outside of town—once tried to run her over with his pick-up."

Loretta began counting on her fingers. "Let's see. There was Nestor Martinez. *Tia* Esperanza kicked his dog Paco for, well, you know, right on her front door. Nestor showed up and started throwing beer bottles at her. Then there was the time—"

I raised my hand. "If you recite the entire list of Vaca Secans who have been aggrieved by your aunt, we'll never fix these tables."

"I'm sorry. I really do love my aunt, but, well, you know how family can be."

"Only too well. Right. Shall we attempt to level these tables?" After an hour of serviette folding and taping, the tables were serviceable. Although the decor was not up to Michelin Guide standards, what with bits of white paper visible under most of the table legs, desperate times called for desperate measures.

Esperanza had not returned from the school and I wondered how she would sabotage this task: a blackboard that would collapse when one wrote upon it? Profanities engraved on the Banda master sheet for the menus? Perhaps she would arrive tomorrow wearing the revealing pink satin robe and clutching a rose between her teeth. Alas, with Esperanza, the possibilities seemed endless.

We popped into the kitchen to check on Maria, who was simultaneously stirring, chopping, and smoking. Suggesting Loretta remain at the cafe to assist Maria and wait for Esperanza, I set off in search of replacement chairs.

My first stop was Rudy's Bar. The ever-present cloud of cigarette smoke biffed the nostrils and lungs as I entered. Joe Garcia was hunched over several empty bottles. Resisting the urge to confront him about the previous day's reptilian encounter, I walked down the hallway to Rudy's office. The door was open. Rudy was leaning back in his desk chair, eyes closed and feet propped upon the desk.

"What do you want?"

"What? I mean, how did you know it was me?"

Rudy sat up and blinked. "Sorry, Bennie. Late night at the bar."

"Quite a talent, sensing when someone is waiting silently outside your door."

"I heard your steps in the hallway. What's going on? You ready for the big day?"

"Well, about that. We've yet another problem on our hands." Rudy sighed deeply. "Shit. What did she do now?"

"Chairs."

"What?"

"Esperanza purchased a lorry-full of wobbly tables and disintegrating chairs. Her niece, Loretta, and I managed to steady the tables with serviettes and tape. The chairs are hopeless. I sat in one and it exploded immediately, leaving me sprawled upon the floor. Worse, when I went over to her house this morning, she was with her, er, boyfriend, Hector, and clad rather scantily. Not for the weak-stomached."

"You're discovering all the town's secrets. She's been seeing Hector for a few years, I think. Gives him money now and then. Was she wearing that pink robe?" I nodded slowly.

"¡*Ay cabrón*! Nobody should have to see that. Once, she showed up drunk at the church in that thing. We had a priest who used to come every two months. That was the last time we saw him."

"I suppose his having taken a vow of celibacy was providential."

"Yeah, I guess. So how many chairs you gonna need?"

"We have nine tables, so thirty-six chairs would be ideal."

"I got twelve in the bar you can use."

"I can borrow four chairs from Uncle Bill. That leaves twenty."

"I'll ask around."

"Thanks, Rudy. I'll return tomorrow morning to borrow the chairs from the Bar." I stood up and stretched.

"You like her, Bennie?"

"Esperanza? Are you mad? The woman's a bloody menace."

"Not her, Loretta."

I felt my throat constrict. "Loretta? Yes, I mean, I just met her. Rather awkward, really. She walked in whilst I lay dazed on the floor. Esperanza had told her we needed to hire a waitress and, well, you must know all of the details already."

"Be careful, Bennie. She's broken some hearts."

"Many are called, few are chosen, eh? Well, she seems charming. As for broken hearts, I would prefer not to have mine torn to bits again. Once bitten, twice shy, as they say."

"Yeah, El Vaquero told me about your wife. If it's any consolation, you're not the only guy who has had it happen to him."

"Thanks, Rudy. Besides, I shudder whenever Loretta says '*Tia Esperanza*,' to say nothing of Joe Garcia being her uncle.

"Bennie?"

"Eh?"

"The cafe's gonna work. I know it. Your uncle thinks so, too."

"I hope you're both correct, but I fear Fate has other ideas."

# Chapter 19

B ack at the cafe, there was no sign of Esperanza or the blackboard. Inured to Esperanza's unique ability to rubbish my suggestions, I sighed and walked into the kitchen.

"What is that awful smell?"

"*Menudo*," Maria said, stirring a large pot like one of Macbeth's witches. "For opening night."

"Did you say 'manure?' Is this another of Esperanza's suggestions to drive customers away? I mean, do people eat this?"

"*Sí, muy tradiciónal.* Especially at holidays. Opening night is special, so we make *menudo*."

Loretta nonchalantly dropped what appeared to be a pig's foot into the pot, reminding me of Daisy. "Don't worry, Bennie, people will really like it."

I glanced into the pot and shuddered. "If you say so. I take it this, ah, *menudo* is boiled pig's feet."

"Pig's feet just for some flavour," Maria growled. "In English, you call *menudo*, I can't remember the word . . ."

"Tripe," Loretta said.

"Ah. Our Scots neighbours have their own favourite tripe-like dish, called *haggis*. One boils a sheep's heart, lungs, and liver in the sheep's stomach until it becomes a gelatinous mass. I suppose that explains why the Scots are the way they are, really."

"You don't got to eat none, Señor Bennie. But people here like it."

I bowed formally. "Maria, I trust that you, better than anyone, knows the culinary likes and dislikes of the local Vaca

Secans. On a different note, I have secured twelve chairs from Rudy. With the four I can obtain from the ranch, we need only twenty more. Any suggestions?"

"How about the school?" Loretta asked.

"Rather small for our clientele, don't you think? Besides, aren't the chairs usually attached to desks?"

Loretta pushed my shoulder playfully. "No, no, Bennie. Folding metal chairs. Why not use those? They aren't real comfortable, but that's probably okay for tomorrow. We're gonna want to move people in and out."

"Folding chairs? Capital idea." I rubbed the shoulder and smiled, pretending I was in pain owing to her assault. "Er, speaking of the school, any word from Esperanza? I mean, how long can it take to retrieve a blackboard and a Banda master?"

"She didn't come back here yet."

I glanced at my watch. "Half four. Do you think I should go the school and find her? I could also enquire of the principal—what was her name again?—regarding the folding chairs."

"School's closed now," Maria said. "You can go tomorrow morning. Loretta, you better go with Bennie. I don't think Carmen's gonna like him."

"*Sí, Tía* Maria."

Loretta remained with Maria, continuing to assist with the culinary preparations. As there was little I could do until the morrow, I departed, returning to the confines of the ranch, and a brief respite of relative sanity.

Arriving at the cafe around eight the next morning, I found Loretta and Maria already at work in the kitchen. "Good morning, all. Did you work all evening?"

Maria looked up at me, the dark circles under her eyes signalling impatience and fatigue. "We got a lot to do. You gonna go to the school now?"

"Sorry, Maria. Are you all right?"

"*Sí*. You go with Loretta."

Loretta removed her apron and hung it on a hook by the back door.

"Ready, Bennie?"

"To see the *gringo*-hating Carmen? Why not?" We slid through the front door and walked towards the lorry.

She revealed the same winsome smile. "Don't worry, she's not that bad."

"It's not that. More of a nod to Fate, really. She seems to be conspiring to nobble us at every turn."

"Huh? What's that mean?"

"Just a bit of slang we have. It means to disable. Something unscrupulous chaps do to horses to prevent them from winning a race."

Loretta raised an eyebrow, no doubt questioning my sanity. "You think Fate is conspiring against you?"

"Well, with Coronado's fusillade that reduced the cafe to rubble, your Uncle Joe binning a rattlesnake into the kitchen to attack Maria and I, Esperanza and her constant sabotage—"

"What did you say about Uncle Joe?"

"We can't prove it was him, of course. However, the morning before last Maria walked into the kitchen and encountered a rattlesnake. It apparently entered through the high window above the kitchen door, although we doubt voluntarily. I arrived shortly thereafter and encountered the serpent. It held us at bay until Coronado arrived and vanquished it."

"You think my Uncle Joe did that?" Loretta's eyes narrowed and became dagger-like.

"Er, well, the evidence is only circumstantial. However, Coronado did mention your Uncle was planning to catch several more to earn a bit of brass."

"Uncle Joe would never to do anything like that."

"Your uncle and aunts are not exactly on good terms. Seems to be a burning dislike that often flares up into aggravated disdain."

"Uncle Joe sometimes would talk about how much money he was owed. But it didn't seem to bother him too much."

"A turn the other cheek sort, eh? Perhaps I've been dealing with a different Joe Garcia."

"Well, they owed him a lot of money. Besides, that snake could have crawled in through the window itself. Or maybe *Tia* Maria left the back door open by mistake."

"Well, Coronado did suggest that perhaps a hawk or owl dropped it through the window. As I said, perhaps it was just Fate. In any case, we must press onward, take the fight straight to the enemy, as Nelson would say."

"What enemy? Who is Nelson?"

"You've not heard of Admiral Lord Nelson?" She shook her head no. I grimaced. "Battle of Trafalgar? H.M.S *Victory*? Still nothing, eh?"

"Sorry, Bennie. Was he important?"

"England would have not defeated the French without him. I suppose such things likely matter little on this side of the pond."

"Sounds like you admire him."

"A fearless chap. One of the ancestors served with him at that very battle. Had he encountered that rattlesnake, I am sure he would have simply dashed it with his sword."

"You didn't have a sword?"

"No, but I did have one of Maria's larger knives. I must say, I was impressed with Coronado's knife-throwing ability. Rather amazing. Anyway, off to the school. Er, where is it exactly?"

"Take a right at that intersection, and then turn left. It's just up the road."

Presently, we arrived at the school. I followed Loretta, who walked briskly inside and up to a door marked "Principal." Loretta knocked loudly and opened the door. "Señora Esposito?" There, behind an ancient wooden desk, sat an equally ancient woman. She wore large, thick spectacles and was snoring peacefully.

"Señora Esposito?" Loretta repeated in a louder voice.

The ancient awoke with a start. Behind the spectacles, her eyes loomed large. She smiled at Loretta. "Who are you?"

Then, as her gaze shifted from Loretta to me, the smile became a deep scowl. "*¿Quien es el gringo?*"

"Señora Esposito, you probably don't remember me. My name is Loretta Alvarez, Esperanza's niece. And this is Benjamin Graves. He's helping to fix the cafe. We reopen tonight."

"Good morning, Señora Flores," I said politely.

My polite salutation did nothing to mollify her. She turned to Loretta. "Loretta Alvarez? *Sí*, I remember you. I remember all the children. You're all grown up now. The boys must be after you, like Jimmy Trujillo. Even when he was ten years old, I knew he was going to chase girls."

I stifled a laugh and saw Loretta blush. "Is this *gringo* your boyfriend?"

Loretta's face reddened. "No, Señora Flores, he's not my boyfriend. He's my boss. I'm going to be working at the cafe."

Señora Flores scowled. "You better treat her real good, *gringo*. What's your name?"

"Benjamin Graves, madam. I, er, assure you I shall treat her like the Queen."

"What did you say? I don't like *gringos*. Why are you here?"

I had asked myself the same question and, as the grand opening drew nearer, often.

Before I could answer, Loretta spoke up. "Señora Esposito, could we borrow some chairs to use at the cafe? Just for tonight?"

"Chairs? Again?"

"What?" we both asked simultaneously. "What do you mean again?"

"Esperanza asked me for some chairs. And a blackboard. And some ditto masters. She starting her own school?"

"Esperanza was here? When?"

"Yesterday, I guess. What time is it?" She peered up towards a large industrial clock on the wall, the hands of which had fallen off.

"Thanks for your help, Señora Flores."

"Loretta?"

"Yes, Señora Flores?"

"Don't never trust *gringos*."

"Um, thank you, Señora Esposito. I'll remember that."

I offered a languid wave of the hand to the old bat, and followed Loretta out the door. As soon as we had stepped outside, she burst out laughing.

"I'm sorry, Bennie. I think she's getting a little senile."

"I believe she's well beyond senility. She must have been sitting at that desk since Methuselah wore nappies. By the way, who is this Jimmy Trujillo chap?"

"Jimmy Trujillo tried to kiss me in the fourth grade. I have no idea how she remembers that."

"And what became of this juvenile Lothario?"

Loretta laughed. "Bennie, you sound almost jealous."

I recalled Rudy's warning about Loretta's trail of broken hearts. She was beginning to dent mine. Then again, admitting I was jealous of a fourth-grader would have sounded daft.

"No, of course not. Merely thinking Jimmy should meet a chap at the bank where I was previously employed. He was fond of mannequins."

"Mannequins? I don't understand."

"An involved and sordid story." I thought it best to change the subject. "It seems Esperanza actually did what I asked."

"Should we go back to the cafe?"

I glanced at my watch. "No. Esperanza will still be home." I started the lorry's engine. "Oh, no," I moaned.

"What's wrong, Bennie?"

"Hector Castillo." I felt the stomach churning as if it was weathering a crossing sea.

"Who's Hector Castillo?"

"You don't know?"

"No. Who is he?"

"He is your aunt's, er, boyfriend, reluctant though I am to use that term."

Her eyes bulged. "*Tia* Esperanza has a boyfriend? Since when?"

"I really don't know. Apparently, he lives in Santa Fe and motors up for periodic, er, visits."

"A boyfriend? ¡*Híjole!*"

I jumped, hearing her use Coronado's ubiquitous expression. "What did you say?"

"*Híjole*. It's just an expression of surprise."

"Yes, I know. I always hear Coronado say it. Is he your uncle, too? It seems everyone in this town is related."

"Coronado? I . . . don't . . . think . . . so. Oh, we're here."

We walked up to the front door. Loretta knocked loudly. "*Tia* Esperanza, it's me, Loretta."

After a minute's silence, I heard elephant-like footfalls from inside. The door opened. Before us stood Esperanza, attired in the same pink satin robe, a smouldering cigarette dangling from her lips. She looked at Loretta and then me.

"I guess you do like girls, *Pendejito*."

"*Tia* Esperanza, don't call Bennie that. It's not nice."

Esperanza shrugged. "What do you want, *Pendejito*? I'm kinda busy. *¿Comprende?*"

I averted my eyes as much as possible. "Er, we were just at the school. The rather aged Mrs. Flores said you retrieved the chairs, blackboard, and banda masters we need."

"Yeah, I got them, *Pendejito*. They're in back of my truck." Her lorry was nowhere to be seen.

"They are?"

"Yeah. Hector took my truck. He went to Rudy's for some more beer."

"A bit early in the day, isn't it?"

"Hector likes his beer."

Loretta's face had turned ashen. "*Tia* Esperanza, you have a boyfriend?"

"*Sí*. You think maybe I'm too old, Loretta?"

Not wanting to become embroiled in a discussion of about the merits of Esperanza having a boyfriend, I spoke up quickly. "Of course, we don't want to interrupt you and Hector. We can load the chairs into Uncle Bill's lorry and be off."

As I spoke, Hector roared into the driveway and stopped suddenly. He staggered out of the lorry, shirtless and inebriated, carrying a large carton of beer.

He leered at Loretta and made a rude gesture. "Hey, *gringo*, who's the little *chica*? She looks real cute."

"¡*Callate* Hector!" Esperanza shouted. "That's my niece." Loretta retreated to the safety of Uncle Bill's lorry.

Hector began to walk slowly towards it. "*Chica*, you don't got to be afraid of me. I can show you a real good time."

"Leave her alone, Hector," I said.

He turned towards me. "What'd you say, *gringo*?"

"I said leave her alone."

"Esperanza's right, *gringo*. Somebody needs to kick your ass, and it's gonna be me." He began to lumber towards me like Frankenstein's monster.

Thinking the death of chivalry was caused by the untimely deaths of the chivalrous, I sought a quick exit and dashed towards the lorry. Fate, however, intervened on my behalf. Hector, whose besotted eyes were staring straight at me, failed to notice a largish hole created by the local gophers. His right foot descended heavily into the hole, causing him to totter, grunt, and fall forward with an audible thud. The box of beer he was carrying exploded upon impact, causing several cans to sail past the cranium.

"Quite the boyfriend, Esperanza." She rushed over to Hector. But instead of helping him up, she pushed him with her foot and, observing no response, walked back inside. I motioned to Loretta, and we quickly loaded the chairs and supplies into the lorry.

"Thanks, Bennie. You're an old-fashioned gentleman." She placed her hand on the right arm.

"I'm afraid bravery is not my strong suit." If he hadn't toppled over, he would have torn me to bits."

"What does *Tia* Esperanza see in him?"

"Probably best not to enquire. Anyway, we have much work to do if we are going to open tonight."

We returned to the cafe and unloaded the chairs and the blackboard. The odour of *menudo* was still strong. I opened the front door and began setting up the folding chairs whilst Loretta returned to the kitchen to help Maria. Not five minutes had passed before Coronado drifted in, apparently drawn by the smell, like a rodentary vulture.

"¡*Híjole*! Is that *menudo*? It sure smells good." He licked his lips, uncomfortably reminding me of Daisy.

"Hullo, Coronado." I wrestled with a folding chair that has so far resisted all efforts to be unfolded. "Yes, Maria is preparing manure, er, *menudo*. You actually like it?"

"*Sí*, Señor Graves. Menudo is real traditional. You got to eat it at Christmas."

"So was keel-hauling."

Coronado licked his lips again, causing a noticeable dyspepsia in my stomach.

"I'm sorry, Coronado, but we have much work to do. After I set up these chairs, Loretta and I need to finish readying the tables."

"Loretta? Is she here?" His eyes widened.

"Yes. She's in the kitchen with Maria. Why?"

"She's my daughter, Señor Graves."

The chair I had been wrestling fell to the floor. "What?" I sat down heavily on the floor, mute.

"I don't remember much, 'cause I was kinda drunk. But Loretta turned out real good, huh?" He shuffled his large feet and looked down at me.

"You okay, Señor Graves?"

I continued to sit on the floor, unable to fathom the unfathomable. I mean, one might as well have heard Adam announce that Eve was the serpent's cousin.

I heard the kitchen door swing open. Maria came over and stood by us. She looked at the chair, then at me, and then at Coronado.

"What the fuck? Did El Gordo knock you down?"

"I'm all right, Maria."

I looked around and saw Loretta standing at the kitchen door. She stared at Coronado, who waved to her gently.

"*Hola*, Loretta." he said.

"Hello, Coronado." She walked over to where I sat immobile. "Bennie, are you hurt?"

"What? No. I'm fine. I was, just wrestling with a particularly recalcitrant folding chair."

"You look real pale. Maybe you should take it easy for a minute."

"*Gringos* always look pale," Maria said, dropping her cigarette butt onto the floor and grinding it into oblivion under her shoe. She walked briskly back into the kitchen.

"I guess I better go, Señor Graves," Coronado said. "What time you gonna open tonight?"

I had been so focused on the day that I had completely forgotten to set an actual time. "Time? Er, what time is it now? Damn and blast, my watch stopped. How about, five o'clock? I should write that down on the blackboard." I began looking for the blackboard, as a feeling of dread descended.

"Coronado turned towards the front door. "*Adios*, Loretta."

"*Adios*, Coronado," she replied. "Why are you staring at me like that, Bennie?"

I felt as if I were in a hypnotic trance as words spewed out of me like a carronade. "Staring? Am I? Sorry, a bit wobbly is all. Shall we continue our preparations? Does Maria need additional assistance in the kitchen? Right, then, we shall need to set up the tables first. Do we have sufficient glasses? . . . I should check the storeroom . . . And serviettes, too . . . Then I need to scribe the menu on the chalkboard . . . Chalk!—"

"Bennie, you need to calm down. Bennie!" Loretta shook my shoulder. "Bennie," she repeated, softly. "We have plenty of time. Relax. Go over to Rudy's and get away from here. Have a drink. It's early, but maybe that's what you need."

I emerged from the trance and exhaled deeply. "I'm sorry, Loretta. Perhaps you're right. I shan't be long."

"Take your time. I'll set up."

I stood up and walked towards the front door and saw Paco trotting casually down the steps. "Loretta, would you mind asking Maria to shoot that damned dog?"

As the eyes adjusted to the dim light inside Rudy's, I espied Coronado at his usual spot, beer bottles arranged before him. I sat down heavily in the seat next to his.

"*Hola*, Señor Graves. You getting a drink before the big night?"

"Something like that." I turned to Antonio, whose diminutive figure stood behind the bar. "Coffee, please, Antonio. And perhaps a little whisky to put into it."

"You okay, Señor Graves?" he asked in a squeaky voice. "You look like you seen a ghost or something."

"*Híjole*. What kind of ghost did you see, Señor Graves?"

"Does she know, Coronado? Does Loretta know you're her father?"

Coronado looked about stealthily. "Nobody knows except Rudy. And you, I guess."

"How could you keep it a secret?"

"I dunno, Señor Graves. I didn't know for a couple of years. Her mom and I, you know, it was just a one night thing. She got married a few months later to Billy Alvarez and they moved to Santa Fe. One day, I was walking out of Joe's store and I saw her with a baby in a stroller. It was Loretta. Then her mom looked at me real funny. I asked her what was wrong, but she just walked away."

"You mean, Loretta's mother never said you were the father?"

"No. But Loretta looks kinda like me."

I imagined her countenance devolving into that of Coronado's. "I don't see any resemblance."

"I guess that's good, huh, Señor Graves, to keep it a secret?"

"Yes, I suppose it is. Let sleeping dogs lie, eh? I finished the whisky-laced coffee and excused myself, then walked to Rudy's office. He was poring over some sort of accounts book.

"I say, Rudy, may I have a word?"

"Hey, Bennie. Thought you were your uncle for a second. Big night tonight, huh? I'm surprised to see you here. Thought you'd be screaming around the cafe."

"Well, I was actually. Loretta suggested I relax for a bit."

"You getting sweet on her?"

"No. Well, I suppose I am, despite trying not to. I can't imagine it's reciprocated. Besides, my track record is rather poor."

Rudy waved his hand dismissively. "Hell, I been married and divorced four times, Bennie. You can't let a little heartache stop you."

"I do have one question for you."

"Shoot."

"It's a delicate matter."

"Just say what's on your mind, Bennie. I can take it."

"It's about Loretta."

"So you are getting sweet on her."

"It's just, with Coronado telling me he is her father—"

"He said that?"

"Well, there is a resemblance. Plus, she said *híjole* earlier today, and Coronado is the only other person I've heard say that. He said you were the only one who knew, so, well, is she?"

Rudy sighed and leaned back in his chair. "Bennie, you want my advice?"

"I suppose so."

"Everybody in this town is related to everybody else. We're all a bunch of mongrels. Coronado told me that story about seeing Loretta in the stroller and her mother looking at him all funny. Is he her father? Who the hell knows? As far as I'm concerned, Billy Alvarez was her father, God rest his soul. I never asked Loretta's mother and I sure as hell wouldn't ask now. So, my advice to you, for what it's worth, is to get your *gringo* ass back to the cafe and make sure Esperanza and Maria don't fuck up everything. ¿*Comprende*?" He leaned forwards and smiled.

I stood there, contemplating his advice. "Thanks, Rudy. That helps."

"No charge, Bennie. That's what bartenders are for."

I walked back outside, squinted in the bright sunshine, and returned to the cafe. The enemy was about to be engaged and I was prepared to lead the charge into battle.

# Chapter 20

F ewer than five hours remained until we opened. Loretta
had set up all of the tables and unfolded the remaining recalcitrant chairs. I had inscribed a menu on the
chalkboard—beef and chicken *enchiladas, tamales de Maria,
menudo, carne adovada*, and green chile stew, as well as fresh *tortillas* and *sopapillas*. The acrid smell of the *menudo* had vanished,
replaced by the warm smell of chile.

As I looked around, I noticed Loretta had set out decora-
tions, hanging strips of red crepe paper along the walls and the
edges of each table. She had even cleaned the pool of urine
Paco had left at the front door.

In the kitchen, Maria and Loretta were preparing some sort
of dough, whilst steam rose from a large stew pot. The heat
was stifling and the back door had been thrown open for ven-
tilation. A small fan spun around loudly. From a radio in the
corner, a voice was jabbering away in Spanish. Both Maria and
Loretta were wiping perspiration from their foreheads.

"Hullo, all. Loretta, the dining room looks spot on."

"Thanks, Bennie. Are you feeling better?"

"I am, and I'm sorry for babbling earlier. I spoke with Rudy.
He offered some comforting advice."

"Could you hand me that can of baking powder behind
you? It's the red one."

I turned around, spotted the red can, and handed it to her.
"Shouldn't I be doing something?"

Maria looked up and scowled. "Don't worry, you gonna be
working real hard tonight. If Esperanza don't show up, I don't
know what we're gonna do."

"Still no sign of her? Maybe that's for the best."

"She wants the cafe to open, she goddamn better show up and help."

"She was with Hector earlier."

"Loretta told me what happened." Maria allowed herself a brief smile.

"Did you go to the bank?" Loretta asked.

"Bank? Right, we'll need some change for the cash register. How much will we need?"

"Maybe a hundred dollars."

"Right, I'll be back soon."

As I stepped out the front door, I espied Paco, who was trotting towards me. He stopped abruptly and growled at me.

"Caught in the act, eh?" I growled back and waived my arms like an orangutan. The dog raised its ears, then dropped its head and retreated down the road towards Rudy's.

As I walked down the steps, Esperanza's lorry careened to stop in front of the cafe, narrowly missing me. She staggered out and slammed the door shut.

"Kind of you to show up."

The pink satin robe was gone, replaced with a pair of grease-stained jeans and a green short-sleeve shirt. The words "Mack Trucks" and a picture of a rather ferocious looking bulldog were emblazoned on the shirt, which also had a large hole that exposed her navel.

"We got any coffee, *Pendejito*? I gotta sober up."

"I don't know. You can ask Maria and Loretta, or make some yourself. Did Hector recover from his, er, accidental fall?"

"He got a sprained ankle and drove back to Santa Fe." Esperanza's eyes drilled into me. "You got lucky, *Pendejito*. He don't remember nothing."

I shrugged. As frightened as I was that Hector would tear me limb from limb, the cafe's maiden voyage was a more immediate concern. "You are going to help us, aren't you? If not, I suggest you to speak with Maria."

"*Sí, Pendejito*. What you need done?"

"Now? Perhaps you could stand guard to ensure that Paco does not urinate on the front door for the remainder of the afternoon."

"Shoot the fucking dog."

"The idea has crossed my mind."

I stared at Esperanza's outfit and shook my head.

"What's wrong with what I got on?"

"You'll be waiting tables, Esperanza. Can't you dress in something a bit more appropriate than grease-stained trousers and that loathsome shirt? Perhaps even something clean?"

"*Vete a la chingada, Pendejito.*"

The Graves spine stiffened. "Not this time, Esperanza. You agreed to do what I said, or have you forgotten that already? Either change into presentable attire or go inside and tell Maria why you won't be helping us this evening."

She extracted a crumpled package of cigarettes from her pocket, removed one, and set it alight, blowing the resulting cloud of smoke into my face. "It ain't gonna make much difference how I'm dressed."

Esperanza paused to refill her lungs with smoke and then blew a second cloud towards me. "We open at five? I'll come back later."

She raised her middle finger and sped away.

Wondering what had possessed me to succumb to Uncle Bill's pleadings, I departed for the bank. It was a small outpost of the same bank at which I had an account in Santa Fe.

I wrote out a cheque. The middle-aged clerk, whose bulk and eyes resembled a fairer sex version of Coronado, sat at her desk reading a magazine.

"I would like to cash this please," I said, mustering artificial cheer, as I handed her the cheque.

She put the magazine on her desk, squinted at the cheque, and threw it back at me. "I can't cash this."

"Why not? I have an account here."

"So? I ain't ever seen you before."

"Nor have I seen you. Besides, I usually conduct my banking in Santa Fe."

"Like I said, I ain't ever seen you." She stared at me over the tops of her spectacles, and then resumed reading her magazine.

"You must know my Uncle? William Graves? El Vaquero?"

"*Sí*, I know El Vaquero."

"Well, I'm his nephew, Benjamin."

"You don't look like him. And, he don't talk funny like you."

"That's because he's lived in the States for decades. Surely you can call the Santa Fe branch and verify I have an account with them."

"I could, but that don't mean you're who you say you are. You got some identification?"

"Identification? Of course I do." I extracted my London driver's licence from the billfold and handed it to her.

She squinted at the licence and returned it dismissively.

"This licence ain't any good."

"What do you mean, no good? It has my picture. Granted, the photography is rather poor."

"Yeah, I guess it looks like you."

"Well?"

"It expired in January."

"It's valid until next December."

"You think I can't read? Your licence expired on January twelfth." I realized suddenly the source of her confusion.

"Madam, if I may explain, in England we write our dates differently than you do in the States. Ours are written day-month-year, whereas you write them month-day-year. That is why you have wrongly concluded my licence expired on January the twelfth. One-twelve. It means one December, the first day of December. My licence is quite valid."

"I don't care, *gringo*. Come back when you got a real New Mexico driver's licence that ain't expired. Then maybe I'll cash your cheque."

"But I need cash now, for the till at the cafe."

"What cafe?"

"Dos Abuelas. We reopen is tonight."

"Esperanza and Maria are opening again?"

"Yes. Tonight."

"Who are you?"

"I just told you, Benjamin Graves. You must know about the cafe?"

"Sure, I used to eat there sometimes, until it closed."

"Well, we're reopening tonight. You can even have dinner. No charge."

"You trying to bribe me, *gringo*?"

"No. We're offering our customers dinner for free. Maria has been preparing for days—*enchiladas, tamales, carne avocado*, even manure, I mean, *menudo*."

The woman's face softened into a far-away, overfed look.

"Maria is making *menudo*?"

"Yes. I say, madam, do you know Coronado de Vaca?"

"Coronado? *Sí*, he's my brother. What'd he do now?"

"He knows me quite well. Perhaps I could ask him to vouchsafe for me?"

"You know Coronado?"

"He was the first person I encountered when I arrived in Vaca Seca. He's helping with tonight's opening."

"Coronado's helping Maria and Esperanza? He told me he tried to shoot a skunk living under the cafe. I don't like skunks. When we were kids, our dog was always getting sprayed at night."

"He did inform me about your unfortunate family pet."

"I hear the cafe is gonna open again."

"I just told you that."

Her mental resemblance to Coronado had become clear, as was the de Vaca ability to set one's blood percolating heavily in the veins. "Coronado said something about a Señor Graves and the cafe. That you?"

By now, I felt as if I were conversing with an overstuffed aardvark. I glanced at the clock on the wall, which was nearing two o'clock.

"Yes . . . that . . . is . . . me. Now, if you will excuse me, I really must get back to the cafe. By the way, does your brother cash cheques here?" She smiled aimlessly. "Sure, I always cash cheques for Coronado.

Sometimes, he buys things for me from Joe Garcia's store—he gets an employee discount."

"How thoughtful of him. Good day, Madam." I turned around and walked out, convinced the de Vaca clan had been cast out from Hell for annoying Lucifer himself.

I sped off in the lorry, bound for Joe's store, where I hoped I would find Coronado. Inside, I espied not Coronado, but Joe himself.

"What do you want, *gringo*? I hope nobody comes tonight and you close tomorrow."

"Thanks for the kind wishes, Joe. Is Coronado is about?"

"Yeah. He's in back. What do you need him for?"

"Er, I have a small favour to ask of him."

"I dunno why he helps you or those two *pendejas*."

"Sorry, Joe, I simply don't have time for this. I was asked to restore the cafe to financial health. Esperanza and Maria owed you a significant amount of brass, and you were paid. Surely you must understand why we are purchasing supplies from Sabrosa Foods. I mean, you purchase supplies for your store, do you not?"

"That's different!" His eyes widened and flakes of spittle appearing on his lips. "I ain't not some big goddamn place like Sabrosa Foods. The owners, the Trujillos, they got stores in Albuquerque and Las Cruces, too. And one of the other brothers, he owns the Coors distributorship and the Coke bottling franchise. You know how they got started?"

"I haven't the vaguest idea. Why?"

"Emiliano Trujillo, the grandfather, was a bootlegger during Prohibition. Everybody in northern New Mexico got their liquor from him."

"Well, an odd bit of history, your Prohibition and all that. But what relevance does that have to our purchasing supplies? Prohibition ended in, well, a long time ago."

"I didn't have no bootlegger grandfather making lots of money for me. I had to work for what I got."

Joe bent down below the cash register and retrieved a bottle of whisky. He took a large pull and stared out the front window.

"Look, Joe, perhaps we can discuss this later. I simply must speak with Coronado immediately."

Coronado had waddled up to the front unseen. "*Hola*, Señor Graves. You ready for tonight?"

I glanced nervously at my watch. It was now half two. "Ah, there you are. Yes, just about. Coronado, could you do me rather a large favour?"

"Sure."

I handed him the cheque. "Would you see your sister at the bank, and cash this immediately? We need some change and your sister refused to accept my driver's licence as identification."

He scanned the check closely, which was odd considering he could not read. "You want me tell my sister to cash your check? She's gonna go to the cafe with me tonight."

"Coronado, your sister will close the bank in one half hour. Can you please go there and cash the cheque immediately? I must get back to the cafe."

"Okay, Señor Graves. You want me to stop at the County Clerk's office and ask Lupe to bring you an ID? She gonna be at the cafe tonight, too."

"What? Thank you, no, Coronado. Just the bank."

I waved him off and ran back to the cafe. The front door was still urine-free, raising hopes that Paco had exhausted his supply for the time being. I stepped inside and found Maria sitting down at one of the dining room tables, cigarette in hand. Loretta sat across from her. In front of each was a bottle of beer.

"Hi, Bennie" Loretta said.

"You got our cash?" Maria asked.

"No. You might have told me that the bank clerk was Coronado's sister."

"How come she wouldn't give you any money?"

"Identification. Well, lack thereof, at least according to her. I couldn't convince her that my driver's licence is valid."

"What are we gonna do?" Maria asked.

"I asked Coronado to cash the cheque for me."

"*Ay cabron.*"

"What? Coronado is always quite sincere."

"I dunno what he is, but when he's got money, he goes to Rudy's."

"Then I'll ask Rudy for some cash. I should have done that in the first place."

Maria took a large pull of beer. "How come Esperanza didn't come in? What you tell her?"

"I told her to change her clothing and wear something more presentable than greasy trousers and a ragged shirt. She promised to return before five o'clock. She might even be sober."

"You want a beer, Bennie?" Loretta asked.

"No thanks. Although I probably will several hours from now." I looked around the room. "Are you quite sure we're ready?"

Maria shrugged. "We just gotta wait until we open. Then it's gonna be hell."

I pulled out another chair from the table and sat down. "Perhaps I shall have that beer after all."

At half four, several townspeople were loitering about hungrily, waiting for the cafe to open.

Esperanza had not returned. Neither had Coronado. Maria retreated to the kitchen to begin her final preparations in anticipation of the soon-to-descend hordes. Loretta agreed to assume the initial waitressing duties, whilst I would help Maria in the kitchen.

Rudy and Uncle Bill walked inside, followed by two of the townspeople.

"You open now?" a largish, middle-aged chap asked with salivary anticipation.

"Not quite."

"How come Rudy and El Vaquero get to come in now?"

"Professional courtesy. Would the two of you care to wash some dishes?"

They looked at me with expressions of horror and quickly exited. I turned to Uncle Bill. "Well, what do you think?"

He inspected the room slowly and grinned. "Looks real good. All of you did great. Are the girls in the kitchen?"

"Maria and Loretta are. Whether Esperanza will return is somewhat doubtful."

"What happened?"

"She showed up several hours ago, in her cups and dressed appallingly."

Rudy looked at me and grimaced. "Not the pink robe?"

"Thankfully, no. Greasy trousers and a torn shirt with a loathsome picture of a bulldog. I mean, if she were in the kitchen, it wouldn't matter. But she is supposed to help serve."

"I dunno, El Vaquero," Rudy said. "What do you think?"

"Hell, I'll help serve if that's what it takes. Goddamn her, anyway."

The crowd on the *portal* was growing in size and increasingly restless.

"Come on, open up," one shouted. "We're hungry." I heard a dog barking, but could not ascertain whether it was Paco, restored of urine and eager for another chance to lubricate the door.

Esperanza arrived and shoved her way through the crowd. "Get out of my way, you fucking *lobos*, or nobody's gonna eat." To my surprise, she was wearing dark trousers and a clean white shirt.

"Glad you decided to show up, Esperanza," Uncle Bill said. "Otherwise, I was gonna have to do your job."

"You see all of those people, El Vaquero? *Estamos jodidos.*"

Uncle Bill looked out the front window. "Bennie, it's quarter till. What d'ya say we let 'em in now?"

"In for a penny," I replied. "Ready, Loretta?"

Loretta stood up, walked over towards the cash register and retrieved two ordering books, one of which she tossed to Esperanza. "Okay, Bennie."

"Esperanza?"

"I don't care," she growled.

"Rudy, would you and Uncle Bill care to greet our guests?"

"Okay, Bennie." They both stood up slowly. Uncle Bill shoved his hands into his trouser pockets. With his bowed legs, he looked as if he were ready to draw his six-guns like a Zane Grey sheriff.

"Right, I'm off to the kitchen."

As I walked through the kitchen door, I could hear the dull roar of the crowd, who now filled the dining room. "Here we go, Maria."

Several minutes passed, as the customers ordered their drinks and reviewed the menu I had scrawled on the blackboard. Loretta was the first to come in with an order. "Two orders of chicken *enchiladas*, one bowl of *menudo*, and one order of *tamales*."

Maria used her cigarette to point me to the cauldron of *menudo* and the large bowls filled with the raw materials for the *enchiladas*. "You remember how I showed you to make *enchiladas*?"

"Er, yes, I believe so. Layer the corn tortillas that have been dipped in red chile sauce, spread chicken, onion, and cheese, repeat same for second layer, place under broiler until the cheese melts, pour over molten green chile sauce, and Bob's your Uncle."

"Who the fuck is Uncle Bob? You get the *enchiladas* ready. I got oil ready for the *sopapillas*. You gotta do those, too. Be careful. Remember what I tell you, okay?"

"Not to worry, Maria." I prepared the plates of *enchiladas* as instructed. Then, after retrieving the bubbling masses from the oven, ladled on *frijoles* and a mix of shredded lettuce and chopped tomato. As I set the completed plates down, Esperanza burst through the door, waving several order slips.

"Two *carne adovada* plates and two *menudos*," she shouted.

Loretta entered immediately behind her, waving about more slips of paper.

"You got my first order ready yet, Bennie?"

"Er, some of it. The *enchilada* plates are ready."

"I got the *tamales* and *menudo* ready," Maria growled. Loretta grabbed one of the large serving trays, assembled the four dishes, and disappeared behind a cloud of steam.

"Bennie, you start cooking *sopapillas*. Esperanza, tell that *pendejo* Rudy to come help me."

I turned my attention to the *sopapillas*. Maria had set out small squares of dough near the fryer, along with green baskets lined with waxed paper ready to receive them.

I picked up a square of dough and dropped it into the fryer. A plume of hot oil rose up, performed a treble somersault of Olympic beauty, paused to accept the adulation of the crowd, and landed on my right forearm.

"Gah! My arm!"

Maria shook her head and biffed me with the large metal spoon we were using to ladle out green chile sauce.

"Gah! My head!"

"*Estupido*. I told you, don't drop them. You gotta let them slip in. Then you won't get burned."

"All right. There's no need to inflict further bodily harm. Where do you keep a first aid kit?"

"What?"

"The first aid kit. Red Cross, Florence Nightingale, and all that. The arm will want burn cream and a sticking plaster."

"We don't got no first aid kit. I think Esperanza took it home. Go to the sink. Put cold water on your arm. The walls are plaster. What you want them for?"

"No, a sticking plaster, er, bandage. For my arm. To cover the bloody burn."

"Oh, *sí*. We got bandages in the cash register."

"Cash register?"

"Sometimes, Esperanza cut her finger on the bills. So we keep bandages there."

I ran cold water over my arm and wrapped it in a towel. The *sopapilla*, which was now a puffy black mass, continued to sizzle in the oil. I picked it up with a pair of tongs and tossed it into the rubbish bin, then walked into the main room, with the towel wound tightly around my arm. A large oaf, who was sitting at a table with his equally large spouse and several oafish-looking offspring, grabbed my newly crisped right arm. "Hey, *gringo*, you got our *sopapillas* yet?" he said gruffly.

"Gah!" I plucked my arm back from his grasp. "I mean, no, just another minute or two, if you please."

"Papa, I want my *sopapilla*," the youngest cried.

"You got to wait, Pedro. This *gringo*, he's gonna bring them out real soon, aren't you?" Papa oaf glared at me.

Arm throbbing and patience evaporated, I raised my voice above the din. "Don't call me *gringo* you larded twit. I am sick of being called *gringo* by you and everyone else."

Silence descended over the dining room as Papa oaf raised his ample girth from the chair. "You know who you're talking to, *gringo*?" he said, emphasizing the offending word.

"You resemble a pig of my acquaintance. Otherwise, no. And I don't especially care. Now, if you will pardon me, I must attend to a burned arm."

He turned to the still-seated members of the oaf family. "We're leaving. Now!"

"But we want our *sopapillas*, Papa," the offspring cried. "Shut the fuck up. We ain't ever coming here again." He turned back to me. "You're in real trouble, *gringo*."

The rest of the family stood up and followed Papa oaf out the door, looking like a brood of ducks.

Esperanza, who had been delivering drinks to a nearby table, stormed over to me. "Jesus, *Pendejito*," she whispered. "Don't you know who that is?"

"No." I rooted through the cash register, eventually locating several old sticking plasters. "He threatened me. I should alert the local constabulary."

"Huh?"

"The sheriff you once mentioned, the one who used to eat in the cafe."

Esperanza boxed my burned arm. "Gah!"

"That *was* Tiny Roybal, *Pendejito*. He's the fucking sheriff." I groaned.

"What happened?"

"I burned my arm. Oil from the fryer splashed onto it when I dropped a square of dough in for a *sopapilla*."

"You just slip them in—"

"Yes, I know. Maria told me. She also biffed me on the head with a large metal spoon."

"You better tell Tiny you're real sorry. We don't want no trouble from him."

"We may be rather beyond apologies."

I returned to the kitchen, just as Loretta was exiting with another tray of comestibles. She looked at the towel-wrapped arm. "Bennie, what happened?"

"Bit of an encounter with boiling oil, I'm afraid."

"Be careful. Do you want to wait tables? I can help Maria."

"I suppose. What does one do?"

"First, ask them what they want to drink. Then, if they ask questions, just tell them everything's good."

"Sounds straightforward. Let me Florence Nightingale my arm first."

I walked into the kitchen. Maria was moving quickly from one spot to another, preparing various plates, ladling *menudo* into bowls, and glaring at Rudy, who was addressing a growing stack of dishes. "Where the fuck you been? I got two plates of *carne adovada* and two *enchiladas*."

"Afraid I had a bit of an encounter with Tiny Roybal."

"What happened?"

"Nothing, really. I mean, well, he was rather upset about the tardiness of the offspring's *sopapillas*. Esperanza told me that you once had an, er, incident, with his father at Rudy's?"

"She did, Bennie," Rudy chimed, his hands buried in the sink. "*Mi querida*, she would have shot him, too."

"I ain't your goddamn *querida*, Rudy. I'm gonna take my gun and shoot you one of these days."

"You've been threatening to shoot me for years. You know you love me too much."

Maria rolled her eyes. "*Vete a la chingada*, Rudy. We got too much work to do."

Loretta came into the kitchen and helped me bandage the arm, then gave me her ordering book. "Stay calm, Bennie. Esperanza's tables are to the right of the door. Mine are to the left."

I walked into the dining room. The din of voices and clattering dishes was overwhelming. Several groups of diners had finished, and a large crowd was pressed against the front door awaiting their seating. I looked around and espied Uncle Bill, clearing off the empty tables.

"I say, Uncle Bill, there's no need for you to do that."

"Never mind, Bennie. I'm glad to help out." He was grinning widely. "I ain't seen the cafe this packed since . . . well, it's been a damn long time."

The line of townspeople outside waiting for a table remained steady for several hours. As fast as we fed and water them, more arrived. The evening was passing in a blur of order slips, heavily laden trays, and the loud din of voices echoing off the walls.

I approached a table with newly seated customers. As I took their drink orders, I heard Coronado's voice behind me.

"*Hola*, Señor Graves. You sure got a good crowd tonight."

I turned around and was met by two sets of rodentary eyes. "I'll be with you momentarily."

He reached into his shirt pocket and extracted a sheaf of bills, then handed it to me. "I got your money for you. I kinda forgot after I went to the bank, though."

"Not a problem, Coronado. Thanks."

"Five dollars is kinda missing. I stopped at Rudy's and I guess I spent it. Sorry. I can get it to you tomorrow, though."

I glanced at his sister, who seemed oblivious to the discussion. "Quite all right. Consider it payment for cashing that check. Would you care for something to drink?"

"Sure. You got iced tea?"

"Of course. And for you, madam?"

"Beer."

"Beer, eh? Do you have any identification? We mustn't serve alcohol to the underage."

"You want ID? From me?"

"Cafe policy, I'm afraid." She handed me her driver's licence, which I glanced at momentarily and returned. "Sorry, I can't accept this."

"Huh? That's my New Mexico driver's licence."

"Yes, I know. But it's expired. Would you care for an iced tea, instead?"

She folded her ample arms across her equally ample bosom. "You're just mad because I wouldn't cash your goddamn cheque this afternoon. I gotta follow the rules—the bank's rules."

"And I follow the rules—Graves's rules. Now, what would you like for dinner?"

She pursed her lips tartly and refused to speak. "Coronado?"

Coronado looked at me like a dog anticipating its supper. "I want Maria's *tamales*."

"Madam? Do you wish to order?"

"No. Okay, bring me some *enchiladas*. Look, *gringo*, next time, I'll cash your cheque. Now can I have a beer?"

"No. And don't call me *gringo*. I've already spoken to one overly rude chap about that."

"Okay, I won't call you *gringo* no more. Now can I get a beer?"

"Sorry, but we don't have a licence to sell alcoholic beverages. You can purchase beer at Rudy's and bring it in here."

"No beer?"

"Not a dram."

She turned to Coronado and muttered something in machine-gun Spanish, rolling her eyes in my direction. Coronado laughed momentarily, then looked at me sheepishly. "Sorry, Señor Graves."

I retreated from their table and retreated to the kitchen, which was ablaze with activity. Maria was madly preparing plates of comestibles. Loretta had tamed the deep fryer, which was now disgorging perfectly cooked *sopapillas*. Rudy stood washing dishes, which Uncle Bill was bringing to him.

Suddenly, I heard a rising commotion that bore the distinct trademark of Esperanza's voice. I bolted into the dining room and observed her standing athwart the front door, yelling outside in Spanish. All other conversation in the dining room had ceased. I delivered the bowls of *menudo* to their owners and hurried over to Esperanza. "What in bloody hell is going on?"

"Fucking Joe Garcia, that's what. *Hijo de puta*."

She grabbed my arm and pulled me outside. In the fading light, I espied Joe, weaving in the middle of the street, his right hand wrapped around what looked like a large bottle of whisky.

"Don't eat here!" he yelled skywards, waving his arms wildly. "Don't nobody eat at the fucking cafe."

Joe pointed the bottle towards me. "*Gringo*! I got my pride." He lifted the bottle to his lips, took a large pull, and continued his rant. "You think you're too good for Joe Garcia? I'll show you."

He started to approach us, ranting loudly in Spanish. A crowd of customers who had been hovering around the front door dispersed. "How about something to eat Joe? Maria has made some rather enticing dishes. *Tamales, carne adovada*, her *enchiladas* of course, even *menudo*."

"I ain't gonna eat nothing here, *gringo*. I'm gonna burn the fucking cafe down." He pulled a match box out of his left trouser pocket and held it up.

I turned to Esperanza. "I suppose calling the Sheriff is out of the question?"

"After what you said? What the fuck do you think, *Pendejito*?" Still tightly grasping the bottle, Joe fumbled with the match box.

Retrieving one, he struck it against the box, looking like a spasmodic symphony conductor. "Gonna burn your cafe, Esperanza. You and Maria, and you *gringo*, you're all gonna be sorry."

He tossed the burning match towards the *portal*. The flame extinguished itself before it landed.

"Joe, please stop. It simply won't do."

"¡*Vete a la chingada!*, *gringo*! You, too, pendeja."

"I'm gonna shoot your *cojones* off, Joe!" Esperanza shouted.

He bent over, placed the whisky bottle on the first step to the porch, stood up, returned the match box to his trouser pocket, undid his belt, dropped his trousers and lowered his underpants to his knees. Then he stood up straight. "You want to shoot my *cojones*? ¡*Aqui estan mis cojones!*"

Esperanza burst out laughing. "¡*Ay, cabrón*! I guess maybe I can't shoot your *cojones*, Joe. They're too small to see."

Under normal circumstances I would have chortled at such derogation, but Esperanza's remarks increased Joe's anger. He recaptured his modesty, belted his trousers, and staggered up the stairs until he stood directly before us. The unmistakable odour of whisky permeated the air.

"Joe, perhaps, you should leave. We can discuss the situation tomorrow, when you are sober."

"I ain't going nowhere, *gringo*. And I'm gonna be here tomorrow and the next day, and the day after that." He glared at me venomously.

Before I could respond, Maria stepped outside, shotgun in hand. The cavalry had arrived.

She levelled the gun at his vulnerable bits. "Maybe I'm gonna shoot you, Joe, 'cause of that fucking snake."

Joe froze. "Don't shoot Maria," he whimpered. "I'm real sorry about the snake. You know I work hard. The store, it's all I got. You always bought from me."

"You think we don't work hard?"

"Sure, but the *gringo*, he don't know nothing."

"Don't you call Señor Bennie *gringo* no more, Joe. We're open again 'cause of him."

Joe stared at me, but said nothing.

"Joe," I said calmly, "how about something to eat?"

Esperanza turned to me. "You gonna let that *pendejo* eat? For free? After this?"

"Well, Joe?"

Joe swayed lightly. "You got some more *tamales*, Maria?"

"*Sí.*" Maria grabbed his arm tightly and walked him inside.

"I don't understand you, *Pendejito*," Esperanza said.

I sighed deeply. "I suppose that makes two of us."

A large group of customers walked out outside. "*Muy sabroso*, Esperanza," one of them remarked. "Just like the old days. Is it gonna be free tomorrow night? I'll come back for sure."

"You better come back and pay for your dinner, Carlos. Or we'll go out of business again."

"*Sí*, Esperanza. We're gonna come back, even if we got to pay."

Esperanza looked over to the corner, where a group still waiting was huddled. "Well, you *lobos* want to eat or not?

Esperanza and I walked back inside. The dining room was again humming. In a corner, Joe Garcia was devouring his plate of *tamales*, *refritos*, and rice. I glanced contentedly about the room. Uncle Bill's dream had been realized.

At nine o'clock, the dining room was still full, and the menu had been reduced to *menudo* and cheese-and-onion-filled *enchiladas*.

Everyone was exhausted. Standing at the sink washing dishes, Rudy complained about his back. Uncle Bill looked haggard from gathering dishes and cleaning tables all evening. Loretta's hair was plastered to her forehead.

"Two bowls of *menudo*, and one plate of *enchiladas* Maria," I said.

"We still got people waiting? I don't got much food left."

"I think we've reached port, Maria. A straggler or two, but no more than that."

"*Bueno.*" She quickly assembled the *enchiladas* and threw the plate into the oven, then grabbed two bowls and ladled out the *menudo*. After she extracted the plate and added the *refritos* and rice, I placed the items on the large serving tray and returned to the dining room. As I walked towards the table of three diners with their order, I saw another couple depart. The woman opened the front door and walked outside, followed by what I assumed was her husband. As he stepped out, another guest—an unwelcome one—bounded through the door. "Gah!" I dropped the tray. The two bowls of *menudo* crashed to the floor, launching white, gelatinous pieces towards the wall. The *enchiladas* lay in a heap. Everyone in the room turned towards me; they had not seen the new arrival in their midst.

From the corner of my eye, I espied our guest heading towards the corner of the building behind the cash register.

"Everyone, we seem to have a rather unwelcome, er, visitor on the premises. Please stay calm."

"What are you talking about?" asked the woman whose *enchilada* plate was now in pieces on the floor. "Who's here?"

I was about to explain, when she screamed—one of those high-pitched sorts of screams one hears in horror films. The other diners looked towards the corner. In unison, they rock-eted out of their chairs and fled through the front door. The woman who had screamed seemed paralyzed; she was carried off by the two chaps with her.

Rudy burst through the kitchen door, followed by Uncle Bill, Maria, Esperanza, and Loretta. "Jesus, Bennie, what happened?"

"Please everyone, stop! Don't move." I pointed towards the corner behind the cash register. They looked in that direction.

"*Dios mio,*" Maria whimpered. She and Loretta ran back into the kitchen. Esperanza vanished out the front door.

Standing before us was the same contented-looking skunk I had seen escape from underneath the cafe, unscathed by Coronado's fusillade. It eyed Uncle Bill, Rudy, and I indifferently, then looked towards the kitchen door behind us.

"C'mon, Bennie," Uncle Bill shouted. "Let's get the hell out of here. If it sprays, we're never gonna reopen." He and Rudy beat a hasty retreat, running out the front door and towards the safety of the bar.

The skunk looked at me with the same skunk-may-care smile I had seen when it emerged from the rubble. It moved towards me, its tail undulating slowly.

"Oh, please, no. We've had a most successful evening. Let's not spoil it."

The skunk smiled and moved closer. Then, espying the fallen mass, it detoured and sniffed.

I gave it a wide berth, moving to starboard towards the kitchen door. "Do please, help yourself. Maria's cooking is highly recommended. There's a good chap."

It lapped up the *enchiladas* greedily, leaving the onions, then consumed the *refritos* and rice. Apparently sated, it walked towards the front door, which was wide open. Reaching the threshold, it turned around and looked at me again. Its tail shuddered and I braced myself for a full-out olfactory assault. Instead, it turned around and walked out into the night.

Exhausted, the nerves still quavering, I turned out the lights and locked the front door.

# Chapter 21

The next morning, I was still recovering from the crisis and the two large whiskies I had consumed for their analgaesic effects. As I arrived at the cafe, Coronado awaited.

"Señor Graves, is it true? ¡*Hijole*!"

I stifled a large yawn. "About the skunk? I'm afraid it is."

"A skunk?"

"Yes. The same skunk you attempted to shoot, but managed to miss whilst destroying the cafe. It returned last night."

"I didn't know about a skunk, Señor Graves. Did the mountain lion kill it?"

"Pardon?"

"The mountain lion. The one that attacked Dora Esquivel? Did it eat the skunk, too?"

The grey matter fought to emerge from yet another thick de Vaca fog. "Mountain lion? Dora Esquivel?"

"*Sí*. Joe said he saw everybody run out and then heard Dora scream. He says God's real mad at you 'cause you're buying supplies from Sabrosa Foods and not him."

"He said that, eh?" The fog was burning off. "Let's go inside, Coronado."

Coronado's glanced about fearfully. "You think it's safe?"

"Well, you would be a most tempting meal for any mountain lion. However, having devoured—did you say Dora Esquivel?—last night, I am certain the mountain lion is sated."

I entered the kitchen, followed closely by Coronado. Maria, who looked far more haggard than I felt, had already begun the evening's preparations, although I doubted anyone would dine with us. The skunk was trouble enough; if the local populace was gullible enough to believe Joe Garcia's idiotic rumours, then we were finished.

"Good morning, Maria. I am going to make coffee for Coronado and me. Care for a cuppa?"

"Coffee? *Sí, gracias.*"

"By the way, Coronado heard a most interesting rumour this morning about last night."

"About the skunk?"

"No, the mountain lion. One which devoured—"

"Dora Esquivel," Coronado interjected. "Joe told me he heard her scream."

Maria looked up from the pot of red chile sauce she was stirring "*¿Que?* Joe told you a mountain lion came in here last night?" She muttered a staccato of obscenities. "When was the last time you seen a mountain lion?"

"Never, I guess."

Maria was spinning into a rage. "Joe Garcia told you a fucking mountain lion ate Dora Esquivel?"

"*Sí.*"

"*Estupido!* It was the skunk. The fucking skunk you tried to shoot!"

"Did it attack Dora Esquivel, too?"

"*¡Ay cabrón!* The skunk didn't attack nobody. And you know Dora Esquivel never leaves her house."

"Oh. I forgot. But Joe said he heard her scream."

"How come you believe whatever Joe says?"

Before Coronado could answer, I said, "Coronado, the only thing the skunk attacked last night was a plate of Maria's *enchiladas* I dropped on the floor. It must have enjoyed the meal, because it walked out the front door afterwards."

"No mountain lion, Señor Graves?"

"No mountain lion. No herd of rampaging elephants. No plague of locusts. Only a single, smiling, shotgun-evading, *enchilada*-consuming skunk."

"Everybody thinks it was a mountain lion."

I sighed, one of my exasperated I-cannot-take-anymore-of-this sighs that had become far too common. "Coronado, do you see blood on the floor? Did you check in on Dora Esquivel this morning? If she never leaves the house, you can easily determine if she's been devoured. She might even tell you herself."

"You think I should ask her, Señor Graves?"

"I do. Let us know what she says."

The coffee was ready, and I poured out three cups. "Would you do me a small favour, Coronado?"

"Sure."

"Would you please tell everyone you see there was no mountain lion? Tell them the cafe will be open this evening and is perfectly safe."

"Should I tell Joe there was no mountain lion, too? I gotta get back to the store real soon."

"An excellent idea."

Coronado beamed, gulped his coffee noisily, and departed.

"I'm gonna shoot that *pendejo's cojones* off."

"Whether you are referring to Joe, Coronado, or both, I understand the sentiment. But perhaps we should be more circumspect."

"*¿Que?*"

"I mean, Joe is angry because we aren't buying supplies from him."

"So?"

"Well, if the cafe were to close because of his idiotic rumours, then we won't be buying anything from him, will we?"

"Some people are gonna believe anything Joe says."

"Then we best have a chat with him soon, before the damage spreads further."

I inhaled deeply. The chile-ish vapours that permeated the kitchen tickled the olfactory like champagne bubbles. "Smells delicious."

"Have you seen Loretta?"

"I told her to come at eleven. She worked real hard yesterday."

I glanced at my watch. It was half nine. "Yes, I know." I paused to clear the throat. "Well, I'll begin washing-up. Once Loretta arrives, you and I can pay Joe a visit."

"I think Loretta likes you. She said you're a lot like El Vaquero."

My face reddened. "Really?"

"*Sí*. She told me last night."

"That's kind of her. Rudy told me she's broken many a heart, and one can understand why. But I will be returning to England soon."

"You gonna leave?"

"Not yet, no. I promised Uncle Bill I would stay until the cafe is under full sail. Unless, of course, we strike a reef and sink or, like some land-locked Jonah, are swallowed by a mountain lion."

I spent the next hour or so cleaning off tables, washing dishes, and scrubbing the dining room floor. As I was finishing, Loretta walked in.

"Hi, Bennie. Have you been here long?"

"A few hours. I was just getting the room cleaned up. It was quite a mess, what with everyone having abandoned ship, as it were, because of the skunk."

"I'm sorry I left you. I was so tired I just went home."

"No apology necessary. It was quite a panic."

She sniffed the air cautiously. "Did it spray?"

"Thankfully, no. Odd bugger, that skunk. It ate the plate of *enchiladas* I dropped and then walked out the front door. Seemed quite content."

"Really? Do you think it will come back?"

"I hope not. Simply won't do to have customers madly dashing for the door each night. Perhaps we should set out a plate by the back door, a peace offering of sorts."

"Like for the *Santos*."

"Eh?"

"We call them *ofrendas*, offerings. You set them out on All Saints Day. It's supposed to bring good luck."

"Is there a patron saint of skunks?"

Loretta laughed. "Not that I know of, but maybe there should be."

"Loretta?"

"Yes, Bennie?"

"Thanks for all of your help. We wouldn't have survived last night without you."

"Of course you would have. Besides, I like working here. It's a lot more interesting than the doctor's office."

She reached her hand out and placed it on my bandaged arm. I enveloped her hand in mine and squeezed it gently. "Nothing about Vaca Seca has been dull. Barking mad, yes, but not dull."

"Does that include me?"

"No, you seem wonderfully sane."

Maria came out from the kitchen and I quickly withdrew my hand. "Er, would you mind taking over in the kitchen? Maria and I need to speak with your Uncle Joe."

"Uncle Joe? Is it another snake?"

"Thankfully, not. A mountain lion."

Loretta's eyes widened. "A mountain lion? In Vaca Seca?"

"Only an imaginary one. Joe has spread a rumour—quite effectively, too—that a mountain lion came into the cafe last night and devoured Dora Esquivel. And Coronado, whose credulity seems boundless, has been doing his bit to spread the rumour."

"Why would Uncle Joe say that?"

"Because I told your uncle we were purchasing goods from Sabrosa Foods, whose prices are rather less than your uncle's. We're going to, er, see if we can reach an agreement of sorts with him."

"I'm sorry about my uncle. He's always been real nice to me. I can talk to him." She looked at me expectantly.

"Er, well, I suppose you could try. Kill him with kindness, rather than a shotgun. What do you think, Maria?"

Maria pulled out a cigarette. "*Sí*. You want to take my shotgun? Then you can shoot him if he don't listen to Loretta."

"No. If we can't convince him, then I'm sure you will."

Maria nodded and turned to Loretta. "You tell your Uncle he better stop if he wants to keep his *cojones*."

"You wouldn't really shoot him, would you, *Tia* Maria?"

Maria inhaled deeply, then filled the room with grey-blue smoke. She looked at Loretta, but said nothing.

"Right, off we go." I grabbed Loretta's arm and escorted her out the kitchen door.

"I've never seen *Tia* Maria look that way. Do you think she means it?"

I had seen Maria look that way on an almost daily basis, but decided it would be cruel to frighten Loretta. "I'm sure Joe will understand the situation. Besides, he should favour what I intend to propose."

We walked to the store and stepped inside. Joe was sitting by the counter, holding a large mug of coffee to his forehead.

"Hi, Uncle Joe," Loretta said. "Are you Okay?"

He groaned. "How come you're here with the *gringo*?"

"You be nice to Bennie, Uncle Joe. And stop calling him *gringo*."

"Why? He's a *gringo* and he don't belong here."

"You're quite right, Joe," I said. "I don't belong and will depart soon. But until then, there is the matter of this absurd rumour you have spread."

"What rumour? I didn't say nothing about no mountain lion."

I sighed again. "Look, Joe, I was hoping we could reach an agreement. The cafe will purchase some of our dry goods from your store. Of course, with this mountain lion rumour running amok, the cafe may soon close, and then we won't be purchasing anything."

"How much we talking about?"

"Perhaps forty dollars each week for supplies. Two thousand dollars a year."

Joe's eyes glittered like diamonds. "Two thousand dollars?"

"But I'm afraid the rumour is spreading quickly. Coronado stopped by the cafe this morning, convinced it was true."

"Coronado? Don't believe nothing he says."

"Uncle Joe, can't you tell everybody the rumour isn't true? If the cafe closes, I won't have a job." She offered him one of those doe-eyed looks for which the fairer sex is so famous.

"Uh, okay, Loretta. So, when do you think you're gonna need more supplies?"

"Ah, well, that depends. I mean, we may close after tonight."

"You can't close. I'm gonna talk to everybody, tell them there was no mountain lion."

Joe paused. "What really happened?"

"Do you remember the skunk Coronado attempted to shoot? It came back last night. Walked through the front door and, well, that was the end of the evening. It enjoyed Maria's cooking—*enchiladas*, *refritos*, and rice."

"You fed the skunk?"

"Not intentionally. I dropped the plate I was carrying. Doesn't like onions."

"A skunk's just a furry rat. I got some rat poison I can sell you. Works real good."

Poisoning the creature struck me as unnecessarily cruel, not that I was fond of rats, furry or otherwise. Besides, it didn't seem to bear us any ill will, despite Coronado's onslaught. Then again, a purchase might further mollify Joe.

"Perhaps a bit of poison would be good to have, just in case."

"I got some real good stuff. Two-fifty a box."

"Er, how about two boxes?" I removed the billfold and extracted a five-dollar bill, handing it over to him with a flourish.

"You need more, you let me know. I've got lots in back."

"Thank you, Joe. I hope this takes care of the problem, I mean, the skunk. We'll keep it to ourselves."

Joe held a finger to his lips. "I won't tell nobody." He looked at Loretta and smiled. "You work real hard, Loretta. Make lotsa money, too."

"I will, Uncle Joe. I like the cafe a lot."

Having co-opted Joe, Loretta and I returned to the cafe. As we walked inside, an especially thickish haze of cigarette smoke announced the presence of Esperanza's foul temper.

"*Pendejito*, you trying to shut us down?"

"I beg your pardon?"

"Three people came to my house this morning, all talking about a mountain lion that attacked Dora Esquivel. What the fuck is going on?"

"Coronado has already been here spreading the news. Joe started the rumour. But we convinced him it could result in our shutting down, in which case we would not purchase anything from his store. He will squelch all rumours and in exchange we shall purchase some overpriced items from his store. Problem solved."

"Where we gonna get the money to pay him?"

"Er, one crisis at a time, I always say. Now, about this evening."

"Nobody's gonna come tonight, *Pendejito*."

"Why not? Joe will tell everyone there was no mountain lion."

"Nobody's gonna believe Joe."

"Why not? They believed him when he said there *was* a mountain lion."

"People here always believe the worst. They ain't gonna come back."

"Not everyone is quite so jaded as you, Esperanza. Your niece is quite keen on the cafe."

"She's too nice to tell you."

I turned to Loretta. "Tell me what?"

"Nothing, Bennie. Really. I like the cafe."

"Loretta's too nice to tell you people here don't like nothing run by no *gringo*."

"Ah, that's it then, is it? Right. I'm bloody well fed up with *gringo* this and *gringo* that. I didn't come here to run your damn cafe, or anything else. I did it as a favour for Uncle Bill—El Vaquero. Who, by the way, is a *gringo*, is he not?"

I stormed out, setting course for Rudy's. Sitting down at the bar, I motioned to Antonio to bring me a bottle.

"You okay, Señor Graves?" He placed a half-empty bottle of Dusty Trail and a glass next to me.

"No, Antonio, I am not."

"My grandfather said the cafe was a big success, just like long ago."

"Yes, I suppose it was. But it needs something more. Or, in this case, something less."

"Huh?"

"Difficult to explain, Antonio. Is your grandfather in his office?"

"Yeah."

"Thanks." I secured the bottle and the glass to my person, and walked down the hall to Rudy's office. His face was drawn and pale, and the creases surrounding his eyes were deep.

"Hey, Bennie. That was a hell of a night, huh?"

"Perhaps the one and only night."

"That explains the whisky. What happened?"

"*Gringo.*"

"Huh? Which *gringo*?"

"Guess."

"I'm real tired, Bennie. Yeah, you're a *gringo*. Unless Tiny Roybal is gonna arrest you because he and those *gordito* kids of his didn't get their *sopapillas*, so what?"

I poured out a full dose of Dusty Trail and made short work of it. "Esperanza told me the cafe will fail."

"So? That's Esperanza. What else is she gonna say?"

"Yes, but this time she said it will fail because I'm a *gringo* and that people in town don't like anything run by a *gringo*."

"The cafe failed before. No *gringos* involved."

"This is different, I mean, I haven't heard anyone call Uncle Bill a *gringo*."

"Hell, everybody used to call him that. But after a while, they started calling him El Vaquero."

"What changed?"

"I dunno. Folks knew how hard he worked at the ranch. He helped Celestina and Ernesto at the cafe a lot, too. Even helped me out, unloading boxes when I there was nobody else around. He always wore a real big cowboy hat back then and spurs. People would see him and say, 'Hey, there goes the *gringo* who thinks he's a *vaquero*.' Pretty soon, it was just El Vaquero. Has been ever since."

I saluted the glass silently and drained the remaining drams. "In other words, gird the *gringo* loins. Stiff *gringo* upper lip, is that it?"

"I guess. But it doesn't mean anything. You could have been Tiny Roybal's brother last night and he still would have been just as mad about the goddamn *sopapillas*. As for Esperanza, I tell Antonio when one of the customers starts yelling or cursing at him, just act like you didn't hear 'em."

Rudy paused. "How old are you? Early thirties?"

"Thirty last December, actually."

"You got your whole life ahead of you."

"I hope the remainder will be less of a cock-up."

"If that means what I think, you got it all wrong."

"How do you mean?"

"If you don't fuck things up in your life sometimes, you ain't trying hard enough. And you sure as hell ain't having enough fun."

"Sounds like the voice of experience."

Rudy passed a hand through his mane of grey-black hair. "I got some stories, Bennie." He laughed quietly. "Maybe I'll tell you some time over a bottle of real whisky, not that shit you're drinking."

"Thanks, Rudy."

I rose slowly, the legs feeling rather wobbly from the morning brace, and started towards the door.

"Hey, Bennie."

"Yes?"

"When are you gonna ask Loretta out?"

"What?"

"Are you blind or just fucking stupid? The whispering's already started. 'Loretta sure likes the *gringo*.' 'I hear that's why she moved back from Santa Fe.' 'I seen that look before. That girl's a goner.' You get the idea."

"I told you. I mean, well, as I said before, 'once bitten, twice shy.'"

"Jesus Christ, Bennie. Just ask her."

"Why? So I can bid her farewell when I return to England soon?"

"What did I tell you about a little heartache? She's here now. So are you."

"What about the *gringo*-haters, like her Uncle?"

"Joe doesn't like *gringos* a lot less than he likes to make money."

"Yes, but he is fond of rattlesnakes and fire. Not a propitious combination, in my view."

"You give Joe money and he'll catch the rattlesnakes for you." Rudy paused, running his hand over his unshaven chin. "And there's one more thing."

"Yes?"

"Try to talk like you live here."

"I was taught French in school. Spanish wasn't an option. I've learned several expressions from Maria and Esperanza, not that one would use them in polite society."

"I don't mean Spanish. I mean English."

"I believe I speak the Queen's English quite well."

"I don't know much about the Queen, but what you just said, that's not how people here talk."

I recoiled. "As best I can tell, the locals' command of the English language is, not to put too fine a point on it, limited. Besides, if I mimicked their speech patterns, they would be offended."

"Bennie, half the time nobody understands what you're saying. So they think you're a *gringo*. You don't need to imitate folks. Just talk like you live here."

"I don't understand."

"How about pick-ups?"

"You mean lorries?"

"Yeah. Don't say lorry, say 'pick-up' or just 'truck.' People understand that."

I pondered Rudy's suggestion, thinking about Uncle Bill's cowboy lingo, which had long ago replaced his Oxbridge accent. "Fine. Consider the word 'lorry' banished from the vocabulary. Anything else?"

"Yeah, don't use so many of those fancy words."

"Such as?" I replied, bristling at his condemnation of my speech.

"I dunno. Just stuff in general you say. It's way too fancy."

"Should I restrict myself to grunting noises?"

"C'mon, Bennie. I'm just giving you some advice. You asked for it."

"I'm sorry. I do want your advice. You've helped me quite a lot. It's difficult to be told not to be oneself."

"I'm not saying that. Just be yourself so folks here can understand it. When you go back to England, you can talk to the Queen again."

I smiled. "Thanks, Rudy. I'll try. I suppose I should return to the cafe—mosey on over as Uncle Bill would say. Do you think anyone will show up tonight?"

"Sure they will. And tell my *querida*, I want some of her beautiful *tamales*. I hope that skunk doesn't show up."

"Joe wants me to poison the little bugger. I purchased some, but it seems rather unsporting. The skunk simply ate the plate of *enchiladas* I had dropped and then walked out. I suggested we set something outside the back door tonight. Loretta called it an *ofrenda*."

Rudy laughed. "An *ofrenda*, huh? I dunno about feeding a skunk, Bennie. But whatever you do, you better keep it out of the cafe."

We opened that evening with far less fanfare, and far fewer customers. Coronado was our first returning customer. He arrived without his identification-obsessed sister and sat at a corner table, scanning the dining room for intruders.

"What would you like for dinner, Coronado?"

"I dunno, Señor Graves. What's good tonight?

"Everything, of course. Would you like to ask Maria?"

Coronado's eyes retreated in fear. "That's okay. Can I get *enchiladas* tonight?"

"An excellent choice." I jotted down his order. "Where's your sister?"

"She went to a church supper, Señor Graves. I'm glad, because I'd have to pay for her, too."

"A Scotsman at heart, eh?"

"*Sí*. What's that?"

"Someone who does not wish to part with his brass, er, money."

"I guess so. Can I have some iced tea, too?"

"Of course."

"Can I ask you a question, Señor Graves?"

I shuddered slightly. "Er, ask away."

"You think that mountain lion is gonna show up again?"

I glanced heavenwards, silently asking for God's mercy. "Well, I'm sure it's still digesting Dora Esquivel. The skunk may appear, but we've devised a plan for it."

"You want me to shoot it?"

"No! I mean, thanks for the offer. Loretta suggested we leave an *ofrenda* for it outside the back door."

"What kind of *ofrenda*, Señor Graves?"

"Well, it had *enchiladas* last night. What would you suggest?"

"I guess if the skunk had *enchiladas* last night, I would give it *tamales* tonight, or maybe some *tacos*. Nobody likes to eat the same thing all the time."

"Excellent advice, Coronado."

"Can I ask you another question, Señor Graves?"

I shuddered again. "Yes?"

"Where you gonna take Loretta?"

"I beg your pardon?"

"I heard you asked Loretta on a date. You gonna take her somewhere real nice?"

Exasperation flooded over me. The entire town appeared to be fixated on my potential romantic interest in Loretta. "Well, I haven't actually asked her yet. Who told you I had? Joe Garcia?"

"*Sí.* How did you know?"

"One has a sense for these things. Would you inform Joe that no wedding date has been set."

Coronado stared at me wide-eyed. "Wedding? You and Loretta are gonna get married?"

"What? No!" A perspiring fear came over me. "A bit of joke, that's all. No wedding. No wedding date. Nothing. Do you understand?"

"Sure, Señor Graves. I can keep a secret real good."

"There is no secret! We're not—oh, fine. Yes, do please keep it a secret."

I retreated to the kitchen, lest he announce the names of Loretta's and my imaginary offspring.

Once his meal was presented to him, Coronado lost interest in matters of the heart. I heard nothing more—neither rumour nor innuendo—that evening from anyone else.

At around half eight, the last customer, a somewhat sullen chap who ordered the *menudo* and chewed it loudly, shuffled out the front door. I checked around the front door, then placed the "closed" sign in the window. Esperanza was at the cash register, tallying the evening's receipts.

"How did we fare, Esperanza?"

"Three hundred seventy-five, plus forty in tips. Pretty bad."

"Not at all. After the opening night, I'm surprised we had as many customers as we did. I should think tomorrow will be even better.

"Not gonna happen," she grumbled. "You think that skunk's gonna show up again?"

I glanced at the clock. We should set out its evening meal, just in case."

"I thought you was gonna poison it?"

"Er, Loretta would rather not. Kind-hearted girl and all that."

Esperanza shook her head and packaged up the evening's receipts in a small bank bag. "You better ask her out soon, *Pendejito*, or she's gonna hit you with that skunk. I already told her don't go out with no *gringo*, but she don't listen to me."

I shook my head and walked into the kitchen. Maria was repackaging the foodstuffs, whilst Loretta was washing dishes.

"I say, Loretta, have you readied tonight's *ofrenda*?"

"I already put it outside. A *tamale*, a broken *taco*, rice, and a *sopapilla*. Do you think that will be enough?"

"Unless the skunk's appetite rivals Coronado's, it should."

"What should we call it?"

"Eh?"

"Don't you think the skunk should have a name?"

"What? You wish to give that malodorous beast a name?"

"That's a great name."

"What?"

"Señor Apestoso."

"Señor what?"

"Señor Apestoso. It means 'Mister Stinky.' Well, sort of."

I exploded in a derisive sort of laughter.

"Why do you think that's funny?"

"I, er, no offense intended, mind you, but you're treating the bloody thing like a pet. If it ever sprays inside the cafe, we'll be rubbished."

"I am not treating it like a pet. And I have no intention of letting it inside."

"Oh, and Loretta?"

"What?" she said with a note of peevishness.

"Would you care for, er, a night out? With me, I mean."

She looked at me sternly. "Are you asking me out on a date?"

I stepped backwards. "No, of course not. I mean, please accept my apologies."

Loretta laughed. "It's about time. When? Where should we go?"

"What? Really? Well, I suppose we must wait until a day when the cafe is closed. You could come out to Uncle Bill's ranch for dinner."

"That sounds great. Thanks." She smiled and returned to the washing up.

At precisely nine o'clock, the newly named Señor Apestoso arrived outside the kitchen door. We watched cautiously as he dined *al fresco*, consuming his meal at a leisurely, skunkish pace. Once finished, he sat down on his haunches, rather like a dog, and looked at us contentedly. After a few minutes, he stretched and walked away into the night.

"You appear to have a new fan of your cooking, Maria," I said.

"This mean we got to feed him every night?"

"Would you prefer he sat in the dining room?"

"You got poison. I can make a chicken *enchilada* for him. He ain't gonna eat no more after that."

"No, *Tia* Maria," Loretta said. "He's a good omen."

"Maybe it's good to have that skunk," Esperanza said, evoking surprise amongst the rest of us.

"What? Of all people, Esperanza, I would think you would favour the poisonous solution."

"Maybe Loretta's right. I don't want to poison a good omen."

Presently, we heard wild barking, followed by a yelp, from outside the front door. We hurried towards the front door. Unsure who, or what, might enter, I peered out, then opened it slightly. Below me was Paco's usual calling card.

Yet the smallness of the puddle suggested he had been rudely interrupted. A pungent odour identified the interrupter. I looked down the road, which was dimly lit by a lone street-light for Señor Apestoso. Then, sensing something watching me, I turned towards the darkened corner of the patio, and espied the skunk sitting calmly. One would have thought he was waiting for a smoking jacket, pipe, wing chair, and ottoman.

"Thanks, old chap, you've earned your *ofrenda*," I whispered. "Per-haps some *carne adovada* shall please the mephitian palate. Until tomorrow night, old chap." I closed the front door gently.

The next evening saw a larger contingent of diners, including, Nestor and Pedro Martinez. As we had no license to dispense spirits, Nestor provided his own six-pack of Best Milwaukee decanted from a large paper bag. Pedro consumed one, whilst Nestor drained the other five in an astonishingly short period of time. When he finished eating, Nestor staggered out the front door, leaving the table, floor, and his shirt coated with a mix of green chile, cheese, *frijoles*, and honey. Esperanza was mollified only by Pedro's large tip and sheepish apologies.

Luis Chavez, wearing his ever-present grease-stained coveralls, also showed. Esperanza cursed when she espied him and, despite my admonishing her to treat all customers well, even those who had insulted her previously, she nevertheless managed to pour a large glass of iced tea into his lap, with only a muted "sorry." Luis howled in anger. Had it not been for Maria waving one of her knives about, as well as my offering Luis dinner at no charge, a brawl would almost surely have erupted.

By nine o'clock, the dining room was empty. Loretta had prepared an *ofrenda* of *posole*, a large *sopapilla* (sans honey), a large serving of *carne adovada,* and a flour *tortilla.* Señor Apestoso made short work of it all, then trundled down the alley into the night.

"I never seen no skunk like that," Maria said, puffing on her cigarette as she watched it disappear. "Maybe it ain't no skunk."

"Perhaps it"s a mountain lion," I replied tartly.

Maria blew a large cloud of smoke into the air. "Maybe it's El Diablo."

"The Devil, you say? One assumes the Devil would appear in a more sinister guise—a poisonous snake comes to mind. Besides, spraying Paco could only have been God's revenge."

The pattern repeated itself each evening. Señor Apestoso would show up at nine o'clock, dine *al fresco* on a plate of the evening's leftovers, and then casually stroll away. Better still, the front door and *portal* were clean and dry.

Against all odds, the cafe had survived its first week. We were exhausted from the efforts, but even Esperanza expressed a grudging confidence for continued success.

# Chapter 22

By unanimous vote we decided the cafe would be closed on Mondays and Tuesdays to provide all of us much needed rest. Loretta and I confirmed our "date" for Monday evening, and Maria agreed to feed Señor Apestoso that night. Esperanza muttered something about driving to Santa Fe, which meant seeing the oafish Hector.

Loretta lived with her mother, whom I expected to upbraid me for various trespasses, real and imagined, regarding the alleged courtship of her daughter. I arrived at the small, neatly painted and trimmed home late Monday afternoon with trepidation. In front, there was a fenced garden that extended almost the entire length of the home containing a small jungle of plants, whose yellowing leaves betrayed the effects of cold mountain nights. I stepped onto the covered *portal* and knocked plaintively on the front door.

Inside, a dog began to bark insanely, sounding as if it would cheerfully tear off my limbs. I heard footsteps approach the door and then found myself staring at a petite, middle-aged woman wearing jeans and a whitish blouse. She was grasping the ear of an enormous black dog, which looked to be a cross between a mastiff and a mastodon. That she and Coronado might have been—well, even the Gomorrahans would have considered it beyond the pale.

"Gah!" The beast continued to bark whilst wagging its prodigious tail.

"You must be Bennie. I'm Loretta's mother, Josefa." Her voice had a pleasant dulcimer tone.

"Er, hullo, Mrs. Alvarez. I'm Benjamin Graves." I extended a hand towards hers, wondering how easily my head would fit in Chata's ample jaws. Perhaps reading my thoughts, the dog barked again, and began drooling profusely.

"Don't mind Chata, she's friendly."

"Gentle as a lamb, I'm sure."

"I had no idea El Vaquero had a nephew. He never said anything."

"You know my uncle then?"

"Everybody in Vaca Seca knows El Vaquero."

Chata continued to drool hungrily. "Perhaps I should wait in the lorry, I mean, pick-up, for Loretta. No sense in upsetting your, er, dog."

"Nonsense. Come inside. Loretta will be ready in a moment."

I stepped into the small sitting room and extended a fearful right hand towards the dog's muzzle. It sniffed the hand, then turned around and flopped down onto the floor. "What, er, breed of dog is it, if I may ask?"

"We're not sure. Part Great Dane, I guess. She likes to meet new people."

"No doubt." I wondered if the dog's fondness for new people would manifest itself as part of a tasting menu. Thankfully, Loretta glided into the sitting room. She looked radiant, wearing jeans, a pinkish blouse, and cowboy boots.

"Hi, Bennie. I see you've met Chata."

Hearing its name, the dog thumped its tail loudly. I nodded. "Yes. Rather a large dog."

Anxious to depart, I eyed the beast warily, wondering whether the tail-thumping was a ruse to lull its appetizers into submission. "Shall we go?"

"Okay. I'll see you later, Mom."

"Have fun. Oh, and Bennie, would you say hello to your uncle from me?"

"Yes, of course."

I followed Loretta out the front door, feeling a wave of relief to escape Chata's jaws. "Your mother seems unexpectedly pleasant. I mean, I was expecting someone different."

"Different? How?"

"I had expected the usual *gringo* admonishments, like Esperanza's or that senile old bat of a school principal."

"She once dated a *gringo*."

"That must have raised several eyebrows."

As we motored off to the ranch, I pondered Loretta's matter-of-fact admission. Other than Uncle Bill and myself, there were no others, at least none I was aware of.

"I say, Loretta, has your mother always lived in Vaca Seca?"

"No. My father was in the Air Force, so we moved around a lot. She came back to Vaca Seca after he died. Why?"

"Simple curiosity is all. You mentioned she had dated a *gringo* after he died. I was merely thinking that, well, the only *gringo* in Vaca Seca is . . . did your mother date Uncle Bill?"

Loretta gave me with one of those dagger-like looks one wilts under. "What if she did?"

I coughed. "Nothing. I mean, rather ironic, what with your mother having dated Uncle Bill and now, well, here we are."

"I don't see what one has to do with the other, but if it bothers you, you can turn around and take me home, Benjamin Graves." She folded her arms tightly across her chest and stared ahead.

"Loretta, I didn't mean . . ." My voice trailed off. "Rather an inauspicious start to the evening, isn't it? Can you forgive me?"

She gradually released the grip she held on herself. "Bennie, I know it's been tough on you. Vaca Seca isn't London, but it's not as bad as you think. I don't care whether you're a *gringo* or a Martian."

I desperately wanted to believe her, but the discordant voices of Esperanza and Joe Garcia remained loud within my mind, despite Rudy's previous advice.

Then again, I did not want to end the evening before it had begun, so quickly changed the subject "You're probably right. Forget I said anything. I am quite looking forward to our dinner."

"Me, too."

We arrived at the ranch shortly thereafter. As I motored around the side of the house, I espied Loretta goggling Daisy, who had raised herself off her usual porcine spot on the patio and was trotting over to investigate.

"¡*Híjole*! That pig's wearing a *sombrero*. Is it friendly?"

"Daisy—that's the sow's name—is, well, I would describe her temperament as mercurial."

"Can I get out of the truck?"

I blew the lorry's horn, hoping Uncle Bill would emerge to retrieve Daisy. "As long as you don't have any luggage."

"What?"

"The day I arrived, Daisy took a strong dislike to my luggage. Afraid they did not survive the encounter. We've reached a *pax porcinus* of sorts. I provide her meals and she tolerates my walking about. I would just as soon convert Daisy into *tamales* and *carne adovada*. Alas, Uncle Bill is rather fond of her."

Presently, Uncle Bill emerged from the house. He addressed Daisy's rump with a swat of his hand, and shouted at her to lie down. The pig complied, trotting gaily back to her usual spot and flopping down.

"Howdy, all," he shouted. "Loretta, don't you worry about Daisy. She's as gentle as a lamb."

"Yes, a twenty-five stone, psychotic one," I added.

"Hello, Señor Graves," Loretta replied. "My mother sends her regards."

Uncle Bill nodded. "That's right kind of her, Loretta. How's she doin' these days?"

"Good, I guess. You should go see her, sometime."

"Yep. I reckon I should." Uncle Bill offered a grin and adjusted his cowboy hat. "She been to the cafe yet?"

"Not yet. She works nights at the hospital in Vista Grande, so it's kinda hard for her. But she will. She promised."

"Good. You tell her I'd be happy to escort her. "

"She would probably prefer you to tell her that yourself."

"Well, I've been mighty busy. And, I don't have a phone. Tell you what, would you give her a note from me?"

"Sure, Señor Graves. I'd be happy to."

I remained curious as to what had transpired during the brief interlude between Uncle Bill and Loretta's mother, but thought it was best to silent for the time being. Instead, I ushered Loretta into the house and the sitting room.

"You have a nice house, Señor Graves."

"Yep, I like it. Kinda different than a London row house, ain't it, Bennie?"

"Indeed. Both have their respective charms, though."

"Well, I'm gonna excuse myself, and give you young folks some time alone. Got a few things to fix in the barn."

"Marjorie again?"

"Yep."

"Who's Marjorie?"

"That would be Uncle Bill's horse, another member of the menagerie. Unlike Daisy, Marjorie isn't mercurial; she's the most contemptuous horse I have ever known."

"Don't listen to him, Loretta. She's just an old gal set in her ways. I can't fault her for that." Uncle Bill walked out the back door, leaving us in the sitting room.

"I hope you have an appetite. Maria was kind enough to provide her recipe for *posole*."

"That sounds great."

"Er, may I offer you something to drink?"

"No, thanks."

We sat in silence and I began to wonder if I had already entered the not-chosen category.

"Er, would you care to take a walk around the ranch? The cattle are quite docile and I must say the sunsets here are quite special."

"Sure. That sounds nice."

We walked out the back door and through the metal gate that led to the sage-filled pasture. Loretta slipped her arm through the crook of my elbow, and we walked slowly north, towards the mountains in the distance.

"Do you think you will return to London soon?"

"I'm not sure. The cafe seems to be on a steady course. I promised Uncle Bill I would stay until then."

"What will you do?"

"Seek employment at another bank, I suppose. Not really qualified for other gainful employment."

"You could open a restaurant."

"What? If I've learned but one thing living in Vaca Seca, it is to never open a restaurant."

"You could stay here."

I laughed. "In Vaca Seca? I rather doubt it."

"What about Albuquerque? They must need bankers."

Loretta stopped abruptly and looked at me with one of those emotive expressions the fairer sex often employs. Despite my slow-wittedness in matters of the heart, I bent down and offered her a brief kiss, which evolved into an extended embrace.

"Albuquerque, eh?"

We sat down on a nearby boulder. "This is all rather unexpected. I came here because I wanted to flee London, what with the ex-wife's running off with a bloody Spaniard and my redundancy from the bank. Really, though, it's all I know."

"You know Vaca Seca pretty well."

I laughed. "And learning more about it all the time." I stood up and took her hand. "Shall we? There are dinner preparations to undertake."

"Good. I'm getting hungry. "

Back in Uncle Bill's kitchen, I prepared *tortillas*, following Maria's instructions, as a still tender lump on the forehead attested. Uncle Bill and Loretta sat at the small kitchen table as I rolled out the balls of dough and cooked them in a frying pan until they were mottled with brownish blisters. From there, a spot of butter and onto a warm plate in the oven.

We were all quite peckish, devouring the *tortillas* and several bowls of *posole* each.

"That was real good, Bennie." Uncle Bill said, consuming a last bite of *tortilla*. "Maria teach you?"

"Well, after asking Loretta to dinner, I realized I needed some cooking instruction. Maria biffed me with her rolling pin a few times, but the Graves hard skull prevented any real damage."

"Biffed?" Loretta asked.

"Sorry. Hit. Clubbed, really." I mimed the action with my arm. Uncle Bill rose from the table.

"Tell you what, Bennie. I'll go put Marjorie to bed, if you do the washing up."

"Thanks, Uncle Bill."

"I'll help with the dishes," Loretta said.

"Hardly worth the bother, really. Why don't you help Uncle Bill and meet Marjorie."

"Do you mind, Señor Graves?"

"Only if you stop calling me Señor Graves. How about just 'Bill?' I been known to answer to that. Been called a hell of a lot worse, too."

"Okay . . . Bill."

They wandered out to the barn. I finished the washing up, then built a fire in the wood stove in the sitting room and sat down on the davenport. The grey matter began to consider the situation, then confessed its befuddlement between London and Loretta: the former the ancestral home, the latter having rather an intoxicating allure.

Presently, Uncle Bill and Loretta returned to the house. "I met Marjorie, Bennie. She seems very nice. Why doesn't she like you?"

"You ought to ride her, Bennie," Uncle Bill said. "I keep telling you."

"And I shall continue to demur. Marjorie is untrustworthy."

"Haven't you ever ridden a horse, Bennie?"

"At the family estate, I rode on several fox hunts."

"Fox hunts?"

"Something only the English could do, Loretta," Uncle Bill said. "They whoop and holler like Indians attacking a wagon train. Chase a fox with a bunch of yapping dogs. Then they get drunk afterwards."

Loretta grimaced. "That sounds awful. Did you like it, Bennie?"

"Not especially. I was nine years old the first time. My father insisted I participate. I rode a rather docile old mare. The next time, I was twelve. I rode the same mare, which by then was quite long in tooth. It was also the first time I shot my father's shotgun. The entire exercise was rather dull, I thought, and I felt sorry for the poor fox. Anyway, there you have it, my equine experience."

"I like to ride horses. Maybe we can go sometime."

"Er, yes, all right." I glanced at the watch. "I should return you home, Loretta. I've promised to help Uncle Bill with more fence-mending and firewood gathering tomorrow.

"Okay, Bennie. Thank you Señor Gr—Bill."

"You're welcome, young lady. Say hello to your mother and give her this." He handed Loretta a small envelope.

"I will."

"I shan't be too long, Uncle Bill."

Loretta walked to the lorry. The air was quite crisp and there was a full moon. The silhouettes of several cattle were discernible against the fence. Loretta huddled against me in the lorry, whilst I started the motor.

We motored down the road, which was deserted, save a deer that ran across at the edge of the headlights. "This has been great, Bennie. It's been a long time since I went on a date. In fact, it's the first time since my divorce."

"You were married?"

"Not the smartest thing I ever did. I was eighteen and right out of high school. Jaime was twenty." She wiped a tear from her cheek.

"No need to discuss it. We both have our pasts."

"I want to tell you, Bennie. We were living in Santa Fe. Jaime was working at a lumber yard. He started going to the bars after work and would come home drunk a lot. Then he hit me. I don't know why." She burst into tears.

I pulled off to the side of the road and extended my hand to her cheek. She straightened up and looked at me. "Loretta, I am so sorry. Only an oaf and a cad would ever strike a woman. I am neither. You must believe me."

"I'm sorry, Bennie. I do believe you. You're so different from any guy I ever met. And not just because of your accent. Sometimes, I think you're a Martian who landed in Vaca Seca and doesn't know what to make of it."

"Many of the locals must think that."

She laughed, wiped her eyes, and kissed me again. "Will you please stay a little longer?"

"I suppose I must. You've certainly complicated matters, Loretta, but it's a most pleasant complication."

In town, Loretta directed me to her mother's house. "What time should I show up for work Wednesday?"

"Would you mind helping Maria with the cooking again? She seems to like yominur presence in the kitchen."

"Sure."

"Thanks."

"You know, we should think about opening for lunch, too."

"Perhaps. But I'm still not convinced the cafe will survive."

"You're a pessimist."

"Merely a realist. Right. Off with you wench, until Wednesday."

"So I'm a wench now, huh?" She laughed and kissed me once again.

"Good night, Bennie."

"Good night."

After dispensing with the morning's care and feeding of the four-leggeds, Uncle Bill and I sat in the kitchen, drinking his cowboy coffee.

"You might have told me she was divorced, Uncle Bill."

"So are you. Besides, it's none of my goddamn business. She would tell you when she damn well wanted to. And she did."

"What exactly went on between you and her mother?"

"It was too soon after Celestina's death, Bennie. I think Josefa understood."

"What about now?"

"Now?"

"What I mean is, still too soon?"

"Nope, too late."

"Eh?"

"There's a fella lives in Albuquerque. She met him a few years ago."

"Have you met the chap?"

"Yep. Jim Pritchard. Works at the Air Force base. Some sort of scientist. Nice guy."

"Sorry."

"I'm glad she's happy. Besides, I couldn't expect her to wait for me."

"I suppose not."

"She's a real nice girl, Bennie."

"Indeed she is. Rudy told me she had broken many hearts. I understand why. Odd, I came here to escape life's complexities. Apparently, Fate had other ideas."

"Yep, she usually does. You sorry you came?"

"There have been moments, quite a few, actually. Then again, if nothing else, I've met the familial black sheep my father still speaks about."

"Vaca Seca would do him some good, too."

"Will you ever come back to London?"

"I dunno. Before you showed up, I would've said 'hell no.' But you took a big chance coming here, so I can't rightly say I wouldn't be willing to do the same sometime." He took a last swallow of coffee and stood up. "Let's get to work. We got a lot to do today."

I arrived at the cafe around nine o'clock Wednesday morning. Maria was already in the kitchen, beginning her preparations, as was, surprisingly, Esperanza.

"Good morning, all."

"You finally decide to show up, huh *Pendejito*?" Esperanza crowed. "You too tired from your date?"

"I beg your pardon?"

"I hear you started at Rudy's, had a few beers, then you and Loretta went to Santa Fe for some fancy *gringo* dinner at La Posada, then dancing, and then . . ." Esperanza made a rude gesture with her hands and laughed. "I guess you do like girls, *Pendejito*."

"What? We didn't do any of those things. Who is saying that?"

"Everybody in town. You're gonna take her away to London." Vaca Seca's gossip telegraph had again, with unparalleled efficiency, spread outlandish rumours.

"If you must know, Loretta had dinner with Uncle Bill and me at the ranch. I made *posole* and fresh *tortillas*, using Maria's recipe."

"*It's true, hermana*. I showed him how to cook *posole* and make *tortillas*."

"That's it?" Esperanza said, with obvious disappointment. "I say, Esperanza, Loretta is your niece."

"Yeah, and she needs a real man, *Pendejito*."

I shook my head in exasperation. "We enjoyed a most pleasant evening. Now, if you are quite finished, Maria and I must discuss supplies for the week, including what we will purchase from Joe Garcia."

"Joe? You said he charges too much money. You gonna buy from him 'cause he's Loretta's uncle? Trying to get in good, *Pendejito*?

"No. As I explained, if we purchase some supplies from Joe, he won't sabotage the cafe. I promised we would purchase one hundred dollars' worth each week. What items do you and Maria believe we should purchase?"

Maria continued to chop onions and peppers. "How about napkins, canned tomatoes, rice, and *frijoles*. He ain't gonna screw those up. Maybe Coca-Cola, too."

"That sounds reasonable. Esperanza? Any suggestions?"

"*Sí*. Shoot fucking Joe. It's never gonna be enough for him. You'll see."

"Fine. You go ahead and shoot him. Then perhaps Tiny Roybal will lock you in gaol, and neither you nor Joe will cause any further problems."

"Look, *Pendejito*, I told you a long time ago this wouldn't work. Maria and me, we know Joe."

"I know Joe's barmy. That's why I want to purchase a few supplies from him."

"Maybe if you marry Loretta, we won't have to worry about it."

"Marry?"

"*Sí*, especially if you knocked her up. Then you got to marry her."

My evening with Loretta had devolved into a maelstrom of marriage and pregnancy, all to placate Joe Garcia's avarice.

Maria growled, raising a large chef's knife flecked with bits of onion. "*No más, hermana*. You making everybody crazy."

Esperanza glared at Maria, but remained silent.

"Bennie, you want me to go see Joe with you?"

"No, let me speak with him first. Oh, and what do you think about opening the cafe for luncheon?"

"We're gonna need more help. Maybe if Loretta cooked and we get somebody to wash dishes."

"There must be someone reliable about whom we could employ."

"How about Luis Chavez's son, Juan?"

"No!" Esperanza shouted, waving her hand. "I don't want to hire nobody related to that *hijo de puta*."

"Please Esperanza. Luis may have had a bit of a laugh at your expense, but that's no reason not to hire his son."

"They're all the same."

"Do you know anyone?"

"*Sí*, Rudy's grandson, Antonio. He's not real busy at the bar. Good kid."

"He's only ten years old. I mean, the lad already tends bar, which is extraordinary in itself. Don't you have child labour laws in this country?"

"So what if kids work? Everybody does."

"Chores about the house, milking the goat before school, yes. Bartending? No. And no dishwashing. Maria, will you kindly speak with Juan Chavez?" I held up my hand, anticipating Esperanza's tirade. "I know, Esperanza. If Juan is not interested, I shall speak with Rudy. Shall we leave it at that? Now, we're off to see Joe."

I had hardly set foot outside when Coronado's distinct voice reverberated in the ear drums.

"Señor Graves," he wheezed. He took my hand and shook it vigorously, whilst displaying a maniacal grin. "*¡Felicitaciones!*"

I retrieved my bewildered hand and continued walking. "Er, thank you, Coronado. I am actually off to the store to see Joe. Is he there?"

"*Sí*, Señor Graves." Coronado waddled unsteadily and continued to wheeze. "You're gonna be real happy. I know it."

"To see Joe?"

"Joe's real happy today."

"Why?" A cheerful Joe was surely an ominous sign.

"You're speaking in riddles, Coronado. Do you mean Joe is happy because I agreed to purchase supplies for the cafe? I've already discussed that with him. Besides, how could he know I was coming to speak with him now? I only just decided myself."

"Everybody knows you're gonna see Joe, Señor Graves."

"How? And why should everyone care about the cafe's purchasing serviettes and tins of tomatoes from him?"

"No, Señor Graves. Joe's happy 'cause you're gonna ask him if you can marry Loretta. Since Billy Alvarez died, Joe's kinda been like her father. Even more than me."

"Marry? What are you talking about?"

"Don't you remember? You asked Loretta to marry you. In Santa Fe, when you went to La Posada."

"What? There's nothing to remember. We didn't go to Santa Fe or dine at La Posada. And I didn't ask Loretta to marry me. Who told you that?"

"My sister, Señor Graves. She heard it from Luis Chavez's wife, Lupe. She's a real nice girl, Loretta. ¡Felicitaciones!"

Apparently, Fate had created a new circle of Hell for my own particular residence.

I fought the urge to verbally detonate. "Coronado, we are not getting married."

"Coronado's brow tightened and he scowled. "I dunno. You got to marry her. That's only right if she's gonna have your baby."

As I was being politely ushered into yet another new circle of Hell, I stuttered, "B-b-baby? Loretta is having a baby? There are rumours swirling about that Loretta is . . . and the child is mine? You're all mad."

"Sorry, Señor Graves, but you gotta do what's right."

"Do you think it's gonna be a boy? I sure hope so."

"How would I know? I mean, there is no baby."

I ran back to the cafe, feeling like a luckless fox being chased by a pack of rumour-addled hounds. Sitting down at one of the dining room tables, my heart pounded loudly. I bent over and enveloped my head with the still shaking hands. "What have these people done?" I thought.

Esperanza walked out of the kitchen, presumably expecting Loretta. "Pendejito? What's wrong?"

I looked at her, still cradling my head, which felt leaden. "Do you know what you've done, you and the rest of the town's chattering magpies?"

"What are you talking about?"

"According to Coronado, Loretta and I are engaged to be married because Loretta is pregnant with my child. Oh, and I am off to ask Joe for his permission to marry her."

Fate, being in particularly rancid mood, chose that particular moment for Loretta to walk through the front door.

"I'm what?" she screamed. "What did you say, Bennie?"

"*Híjole.* I better go help Maria," Esperanza vanished into the kitchen.

"Did you just tell Esperanza I was pregnant? With your child?"

"What? No, I mean, Loretta, before you say anything more—"

"You're damn right I'm gonna say more, Bennie. What were you thinking?" She burst into tears.

"Loretta, please—someone is spreading rumours again. Coronado told me. He was told by his dim-witted sister, who was told by Lupe Chavez, who was told by God knows who, that we are to be married because you are pregnant. All of this because of our romantic dinner in Santa Fe Monday night at La Posada. Oh, and we went dancing after dinner, too"

"Santa Fe? Dancing? What are you talking about?"

"The Vaca Seca rumour mill has turned our dinner at Uncle Bill's ranch into . . . well, a depraved bacchanal."

"What are we going to do?"

"I haven't the vaguest idea. The more outlandish the rumours, the faster they spread in this town. I'm surprised our dinner in Santa Fe wasn't interrupted by the same mountain lion that ate Dora Esquivel." At the mention of the non-exist-ent mountain lion, Loretta burst out laughing.

"I'm sorry I got upset with you, Bennie. What are we going to do?"

"I don't know. We could—gah!"

"What is it?"

"The mountain lion."

"I don't understand."

"It's your bloody uncle again. He must have started this, just as he started the mountain lion rumour."

"Why would Uncle Joe do that? You promised you would buy supplies from his store."

"Why indeed?" I turned to the kitchen door. "Esperanza, Maria, would you be so kind as to step out here?"

Esperanza, who had quite obviously been listening by the kitchen door, burst through immediately, followed by Maria.

"I presume you heard me, Esperanza. Did you know he started this rumour?"

"Uh, *sí*." Esperanza turned her gaze away from me.

"I thought so. Maria, I need your shotgun. It is time to deal with Joe once and for all."

"Bennie," Loretta cried. "What are you saying? You can't shoot Uncle Joe."

"A Graves can only turn the other cheek so far, Loretta. I've reached the end." I glared at Esperanza. "Where is it, Maria?"

"You sure, Señor Bennie? Tiny ain't gonna like it."

"I don't care, Maria. Loretta's and my honour are at stake. If it means gaol, then so be it."

Maria returned to the kitchen and soon emerged cradling her shotgun. "Be careful, it's loaded."

"Thank you, Maria." I picked up the shotgun and began walking towards the front door.

"Wait, *Pendejito*!" Esperanza shouted. "You can't shoot Joe."

"Why not? You said yourself he started these contemptible rumours."

Esperanza moaned. "Joe didn't say nothing."

"Who did?"

"Nobody. Me."

"*Tia* Esperanza, you started this? Why?" Loretta's eyes welled up. Esperanza sat down heavily.

"I dunno. I'm real sorry, Loretta. I thought, maybe if you heard this, you would go, 'cause he don't belong here."

I retrieved a nearby chair and sat down, laying the shotgun on a table. "Odd thing is, you're right. I don't belong here. I understand that now."

"Bennie, no, don't leave." Loretta turned to Esperanza. "*Tia* Esperanza, how can you be so selfish?"

"Don't blame her, Loretta. At least she's honest. I am the *gringo*, after all."

"Then I am going with you." Loretta attached herself to my arm.

Maria, who had remained expressionless, spoke calmly. "*Hermana*, no Señor Bennie, no Loretta, no cafe. *¿Comprende?*"

"We can work together, just like always."

"*No más, hermana.* Loretta, she's my niece, too. And Señor Bennie, he's kinda like *mi hijo.*"

"I appreciate the gesture, Loretta, really I do. But you would probably find London a rather frightening place. Besides, Maria is going to need your help. Right, I'm off to the ranch to pack."

"Bennie, please, don't go."

I shook my head and walked out the door. I climbed into the lorry and started the engine, which sputtered to life in a defeated way, much as I felt. As I motored around the corner, Coronado espied me and waved his hand cheerily. I waved back, and turned down the rutted road to the ranch house.

Walking inside the house, I proceeded to the side cupboard in the drawing room, retrieved a bottle of Dusty Trail, and poured a large glass, which I downed greedily. As I began to pour a second glass, I heard the back door open.

"Bennie, Is that you?"

"In the drawing room, Uncle Bill."

He walked in, espied the bottle and glass, and cocked an eyebrow. "Little early for that, ain't it?"

"Given this morning's events, I should have started hours ago. You haven't heard the news?"

"What news?"

"About the rather extraordinary evening Loretta and I spent in Santa Fe Monday: dinner at La Posada, dancing afterwards, my getting down on bent knee asking for her hand in marriage because, after all, she is carrying the next generation of Graves. That news."

"What the hell are you talking about?"

"Apparently the Vaca Seca rumour telegraph hasn't yet arrived this far."

Uncle Bill sat down upon the davenport. "Jesus. What happened?"

"I had no sooner arrived at the cafe this morning, when Coronado offered his congratulations on Loretta's and my impending nuptials. He then enquired whether we were expecting a boy, which he hopes for."

"Who told him that?"

"A long and sordid train of individuals."

"Did Joe start this one, too?"

"Actually, no. Esperanza was the instigator."

"Esperanza? Why?"

"Well, I cannot condone her methods, but at least she was rather honest about the situation. And I agree with her."

His voice rose in anger. "What situation? Goddamn it, Bennie, what's going on?"

"My situation. The *gringo* who should return from whence he came."

"You've heard Esperanza spout that nonsense before. Didn't Rudy tell you to ignore it? Why now?"

"Uncle Bill, I did as you asked. Against all odds, the cafe is functional again. No need for the *gringo* with the funny accent to overstay his welcome."

"What about Loretta? She's one hell of a nice gal. Are you giving up on her, too?""

"It's because of Loretta."

"Loretta agrees with Esperanza? She wants you to leave because you're a *gringo*?"

"No, of course not. She offered to return with me to London. I told her no. She would be miserable in London, fitting in as well as I fit in here. Besides, can you imagine what my father would say?"

"Who cares what that pompous brother of mine would say? You like her, don't you?"

"Very much so."

"But you're gonna throw it all away because of Esperanza's stupidity?"

"Esperanza was the final straw, as it were."

"C'mon, Bennie. You were called names in school. We all were. You didn't quit then."

"Uncle Bill, I'm truly grateful for your hospitality. But I'm not a cowboy like you. I'm not El Vaquero and never will be. I'm just the *gringo* with the funny accent. I don't want Loretta ridiculed because of me. She deserves far better."

"At least think about this for a day or two? Don't go off half-cocked."

"Fine. I need a few days to arrange my affairs, make arrangements with the travel agent in Santa Fe, that sort of thing. As for the cafe, I presume it can operate this evening without me. And if not, well, bugger all, I say."

Uncle Bill pondered the situation. "Well, if you need something to keep you busy today, there's more fence that needs repairing."

We gathered our tools and headed into the pasture. The cattle had made a hash of another large section of fence, which lay on the ground. By the time we finished the repairs, dusk was falling upon us. I felt exhausted, yet oddly refreshed.

I returned the tools to the barn, under the baleful eye of Marjorie, whilst Uncle Bill walked to the road to retrieve the day's post. After a wash and brush up, I returned to the drawing room. Uncle Bill was sitting on the davenport, looking pensive.

"Are you all right?"

"I got a letter from your mother today."

"A letter? Is she all right? What about my father?"

"Yep, she's fine. So is your father. It's, well, your mother asked me to give to you this." He pulled out a small, sealed envelope and handed it to me.

"What's this?"

"It's a note from your ex-wife."

I held the letter in my hands, which began to shake.

"Apparently, she contacted your mother, asking what had become of you. Your mother told her you were staying with me, and didn't know when you would return. Apparently, she asked your mother to forward that letter you're holding to me."

Despite a sense of foreboding, I tore open the letter.

*My dearest Benjamin,*

*I hope this finds you well. Your mother has told me you are living in New Mexico with your uncle, although I have no idea where. It all sounds terribly primitive.*

*I made a terrible mistake with Rodrigo and I dearly hope you have it in your heart to forgive me for my horrid behaviour. I was impetuous and tossed common decency out the window. I know I have hurt you and you have every right to hate me, but do please forgive me and let me make it up to you. I miss you.*

*I asked your mother to send this letter to you. I've already spoken with a travel agent to make the arrangements. I must see you, Benjamin, and hope you will return to England with me, where you belong.*

*Love,*

*Cynthia*

"What's happened? You look white as a ghost."

"Cynthia says she made a mistake running off with Rodrigo and is coming here to take me back."

"Your ex-wife is coming here?"

I thudded down onto the davenport, stunned, and reread the letter. "Uncle Bill, the letter from Cynthia was written over a fortnight ago. Good God, she could arrive anytime."

"Bennie, you're not gonna leave before she arrives, are you?"

"Disappearing into the mountains seems a prudent strategy."

"What's she like?"

"Cynthia? A bit like me, I suppose, other than the fondness for Spaniards. She's quite cosmopolitan. I'm sure she will loathe Vaca Seca."

"You want her back?"

"Had you asked me several months ago, I would have responded with an emphatic 'yes.' Now? Not especially, no. That probably sounds heartless. I wish her well and all that. But start anew, as if Rodrigo never happened? No."

"What about Loretta?"

"Eh?"

"What are you gonna do when Cynthia meets Loretta?"

The mind pictured such a meeting—with Coronado providing the introductions—and winced.

"Can one hope their paths will not cross?"

"Here? Are you kidding?"

"What should I do?"

"I dunno. Listen to your heart, not your head. Why the hell do you think I came here in the first place?"

"I am listening to my heart, which is shouting 'The end is nigh.'"

# Chapter 23

I expected Cynthia would send a telegram to Uncle Bill telling him when she would arrive, which would at least provide me a bit of advance warning. I motored into town the next morning and reluctantly stopped at the cafe. Inside, I beheld the remains of a typhoon.

Tables lay on their sides and chairs were strewn about. Dishes were piled high on trays, the remains of various meals were scattered on the floor, and Señor Apesotoso's calling card permeated the room.

I threaded my way to the kitchen. Maria looked especially haggard, a half-smoked cigarette dangling from her lips. She stood next to her usual counter, chopping vegetables, and looked icily at me. "You see it? Where the fuck were you?"

"My God, what happened last evening?"

"You got eyes. *Estamos jodidos.*"

"Yes, I know. I mean, why did it happen? The dining room looks as if there was a brawl of sorts. And the smell . . . "

"Yeah. Everybody was real busy 'cause you weren't here to help. I guess the skunk came to the back door, but we didn't have no plate for him. So, he went to the front door and ran inside."

"Yes, but he didn't spray the last time."

"He sprayed 'cause Paco was inside."

"What? How did that happen?"

"He came in with Nestor."

"Surely Esperanza told him to remove the dog."

"*Sí*, she told him. So did Loretta. Nestor was drunk. He ignored everybody. Esperanza tried to grab the dog, but it bit her."

"Paco bit Esperanza? How bad?"

"I dunno. She screamed at the dog, then ran into here. I didn't see no blood or nothing, but Esperanza ran out the kitchen door. I guess she went home. I was gonna shoot it, but we still had a lot of customers who wanted to eat."

I grimaced. "So, it was just you and Loretta?"

"*Sí*."

"But why was Nestor here at nine o'clock?"

"Nestor was here early. But Paco wouldn't leave. He just lied down under a table and growled."

"Did you call the Sheriff?"

"Tiny? He's scared of fucking dogs."

"He would be. So, Señor Apestoso's evening meal was not waiting by the back door and he wandered through the front door. Then Paco unleashed a sneak attack."

"*Sí*. Paco went crazy, started barking real loud. People were still eating, but they all ran out real fast, knocking over tables and chairs. Then, I heard a yelp. Loretta ran into the kitchen and out the back door. I looked into the dining room. Paco was gone, but I smelled skunk real bad. What we gonna do? Nobody's gonna want to come back again."

The urgency of my departure suddenly vanished.

"Right, we need a plan of action. No retreat, battle we must. There must be something we can use to remove the stench."

"Tomato juice works pretty good."

"All right. Joe must sell tomato juice. If not, well, perhaps Rudy has some. I'll return as soon as I can."

"*Gracias*. We need your help."

"Thanks, Maria. But had I been here last evening, as I was supposed to have been, perhaps none of this would happened."

Maria shrugged. "¿*Quien sabe*? Maybe it's just the cafe."

"Can you find Esperanza? We need her help, too."

"*Sí*, I can go get her."

I paused. "How's Loretta?"

"I dunno. She was crying last night when she left. She don't want you to go, Señor Bennie. Me neither."

"Thanks, Maria. I won't leave with the cafe like this. I promise."

I manoeuvred through the dining room and ran to Rudy's. Inside, I passed through the bar quickly and walked down the hall to his office, whence I banged on the door.

"Yeah?"

I barged inside. "Rudy, we need your help. The cafe is—"

"A disaster. Yeah, I heard. How bad?"

"Disaster is an apt description. The dining room is a complete shambles and reeks of skunk. Maria told me tomato juice can eliminate the odour. If not, well, I don't know what we shall do."

"How can I help?"

"Can you spare Antonio for a bit of clean up? We need all hands, I am afraid."

"I'll go over there myself. I've got some tomato juice in the storeroom."

"Thanks. I'm going to get Loretta, then stop at Joe's. Surely he must stock tomato juice."

"I heard the rumours about you and Loretta. Crazy shit."

"All courtesy of Esperanza. No time to explain now."

I dashed outside, then ran back to the lorry and motored towards Josef's house, where I hoped to find Loretta. When I arrived, Chata lumbered over, tail wagging and tongue lolling. It rose up and placed its two massive front paws on the door. I pushed the door open and stepped out. The dog barked loudly, then followed me to the front door.

I knocked on the door and waited. Josefa opened it, her face displaying one of those withering, motherly sorts of looks.

"Hello, Bennie"

"Er, good morning, Mrs. Alvarez. I know you have heard the rumours. I assure you they are all untrue. May I speak with Loretta?

We have rather an emergency at the cafe and I desperately need her assistance."

"Loretta told me what happened last night. She also told me about the rumours, and that you've decided to run away like a frightened child because of them."

I lowered the head in shame.

"I'm sorry, Mrs. Alvarez. I do want to speak with Loretta about it. For now, we need her help—I need her help. The cafe is a disaster."

"You're abandoning my daughter but not the cafe? Is that it?"

"No. I mean . . . I don't want her to be ridiculed because of me."

"That sounds like a pathetic excuse. Very well, come inside."

"I stepped into the small drawing room and waited nervously for Loretta to appear.

"Hello, Bennie," Loretta said softly as she walked into the drawing room.

"Hullo, Loretta. I've been to the cafe. Maria told me what transpired. I—I am sorry . . . about everything. Are you all right?"

"I guess so. What do you want?"

"Your help. The cafe will sink without it."

"You didn't want my help yesterday. You didn't want me."

"I'm sorry. I would prefer to forget yesterday, actually."

"Me, too, but I can't."

"No, of course you can't. Look, I'm not very good at these sorts of things. Awful, really. Esperanza has been the proverbial thorn in the paw since I arrived here. I didn't mind particularly—well, I did—but what she did yesterday, spreading rumours about you and me . . . well, I can't allow you to be exposed to such ridicule."

"And expose you too, Bennie?"

"Yes, I can't deny it, especially living here."

"I meant what I said about going to London with you."

"I know. But when I saw the cafe this morning, all my thoughts of returning to London vanished. I want the cafe to survive, not only for Uncle Bill's sake, but for mine as well. Besides, I don't think I could bear never seeing you again."

She walked over to me and let me take her in my arms.

"You know, Bennie, I'm an adult. You don't have to protect me."

"Part of the Graves code. A chap must always defend the damsel in distress."

"So, now I am a damsel in distress and not a wench. Does that make you my knight in shining armour?"

"I was rather a proficient fencer at Cambridge. But if you're attacked by a rattlesnake, Coronado's your knight."

She laughed and kissed me. "Is everybody in England as strange as you are?"

"Have you ever met a Scotsman?"

"No. Are they strange, too?"

"Much, much worse. They do know their whisky, however. Now, there's much to be done."

"What about the skunk smell?"

"Maria says vigorous scrubbing with tomato juice. Rudy was bringing bring some over immediately. Our next stop is your uncle's store. Maria has gone to fetch Esperanza."

We hurried over to Joe's store and found Coronado standing behind the counter.

"*Hola*, Señor Graves. *Hola*, Loretta. I hear the skunk showed up last night 'cause of Paco."

"Er, yes, Coronado. We've much work to do. Does Joe sell tomato juice?"

"Tomato juice? I think we got some on aisle three. How come?"

"Maria told me tomato juice would remove the skunk odour."

"Is it real bad?"

"Bad enough, Coronado."

"You want me to help? I can if you need me."

"Thanks, Coronado. Shouldn't you remain at the store?"

"I dunno. You think I should?"

"Well, I assume that's what Joe pays you for."

"I guess. But if you need help, let me know. You ain't gonna close the cafe 'cause of the skunk, are you?"

"Not hardly. We remain steadfast. You shall dine again on *enchiladas* and *tamales* soon enough."

"I get hungry just thinking about them."

Joe had four large tins of tomato juice, which we purchased. Returning to the cafe, we observed the dining room transformed. The front and back doors were both wide open, and a coolish breeze streamed through, which lightened the odour. The dishes had been removed and the tables and chairs were set up properly. Rudy was wiping tables and chairs with a large rag.

He stood up and stretched. "Good to see the two of you together. Loretta, can I ask you a favour?"

"Sure. What do you need?"

"Esperanza's in the kitchen washing dishes. Before you kill her, let her finish them. Otherwise, Maria will make me do them. I'm gonna sneak back to the bar now."

Loretta laughed. "That sounds fair."

"Bennie, did Joe have any tomato juice?"

"Four tins. I'll start in the corner. The odour seems to be strongest there."

"What do we do, Bennie?" Loretta asked.

"I suppose we wash the floor and walls with the tomato juice."

Leaving Esperanza to wash dishes, we scrubbed until, several hours later, our hands and forearms possessed a distinctly reddish hue.

The odour was much less noticeable, or at least masked by a tomatoish one. After a rescrubbing with soap and hot water, the cafe seemed almost presentable.

Loretta and I walked into the kitchen, which smelled heavenly. Esperanza was still washing dishes.

"Are you almost finished with the dishes, *Tia* Esperanza?"

"*Sí*," she replied softly.

"I think you owe Bennie and me an apology. Rudy cleaned all the tables and chairs, and we spent the last several hours scrubbing. If you hadn't started that stupid rumour, none of this would have happened." Esperanza looked at us. Her grey hair was matted from the steam of the hot water. She brushed back a strand that hung over her face.

"I'm sorry, Loretta. You, too, *Pendejito*."

"And stop calling him *Pendejito*. His name is Bennie. Or maybe we should call him El Vaquerito."

I laughed. "El Vaquerito? I definitely prefer that to *Pendejito*, although Bennie is quite acceptable"

"Okay . . . Bennie, El Vaquerito, I'll try."

"Thank you, Esperanza. You may yet be rid of me, but I could not let El Vaquero down. When I heard what happened last night, well, I decided to stay a bit longer. Right the ship and all that."

I saw Maria smile whilst she stirred a large pot of green chile sauce. "El Vaquerito," she muttered.

"Esperanza, may I ask a favour?"

"What do you want now?"

"If you see that bloody cur of Nestor Martinez's so much as look at the cafe, would you please shoot it?"

A smile escaped from Esperanza, despite her attempt to suppress it. "Okay, *sí*. How about shooting Nestor?"

"If he ever sets foot in the cafe again, yes. Maria, can we open tonight?"

"Do you think anyone will show up after last night?" Loretta asked. "We could offer half-price meals. Have Coronado tell everyone.

What say you, Maria?"

"*Sí*. I got enough food, but somebody's got to go to Sabrosa Foods tomorrow. And I need more canned tomatoes. Joe's always got some." I groaned at the mention of the word tomato. "Right, back to Joe's.

I'll ask Coronado to spread the good word."

"What about Señor Apestoso?" Loretta asked. "We can't risk having him come to the front door again."

"Perhaps we should offer him an especially large ofrenda at the back door this evening, a bit earlier, too, say half eight."

"I never know nobody who liked a skunk before," Maria said.

"A bit of bribery to keep the peace. Besides, he is an odd duck, er, skunk, our Señor Apestoso."

Leaving Loretta to help Maria, I returned to Joe's store for the canned tomatoes and Coronado's ability to disseminate information, real or imagined, in record speed.

"*Hola*, Señor Graves. How's the cafe?"

"I believe we've recovered Coronado. But we need your help with two items."

"Sure. What are they?"

"First, I need tinned tomatoes. Well, Maria needs them as we have run out."

"Tinned tomatoes? We got canned tomatoes on aisle two, next to the motor oil and cat food."

Despite an intense curiosity to know why one would place tinned tomatoes next to motor oil and cat food, I thought it best to not ask. "Yes, canned tomatoes is what I meant. We call them tinned, because the cans were once made of tin."

"What's the second thing you need?"

"I need you to spread the word that, just tonight, everything on the menu is half-price. Can you do that?"

He licked his lips. "Half-price? Is Maria gonna have *tamales*?"

"If not, I know she is making a fresh batch of green chile sauce for her *enchiladas*."

"That sounds real good. Can I bring my sister, Señor Graves? She won't bother you. I promise."

"Of course you may. And I promise not to ask her for identification." I retrieved five tins of tomatoes and delivered them to Maria. Promising I would return later, I motored to the ranch to inform Uncle Bill of the morning's events and my resolve to stay on. I found him in the barn, hammering away at some sort of longish piece of metal.

"Bennie, I thought you'd be gone all day. Something happen?"

"Er, yes. I stopped at the cafe this morning out of, well curiosity, really to see how things fared last night."

"This doesn't sound good. What happened?"

"It started with Nestor Martinez, who decided he would grace the cafe with his horrid table manners, as well as that bloody cur. Esperanza attempted to remove the dog, which responded by biting her."

"Bet that left a bad taste in Paco's mouth."

"One can only hope. After being bitten, Esperanza went home. Maria and Loretta were left to pilot the ship. Furthermore, Paco remained, curled up under the table where Nestor had sat."

"Well, Maria and Loretta forget to leave Señor Apestoso's evening snack outside the back door. Thus, because he is fond of Maria's cooking—"

"Oh, no."

"Oh, yes. Señor Apestoso strolled through the front door again. Under normal circumstances, if one can call an *enchilada*-consuming skunk normal, this would have been no problem. However, when Paco espied Señor Apestoso, the chase, albeit short-lived, was on. Señor Apestoso defended himself and, well, you can imagine the rest. The cafe was a disaster this morning."

Uncle Bill shook his head. "I guess it just ain't meant to be. Maybe I should just sell the building and forget about this."

"Perish the thought. We open this evening. All menu items half-price."

"What about the mess? And the smell?"

"A morning's worth of vigorous scrubbing by all."

"Maria and Esperanza?"

"And Loretta. Rudy assisted as well."

"Loretta? You two—"

"Are fine, thank you."

"London?"

"Not now. I made a promise to you, after all. I can't walk away, despite what little sanity I have urging an Olympic sprint. I suppose the cafe not only means something to you, but to me as well."

He put his hand on my shoulder. "I'm real glad, Bennie. For everything. Wish I didn't have to tell you the bad news."

"Eh?"

"Cynthia arrives tomorrow. Telegram came this morning."

I groaned.

"Bus arrives about two o'clock. You can pick her up and bring her here, if you like."

"I don't suppose you would care to act as chauffeur?"

"Nope. Some things you just gotta do yourself. You gonna tell Loretta?"

"That the former spouse has travelled half-way around the globe intending to take me back to London? How?"

"I dunno. But you better say something to her. You don't spring that kind of surprise on a gal like Loretta."

"I'll tell her this afternoon before we open and hope for the best, as they say."

"Your ex-wife is coming here?" asked Loretta incredulously.

"Yes. Uncle Bill showed me the telegram earlier today."

"And she wants to take you back with her?"

"Her letter said she had made a terrible mistake, running off with that bloody Spaniard. She wants me back in England where I belong."

Loretta slumped down into a chair. "So you are leaving. Did you lie to me this morning, about wanting to continue seeing me?"

I took Loretta's hand. "I'm not returning to London. Not now."

"What will you tell her?"

"Well, Cynthia has always been most persuasive, in her own way."

"If you leave with her, I'll shoot your *cojones* off. Better yet, I'll ask Hector to do it for me."

"Hell hath no fury, eh?" We kissed quickly. "We open in two hours. I hope Coronado has spread the news."

I need not have been concerned about Coronado's ability in that respect. By five o'clock, a crowd was already in place, led by Coronado and his sister. The evening proceeded without incident, almost frighteningly so. At half eight, all of the tables were still occupied. I dashed into the kitchen, reminding Maria we needed to set out Señor Apestoso's meal.

Maria shook her head in disbelief. "I got a *tamale, carne adovada*, half a *sopapilla*, and some *frijoles*. You think that's enough?"

The plate was overflowing. "It looks rather substantial."

She set the plate outside the back door. With Royal Navy-like punctuality, Señor Apestoso arrived at the back door precisely at nine o'clock, and tucked into his repast. The four of us stood by the back door observing him eat. After he finished, he sat on his haunches and looked up at us with his usual wry grin—I should think he would have tipped his hat, had he worn one. Then he walked down the alley and again disappeared into the darkness.

By half ten, the dishes were cleaned and the dining room swept. Loretta and I walked outside into the cool night air. "Shall I give you a lift to your mother's house?"

"Thanks."

When we arrived, Loretta looked at me. "Bennie, I wish—"

"What?"

"Could we just skip tomorrow?"

"A grand idea. Unfortunate that Mister Verne's time machine is in the garage for service. I would add one other item to the wish list."

"What's that?"

I took her hand in mine. "How about dinner and dancing in Santa Fe? Rumour has it we are rather disposed towards both."

At breakfast the next morning, Uncle Bill pawed at his coffee. "You let Loretta know?"

"I did."

"How'd she take it?"

"Well, both of us would prefer to simply skip today. Fate, however, appears not to allow for such dodging."

"Yep. Some days you gotta grab the bull by the horns."

"Well, I wouldn't consider Cynthia a bull, but I take your meaning. Anything you need from town, Uncle Bill?"

"Better get us a few bottles of Dusty Trail from Rudy's. I gotta feeling we're all gonna need it."

Preparations at the cafe proceeded uneventfully. I helped Maria make *tamales*, Esperanza had already left for Santa Fe with the shopping list for Sabrosa Foods. Loretta would come in later in the day.

"You don't look real good, Señor Bennie."

"Eh? I'm fine, Maria. A lot on the mind is all."

"*Sí*. That's what happens."

"What?"

"You got a girl now. Lots to think about. *¿Que no?*"

"More than you can imagine."

"How come you keep looking at your watch?"

"Er, Uncle Bill and I are expecting a visitor from England. She is supposed to arrive on the bus from Santa Fe, and I will escort her to the ranch."

"She? Somebody El Vaquero knows?"

"Not really. I mean, well, it's my ex-wife, if you must know."

"You divorced?"

"Yes. That's partly why I came here. Cynthia ran off with another chap. They went to Seville or some such place. Well, to make a long story short, I received a letter from her. She told me she had made a terrible mistake, asked my forgiveness, and announced she was coming here to bring me home."

Maria inhaled deeply on her cigarette, then blew a large cloud of smoke skywards. You tell Loretta?"

"Already done."

"Loretta—she's been through a lot, Bennie."

"I know. She told me about her marriage, Maria."

Maria nodded, then attacked an onion.

As two o'clock neared, my nerves sizzled. I stepped outside onto the *portal*, gulping in quantities of cool air, and heard the bus approach. It drew to a stop, raising a large cloud of dust.

The dust cleared and the door opened. An ancient and stooped old chap, wearing an enormous black cowboy hat, stepped off slowly. He immediately shuffled towards Rudy's Bar and disappeared.

And then Cynthia stepped down. She was wearing a blue floral skirt, cream-coloured blouse, and whitish heels, looking, as ever, fabulous. She looked shell-shocked, much as I had looked when I first arrived.

I walked up to her. "Hullo, Cynthia."

"Benjamin!" she cried, grabbing me like a life vest. "This is where your uncle lives? It looks like a Calcutta slum."

"It's really not all that bad. Not London, of course."

"Well, you can return home now. You did receive my letter?"

"I did."

"We have so much to discuss. Are you going to introduce me to the infamous Uncle William?"

"Indeed I shall." I retrieved her valise and we walked over to the lorry, which was parked in front of the cafe. I could sense untold pairs of eyes gazing upon us stealthily, and new rumours being drafted for review and dissemination. "Would you like to see the cafe? I'm rather the manager, you see."

She stared at the painted sign. "Dos Abuelas? Two what, exactly?"

"I would have thought your experience in Spain would have perfected your Spanish. It means two grandmothers. They're two sisters who own the cafe. Well, it's rather a long and complex story. The cafe opens at five o'clock, but if you are feeling peckish, I am quite sure I can prevail upon Maria to offer you something."

Cynthia lowered her head. "Thank you, no. And there is no need to remind me about Spain.

"Sorry."

"Perhaps we should go see your uncle straight away."

I placed the valise in the back of the lorry and we motored off. By the time we arrived at the ranch, Cynthia looked even more shell-shocked. I pulled around to the side of the house. As we passed, Daisy rose up, *sombrero* athwart, to investigate.

"Benjamin, was that a pig on the porch?" Cynthia asked, craning her head towards the house. "Why is it wearing a hat?"

"That's Daisy. Uncle Bill will make the introductions."

She glanced out at the fenced pasture. "Are those cattle?"

"Yes. Uncle Bill has fifty head. He's quite proud of his stock."

"The smell here is quite horrid. How do you bear it?"

She held her nose until we were safely inside the house. I escorted her to the davenport in the sitting room. "Uncle Bill must be in the barn. Would you care for a drink?"

"Thank you. A gin and orange."

"Afraid we have neither gin nor orange. Would you care for a whisky?"

"Whisky? Yes, that would be fine. With a bit of tap water. I'm feeling quite light-headed."

"I remember how you take it." I poured out a measure of Dusty Trail and added an equal amount of water. "Here you are."

She took a largish sip and began to cough violently. "What is this?"

"Dusty Trail. It's the only whisky Uncle Bill drinks."

"Dusty Trail? God, it's horrid." She placed the glass down on the table in front of the davenport.

"An acquired taste, I admit."

Presently, I heard the back door open. "Bennie, you there? You got Cynthia with you?"

"Yes, Uncle Bill. In the sitting room."

Uncle Bill walked into the sitting room, wearing his cowboy hat and boots. He looked at Cynthia, removed his hat with his left hand, and extended a rather dirty right one towards her. "Howdy, little lady. You must be Cynthia. I'm Bill Graves, Bennie's uncle. Otherwise known as the black sheep of the family."

Cynthia eyed him coolly and extended her hand to his.

"I've heard, ah, so much about you, Mister Graves."

"Call me Bill. And what you heard is probably all true, especially if you heard it from that pompous ass brother of mine, Bennie's father."

"A bit different than London, ain't it?" he said.

"Quite. You actually chose to live here?"

"Damn right. All I ever wanted was to be a cowboy. That's what I got here."

"But it is so primitive."

"Yep. I guess if you like all that high-falutin crap in London, it is. But I don't, and it ain't."

"I beg your pardon?" Cynthia appeared to be suffering from both the shock of Vaca Seca and Uncle Bill's mode of speech.

"Vaca Seca is a most interesting place, Cynthia," I said. "There's much more here than meets the eye."

"There could hardly be less than meets the eye, Benjamin. In any case, Mister Graves, would you excuse us. Benjamin and I have much to discuss."

"I reckon you do. Well, I got to get back to the barn. Marjorie has kicked out some of the boards in her stall."

"Marjorie?"

"Marjorie is Uncle Bill's horse," I replied, A rather baleful one, I might add."

"Would you like to meet her, Cynthia? She's a good ol' gal, despite what Bennie says."

"No thank you."

"Well, I'll leave you two to talk." Uncle Bill put on his hat and walked out of the room.

"This place is a menagerie, Benjamin."

"Yes, I suppose it is."

"I've missed you. I know that may difficult for you to believe after, well, after what has transpired, but I truly have."

"I"ve missed you too, Cynthia. Despite what transpired."

"If you mean, was I a fool, then, yes, I was. That is why I so wanted to see you Benjamin. Can you ever forgive me?"

"I'm not angry at you. I was, but not anymore."

"I'm glad, Benjamin. I want our life back, together, the way it was."

"You know I was made redundant by the bank?"

"Yes, your mother informed me. It doesn't matter. There are always other jobs, as long as we are together. We can even start a family."

She took my hand in hers and looked into my eyes. Cynthia had stunningly beautiful eyes; they beckoned one and easily melted the stoniest of hearts.

"Start a family, you say?"

"Good. We can leave for London tomorrow."

"I'm sorry, but I can't leave just yet."

"Why ever not?

"The cafe for one. I made a promise to Uncle Bill that I would restore it to its former glory, as it were."

"What on earth do you know about running a restaurant?"

"When I began, nothing really. However, ignorance has proved to be rather an asset in this case."

"Surely, there are others who can run a dingy cafe."

"It's not a dingy cafe at all, especially for Uncle Bill. His late wife helped run it. She died there, as a matter of fact."

"Died? Rather morbid, that. Was it the food?"

I sighed. "I should not say that in front of Uncle Bill."

"I'm sorry, Benjamin. I just want you to come home so we can start anew. Please."

As she looked into my eyes, and kindled memories of our life together, the Graves resolve weakened. London was home after all, a home in which I would not be called *gringo*. Nor would I be confronted with rattlesnakes, copiously urinating dogs, and grinning skunks.

As I pondered my future, I heard a lorry coming up the road, its horn sounding wildly. It stopped in front of the house with a loud thud.

"What was that?" Cynthia asked, standing up and peering through the window.

I rose up from the davenport and through the front door. Daisy was on full alert. Coronado's lorry had smashed into the fence and snapped a post. Coronado and Loretta were walking towards the gate.

"Has something else happened?" I asked.

Coronado looked at the broken fencepost. "Sorry about the fence, Señor Graves. I hope El Vaquero don't get too mad. I can fix it, if he wants."

"Never mind the fence, Coronado."

Loretta opened the gate and ran into my arms. I felt her tears dampening my shirt.

"I'm sorry, Bennie. I asked Coronado to drive me up here. I had to see you."

"Loretta made me drive real fast, too, Señor Graves." He walked past me and towards the house.

"Never mind the fence. Loretta, why are you crying?"

"I had to see you once more before you leave."

"But I told you, I'm not leaving."

"I saw her, Bennie. She's really beautiful, your wife."

"So are you."

"Not like that, I'm not." She began to sob.

I stared into her eyes. "Loretta, truly I am not leaving. I made a promise to Uncle Bill and a promise to you."

"I can run the cafe, Bennie. I already spoke to *Tia* Maria about it. Uncle Joe isn't going to overcharge me for anything, either. And *Tia* Esperanza, I think she learned her lesson. So you don't have to think about the cafe, I promise."

"Do you want me to leave, Loretta?"

"No, but if you are going to anyway, I want to get it over with."

"I understand."

I turned towards the house and saw Cynthia emerge from the front door, followed by a grinning Coronado.

"Benjamin, who is this horrid little man?"

As she stepped out, Daisy grunted loudly.

Cynthia stared at Daisy and cried out. "My God, it's that hat-wearing pig!"

Daisy grunted again and walked towards Cynthia, who remained frozen. "Benjamin, help me!"

I walked towards the *portal*. "She's usually friendly, well, not unfriendly, at least. Scratch her behind the ears. Daisy's rather fond of that."

"You expect me to pet it? It smells absolutely horrid. Benjamin, please!"

"All right, Cynthia." I walked up to Daisy and scratched behind her ears. "Avast, Daisy, or no supper for you." On hearing the word supper, Daisy sat on her hind legs.

"*Híjole*, Señor Graves," Coronado said. "Daisy's a real smart pig."

"We all tend to respond to culinary signals, Coronado."

With her ears satisfactorily scratched, Daisy flopped down. I escorted Cynthia into the house, followed by Coronado and Loretta. Once inside, Cynthia collapsed in my arms. "I've never been attacked by a pig. This place is horrid. Please take me home, Benjamin."

"What do you mean 'horrid?'" Uncle Bill growled, walking inside.

"I'm sorry, Mister Graves, but surely, allowing a filthy pig to sleep on the porch? I could have been killed."

"Daisy's as gentle as a lamb."

"There is a most pungent barnyard odour about it, as well."

"Sorry, little lady. That's part of ranching."

"Benjamin, how can you possibly live here surrounded by all of these . . . animals?"

"One adapts, I suppose. Anyway, you're quite safe now."

Coronado walked up to Cynthia, and extended a pudgy, dirt-strewn hand. "*Hola*, Señora Graves. I'm Coronado de Vaca. Are you okay?"

Cynthia eyed Coronado, much as she had Daisy. "No, I am most certainly not. Why are you here, anyway?"

"'Cause Loretta asked me to bring her. She and Señor Graves are gonna have a baby."

"What? Benjamin!" Cynthia looked at Loretta. "Her?"
Gah! No! Esperanza started a nasty rumour. It's not true."

"Who is Esperanza?"

"Esperanza is one of the *abuelas*. She, well, she's never been overly fond of me."

"You like *tamales*, Señora Graves?" Coronado interrupted. "Maria makes the best *tamales*."

Cynthia ignored Coronado's entreaties and continued to stare at Loretta. "Excuse me," she said. "My name is Cynthia Graves, Benjamin's wife."

"Yes, I know," Loretta replied softly.

"Well, what do you have to say for yourself?"

"Excuse me?"

"Rumours are started for a reason. Smoke and fire, what. So I shall thank you to leave my husband alone. He's returning to London, where he belongs."

"¡*Vete a la chingada*!"

"What did you say?"

"Cynthia, please." I did not want Loretta to respond further.

"I need to see Bennie."

"You mean Benjamin? Why?"

"Cynthia, please, sit down whilst I speak with Loretta."

"Benjamin, what is going on? I've travelled thousands of miles to see you. Now this horrid man informs me you and this trollop are going to have a baby? How could you?"

"How could I what? It's an unfounded rumour. Besides you're in a position to lecture, what with your having run off with that idiot Spaniard."

"I have already apologised. There is no need to bring it up again. We should move forward, not dwell on the past."

I paused. "You're quite right. We should move forward. Only, my moving forward means not returning to my past— neither to London nor to you."

"Benjamin, we can move forward. We can go somewhere else. What about Paris? Or even New York, if you must stay in America."

"I'm sorry, Cynthia, truly I am. But I'm staying in Vaca Seca."

"Because of her, Benjamin? You want to stay in this God-forsaken place because of her?"

I placed an arm around Loretta's shoulders. "Yes, actually. And, well, because despite Vaca Seca's unique ability to drive one barmy, I rather enjoy it."

"What happened to the sensible man I married?"

"Sensible? I consider myself quite sensible. Only, I have been told we all have to fuck up now and then."

## THE END